# SPARE PARTS

R. E. Laurence

ISBN: 0692373500
ISBN 13: 9780692373507
Library of Congress Control Number: 2015901215
Four Paws Press, Laredo, TX

The characters and events in this book are fictitious. Any similarity to real persons, living or dead, is coincidental and not intended by the author.

*Berkshire Crier*
**POSTED:  08/08/2034** 03:00:26 PM EDT
|UPDATED:  15 MIN. AGO

New Burford, MA – Hikers in the old New Burford quarry discovered on Wednesday, August 7 a plastic container with a clearly legible label, "Heart - Male - 47." The container, identified as turn-of the-century Tupperware, and its contents were turned over to the Berkshire County Medical Examiner's Office. An investigation was authorized.

# 1

*New York City*

On West 64th Street a black, mud-splattered, 1999 Range Rover turns in at the parking sign, slowly descends the ramp into a subterranean garage and stops at the attendant's booth where, against a glossy white cinderblock wall suffused with harsh lighting, expensively dressed metropolitans are waiting to retrieve vehicles. Hunter Barnhill gets out of the Rover, takes a receipt and, checking his watch, heads for the street. Quarter to eleven. Great time—less than three hours to midtown on moonlit highways—and perfect timing.

Concertgoers are streaming from Lincoln Center across the plaza to a swarm of idling taxis and limos. Hunter walks fast, weaving through the crowd, through choked traffic, through foul exhaust clouds spewed from transit buses, crossing Broadway to Café My Way.

Above table noise, strains from a string quartet resound on the domed ceiling. *Meechelle, ma belle.* Every word of the song comes back to him as he skirts the parties waiting for tables, and at the bar takes the one available seat facing the screen ensconced among floating shelves of bottles. On the screen CNN's Aaron Brown, in striped tie and rolled shirtsleeves, is looking especially somber.

"Hey squire," says the bartender, salting margarita glasses, "I'll change it in a sec. What'll it be?" He wipes his hands, takes Hunter's order and punches the remote.

Graphics for the Eleven O'clock News fill the screen, then cut to Melanie Atwood's classic features and bright blonde hair, her pronouncements barely audible through the din. "—with one month till election day, races are tightening—" A burst of hilarity at the end of the bar momentarily drowns the audio. "—and in Massachusetts, Lawrence Balk, counsel for Senator Richard Donnelley, disclosed in a press conference today that a series of developments now casts different light on how the *MetroInquirer* obtained the controversial photos of Senator Donnelley with Washington journalist Kyle Ludger. According to Balk, there is evidence that the efforts of more than one person associated with—."

"*Haaaappy Birthday tooo yooou*—" At the end of the black granite bar an advanced belter, ready for Broadway, leads his friends in a show-stopping rendition, concluded with cheers, hoots, whistles and applause. Hunter's bottle of Bud lite arrives. Melanie's audio re-emerges.

"—shutting down La Guardia for five hours today. Despite new regulations, this is the third incident in as many weeks attributed to sky rage, as the surge in private air traffic continues and commercial flights decline. A spokesman for the air-charter business—." Again, talk covers the audio. The video cuts to a commercial showing a Lexus speeding through desert dunes to a cragged pinnacle. Melanie returns, still inaudible.

Sipping the beer, he wonders how long he'll keep making these trips. When they met, Melanie's husband had just left for France with his secretary, eight months pregnant and Melanie made it clear that all she wanted from a relationship was good sex, reliability, and freedom. Monogamy, possessive lovers, and petty jealousies were not for her. She never even mentioned marriage, except that first Valentine's Day, when, after too much wine, she asked if she could tell people they were abstractly engaged. He wasn't sure what that meant. Neither was she, but she said it somehow made things special for them.

"—and in Washington, the National Lawn Care Bill moved closer to becoming law when, late this evening, it passed in the Senate by a close margin." Her tone is deeper now, more authoritative. "Forming a Federal Lawn Maintenance Organization to oversee state networks of local crews, the law will minimize gasoline usage by assigning crews to territories, thereby reducing distance traveled between jobs, and by licensing fuel-efficient mowers and other equipment. Use of manually operated equipment will remain unrestricted for those opting for self-service. The new legislation will create thousands of entry-level employment opportunities and will free up for lawn care recipients, on average, one hour a week spent on yard work. Environmentalists praise the Lawn Care Act, which will conserve fossil fuel resources, reduce oil and noise pollution, and improve air quality. Opponents say the bill is a costly substitute for a middle class tax cut. With approval in both houses, the bill now goes to the President who is expected to sign it into law next week."

The bartender delivers Hunter's bruschetta, "So, you got a big lawn up there?" and moves on without the answer.

He ponders, No, not big. But she could never understand why he wanted to mow a lawn. Or cut wood, or turn soil for a vegetable garden. For that matter, she couldn't relate to any aspect of country living. When he bought the house, she wasn't even sufficiently curious to check it out. She always had to stay in town so she wouldn't miss any opportunity to network toward her goal which was, at that time, to anchor network evening news.

Then, the Saturday after September 11, a different, vulnerable Melanie showed up at the old Hamilton house. It was the only time she didn't act as if she were immune to the events she reported. Her protective bubble of TV news celebrity had burst. She cried, telling him she didn't feel safe in the city any more. She said she wanted to stay there with him, forever, but, around midnight, rolled over in bed, sat up with a straight back, and announced, "In New Burford,

Massachusetts, this is Melanie Atwood, ABG News." With that, she dropped back onto the sheets, eyes closed. He thought she was playing around. Spoofing. Possibly even mocking herself, which would have been a first. She wasn't. She had fallen sound asleep, or so it appeared. Unable to sleep, as usual, he got up, dressed and, with the dog, walked to the edge of the woods where he sat, thinking until daylight slivered through lofty branches. When he got back to the house, she was gone. The next morning, she called to say she didn't want anything to change between them, but would only see him in urban or resort locations—never again New Burford.

He picks at the bruschetta. She pauses, shifts expression and in a tone of controlled alarm continues, "Tornadoes swept through Central Texas today leaving—"

When he quit his job, announcing that he was making the "old Hamilton house"—so called in New Burford—his primary residence, she was incredulous, told him to see a shrink and trade the Berkshires house for a place in the Hamptons where they knew everyone. That was precisely what he didn't like about the Hamptons, he reminded her. She did, however, convince him to rent his apartment instead of selling it.

She laughs. Time for weather. A perky, amiable Melanie asks, "So, Mr. B, is this beautiful weather going to stay with us through the weekend?" Mr. B presents his radar displays and weather maps decorated with smiling sunbursts. The camera pulls back to include Melanie. She banters with Mr. B about the drop in temperature and the probability that everyone would need a warm jacket in the morning. The last word is hers. The camera is hers. She purrs, "This is Melanie Atwood wishing you a good night from all of us at WABG News."

The weekend after Melanie's New Burford experience, he went back to New York. But that weekend, for the first time, her enthusiastic reports of career-advancing flings really irked him. He went back to New Burford and invited an old flame, the first in a succession, to the old Hamilton house. None re-ignited. Locally, he had met few people, mostly merchants, certainly no attractive women—with the possible exception of the head teller at the New Burford Bank & Trust, a friendly redhead who dressed to accentuate her ample chest and always came on to him. She had said she was getting a divorce, but, in fact, was still very married to a very large husband who drove very large trucks for the St. Catherine Sand and Gravel Company, just a few miles from the old Hamilton house. He resumed overnighters and weekends with Melanie.

"Another beer?" The bartender eyes Melanie approaching.

"No thanks. I'm all set," he says as she wraps her arms around his chest, plants a kiss on the hollow of his ear and whispers, "You're not really going back tomorrow."

He almost smiles, kissing her cheek. "Town Meeting."

"Oh, please," she smirks.

"It's a big deal up there and I have yet to make an appearance. Hungry?"

"Famished. Let's go." She strides to the door as he leaves cash on the check and follows.

# 2

*New Burford, Massachusetts*

Exhaling heartily, Emma Peters Pell plunks herself into one of the twin ladder-back chairs nestled in the bay window looking out on her back lawn, and places a mug of hot tea on the butler table between them. She leans over, unlaces her jogging shoes, yanks them off, then the sweat socks and, bending her knee, grabs her foot to inspect her toes for athlete's foot.

Eight years ago she ran her last marathon. Since then, her daily mileage steadily dropped to one mile but still, without fail, she goes out every day for a run, or, more accurately, a shuffle. At ninety-four, she knows she's beaten the actuarial charts and doesn't need to give a damn about exercising, or much of anything else. But she does, resolved to live each day healthfully and with a chuckle. She's lost two inches in height since her seventieth birthday, but still stands tall, not a bit stooped, at five feet, seven inches. Her vision is keen, reflexes dependable, and she capably drives herself around town in her vintage Mercedes—although now and then a bit too fast and, on occasion, parking wherever she happens to be. The founding owner of the Colonial Cable Company, she has managed the operation since 1960, and, on the side, runs a Tupperware franchise. She keeps a firm hand in local politics, and a sharp eye on state and national politics.

Emma grabs the other foot and checks it. Not a trace of athlete's foot. Good.

On the Bokhara rug a red dog, a mix of foxhound, spaniel, and Irish setter, stirs from a nap, stretches its long, feathered legs, and ambles over to her. "Salty, eh, Jenny?" Emma strokes the dog as it licks her feet. Jenny yawns, circles, and, with a fifty-pound thud, resettles on the rug.

She picks up the steaming mug and, holding it under her nose, enjoys the fragrance and warmth. It's one of her own herbal blends, mostly lemon verbena and anise hyssop from her garden and, by her standards, far superior to any commercial tea.

The Seth Thomas mantel clock chimes four o'clock. Quiet time. Time to stop and count the blessings of the day. A few years ago she resolved not to indulge in distant memories during her daily reflection. Like chocolate, they are delectable, sometimes comforting, sometimes unsettling, but certainly addictive, and best reserved for the occasional splurge.

She sips the tea—still too hot—and sets it back down with a sigh. Things are ticking smoothly here in town but she is not pleased about the passage of the Lawn Care Bill. She can't imagine the Federal Government in charge of lawn mowing, let alone hedge trimming, leaf blowing, fertilizing, pest control, and the like. "Humph. Come what may, they'll not cut my grass. No sir-ee. I'd sooner let it go to wild flowers, like the old days."

The phone is ringing in the center hall. Emma scurries barefoot into the hall. "Yes, yes, here I come." The dog lifts its head as if curious about the caller.

"Emma Peters Pell speaking. Agatha? For goodness sake!—Oh, dear." Agatha Peters Warwick, Emma's cousin in Boston, her friend since childhood, is sobbing uncontrollably. "Have yourself a good cry, my dear—. Oh, my, my." Agatha telephones Emma whenever her distress becomes unbearable and, invariably, the cause is her daughter's discovery that her husband has strayed yet again. Over the years, Emma always calmed her, saying it's in everyone's best interest that

Millie turn a blind eye to her husband's fleeting dalliances with the likes of the summer stock actress in Dennis, the third runner-up for Miss Massachusetts, countless secretaries and aides. However, Dick Donnelley's current affair defies denial.

Emma feels torn. She has championed Dick Donnelley since his first race for Congress when she detected his knack for claiming the ethical high road, graciously knocking others from it. Whatever his indiscretions, even back then, he was always scrupulous about safeguarding his privacy for them and that, in her opinion, made him rock solid. But when recently he took up with the young, attractive, well-endowed member of his own set, Emma was astounded, and furious. She knew immediately this affair couldn't be kept quiet, and, in the middle of a re-election campaign, that spelled political suicide. Photos of Dick and Kyle hit the front pages of the checkout counter rags, and the next morning the story hit national headlines, making it the focus of the Senate campaign. Dick Donnelley crashed in the polls, hitting rock bottom. Yet, despite all odds, Emma stubbornly believes that Dick might still come up with the tactics to reverse the situation and seize victory. Agatha's sobs now signal another turn for the worse. "Agie, dear, what's happened?"

Agatha gulps, then whimpers, "They're—"

"They're what?"

"—slandering—"

"They? Slandering *whom*?"

"My Millicent!" Agatha snivels, then blurts, "Millie is *not* a—" she whispers, "—a lesbian. "

"Lesbian?"

"You heard me."

Emma hesitates, her thoughts racing. Could it be a set-up? Part of a scheme to salvage the election? "You know, I dearly love Millie, and that wouldn't change one bit if she were to come out and—"

"Come *out*?! You believe them!" She wails.

"I meant to say come forward." Emma is about to warn that if Millie were to protest too vociferously, her defensiveness might give credence to the charge. Instead, she says, "But I can tell you, she and Dick never had much of a marriage."

"That's beside the point."

"Fiddlesticks, Agatha. Have you ever seen any spark between those two? Sometimes I think their most intimate moments are when they stand next to each other in receiving lines."

"That doesn't make her a lesbian!"

"True. Now where did you hear this?"

"E-mails. Friends forwarded them to Millie, she faxed them to me. Millie said it's all over Washington, which means she again will be shamefully dragged into the evening news. Emma, this affair is preposterous. Kyle Ludger is a child."

"Kyle is no child, m'dear. It's easily ten years since she got out of Princeton. Open your eyes." Having married a man of considerably greater seniority, Emma isn't about to criticize the age difference between Dick and Kyle.

"I see quite well, thank you. Even as I saw clearly before Millie married him that Mr. Dick Donnelley was nothing but a parvenu, an opportunist. He wouldn't be where is today if it hadn't been for the Peters Warwicks. The least he can do is show loyalty—and put an end to this slander."

"Agatha, I strongly sense that it was Dick or one of his people who planted the rumor."

"Wh-what—?"

Emma thinks aloud. "For as long as Dick's been in politics, the opposition has been trawling, unsuccessfully, for embarrassing secrets to hurl at him on his moral high ground. Now, suddenly, at this critical moment, he's a sitting duck, gallivanting about with Kyle. Seems to me he's deliberately set himself up as an easy target, figured out how to snatch victory from the jaws of defeat by enlisting the help of the unwitting opposition. That's it! Consider, what could better exonerate our beleaguered senator than news that his wife's a lesbian?" She pauses, realizing what this means for Millie. "Agatha —? Are you there?"

"He is truly contemptible."

"Is Millie granting him a divorce?"

She moans, "It's the only option."

"She's better off without him."

There is silence. Agatha heaves a sigh. "Well, if you acknowledge that Richard Donnelley is capable of such deviousness, then I suggest you start keeping an eye on your back forty."

"What are you implying?"

"You know Brew's campaign promise to grow the economy in the western counties by constructing a highway?"

"Of course I do. I've had quite a few talks with him about it."

"Well, Millicent said that highway's going to go east out of Barrington."

"Impossible!" Emma is stunned.

"Doesn't it sound a lot like the old plan? Back in the fifties, that's precisely where they wanted to put Interstate 50. From Barrington through New Burford and—"

As Agatha rambles on, Emma tries to recall her discussions with the governor when he detailed his plan to boost the economy of western Massachusetts with a new highway. He gave the distinct impression that the highway would be some thirty miles north of Barrington, a good distance from New Burford. He also said any number of times that he knew she'd fight tooth and nail if the highway were to impact New Burford. She interrupts. "What's her source?"

"She discovered it when going through some of Dick's papers. Snooping. She also overheard him and Brew talking about it."

Emma bows her head, pinching the bridge of her nose, closing her eyes. Unlike scandals, a highway, once it materializes, will not go away. "Agatha, I've got to run. There's a town meeting this evening. Tell Millie to batten down her hatches. She's going to weather this storm just fine. And I predict it will all blow over before Election Day. Trust me," she says with such resounding affirmation that Agatha takes comfort from it.

Emma hangs up. Chin in hand, cogitating, she walks back to her chair and picks up the mug. Had Brew Pease deceived her? Is it possible that they have come to cross-purposes? They've always seen eye to eye and she's given him considerable and unwavering support. He owes her too much to even contemplate going behind her back, particularly for something as monstrously onerous as building a highway through her town. He and Dick both know what she did back in the fifties to block construction of Interstate 50 in New Burford, mustering the entire community in protest until the plan was revised. And, if necessary, she'll do it again in a heartbeat. It is her duty today, as it was then, to protect the town. She owns the most real estate, pays the highest taxes, and, most important, she is the only remaining member of the Peters clan in the Valley of Runs-On-Toes-Into-Wind. It was her eighth great-grandfather, Captain Duty Peters and his wife Rebecca, who in 1638 set out from Hartford, ventured into the Valley of Runs-On-Toes-Into-Wind, bought the land from Chief Agitated Bear, and founded New Burford, naming it after their hometown in England.

She gazes out the bay window. Late afternoon sunlight is beaming over the treetops, onto the lawn enclosed by ancient stonewalls. Beyond are the pines, the mountains, four hundred acres of family homestead. She loves every inch of it. Always has. Even when she was a very little girl, she knew she would never leave this special place— not for long, anyway. She tries to imagine a highway cutting through the township. Corporate parks would follow, and shopping malls, condos, more people, more problems. There'd be accidents on snowy nights. And who would go out in the snow and sleet to deal with the mutilated cars and broken bodies. The town constable? The county sheriff? State police? They would all bicker about who is responsible while some poor soul might be departing this life out on the cold highway. Not in New Burford, she vows.

She sets the mug on the butler table and listens to the crickets, feebly chirping, forecasting frost. If a plan were going forward for constructing the highway spur through New Burford, it would have been on the warrant for tonight's town meeting. Or it could be introduced from the floor as new business. Either way she would have had prior knowledge of it. Furthermore, Brew had said there'd be a public announcement as soon as the plan is finalized. So, clearly, the plan isn't yet in place. When it is, if it impacts New Burford in any way, a public hearing will be scheduled, and, at that point she'll muster forces.

She briskly rubs her hands together, and cups them over her eyes, enjoying the penetrating warmth. Suddenly, the dog springs to its feet and, baying like a foxhound, lunges at the window, front paws on the sill.

"Who's there, Jenny?" Emma goes to the window. A white Volkswagen Beetle squad car with a wide green stripe is coming up the drive, lights flashing. "Hmm, Turbo's checking up on me a little early today, but goodness-gracious, why the lights?" She watches as Constable Turbo Bull, all 240 pounds of him, squeezes out of the cruiser, grasping a metal milkshake container. He takes a draining swig of the milkshake, tosses the container into the squad car, and shuts the door. Emma scurries into the hallway and opens the front door. The dog quiets. "Constable Bull, what can I do for you?"

In his wrinkled uniform, Turbo fills the doorway. Sweating at the brow, nails chewed, a rusty .357 magnum revolver at his hip, he is repulsively disheveled yet oddly imposing and friendly-looking. Stepping inside, he removes his hat. "Sorry to bother you, Mrs. Pell, but I just seen something I think you'd want to know about. Out on Route 22. I was just coming around the bend past Miller's barn, you know, just before the Haystack Motel there, when I seen this truck with a little American flag on its door."

"A truck?"

"Yes, ma'am. First, I saw just the one, going real slow, heading into St. Catherine's Sand and Gravel. I didn't think much of it, but I was kinda curious about the flag."

"—the flag on the door."

"That's right—because that's how I could tell it wasn't a St. Catherine's truck. Actually the little flag is on the driver and passenger doors."

"Yes—."

"So I go for a closer look, drive into the gravel yard and what do I see but a whole mess of 'em. Lined up all the way back into the field."

"Oh my, no." She presses her fingers to her forehead.

"Are you all right, ma'am?"

"Yes, yes. Just a headache coming on. Tell me about the trucks. What kinds?"

"All kinds. Dump trucks, flat-bed trucks, bulldozers, road graders. Every one of 'em with a little American flag painted on each door. Guess I had just seen the last of 'em drive in there because none came in behind me. I got out and looked around. All those drivers had taken off. Could be they're about to do another Homeland Defense project up at the dam. I alerted the State police. They're checking it out and will get back to me. I've also got a call into St. Catherine's."

"You saw no one?"

"Not a soul. You can be sure I'll keep checkin.' If everything's fine here, I'll see you later at the meeting."

"Yes. Thank you, Turbo. See you at the meeting." Emma closes the door and listens as the Volkswagen engine starts up and trails off. "Damn if this doesn't sound like highway building gear!" She marches over to the ladderback chair, followed closely by Jenny, and puts her Nikes back on. "Damn you, Dickie Donnelley. And you, Governor Brewster Pease, you damn Yalie, you deceitful, manipulative, self-centered sneak. Well, mark my words, Mr. Pease, I knew your father. And your grandfather. I taught each of them a thing or two in their days. And, by God, if you're up to what I think you're up to, I'm about to teach you a few more things. But first, I've got to do some research."

She hustles into the dining room and looks out the bay window at the western sky. The sun is touching the hills. Enough time, enough light for reconnoitering. She whistles to Jenny and grabs her purse. Shoulders back, smartly outfitted in a royal blue sweat suit, Nikes, and a navy windbreaker jacket on her ninety-four-year-old frame—she always said gym clothes take away twenty years—Mrs. Waldo Peters Pell, is primed for another good fight.

The Mercedes tears down the driveway. Jenny, seated in the back, looks straight ahead through the windshield at the road, and growls.

Back at the old Hamilton house, Hunter stares into the clutter on his desk, struggling to contrive a rational excuse for not showing up at Ben's for the nine o'clock meeting with the packager—or calling to cancel. Truth is that Melanie had greeted him first thing in the morning with a velvety-voiced harangue about his sinking into bucolic oblivion. After hearing what she had to say, he was in no mood for that meeting and couldn't leave the city fast enough. He went directly to the garage, got in the Rover, and drove north. But he can't say that to Ben.

This is like presenting copy to a pain-in-the-ass client, he says to the spaniel asleep on the sofa, and reaches for the phone.

Ben's tone is icy. "Where the hell were you?"

"I would have called but I lost my phone."

"You left it at Melanie's. I called her when you didn't show. You can't walk out on this, Barnhill."

That is precisely what Hunter wants to do, because the whole thing is nothing but a dumb practical joke run amok. He had come up with it back in the eighties when the *Times* ran photos of Kennedys with their rosaries kneeling at family graves on anniversaries of the assassinations and other tragic deaths. He collected the photos, researched the size of the family, estimated the probability of more dramatic deaths, wrote something about the evergreen Camelot market, assembled it all in a mock proposal for a coffee table book, The Kennedy Memorial Graveside Companion, and gave it to Ben as a gag gift when he struck out on his own as an independent literary agent. Hunter had completely forgotten about it until Ben called, a few months ago, saying the market is now ready for it. You're out of your mind, Hunter told him. But Ben had all but closed the deal. "Don't worry. I won't walk." The spaniel stirs, its legs twitching as if running in a dream.

"Forget the assurances. Just show up when you're scheduled. Some of us, Melanie included, would like to know when you are going to snap out of this reclusive phase."

"Perhaps never. And I've shared that with her. So tell me about the meeting."

"It went well. They see it like an annuity with sales peaking every time a member of the clan goes under. Like, imagine if this had been done in time for John Jr.—"

Hunter winces. "So you reminded them there are twenty-six surviving grandchildren of Joe and Rose."

"Certainly I did, which is why they're talking deluxe edition, a leatherette cover, detachable for adding supplemental photos, a certified limited edition registration number embossed on the cover and inside a glassine envelope containing a paint chip—oh, I didn't tell you—they found this guy on the internet, a retired janitor who swept up paint chips from the Texas School Book Depository. They bought 'em up."

Hunter groans. "Hard core crass."

"You've got to stop saying that. The recreational mourning market is very big now and growing. They think this is a winner. And you should have seen them trying to figure out if they could do a pre-launch on November 22.

"No way."

"Of course not, but I love the enthusiasm. And we're looking at DVD possibilities, but you've got to get in on this. Let's set up a meeting, and I'm nailing you to it. How about a Monday or Friday. Stay the weekend."

"Fine," he lies, remembering his first winter in the old Hamilton house when he drove to New York every Friday and returned on Mondays to a cold house. In three days' time, cold permeated everything, the upholstery, mattresses, even walls, and it took as many days to re-warm the place. That was before he installed the new furnace, a fourteen-inch layer of fiberglass insulation in the attic and a wood stove in the fireplace. He'd get back from the city, light the kerosene heaters—risking fire, and carbon monoxide poisoning— and wear an electric blanket with a hundred-foot extension cord, tying it on with a piece of scavenged clothesline. Just to get warm. "How about the week after next? Monday."

"Be here or Melanie and I will go up and drag you here."

With a laugh, he hangs up. Melanie. Sometimes he wants to end it, and sometimes he wishes he could just hail a cab to be with her. He sits next to the spaniel on the sofa and strokes it. He doesn't have to worry about heating the house any more. But he still has lots to do before winter, caulking windows, wrapping pipes, splitting firewood for the stove. As for showing up, he's got to do that here in New Burford. Tonight. And tomorrow night he's invited to dinner on the other side of town at the home of the president of the military academy. No doubt a fundraising set-up, but no matter.

And what does it matter if Melanie or anyone else can't understand why he left New York? He never understood why he had settled there. Or in the ad business, for that matter. Sheer chance connected him to Ruggie Wilmot, and Ruggie offered him a job. In his gut he always knew he wanted to do something other than advertising but never figured out what. Until he ended up in New Burford where his priorities became wood splitting and pipe wrapping. He scans the bookshelves lining the room, all filled with books he had collected in the city to read someday in the country— Shakespeare, Doctorow, Halberstam, Hemingway, Tolstoy, Tuchman, Plato, Proust, running yards of Agatha Christie, home improvement, photography, and gardening books.

The clock strikes. He goes to the kitchen, the dog at his heels, opens a can of black bean soup, pours the contents into a pan and, as it simmers, gets a bottle of sherry from the parson's cabinet in the living room. There, on the shelf next to the sherry, is his Academy of

Advertising Golden Ladder Award, a solid piece of Plexiglas, about the size of a brick, with a little golden ladder embedded in it. He picks it up, recalling what Bert Lohman, over at Lohman's Hardware, said the other day about keeping a brick in the toilet tank to conserve water. Bert is one of his best sources for home maintenance tips. He reads the inscription on the little golden rungs,

*If we can see farther it is because*
*we climb on the rungs of a ladder*
*built by those who climbed before us.*

At the foot of the ladder, is the tribute, engraved in brass,

*With the industry's gratitude to*
*Hunter Zelotes Barnhill*
*The Advertis*ing Hall of Fame.

Another mystery, he recalls, bringing the sherry and the brick into the kitchen. Everyone who had won the Golden Ladder before and after him was either dead or retired. He was only thirty-five when elected and his work was nothing special. But once branded a winner, more kudos just kept rolling his way. More awards, along with more promotions, salary increases, bonuses, and perks till he became one of the highest paid in the industry. *Advert*'s annual salary review articles used to list him with an asterisk, designating compensation packages estimated at $10 million and up. Ruggie always told him he was worth every dime so the agency could sell itself as the home of a Golden Ladder winner. He could never buy that. Nor could he ever equate the work he had done with the remuneration and he always sensed the unrealistic salary would ultimately make him unemployable.

The black bean soup is steaming. He adds an overflowing tablespoon of sherry, turns off the flame and starts upstairs with the brick. Eerie light is spilling into the stairwell from behind the partially opened bathroom door. He pushes the door open, drawn into the bright, bluish white light streaming through the window and looks out over the illuminated lawn, rail fence, the field, the horizon of dark, wooded hills to the enormous, golden harvest moon. It is so close to the earth, its giant facial features so distinct, he wonders if he is looking at Ptolemaeus, the only crater name he knows. And somewhere in the lunar dust is a plaque with Richard Nixon's name on it. He chuckles, lifts the lid off the toilet tank, and installs the Golden Ladder Award between the floater ball and the return pipe. Pleased, he returns to the kitchen for his supper. After the dog has licked clean the empty soup bowl, he washes it, puts on a jacket, and leashes the dog for a walk before the meeting.

Heading into the field, into the effulgent moonlight, he freezes. Listening. At first he isn't sure. But the unmistakable drone of a helicopter grows louder. He shuts his eyes, gulps his breath. Dropping the leash, he presses his hands to his ears and starts counting, certain that before he reaches 500 the sound will be gone. The dog skittishly scampers around him, then jumps, pawing his legs. Hunter takes the leash, and pats the dog.

Long ago, he and his buddies had joked that when a chopper got hit, it assumed the characteristics of a flying safe. Then, on a very hot day, back in 1972, he was in a Huey—and it happened. The instant it blew up, he was thrown into luxuriant foliage. When he came to, he learned he was all that remained of the 2nd Squad, 1st Platoon, Charlie Company, 3rd Battalion, 7th Regiment, 1st Brigade, 2nd Marines. The noise trails off. Silence.

Wiping sweat from his cold brow, he starts back to the house. Enervated, he does not feel like going to the town meeting, or anywhere.

Racing against a setting sun, Emma slams the brakes at Wilken's Apple Farm. The Mercedes makes a sharp turn onto the old harvest road and barrels along furrowed tracks through a golden meadow flecked with bittersweet. At the grazing fields, she slows the car to a crawl in deference to an approaching line of cows ambling back to the barn. Jenny barks.

"Quiet, Jenny. Let's not sour the milk." She checks her rear view mirror for the rump of the last cow in the line, then picks up speed.

Emma knows the terrain like the back of her hand, having walked it countless times since Waldo first took her there seventy-five years ago. That was the day he told her about General Custer and the Little Big Horn, which, he said, was like the contour of the promontory at the end of this harvest road. She was wearing a white middy blouse and long slim skirt, and held Waldo's arm as they strolled.

The car comes to a stop in a stand of white oaks. "Here we are, Jenny." She turns off the engine, leans against the steering wheel and peers up through the windshield. "Goody. Old man Wilken's bird-watching seat. Still here." She takes binoculars from the glove compartment, gets out of the car, opens the door for Jenny, and they walk over to the razor strop, hanging from a sturdy branch and attached to block and tackle.

"Now, let's see what condition this is in." She loops the binoculars' strap over her neck and gingerly perches herself on the strop, gets up, examines the leather, tugs at the ropes, and then drops herself heavily onto the strop. "We're in business," she exclaims, pulling on the lift ropes, hoisting herself into the branches, into a panoramic view of St. Catherine Sand and Gravel Company's entire operation. Jenny sits, looking up at her.

Wrapping her arms around the ropes, she lifts the binoculars to her eyes, and slowly scans the metal-roofed buildings and the yard. Nothing strange. Then, on the northern perimeter, a bulldozer comes into view. And another bulldozer. Then a dump truck. Another dump truck. A power crane, grader, bulldozer, crane, ditcher, trencher, paver, an office trailer. All lined up in the same direction—a little American flag on every door. Thirty-two updated versions of what had arrived in the fifties just before New Burford got its court order to reroute Interstate 50.

The strop painfully squeezes her legs as she retraces the line of vehicles. She is about to lower the binoculars when suddenly there appears, from behind a bulldozer, a soldier in camouflage battle dress and campaign hat, a swagger stick tucked under his arm. Quite odd, she mutters. That outfit looks like a hodgepodge of uniforms. The campaign hat belongs with leather puttees—like Waldo's, in the photograph taken the day he left for World War I, a small rolled up Oriental rug at his side. Before the photo was taken, his mother insisted he press to his chest adhesive tape with his name and address printed on it, which is how they would identify him. Long ago. She refocuses. However, this chap is wearing that old campaign hat like a drill instructor's. She makes out the name over his right breast pocket: CLAPPSADDLE. Humph, Clappsaddle.

Clappsaddle turns his back to the binoculars revealing steely gray hair. He commences pacing the line of vehicles, randomly checking tires, fuel caps and locks, moving like a martinet, his right arm swinging metronomically, his left rigidly gripping the swagger stick. At the end of the line, Clappsaddle leans over and takes something from his sock. A cigarette. He lights it with a gleaming, silver lighter, coughs, rasping, and spits out a large glob of phlegm. "My word," Emma gasps, dropping the binoculars to her chest.

A chilly breeze rustles the turning leaves. She cocks her head, hearing a distant drone over the black hills. In seconds, the sound crescendos to a deafening roar. A helicopter looms in the crimson sky, heading directly toward the promontory. At about one thousand feet above the white oaks, it hovers, port and starboard lights flickering, then descends into the yard. The letters on it are huge, MAARNG.

The rotors slow, the hatch opens. Emma takes up the binoculars. A stocky guardsman in camouflage battle dress leaps out, hunches under the rotors, arm bent in a salute, and waddles out of decapitation range, where he immediately straightens rigidly. Clappsaddle returns the salute, touching the rim of his campaign hat with the tip of his swagger stick, follows the guardsman under the blades, and they climb aboard. The helicopter lifts off. Emma lowers her binoculars.

Quiet again. From Wilken's farm, the comforting aroma of ripe apples and fragrant applewood smoke wafts through the crisp air. Emma closes her eyes, gathering strength. Suddenly she senses that she is not alone. She looks over her shoulder. There, behind her, gleaming through the trees is the rising moon, a huge orange orb. "What a presence you are tonight," she marvels, gazing, then takes a deep breath, and releases herself to the ground.

The car is still warm inside. She starts the engine, turns on the lights, backs around, and takes off down the old road, recalling the time her man from the Chase Bank came up from New York City in a helicopter and landed on her front lawn. Turbo had sped up the driveway in hot pursuit, ready to make an arrest.

She leans into the steering wheel, squinting through the windshield, and slows the car. Ahead is the unmistakable lanky frame of Alvin "Speedy" Serika, his gawky stride and long walking stick. He faces the headlights.

"Good evening, Speedy."

He nods, warily. Jenny pokes her nose out the window.

"Did you see that helicopter?"

He nods, reaching into his Army surplus field jacket for a pad and pencil. "In gravel yard," he scrawls and gives her the pad.

"You saw the helicopter land?"

He nods, nervously peeling a bit of bark from his walking stick.

"Why don't you get into the car? Then I won't have to twist my neck to read you. I'll give you a lift to the meeting." He had never accepted a ride from her or, as far as she knew, from anyone else, but neither had she ever seen him look so anxious. "Please."

His eyes narrow.

"You'd be doing me a favor. I'd like to talk to you."

He clutches his walking stick.

"The stick too. Hop in."

He gets in, angling the stick between them. The lighted dashboard, the leather seats, the unfamiliar scent fascinate and intimidate him. He hadn't been inside a vehicle for maybe thirty years. Not since the day he got off the Greyhound Bus headed for a Veteran's Administration hospital in northern New York where he was to have received care for the rest of his life, compliments of the United States Government. At the Barrington rest stop he wandered off into a pine grove and while gathering sappy, fragrant cones from a thick carpet of needles, the bus drove away without him.

Jenny sniffs his jacket, and settles down in the back seat.

"Did the helicopter noise upset you?"

He shrugs.

"Something's troubling you. What is it? There's a flashlight in the glove compartment. Take it out so we can see your writing."

He carefully removes the flashlight from under the binoculars. He trusts her. When he works for her during the summer doing handyman jobs at the house, she sometimes invites him to have lunch with her at the kitchen table or on the terrace, and she would say, "—but don't you know," as if she really believes he understands things. And before eating, she always takes his hand and says grace. Maybe a miracle brought her to him on the old harvest road. He reaches into his pocket for an envelope and gives it to her. She reads it.

> *Lady and Gentlemen of The Board: I am a senior citizen and have dignity. I cannot go into the girls' bathroom and locker room at New Burford High School. I ask you, please, get somebody else to clean there. I do not mean any disrespect.*
>
> *Sincerely yours, Alvin A. Serika*

"You wrote this?" It is more an exclamation than a question. As she rereads it, he opens his hand for her to return it. She looks into his anxious eyes and asks, "Would you like me to present this for you?"

He nods—hesitantly, then vehemently.

"I'll be glad to do that for you. You know how business is conducted in town meetings?" He nods but she explains anyway. "Residents bring business before the selectmen who act as the Town Board, Zoning Board, Planning Board, School Board, Highway and Road Commission. If a resident presents a petition they don't like, or if they don't like the petitioner, business simply is not conducted."

Speedy knows this, which is why he's worried about his chances with the selectmen. He can hear their questions—Who is going to take over as custodian for the girls? How do we pay for this? —. He doesn't have any answers. It also worries him that they might finally make him retire—even though he does his job well. Maybe a little slower these days but well, and possibly better than ever.

"Don't worry about a thing. I'll take care of it." She secures the letter in her purse. "Now, I'll take you over to Historical Hall. Would you save my seat? I'm running late and still have to stop by the house."

He writes huge letters, filling the page. "Yes. Thank you."

"Glad to help." Emma grabs the steering wheel with both hands and the gray Mercedes speeds off to Historical Hall.

*Barrington, Massachusetts*
The Black Hawk hovers above the juncture of Main and Church Streets, then banks for an impressive landing on the sprawling back lawn at the Millrace Inn where Palumbo Construction's president, Lieutenant General Bunker T. Clappsaddle, US Army, Retired, is staying. The general and Lieutenant Colonel Marvin P. Norwocki, Massachusetts Army National Guard, leap from the helicopter, and trudge across the lawn, through the inn's charming lobby, and into the oak-paneled barroom, drawing sidelong, disparaging glances from guests and management, and reveling in the impression they are making in their camouflage uniforms.

A libation is in order because the Guard officer, compliments of the governor, has just been assigned to escort the general for the duration of the highway job. The general sets his swagger stick and campaign hat on the bar, and noisily clears his throat. "I'm having Daniel's on the rocks. What's your pleasure, Colonel?"

Norwocki pops out his chest, bracing, and responds in an official tone. "General, I'll have the same, Sir."

Clappsaddle's nostrils flare slightly upon hearing this use of ersatz command voice to express cocktail preference. It's as irksome to him as those exaggerated salutes, and both mannerisms are clear markers of his old pet peeve, Gilbert and Sullivan-esque Guard officers. Nothing used to grate him more, and he had assumed that since his retirement this breed had been relegated to extinction through the ongoing deployments of the Guard with the Active forces. Now he's not so sure. "Bartender, we'll have two Jack Daniel's on the rocks."

The drinks arrive. Bunky raises his glass. "To the President."

"To the President," Norwocki boldly responds. They drink to the President. Norwocki has been working on his image ever since his requisite few days on active duty when it became very clear to everyone that the Guard was inferior to the Regular Army. Years later, Bosnia and the joint training mission in Egypt boosted his Guard esteem, but there's no getting around it, his job is logistics, homeland security, flood and fire control, disaster rescue and relief—not combat. And every day it looks less likely that he'll ever get sent to any hot, sandy location before retirement. Now, with this fluke of an assignment to escort a retired Regular Army general, he is determined to pass as a "real" soldier.

Marvin Norwocki raises his glass. "To the Governor." They toast the Governor, the United States Army, and the National Guard. The ritual concluded, Norwocki waits for the general to speak.

"So, everything is all set for tomorrow morning?" The general hammers his question with the inflection of a command.

"Yes, sir. The chopper will be here at 0915 hours for arrival 0920 at Western Massachusetts Military Academy."

"My vehicle will be at the campus before my arrival?"

"Yes, sir. Your POV will be there 0900."

Clappsaddle is pleased with the change of accommodations, although at first he was mystified by the invitation to stay at the home of the academy's president, Brigadier General Roy Bolton Farrand, for as long as he has business in the area. After checking it out with the governor's office, he accepted—the arrangement is ideal—but has yet to determine how Farrand learned his whereabouts. "Where do you live, Norwocki?"

"Springfield, Sir."

"Do you know New Burford?"

"I know where it is, Sir."

"I've got four million dollars of road-building equipment parked in the middle of that town and a highway to build. The road essentially traverses that town on state land so there should be no problem but I've been alerted to expect trouble if the town gets wind of the job before the bulldozers roll."

"Trouble, Sir?"

Bunky clears his throat. "Did you know Governor Brewster Pease studied ROTC at Yale?"

"Yes, Sir."

"Well, the governor said to me, 'Bunky, you're an old Army man. Fire and movement. Mop-up. You may need that background when you get to New Burford.' Now, that's a gross estimate of the situation, but it's clear the town is eccentric as hell. Evidently, an old battle-ax has a lot of clout there. She's one of the Peters clan, related by marriage to Donnelley, Senator Dick Donnelley, and she is vehemently opposed to the highway—at least doesn't want it anywhere near her town. I was told she'd go to any length to get it rerouted and might even manage to deep-six the whole project. To date, our covert set-up operations have gone smoothly. The old lady knows nothing and has to be kept in the dark only twenty-four more hours. However, I understand she can't be underestimated for a moment."

"If she doesn't know the plan, how can she present a problem?"

"That was my thinking."

"Sir, you say the equipment is at the gravel company. Wouldn't people in the town know it's there?"

"Certainly, but they have no way of knowing why it's there. And the State Director of Highways, Bruno Fitzsimmons, informed me the Highway Patrol is keeping an eye on things. Governor's orders."

"I can confirm that, Sir. State trooper, Sergeant Tim Monahan got the call at Briggs Barracks. The troopers are checking out the entrance to St. Catherine Sand & Gravel every few hours as a part of their regular run down Route 22."

"Good."

Pumped up by approval, Nowocki says, "You know, Sir, Briggs Barracks was named in memory of State Trooper Brad Briggs, killed in Vietnam in '68."

"Interesting."

"Yes, Sir. And, you know, Sir, on the wall right behind Monahan's desk there's a framed clipping from *The Global*. A front-page pho-to of Brad's funeral. And Brewster Pease is in it, consoling Briggs' mother, next to the casket with the flag. Pease was running for State Representative at the time. I remember, 'cause he was just out of law school. I went to high school with Briggs."

"Is that right?" Clappsaddle is ready for a cigarette.

"Yeah. Briggs died out in the jungle. Another patrol found him a week later."

Clappsaddle coughs, and swigs the last of his bourbon. "Ever see combat, Norwocki?"

"No, Sir. Came pretty close in Bosnia. But I read a lot. Clausewitz, Thucydides."

"Admirable."

Marvin takes the compliment as permission to further distinguish himself, which, he understands, is most effectively accomplished by kissing ass, and, having checked out the General's bio on the Internet, he is prepared. "General, that paper flow you had in Vietnam was a first, was it not?"

"Yes, Colonel, it was. Revolutionized after-action reporting. It cost the lives of some brave troopers, but we never lost a single sheet of paper. Not a single order, memorandum, morning report, or after-action report. Not one single damn sheet of paper. I came out of Vietnam with more paper than any other officer in the history of warfare." Bunky envisions the 8,765,000 sheets, stored in footlockers at the Army War College, Carlisle Barracks, Pennsylvania, in the basement of the motor pool.

"That was in '68, I believe."

Clappsaddle signals for another drink. 1968. He was so frustrated by new communications requirements and persistently negative press that he finally wrote to the director of research and development at Xerox, a West Point classmate, telling him he needed field photocopy capability. Six weeks later, the first field Xerox copier was delivered to him in Saigon. It was portable in specially designed backpacks and operated by a team of eleven—ten carrying car batteries, power cords, paper and toner and one machine bearer, who would get on his hands and knees to form a work table. "Yep, '68." When he first asked for volunteers and no one came forward, he ordered the sergeant major to pass the word that anyone who volunteered would get promoted one grade and receive a Bronze Star. The team formed. "I'm proud of those boys to this day. On command, they'd form a circle and go to work, copying, collating, stapling. Every operation, they were first in, last out. I'd walk into briefings, ready to distribute after-action reports to anyone and everyone. And whenever a reporter came up to me, I'd just jab him in the chest with my swagger stick and say, 'You want to know what the fuck happened? Well, here, you smart-assed, preppy yellow-spined dummy. Here's what happened. Read it. And get the fuck out of here.'"

"I've read you gave the press corps a work out."

The second round arrives and Clappsaddle downs half of his, deciding he had misjudged this guardsman. "Colonel, it's time I call it a day." He picks up the swagger stick and tucks it under his arm.

"That's an impressive swagger stick, Sir. A trophy?

"Trophy?" Bunky peers at Norwocki. "No. But it's one of a kind. The shaft," he points, "is the ulna from a Japanese forearm. Guadalcanal, World War II. My father, Gunny Clappsaddle, shellacked it, passed it on to me when I was old enough to understand. I added this part, the occipital bone from a North Korean cranium. Used epoxy glue."

"Imposing." Norwocki's eyes bulge. He gulps some whiskey.

"I was a second lieutenant, then." He pauses. "The tip here is a North Vietnamese meta carpus. I was commanding a Brigade then." He drains his glass, reading Norwacki's horror and disbelief.

"Uh, not everyone would understand what you've got there, Sir." His voice is muted.

"Keen insight, Norwocki. Until I retired from the United States Army, this stick was the bane of a number of young lieutenants, aides-de-camp who failed to keep it out of camera range during my press briefings. However, any criticism, whatever the source, got my standard response: 'They could shove it'—a sentiment some would say pretty much characterized my entire career." He tucks the stick under his arm, signs the check, and picks up his campaign hat. "See you in the morning, Colonel."

Norwocki salutes, perfectly. "Yes, Sir. Thank you, General."

"One more thing, Norwocki. Check on those troopers. I'm reasonably confident I can manage the battle-ax of New Burford but just the same I'd like to be assured tomorrow that she had slept soundly tonight."

"Yes, Sir." Norwocki salutes again.

"Continue to march."

Marvin gapes as the general leaves the barroom, then empties his glass, salutes the bartender and, somewhat bewildered, ambles across the great lawn to wake up the pilots and take off for home.

Not a trace of modern technology is visible on the Common—no telephone poles, electric lights, or automobiles. Light flickers in gas lampposts along the walkways as villagers gather for the town meeting. Leaves drift from stately oak, maple, and sycamore trees. At one end of the central gravel walkway, Historical Hall is radiant, its twelve over twelve paned windows brightly lit from within, while the similar, somewhat smaller white clapboard Congregational Church at the other end of the Common is dark. Prominently displayed between the two buildings are the town's relics, a highly varnished iron cannon, cannonballs stacked beside it, and the ancient pillory, a reminder of the method of punishment, exposure to public scorn, in effect a century before 1757, the date over Historical Hall's entrance.

Massive chestnut doors swing open into the aroma of mulled cider and a commotion of greetings, seat saving and coat stashing. Hunter, among others who have arrived too late to get a seat, is wedged into the back of the meeting room, against a brass wall plaque—*Two hundred Windsor chairs donated by Waldo Pell, September, 1930.*

At precisely eight o'clock the gavel is pounded. People are still arriving. Emma hustles down the center aisle to her seat—right side, fifth row, where Speedy is watching for her. "Now don't you worry," she whispers to him as she takes her seat and reaches into her purse. Deftly, she places an air mouse on her shoulder, pointing it toward the back wall where a little red light flashes near the ceiling, assuring her that Colonial Cable's cameras are operating.

"Order. The meeting will come to order." Town Moderator Worthington pounds the gavel, and signals the lamplighter who signals Turbo to come inside. The room quiets. "Ladies and Gentlemen, the meeting will come to order. All stand for the presentation of the colors by the United States' oldest military command in continuous service, the New Burford Defense Battalion, founded in 1638, now under the command of Colonel Hamilton Goodwill."

Everyone stands, turning to face the entrance. In a deafening eruption of snares and dull, penetrating thuds, drummers lead a procession to the front of the hall, followed by eight fifers playing "Yankee Doodle" in shrill unison, then the solemn Colonel Goodwill, the color guard carrying the Betsy Ross and Massachusetts flags and the Battalion's Battle Colors, and, finally, two militiamen clutching Brown Bess muskets with thirteen-inch bayonets—all in colonial militia uniforms. At the selectmen's table, they turn and face the assembly.

"Ladies and Gentlemen," Worthington intones, "Our National Anthem performed by Willard Cornwall, deformed at birth, thereby gifted, and blessed with perfect pitch."

A trim, middle-aged man in a dark blue suit, starched white shirt and red bow tie, steps forward, places his hand on his heart, takes a deep breath and, accompanied by a soft, continuous drum roll, whistles pure, resonant tones. —*And the land of the free-e-e-e-e*— Willard holds the high note, enrapturing his audience, then quickly catches more breath for the conclusion. Applause is thunderous, women sniffling, drying their eyes, men cheering.

A craggy faced man elbows Hunter and comments, "Fine whistling, eh, Barnhill? It's the harelip, ya know." Hunter nods, applauding, smiling at the performance, at the odd references to the unfortunate cleft palate, and at the realization that this guy knows his name.

The applause gradually subsides, the color guard sets the flags in their stands, the Defense Battalion recesses, Turbo hustles down the aisle to his front row seat. At the fireplace, Tom Kindle, lamplighter, adds logs until flames lap the suspended kettle of cider. Worthington announces. "Be seated. The meeting will come to order. All selectmen are present, together with the Town Moderator, Secretary, and Town Clerk. Those with business to present before this governing body of New Burford may come forth."

Emma cranes her neck for a better look at a man in the second row, far left. Yes, it's Percy. Percy Standish, Secretary of the Commonwealth, Brew's buddy through Yale and Harvard Law, and a most trusted adviser since he managed Brewster's first and victorious political campaign. So what's he doing here tonight? Standish glances, uncomfortably, over his shoulder at her. Emma averts her eyes.

Hamilton Goodwill, hand upon scabbard, struts to the trestle table and clicks his heels.

"Mr. Goodwill is recognized."

"Mr. Worthington, honored Selectmen, friends and neighbors, I come before you to petition special funding for the Memorial Day Parade, which, by tradition, is led by our oldest living veteran. Montgomery Gerard, hero in the Spanish American War, did so till he passed on in 1979 at the age of 101, yielding the honor to Perkins Haight, who served with the first U.S. combat troops in France in the Great War. As you know, Perkins is at the Heavenward Rest Home where he's been pretty much unconscious for years. But for two years now, in a wheelchair, he's lead the parade." He pauses. "Unfortunately, Doc Barnes says Perkins is on life supports and can't make it in the wheelchair this year."

A low grumble ripples across the room.

"However—!" He waits for the room to quiet. "However, if we were to rent a portable life support system—you know, on casters—we could push Perkins in his bed, with the equipment, down the parade route." His voice is ebullient. "A Heavenward nurse would accompany him and we'd assign Boy Scouts to help him salute."

The assembly murmurs in accord.

"The cost is $3,500 for the equipment rental, shipping and insurance. A considerable sum, but a small price to continue our tradition." He bows his head.

Worthington moderates. "This is a simple matter of approving the expenditure from the General Fund. Is there discussion?" Someone yells, "How do you know he's alive?" Generalized mumbling ensues. Worthington bangs the gavel.

Hunter has heard enough, wants to leave, imagines himself squeezing through sardine-packed villagers to open and escape through the huge doors, and decides it would be regrettably poor form. Captive, he scans the crowd, checking out the women. They all look very married, too young, or much too old for him.

Then he sees her across the aisle. Shiny, long dark hair, in a single thick braid, her head held high on a graceful neck, like an exotic flower. She looks his way, for an instant. Beautiful. Great cheekbones. Maybe late thirties. Hard to tell. He looks at the speaker, trying to pay attention. There is a petition to light the inside of the church whenever there are activities at Historical Hall. A complaint about the military academy's reveille cannon going off at 5:45 a.m. A proposal to disallow that complaint because it comes up at every meeting, to no avail. A petition to restore Mildred's Coffee Shop to its original purpose triggers heated comment; "Let me remind you that Mildred's was originally the town's arsenal until her avaricious great-grandfather converted it into a general store back in the mid-1800's. For years some of us have endeavored to explain to you all the importance of preserving authenticity. Now, in these terrible times of attack on American soil, we have yet another and, I daresay, compelling reason to restore our town arsenal for—"

"Sit down, George," someone shouts. Others boo. Worthington strikes the gavel. Hunter gets another elbow jab and comment from his neighbor, "Don't worry, this talk about restoring Mildred's is just a lot of blather."

Hunter glances at her again. Again she looks his way, this time with smiling eyes, telling him they will meet after the meeting. She is exquisite, with a kind of energy, even as she's just standing there. He forces himself to listen to the speaker so he can talk about it with her. A husky woman in a green corduroy dress stands to announce that OSHA investigators showed up at Grandmother Tucker's Chocolate Chip Cookies Cooperative to check the commercial baking kitchen and assessed that the countertops are too high for the workers, posing health risks. She whines, "It will cost the town $10,000 to lower them but the minimum penalty for willful violation is $7,000."

Opinions fly. "The grandmothers don't use that kitchen for baking cookies, they play bocce ball there, and make the cookies in their own apartment kitchens." Another says, "Don't mess with OSHA." The husky woman continues, "We're all very proud of our town for having realized Olive Tucker's dream of converting the condemned shoe factory into a place where senior widows can live comfortably and choose to work, doing what they love—baking chocolate chip cookies. They get flex-time, three months vacation a year, and excellent medical care for life. And the ladies are proud of their cookies, personally signing each bag, pledging that a real grandmother baked the contents. We keep on file copies of all the grandmothers' birth certificates and family trees, available for inspection at the Attorney General's Office. We simply must comply with OSHA or it's all over for the cookies!"

Like Hunter, Emma is having difficulty paying attention. Her thoughts circle and re-circle the possible reasons for Percy Standish's attendance at this particular meeting. And the trucks. Suddenly, the gavel bangs with the final call for new business. Remembering Speedy, she jumps to her feet and composes herself, standing with back straight, sternum elevated, chin raised, hands clasped, and projects her voice. "Mr. Moderator, I have two items, but before presenting them let this assembly recognize, as a courtesy and for the record, the presence of the Honorable Percy Standish, Secretary of the Commonwealth." She captures the full attention of everyone in the room, including Hunter who imagines her delivering a formidable new business presentation in New York.

"Quite right, Mrs. Peters Pell. On behalf of the Town of New Burford, I extend a formal welcome to the Honorable Percy Standish, Secretary of the Commonwealth of Massachusetts, who is visiting here tonight as part of the governor's initiative to explore more adaptable organization frameworks between state and local governments. Mr. Standish."

Standish stands, waves perfunctorily, and hastily sits down.

Emma continues. "I'm so glad the secretary is here tonight because he can address my first item: the governor's new highway. Secretary Standish, please tell us, the people of New Burford, the exact location of the highway and assure us that this highway will not, in any way, impact New Burford."

There is mumbling.

Worthington brings down the gavel. "Silence! Mr. Standish, would you be kind enough to respond to that."

Percy stands. "I'm afraid I can only say that the highway route is not yet finalized. However, as far as the people of New Burford are concerned and especially with deference to you, Mrs. Peters Pell, I can affirm that in planning the highway, the Commonwealth of Massachusetts has taken into account New Burford's history of active intolerance of highway construction within its borders."

The assembly chuckles as he takes his seat. Emma smiles, pleased that so many still know about her crusade back in the fifties. "So then, Mr. Standish, explain why today road-building equipment arrived at St. Catherine's Gravel."

Percy gets to his feet again. "Uh—, you know, I can't explain it. I suggest you ask the people at the gravel company."

"Anything further, Mrs. Peters Pell?" Worthington asks.

Emma doesn't like his slick, evasive answer and particularly it's condescending edge. From the corner of her eye she can see that Speedy is wringing his hands. "Yes, Mr. Moderator, may I speak privately with you for a moment? This item needs to be presented and handled with discretion?"

Worthington agrees, Emma goes forward, withdrawing Speedy's note from her purse. As they speak quietly at the side of the room, conversation rises. Turbo unwraps trays of finger sandwiches and Grandmother Tucker's cookies, while the woman in the green corduroy dress ladles hot cider into cups. Tom Kindle stokes the fire. Worthington shakes hands with Emma and signals Willard, who comes forward and whistles "Good Night Ladies."

The center aisle fills with chatting villagers, wending toward the refreshment table, blocking Hunter's approach to her. For an instant, he loses sight of her, then sees her at the door as she turns to glance into the crowd just before disappearing. Unable to butt through the crowd, he calms himself and affably returns neighbors' greetings and small talk, while fully expecting to find her waiting outside.

She isn't. She's nowhere on the Common. He dashes to the parking lot and walks the length of the lot, looking around as cars drive away. She's vanished.

By 11:00 p.m. everyone has left Historical Hall except Tom Kindle and Constable Turbo Bull. They place a spark guard screen on the fireplace, check the window latches and leave together, ceremonially closing the massive chestnut doors. Turbo inserts the brass key in the wrought iron rim lock and, turning it, listens for the hollow clunk of secure closure.

The room is still. The camera sensor responds to the silence and the videotape recorder at Colonial Cable shuts down. Moonlight casts shimmering shadows on the luminous whitewashed walls.

In his room at the Millrace Inn, Bunky Clappsaddle is in bed, rereading *War As I Knew It*, George Patton's diaries. It's his gospel—good, tough, don't-fuck-around-with-it military logic. He lifts his reading glasses onto his forehead to rub his eyes, then lets them slip back onto his nose and checks the time. Eleven o'clock. He swings out of bed, puts on his West Point bathrobe, throws open his old footlocker scarred by bullets and incendiary bombs and takes out a shoe-polish kit.

Wrapping a stained rag around his index finger, Lieutenant General Bunker Terhune Clappsaddle, US Army Retired—recipient of thirty-seven personal decorations for bravery and gallantry, commander of thirty thousand troops, holder of two advanced degrees—commences smearing black polish on his sturdy black shoes, just as he has every day since his enlistment in the Marine Corps, which was two years before his appointment to West Point. Shoe shining is his particular ritual whereby he grants himself permission to go to sleep. It is also somewhat humbling—just enough to remind him of how he fits into the scheme of things with everyone, including enemies. Yes, that's what he'll say to the cadets in the morning if asked to address them after the parade. He'll tell them humility is an essential part of the military psyche. Yes, he's looking forward to his stay at WMMA.

Speedy sprints up two flights of stairs, into a classroom, to his favorite computer. As Emma was driving him home and telling him about her meeting with Worthington, he couldn't remember if he had deleted the letter from the hard drive after transferring it to his floppy disc.

The computer is taking forever to boot. His heart is pounding. Emma told him Worthington is handling his matter with the selectmen. But what does that mean? If they turn it down, he will have to take his pension and find a place to live. So be it. He simply will never again clean the girls' rest rooms, their locker room, or showers, or, most shameful, load tampon machines, which are all about girls' bodies and sex and indecent, sinful things. Even if nuns and the Virgin Mary herself had been girls once, they never would have used a girls' rest room. And no decent Lithuanian Catholic man should ever have to go there.

A few clicks take him to the file. There's the letter! He deletes it, shuddering to imagine if some kid had found it. He turns off the computer, and carefully, to avoid scuffing the newly waxed floor, replaces the chair under the desk. In the hallway, walking down to the stairs, he feels secure again. For years he's washed, waxed, scraped and painted every inch, so many times. Here, after everyone's gone home the school feels like an empty church—the words, the discipline exacted by the teachers, linger in the stillness, letting him know he's part of something important. He doesn't want to retire.

In the basement he unlocks the door to his apartment. A large orange cat greets him, meowing insistently. It would be very hard to leave the home he built himself, starting construction the day he moved in, which was the day after he arrived in New Burford. He first subdivided the cavernous area between the boiler and the storage rooms into a kitchen, a bedroom and bathroom, rerouting pipes and installing a shower with a steam bath tap from the boiler. Then he created a living room and dining area for guests, though no one ever came for a visit, except the sweet kitten he named Fiona.

He replenishes Fiona's kibble and water, replacing under them a fresh paper placemat celebrating the United States' Bicentennial, and then goes about replacing the Bicentennial placemats on his dresser and the arms of his TV chair. He drops into the chair, gazing at the wall art behind the TV screen, five girls' bicycle seats arranged in a circle, like petals on a daisy. Years ago, he stole them from the bike-racks. He knew it wasn't right, but, looking at them, he could feel, if only for a moment, as if he knew something about women and sex, and not quite so embarrassed about things.

Fiona leaps onto the arm of his chair and licks her paws as he pulls off his heavy shoes. From under the chair, he drags a metal box full of rags, brushes, and shoe polish tins. His first pair of shoes, from the Montgomery Ward catalog, never got shined. In catechism class, when their chairs were in a circle, he'd compare his scruffy shoes with the other kids', thinking his were like nice old dogs. When he outgrew them, his older brothers weren't ready to pass theirs on to him, so he went barefoot that summer. He loved running barefoot, feeling free and brave, even on dirt roads, toughing out the impact of pebbles on his tender soles. A few summers later his feet were too big for the shoes left behind by his brothers when they got drafted, and even the shoes left by his father were too tight. Realizing how big he was for fourteen, he hitched a ride down to the draft board in Scranton, lied about his age, and enlisted. Next thing he knew he was at the induction center, where he was put on a bus to Louisiana with a new pair of shoes, free shoes, provided by the Government, and he was told that if he didn't take care of his free shoes, he would be punished. Ever since, he continued polishing his shoes every day, even at the V.A. hospital, where nobody had to tell him to do it, but he figured the terms for free shoes were the same.

He brushes off the dust before applying polish.

Hunter can't quite believe she had fled, that they hadn't connected. How is it possible that after years of reading New York women signaling attraction, he could completely misinterpret that smile in New Burford, Massachusetts? Not only did he misread her, but now he's feeling like an insecure adolescent, rejected by the girl of his dreams. This is lunacy, he says aloud, tossing a biscuit to Freddie. Maybe she had to get home to kids. Or to a husband or some other.

Spreading a yellowed section of *The New York Trib* on the kitchen table, he suddenly thinks of Jefferson who hadn't entered his thoughts for years. Jefferson used to work the buildings between Madison and Sixth Avenues, making office rounds with his shoeshine stand, always smiling and humming. Hunter never let Jefferson shine his shoes. Instead, he'd take the polishing stand from him and shine his own shoes while Jefferson sat at his desk, telling jokes, hot gossip, and insider information picked up at the other media companies he serviced. Great jokes, fantastic stock tips.

He places a pair of highly shined black dress shoes on the newspaper, suddenly remembering the day he was in the Luz-Werner Building for a meeting, walking by the office of the icon of New York ad women, Babs Mahoney. There she was, cosseted in her leather armchair, lifting her skirt, swinging her long leg to place her Bottega Veneta-clad foot onto Jefferson's stand while Jefferson, at her feet, sat bantering away, smiling, polishing, looking up her skirt. Amused, Hunter said hello to Jefferson, who called him in for an introduction. Babs Mahoney hardly needed an introduction. Smart, tough, fiercely tenacious, she was one of the company's top advertising salespeople. It was said that she never asked for an order—she demanded it. Their affair, if it could be called that, started that afternoon and ended almost as quickly, but, for some inexplicable reason, they remained friends.

He pauses, momentarily closes his eyes, then opens a can of polish and smears some on the shiny shoe, just as he was taught under the hot sun of Parris Island, South Carolina. After he recovered, physically, from the helicopter crash, shoe shining became his private ritual for keeping alive the memory of buddies he had survived.

The town secretary stands by, watching out across the moonlit Common as Worthington inserts the heavy brass key into the rim lock. With a loud clank, it unlocks Historical Hall's massive door.

Silently, they step inside, into shadows of mullions, branches and falling leaves dancing on wide, moonlit floorboards. They move through the shadows, to the front of the room, without removing coats or hats and, without making a sound, seat themselves at the trestle table.

Minutes later, the door creaks open again, admitting the town attorney, the town clerk, and the three town selectmen, all wearing brimmed hats, coats, and scarves. In silence, they join the others at the table. In silence, they wait. Worthington reaches for his pocket watch, its steady tick intensifying each second.

They wait, nerves on edge, wrestling with conflicted loyalties, pangs of conscience—the very feelings each had experienced when first approached, individually, by the governor's envoy. Independently, each had said: No—it would destroy the town. Then, the next morning, Governor Pease himself had telephoned each of them, expressing his gratitude for their public service in weighing complex factors affecting the future of their town and the Commonwealth. He had asked their opinions on state and national issues, and listened. He had confided, letting them know his goals and dreams for the people of New Burford, how much he cares, and how grateful he is to the Widow Pell, his mentor and champion. Charmed, each council member had caved. However, each also had insisted that the matter go before a town meeting. That evening, an aide to the governor, had phoned Worthington proposing, "Dispense with adjournment and keep the meeting open for continuance after the people go home. The council can then legitimately proceed with official business." He had assured Worthington that no record of the transactions would be accessible to the public, and promised that each council member would be handsomely compensated at the close of the meeting for meritorious civic service. It was agreeable to all. Two days later, each received a blazer patch of the Massachusetts State Seal, a token of the governor's appreciation.

A hot coal crackles behind the fireplace screen, startling them. They resettle, again bowing their heads, tugging at hat brims, averting their eyes. Worthington had thought it fortuitous when Emma approached to speak privately. Their discussion had provided a perfect cover for suspending the meeting without adjourning. At the time, he had felt it was a sign that the council was doing the right thing by going around her. He doesn't feel that now, but there is no turning back. He tries to focus on the positive, imagining the town council buying new blazers for their new Massachusetts patches.

The door opens. Two men in long coats and brimmed hats, one tall, easily six feet, the other short, stocky and carrying a briefcase, walk silently through the shadows to the long table and seat themselves. The selectmen recognize Percy Standish as he eyeballs Worthington, but not the stocky guy who excruciatingly grimaces as he fingers the combination lock on his briefcase. The case opens without a sound and he withdraws stacks of papers flagged with yellow stickers. One by one, he passes them to Standish, who starts them around the table for the required signatures. One by one, the papers return to the short guy who looks them over and checks them against a list. It's all there—the Commonwealth's environmental impact statement, rights of way, blasting permits, contracts for the Palumbo Construction Company, sole source purchase orders for St. Catherine Sand and Gravel Company, an executive order from the Governor, a Federal order from the Department of Transportation and all other instruments required legally to permit construction of Interstate I-51 through the Township of New Burford.

Percy shakes hands with Worthington. The entire route for I-51, including the stretch through New Burford, is now clear—from New York's State Parkway to the turnpike into Boston, and, under authorization of the Federal Highway Administration, the highway will run in one direction only—east—facilitating entrance into the state and slowing egress. He yanks at the brim of his hat, acknowledging the council, and silently leaves the building. The short guy piles seven envelopes, each about two inches thick, in the center of the table, and chases after Standish.

The town leaders sit motionless, each waiting for someone to make the first move. Worthington leads, easing up from the table. He takes an envelope, silently exits, and stations himself at the door. Like a spotlight, the moon is shining on the Common. The recording secretary emerges, then the town clerk, the town attorney and finally the selectmen—all pass by, into the night. Worthington looks in to be sure all the envelopes have been taken, then secures the door, replaces the brass key in the bore of the cannon, and flees.

Historical Hall is still. At Colonial Cable the video recorder stops.

Speedy rubs his eyes. The dark screen had lit up, brightening the room, awakening him. Shadowy figures. In Historical Hall. Was it a dream about the meeting? He had turned on the television to calm down, watching *New Burford's Best Home Videos*, and pressed record just before dozing off. He draws his hands over his rough chin, then hits replay. This was no dream.

The picture is dim, blurry, but very real. Seven shadowy figures gather at the selectmen's table. Speedy studies their shapes, their movements, how they walk and sit. One by one, he identifies them. Two more enter. It's the guy Emma introduced at the meeting. Percy Standish, Secretary of the Commonwealth. The one with the briefcase is a stranger. The briefcase opens. Paper flows from it, streams around the table, momentarily stopping at each person, and returns to the briefcase. Then, in reverse order of arrival, the players leave.

The screen darkens. What were they doing? Speedy vigorously scratches his scalp, gets up from the edge of his chair, and goes to the kitchen to heat a cup of Wilken's raw milk, his sedative.

# 3

*New Burford*

Her face buried in plump feather pillows, Emma ignores the brilliant, insistent morning sunlight, the furnace's muted rumble, the clock radio's dulcet market report. Jenny paws at her shoulder. The phone is ringing. She rolls over, spilling pillows to the floor, and reaches for the phone. "Emma Peters Pell speaking."

"Mrs. Pell, it's Samson. Something's amiss here."

"Samson. For goodness sake. Hold just a second. I've got to let the dog out." Samson Feddicker works at Colonial Cable every morning from 5:30 to 7:30, when he goes off to teach physics at New Burford High. He's never met a problem he can't solve, and certainly never phoned her with an alert of any kind. Tying on her red tartan robe, she bounds down the stairs after the dog, lets her out, and picks up the phone in the front hall. "Okay. What's up, Samson?"

"Mrs. Pell, I'm not quite sure what we've got here but when I came in this morning, I discovered the back-up tape for Historical Hall had been running for some time. Kicked in a few hours after the meeting last night."

"Technical difficulty."

"I thought so, too. So I rewound and played some of it back. Now, I can't tell you what was going on because the picture isn't clear, but—"

"Maybe that home video show went off trolley."

"No. That show ended at 11:30 without a problem. This was going on around two a.m. Looks like phantoms but they blur into the shadows."

"What's the audio?"

"Nothing much. Seems the key in the lock may have been loud enough to trip the tape. And noise of some sort was continuous enough to keep the tape going. At one point it sounds like a coal pops and the phantoms seem to jump a bit. I don't know."

"So, those phantoms knew enough to avoid audio detection."

"I'd say. But, Mrs. Pell, it's all very unclear."

"What's clear is that phantoms didn't trigger the tape." She's pacing, tethered to the telephone. "And, if nothing else, the video is proof that a meeting took place, and nails the time."

"I'm about to see if I can enhance it, bring up some of the images."

"Excellent. Make dupes, too. I'll be down right away, in two shakes of a lamb's tail. Thank you, Samson."

She hangs up, touches her toes five times, opens the door, letting Jenny in, and dashes upstairs to get dressed, muttering the whole time. "Percy Standish, road-building equipment, weird-looking soldiers in a Guard helicopter, phantoms at Historical Hall—all under the light of the Blood Moon. This is highly unsavory, and I'm going to get to the bottom of it."

*Boston*

Despite a sleepless night, Governor Brewster Pease is energized when Senator Dick Donnelley arrives for breakfast in his office at his residence. With the Senate's passage of the National Lawn Care Bill, and the right of way approved in New Burford, the major obstacles to delivering on his campaign promise are cleared. Western Massachusetts will get its federally funded highway, a new conduit for pulling in more tourist dollars and vacation homebuilders. Little did he know during his campaign that immediately after his election the federal government would put a tight squeeze on highway funding, shifting the financial burden for new highways to state taxpayers. At that point he had no option but to find alternative federal funding for the highway. And he did. Pork. Donnelley agreed to attach the highway to the National lawn Care Bill and now he owes him—big time. He presumes the senator, lagging miserably in the polls, has come to discuss payback.

Pease pours coffee from a Victorian silver pot, first into Dick's cup, then into his own. "So I understand it'll be signed next week."

"That's right. I got the President's congratulatory call last night. The bill and everything attached to it will be signed into law on Tuesday."

"Thank you," Pease says sincerely. "Too bad the bill itself is such a monstrosity."

"Nobody on the Hill had any enthusiasm for it," Donnelley admits, tearing off a piece of croissant. "And right up to the vote, the chances for passage had been anyone's guess."

"But enough of you had stakes in the stuff attached to it. Marmalade?"

"Please."

Pease leans back against pale yellow brocade upholstery and presses his fingertips together, "Now a jillion lawyers and bureaucrats—federal, state, local—will trip over each other trying to make it work."

"It'll be something of a mess, definitely, but there's an up side."

"What's that?" Brewster uncrosses his leg and picks up the paper Dick had laid beside his water glass. It's a schedule of stump speeches and appearances.

"First, it's going to employ a hellova lot of people just to set it up. And, since it's considered a middle class bonanza, it'll give us leverage to pass some of the tougher legislation we want."

"If you get the job again." Brewster can't figure out why Dick is so composed, so confident, as if unaware of his numbers.

"I'm not going to lose. And you're a great support—."

"You know I'll get more votes for you." Brewster reviews the schedule. "I see here you're putting me on a diet of rubber chicken for a month."

"Right up to Election Day. Your chief of staff already has that schedule."

He puts it down. "I'll work hard for your reelection. I'll give you all the credit you deserve and then some. I'll focus on your achievements, your ongoing legislative work to improve the economy and assure public safety. But—I'm not a magician."

"I know that and I greatly appreciate your support. But the silver bullet required to win this campaign is in a plan that's right on the zeitgeist. It's in place and already working."

Brewster is put off by his smug, irrational confidence. "You're barely scraping nine percent with less than four weeks to go."

"You know very well things can change overnight in this game. Also, bear in mind, had I not orchestrated some things, you'd now be marked as a one-term governor. The challenge I face in this campaign, and in my personal life, is daunting but no more so than yours in delivering the highway."

"That's not a valid comparison. For starters, I could not have predicted the shift in federal policy on highway funding—and certainly not the timing of it. However, you should have known that once the media got wind of you and Kyle, the affair would go to the top of the news."

"Yes, I knew that."

"And you knew damn well that your effectiveness set you in the crosshairs, an ostensibly upstanding target to be brought down by scandal, fabricated if necessary. And surely you know that Kyle Ludger is not the kind of gal you keep quietly tucked away in Georgetown."

"She certainly isn't," Donnelley affirms with a wide smile. "She's about as high profile as it gets. And yes, Brew, I very much considered all the factors—she's gorgeous, has a great body, great family, even has a relative on the other side of the aisle. Farmington, Princeton, Columbia School of Journalism. And, you could say, she is the media. What's more, she has an uncanny instinct for psyching out voters, an extraordinary talent for lovemaking, and I have every intention of divorcing Millicent and marrying her."

Pease smirks. "And if you lose, where does she stand?"

The door opens. An expressionless woman in a black dress steps in. "Governor, the people from *Folks* are her for the eight o'clock interview—I told them you'd be a bit longer."

"Thank you."

Donnelley spoons orange marmalade on a piece of croissant, pops it into his mouth, and drinks some coffee. "You asked me to speculate where Kyle would stand if I were to lose."

"You've thought about that, I'm sure."

"She and I have discussed it. If I lose, I'll land a post like ambassador to France or Italy."

"So, win or lose, you get the girl."

"Look. You yourself said the opposition dredged up those photos because I built my political career on high ethical standards. I got plenty of mileage out of that. But it actually became a liability. The longer it took to get any dirt on me, the greater their imperative to do so and, as you also pointed out, it was just a matter of time before I'd find myself in a trumped up scandal. So I took control, set it up myself, arranging it so that they'd get their scandal but I'd still come out on top, having my cake and eating it, too."

"Clever. You set yourself up to get knocked off the moral high ground."

"Correction. I haven't yielded the moral high ground—not yet, anyway."

Pease shakes his head. "You're delusional."

"As I said, things are about to turn around."

"Dick, you can't spin out of this one."

"People see photos of Kyle and me—and they wish."

"Indeed. But they won't vote you out of office because you're a philanderer. Rather, it's because they now see you as a blatant hypocrite. Voters want a scapegoat. This time, you're it."

Donnelley is unperturbed. "Not so fast. As it happens there's a rumor on the Web that's reframing this entire situation." He pauses, wipes his hands on the linen napkin and, dropping it on the coffee table, announces softly, "It is rumored that Millicent has had several lesbian affairs over the past twenty years."

"That's low," says Pease. "And brilliant. Millicent will soon be very eager to get this out of the news cycle."

"Exactly."

Pease contemplates momentarily. "You will get votes out of this."

"No doubt," Donnelley understates. "It's being positioned that it was because of my ethical standards that I suffered a dead marriage to a lesbian for all those years—for the sake of our daughter. There will be plenty of sympathy for me, and for Millie, for each of us, in our own separate ways as we finally move on to experience real marriage. And I expect I'll even be forgiven any past affairs that might surface in all this."

"It'll work. No one's quite done this before." Brewster says with some amazement. He crosses his arms. "You're betting Millie won't respond."

"Millicent won't know how to deny it and, if she does deny it, people will think she's protesting too much."

"Your daughter gets a bad deal."

"She's twenty-four. She's a good kid. She's tough. Couple of weeks, she'll be fine."

The expressionless woman again opens the door. "Governor, Mrs. Peters Pell is on the line."

"Maybe she's found out about the highway," quips Donnelley.

"What's on her mind?" asks Pease.

"Wouldn't say, except that it was just between you and her."

"I'll take it."

Donnelley looks at his watch. "I've got to run. I'll see you at the Copley, then, 11:45," and, as he leaves, cocks his head toward the telephone. "Good luck with her."

Brewster picks up the phone. "Emma! Good to hear from you."

"Oh, bullshit, Brewster. I'm calling to let you know I'm on to your chicanery. And I'm not going to let you get away with it."

"Emma, Emma. There's got to be a misunderstanding here."

"I'm talking about the special meeting last night in New Burford's Historical Hall, the clandestine meeting around two in the morning when most citizens are home in bed."

Brewster flinches. How in hell did she find out? "Meeting? At two in the morning?"

"Furthermore, I personally counted the road building trucks over at St. Catherine Sand and Gravel. You're aiming to ram that damn highway through New Burford—and I won't stand for it."

Brewster quickly assesses she's pieced together a few flimsy, sketchy facts, and formulated a hunch, nothing more. "Emma, please, calm down."

"Brewster Pease, I've handled this kind of cheap political crap before. You know that. This time you've gone too far."

Brewster lets out a sigh. The paperwork was signed and reviewed by the attorney general. Nothing had been overlooked. It would be impossible for her to stop things now but he doesn't want her to know the details until the work is underway. "Emma, you know the Commonwealth of Massachusetts is about to get a much needed piece of the Federal interstate highway system. Now, I know you don't want it anywhere near New Burford, so that's the last thing I would permit."

"The last thing? Point blank, Brewster Pease, precisely where is the route?"

"I've told you, Emma, I will personally let you know just as soon as it's nailed down."

"I know you, Brewster—"

"And I know you and respect you tremendously, Emma. But I'm beginning to think you'll oppose the new highway no matter where it's built."

"That's not true, young man. I believe as you do that it's high time for the rear end of our state to catch up with the front end. But I think this is about something else."

"Progress, Emma. It's about progress."

John Cassler, media adviser, comes in. Brewster signals for him to be seated.

"Progress? Nonsense," Emma vociferates.

"Mrs. Peters Pell, a lot of good people did a lot of work to get this highway. It's fully approved, funded, and there's nothing you can do to stop it. So I wish you'd just relax and appreciate that the day the highway opens will be a great day for Massachusetts."

Cassler cynically rolls his eyes.

"A great day, all right. For advancing yourself to the Presidency, and you know I'll support you, but only if you behave like a public servant, not some self-centered brat."

"I'm doing what's right for the people. And they know it. Emma, don't become an anachronism. It doesn't suit you."

Cassler strikes his forehead with the heel of his hand, scrunching his mouth.

Emma is indignant. "Pease, whether or not I'm an anachronism is irrelevant. But if you're operating like a scoundrel with me, and I believe you are, then I'm going to see to it that you are ground out like a cheap cigar." She hangs up.

"Emma, let me assure you—" Brewster, stone-faced, hangs up on the dial tone.

"Trouble," says Cassler.

"Not at this point. Everything's in place."

"I'll say. Wait till you see what I'm pulling off the Internet." He opens a thick file. "Our Dick Donnelley may be golden, after all. Would you believe Millicent—"

Pease cuts in, "—is a lesbian."

"I'm betting Donnelly rides this right into the winner's circle."

*New Burford*

As usual, downtown New Burford is bustling at eight o'clock. Shopkeepers have opened for business, displayed their American flags and many have hung on the door a little sign printed in Baskerville, the town's official typeface—*Browsers welcome. Back in five minutes—* which means the proprietor is over at Mildred's.

As usual, Mildred's breakfast crowd is buzzing, every overheard statement open to anyone's comment. As usual, town officials are all there, though not, as usual, sitting together. As usual, Mildred's cat, Peachpie, is stretched out under the butter dispenser at the end of the counter near the front window, which, for the first time since early June, is masked with steam on the inside against the frosty morning outside. At the other end of the counter, by the back door, Constable Turbo Bull is perched on the first red-cushioned stool, his rusty .357 magnum revolver, drooping from its holster belt. Speedy is on the next stool, then Hunter, a new regular at the counter.

"Here we go, Constable, the He-Man Special. Go easy on the butter," Mildred warns, delivering Turbo's three fried eggs, hash brown potatoes, bacon, ham and sausage, and a stack of blueberry pancakes. She refills Hunter's coffee cup, then Speedy's, and dashes off. Like a Norman Rockwell model, Mildred is wearing a tailored gingham dress, starched lace handkerchief in its chest pocket, crisp white apron ruffled at the hem, a hairnet over her permed coif, and half glasses hanging from a cord around her neck. Along with good home cooking, she dispenses instant advice on anything to anybody, including her husband, Hank, who works the grill. She claims her food is farm fresh and admits to having bought only once from a fast-talking restaurant supplier—that was back in 1976, when she bought 2,500 Bicentennial paper place mats, which she trashed because customers said they were ridiculous in a town more than 300 years old.

She delivers Speedy's soft-boiled egg, blueberry muffin, and a large orange juice, and gets back to Turbo. "Now what's this about the Widow Pell speeding on Hawk's Road this morning?"

"Like a Lyme Rock racer," he says, dropping butter pats on the pancakes. "Said she was on her way to check some problem at Colonial Cable."

"Maybe she's getting too old to drive," someone remarks.

Turbo responds without looking up from his breakfast. "I've had that thought from time to time. But this morning she was driving like a pro, accelerating on the curves, hugging the road."

Speedy breaks open the steaming muffin, dips it into a warm egg yolk, and peers straight ahead into the long mirror behind the marble counter. He watches reflected activity every morning, but this morning his eyes are glued to specific subjects.

Hunter senses it and looks in the mirror. Nothing unusual. He finishes his over-easy eggs, folds his *Wall Street Journal* and, reaching into his pocket for a tip, glances again into the mirror. There she is. That exquisite face, shiny black hair pulled back, a red jacket unzipped over a tight, black jersey, stretch pants on fantastic legs. She catches his eye in the mirror, smiles and, with incredible presence, walks directly to him and says, "We almost met last night."

Smiling, he swivels off the stool. "I looked for you after the meeting, but you had left."

"Had to move my car—fast. It was blocking others. You're Hunter Barnhill."

"I hardly know anyone here but the whole town seems to know my name."

"Well, you're what people here call a Damnewyorker, and everyone knows who they are, even when they keep to themselves. I'm Jean Glick, the self-appointed welcoming committee for Damnewyorkers. Have time for another cup of coffee?"

"Sure. Thanks." He follows her to a table by the window. You know, I can't say I'm wild about being known as a Damnewyorker. How do I shake that stigma?"

"You don't. Even if you weren't born in New York, if you arrive here from there, you're a Damnewyorker. It's who you are. Nothing you can do to change that. However, if you were to have kids born here, they'd be natives."

"Pretty tough admission policy," he says, as Mildred appears with a pot of coffee, two cups, a blueberry muffin for Jean, and hurries off.

"I didn't say they wouldn't accept you. As long as you're sort of like them, they'll accept you."

"That's encouraging." His small smile is now indelible.

"You see, New Burford people believe a typical New Yorker would never even want to settle here, so they cut you slack right from the start, during probation—"

"Probation?"

"For a while, they watch to see if you ever act like their stereotypical New Yorker."

"Aggressive, frenetic, flashy, glitzy, brash, arrogant."

"That sums it up," she laughs, breaking the warm muffin and spreading butter on it. "They don't want that here."

"Well, neither do I—nor do you, I presume," he pauses, puzzled. "Why do you refer to New Burford people as them and they—not us and we—when you're one of them?"

She licks melted butter from her finger and grabs a napkin. "It's the way Damnewyorkers talk to each other."

"You're from the city?"

"Born, raised, and educated on Manhattan. Worked there, too. M-m-m, I adore these."

He had never seen such a fantastic-looking woman, and so unconcerned about fat calories as she's thoroughly enjoying an ordinary muffin with gobs of butter.

"The food is terrific here," she continues. "You just have to overlook a few things."

"Like that cat hanging out under the butter dispenser?"

"Peachpie? Perfect example. And whenever someone complains that the cat's unsanitary, Mildred tells Billy, you know, the busboy. And he puts on gloves, so everybody can see, grabs poor Peachpie, and washes her, suds her up. And, get this —he holds her down while Mildred brushes and flosses the cat's teeth. Poor Peachpie is just— stunned." She's holding up her hands, fingers curled like trauma-tized paws gripping the air. They laugh.

Hunter is charmed by every word, every gesture. "How did you end up here?"

"My parents bought a place here when I was a kid. We used to come every summer, weekends the rest of the year. When they retired to Florida, I kept the cottage, winterized it. Came up from New York whenever I could, which wasn't often enough. Then one summer, I danced at Jacob's Pillow, and stayed. But enough about me. What about you?"

"You were a dancer?"

"I dance. For some years, I danced with New York City Ballet. Now I do festivals, benefits, workshops at colleges, things like that. Mostly I teach. I have a dance studio here—But tell me about you? They say you're in advertising."

"Used to be in advertising. Now I'm working on a book."

"Really. What about?"

"Uh, the Kennedys."

"Fascinating. I would have thought it's all been said about them."

"It's not that kind of book. It's more, well, a coffee table book. Photos. Short essays, about the Kennedy funerals, mourning, remem-bering the deceased on anniversaries, visiting the graves. There are more of them all the time."

"Graves?—or Kennedys?"

"Kennedys. Graves, too. Anyway, people never get tired of them. The Kennedys." He can see that she's less than impressed. Regretting that he mentioned it, he tries to redeem it with a little bravura. "It's a new concept, a repackaging strategy for an emerging market."

"Careful—," she teases. "You're sounding like a New Yorker."

While Hunter and Jean talk, Speedy is staring down the late night TV performers, unnerving them, one at a time, starting with Bertha Harper, the town clerk. He glares at her till she feels it. She glances into the mirror and shifts in her chair, rearranging her bottom under her matronly torso. Never before had he even looked directly at her. Fiddling with the ear of her coffee cup, she flashes an intimidating smile at him. He squints back at her reflection. She was the one at the end of the selectmen's table.

The audacity of him, Bertha says to herself. Maybe the idiot simply noticed that today I'm not sitting with the other town council members.

Bertha couldn't bring herself to do that this morning. They had all assured each other that they were doing the right thing, but now she isn't sure. Isn't sure of anything, except that Speedy is staring at her—almost as if he knows everything, even about the envelope she hid in a hatbox at the back of her closet. Unable to tolerate it any longer, she takes two quarters from her purse, slips them under her saucer, gets up, smoothing her skirt, and marches out of Mildred's.

As soon as Bertha is out the door, Speedy starts on the town attorney, Carson Lynch, who is sitting with Harriet Holcombe, administrator of the Heavenward Rest Home. Carson immediately senses Speedy's glare and scowls back into the mirror at him. Speedy doesn't blink. Carson looks away, gets up from the table, telling Harriet he just remembered an 8:30 appointment, and walks out of Mildred's.

Finally, it is Worthington's turn. The moment Speedy shifts his eyes him, Worthington pushes himself away from the table, gets up and leaves. Mildred appears, presenting Speedy's check, "I ought to charge you for a full pot of coffee this morning. But I figure you just made up for all the times you never had a second cup."

Speedy isn't paying attention to her. There's new action in the mirror. Jean is running to the door, easily five minutes later than usual. Hunter's standing, looking after her, then he starts for the door, but turns back to the take-out counter, gets two blueberry muffins, and leaves.

＄

"Damn him!" Emma mutters while making her oatmeal and whole-wheat toast. Before calling Brewster, she had viewed the videotape with Samson at the studio, brought home a dupe and looked again, fast-forwarding and freezing it to study the shadows. She couldn't identify anyone or anything, but, intuiting that the video captured a secret meeting about the highway, she had played her hunch with Brewster. And got nowhere. "Damn him."

What has happened? She's known Brewster since he was knee-high to a grasshopper. She has mentored him, supported him abundantly. He calls often, asking her advice, and never turns down her invitations. Lately her harshest criticism of him has been directed at his wardrobe—too much Dunhill, not enough L.L. Bean. He's a good leader, has excellent people skills, and accomplishes short-term projects without losing sight of long-term goals. Certainly, he has to be manipulative in order to get things done. But never, in all the years she's known him and his forebears, has she seen this deplorable streak of unbridled arrogance, and inexcusably myopic selfishness.

She scoops the oatmeal into a bowl and butters the toast. She has no appetite. At least she let him know she's on to him.

Jenny barks to be let out. Emma opens the kitchen door, and the dog dashes out, across the lawn into the field, barking frantically. Probably deer, she guesses, about to close the door. No. Someone's out there. It's a man, walking toward the house. Jenny is prancing alongside him. Why for goodness sake. It's Speedy. Why would he be coming here now? He should be at the school at this time. She waves to him.

＄

Thundering over russet hills, the Black Hawk helicopter lifts, clearing New Burford's northern ridge, and sweeps toward the campus of Western Massachusetts Military Academy.

"Remarkable," Clappsaddle says under his breath as the chopper approaches a patchwork of green playing fields, lawns, golf course, a quadrangle of gray stone buildings, and two rows of white houses at one end. On the drill field are the corps of cadets—six companies of one hundred cadets each, in formation, polished brass buttons and breast plates on gray uniforms, flags unfurled, sabers glistening in the sun—and a fifty-piece band.

The Black Hawk hovers before settling down. Blades spinning, the hatch opens, and Lieutenant Colonel Marvin P. Norwocki, Massachusetts Army National Guard leaps out, followed by Lieutenant General Bunker Terhune Clappsaddle, US Army, Retired.

The first of fifteen blasts is fired from the academy's reveille gun, a 75-millimeter pack howitzer. Bunky brings himself to attention, the bony swagger stick neatly tucked under his left arm, and stands rigidly as the band plays three ruffles and flourishes.

Brigadier General Roy Bolton Farrand, President of Western Massachusetts Military Academy, walks up to Clappsaddle and salutes. "On behalf of the Corps of Cadets, I welcome you to Western Massachusetts Military Academy, General. Would you care to troop the line?"

The two generals march to the end of the formation where the cadet first captain meets them and the three proceed down the corps' gray line. The band strikes up, plays a few bars of "Hello, Dolly," suddenly silences, and resumes with the "General's March."

Clappsaddle clears his throat. "Tell me, Roy. How did you find me at the Millrace Inn?"

"The Renegade gave me the heads up."

"Is that so." Clappsaddle ponders the unlikely fortuity of the arrangement. Before checking out of the Millrace Inn, Standish had called, informing him that all rights of way are now secure, but construction is not to proceed until he is directly authorized by the governor. The timeframe, he said, is uncertain. Bunky hates delays, especially in the covert phase of an operation. On this highway job, a delay of any duration will be pose problems. And if the postponement is for political reasons, there's no telling how long the operation will remain on hold.

Farrand cracks a smile under his waxed mustache. "As a matter of fact, General, Constance and I are hosting a small dinner party this evening in your honor."

At the end of the line of cadets, the generals exchange salutes with the cadet first captain and head across the drill field for hot coffee at the administration building. Norwocki marches behind them, two steps to the left and one to the rear.

Constance gently folds chunks of canned salmon into a fluffy, beaten egg white mixture, licks the spatula, and groans, "Uh, to die for." AnnaBelle grabs the spatula from her. "Enough, Constance."

The two women are about the same age, but statuesque AnnaBelle with her strong chin and silver hair is clearly in charge. AnnaBelle pours the mixture into a fish mold, secures it in the refrigerator and hustles Constance into the dining room. "How many civilians this evening, Constance? Where are your place cards?"

Constance Farrand hands her the nested place cards, folded like tents. She had carefully printed, with her calligraphy pen, each guest's name below the engraved, single red star for her husband's rank. On the other side, she had printed the date of the dinner party and the name of their home, Brass House. "Maybe tonight after dessert my general will ask the guests for their place cards and he'll do his recreation of the Crimean War tent problem."

"I need to know how many civilians."

"Civilians, yes. Now, let me see." She reads the names on the little tents. "Emma Peters Pell. Doctor Barnes, Ham Goodwill, Hunter

Barnhill. We don't know about him. But my general thinks he might support the academy. He's a former Marine, was in Vietnam, has some money, and no family."

"The Damnewyorker."

"Yes, he's that, too. I wasn't so sure about inviting a former Marine to Brass House but I understand advertising people are clever with words, like in that movie—. Oh, dear." She sighs, accustomed to memory lapses. "Well, at least we know Mr. Barnhill isn't one of those Vietnam Marines who ended up down and out, all messed up, running around shooting people and the like."

"Constance, enough."

"But I must tell you, when he accepted my invitation, he said there is no Mrs. Barnhill, which I said is fine. And then, this morning he called asking if it was too late for him to change his acceptance and bring a guest. Well, AnnaBelle, you won't believe this, he's bringing Jean Glick!"

AnnaBelle raises her eyebrows. "Hm-m. Who else is in your stack of cards?"

"Ed Broker and Ursula Broker. Civilian. Ed is smart. Has an MBA from Wharton, Ursula's from Akron. They're new summer people. Bought the old Putt house. They go to some fancy place in Florida for the winter. Ed used to be a big executive with Giant Foods. Ursula told me Ed is the one who invented those frozen pop-up soufflés that come with freeze-dried sauces. We should try them."

"I make a real soufflés."

"Of course. Ursula is a paddle tennis champion. Did you know they have ranks for that?" Her voice drops to a confidential hush. "My general thinks they might make a very generous donation to Western."

"So, with Jean, it's ten. Four on each side."

"You still don't want to join us? Lucy can manage everything."

"No, thanks." The widow of Western's former dean of admission, AnnaBelle has had three decades' experience with the Farrands and knows her help is especially needed on occasions such as this dinner party. When her husband died she had agreed to stay on as a companion for Constance. Before long and by default, she was running the Farrand household. "Now, back to the kitchen, Constance. You've got potatoes to peel."

"It's going to be a lovely evening," Constance muses at the kitchen sink, potato in hand. "After cocktails, we gather at the table, my general will say grace, and then he'll ask General Clappsaddle to toast the President." She gazes out the window.

"Peel."

"Yes, yes." She rinses the potato. "There'll be more toasts, surely a toast to the Seventh Cavalry in respect for Emma's dear Waldo. And after dinner, my general's surprise."

"Hmm." AnnaBelle is only too familiar with the routine.

"At precisely 9:30 there will be a knock at the door. My general will lightly tap his water glass—ding-ding—and announce, 'Ladies and gentlemen, I have a surprise for you. Please join me on the porch.'"

"Peel."

"We'll stand in the beautiful fresh air and there on the lawn will be the Cadet Glee Club, in full dress coats, singing all the wonderful songs, "Let's Remember Pearl Harbor," "Coming In on a Wing and a Prayer," "Army Blue." There won't be a dry eye on the porch."

"Hmmm."

"AnnaBelle, did you ever notice—? After the bomb over Nagasaki, it seems they stopped writing romantic songs about coming home from war."

"Come in I'm on the phone have a seat I'll just be a second," Jean explains, letting Hunter in the front door, and, barefoot, running off to the next room, her shiny long hair falling on the shoulders of a classily snug knit dress.

He looks around, trying to hear her conversation—something about going to Boston. A fieldstone fireplace dominates one end of the living room, which smells like cinnamon, cardamom, maybe both, and at the other end is an old baby grand piano covered with sheet music. Overstuffed chairs face an equally overstuffed couch, and on the wall is a huge abstract watercolor of a horseshoe crab. He sits on the edge of the couch, imagining himself sinking into it with her. The coffee table is cluttered with dried pomegranates, acorns, chestnuts, cinnamon sticks, bowls of acorns, hazelnuts, a small vice, an electric hand drill, spools of satin and metallic cords. He picks up a cardamom pod, rolls it in his fingers, and, sniffs its clean spicy fragrance.

"Sorry, had to take that call," she says, her arms reaching behind her neck to clasp a choker of chunky, shiny, reddish-brown beads, the knit dress moving with her amazing shape. "Could you help me with this?" She turns her back to him, sweeping her hair away to reveal the ends of a satin cord drawn through the beads. "Just tie a secure knot. Hold it, just a sec. Let me make sure they're not strung too tight—good."

Tying the satin cord, he memorizes the contours of her neck. She is the highest concentration of elegant sensuality he has ever seen. "That should do it."

She turns. "How does it look?"

"Perfect."

"Thank you. Horse chestnuts. Found them this morning. All set. Except shoes." She hurries off, and reappears in stocking feet, sling-backs dangling from two fingers. She drops the shoes, and slips into them. "I spend as little time as possible in gear like this, but the Farrands are pretty formal. Also a little weird, I should warn you. Constance, especially, but AnnaBelle keeps her in check."

"So you know them. What about the general?"

"Eccentric, old school, but nice enough."

"I'm wishing we had decided to go to Sparkie's instead."

"Oh no. Emma Peters Pell will be at the Ferrands. She's looking forward to meeting you."

"The one who confronted the secretary of state at the town meeting?"

"You'll adore her."

They're the last to arrive. Constance, bubbling with enthusiasm, leads them into the living room where the party has assembled for drinks, and introduces them. Emma greets Jean with a hug and, shaking hands with Hunter, dismisses Jean with a wink. "Glad you've decided to settle in New Burford, Hunter." He senses he's about to undergo an evaluation as Dr. Ralph Barnes hands him a rum and tonic, and instantly retreats.

"So tell me," Emma begins, "are you from New York—originally?" It is the first of a steady barrage of personal questions, prying questions he would have considered rude, had it not been for her gentle voice and manner. He answers plainly, more convinced with each question that she's not merely checking him out as a new resident but as Jean's date. Something about the way the old lady carries herself, her poise, her presence, suggests that she and Jean might be related.

"And you never married?"

"Never found the right woman in New York."

"Then it was indeed high time for you to relocate. Now tell me, have you done any blogging?"

Constance interrupts, presenting a tray of canapés. "You know, Hunter—" she effuses, "AnnaBelle— over there, talking to Jean— her granddaughter is Jean's best pupil—."

Jean and Annabelle are politely auditing Ursula Broker's exhaustive comparison of ballet and racquet sports while Ed Broker and Ham Goodwill discuss large-cap, global food companies, and the generals delve into a discussion of Russian oil reserves. Dr. Barnes, having offered to tend bar, darts about, attentively refreshing drinks, and topping off his own on every return to the bar.

At exactly 7:30, General Farrand rings a silver bell, calling everyone to the dining room. The guests are seated, toasts are made, and the soup is served, just as Constance had envisioned. Then, with Farrand's announcement that Hunter had been awarded a Silver Star in Vietnam, the evening begins to deteriorate.

"It's kismet," Constance cheerily announces. "Jean was in the Corps de Ballet and Hunter was in the Corps de Marines."

Hunter smiles, swallowing a laugh, and raises his glass to Jean. "To the Corps."

"To the Corps," they all toast; Jean, amused, raising her glass to Hunter.

"The broccoli soup is divine," Ed Broker compliments Constance, who beams.

"Hunter," Farrand intones, "I do hope you'll come as an honored guest to our Old Boys Alumni Dinner, wear your decorations, show off your Silver Star."

"Uh, actually—," he hesitates, "—I don't have my medals any more."

Farrand, Constance, and Clappsaddle, wide-eyed, wait for his explanation.

"—Sent them back. Years ago. Um, protesting U.S. involvement in Nicaragua."

"Jesus Christ!" Clappsaddle exhales through clenched teeth.

"Salmon mousse!" AnnaBelle bursts from the kitchen with a large platter and presents the decorated fish mold.

"Beautifully garnished," comments Ed.

"Sending your medals back doesn't diminish the honor they represent," says Ham, tactfully. "It was a lousy war, you did your duty, honorably."

Ursula pounces. "Oh, wow, how can you say anything associated with Vietnam was honorable? It was completely uncivilized."

"War is hell, Madam, as no doubt you've heard." Clappsaddle doesn't like what Hunter did with his medals but he abhors inane remarks like Ursula's. Since retirement from the Army, he learned to tolerate them, much as he had learned to accept women at West Point—without comment. Occasionally, however, he feels compelled to interject a smattering of his views. This is such an occasion. "But anyone who fought in that damn jungle deserves to be honored."

"For what? Did we learn anything from it? No!" She gloats. "We're just at it again, up to our eyeballs."

"You're almost absolutely right, madam," Clappsaddle strikes his fist on the table, bouncing the silverware. "When we got into Vietnam, the Pentagon still hadn't figured out that we weren't fighting World War II anymore. What's worse, it took another twenty years before they even started catching on." He glares at Ursula with the fervor of a revivalist preacher and coughs. "We've got great soldiers, fantastic new technologies but if we don't speed up in getting new force designs with diversity capabilities, we'll be even more vulnerable than you could ever imagine."

Ursula doesn't flinch from his glare, her brows angled. "Are you agreeing with me?"

Hunter clarifies. "He's saying the Pentagon should listen to guys in combat, stop writing plans to yesterday's threats and reorganize to beat them at their own game, whoever they are, however they may play it."

"Exactly!" Clappsaddle considers telling Hunter he had been an enlisted Marine before his appointment to West Point.

"What do you mean, Beat them at their game?" Ursula demands. "You're the aggressor, with your gunboat diplomacy, nuclear arsenals, military interventions in support of wretched dictators. You trample poor countries, with no regard for innocent lives—" She is ignoring Ed's less than subtle signals that she back off, as Emma and Ham exchange disapproving glances. Ralph Barnes pours himself more wine and shrugs. Farrand leans forward, saying, "I'm sorry I didn't quite catch that."

Emma treads into Ursula's diatribe, "Who's this you ? Who's trampling poor counties?"

"United States imperialists, of course."

"Bullshit!" Clappsaddle and Emma retort in unison.

"We've got our flaws," Emma protests, "but the lion's share of blame belongs squarely on the radical Islamic leaders who are faulting others for their self-created fiasco."

"Brace yourself, Ursula," Hunter cautions amiably, "what's coming may make Vietnam look like a picnic."

"Picnic?" Farrand repeats loudly.

"Ugh." Ursula is somewhat subdued. "Why can't we all be impartial?"

"Ah, impartial," Ralph Barnes mimics, then offers a quote, "'I decline utterly to be impartial as between the Fire Brigade and the fire.'"

"Winston Churchill!" Ham exclaims, identifying the quote.

Ursula persists. "At least, during Vietnam the media showed the whole reality."

"What's that?" Farrand shouts.

"That wasn't reality." Hunter mumbles.

"How can you say that?" Ursula demands as Jean asks, "What are you saying?"

"I'm saying—." Looking at Jean, who is even more beautiful in the candlelight, he wants to say let's leave, immediately, and go to my place. But they are all looking at him, expectantly. He grins, itching to abort the conversation with a flip or outrageous comment. "I'm saying—if they had listened to Goldwater, we might not be having this discussion." Instantly, he regrets it. Miraculously, AnnaBelle appears, "How do you all like your roast beef?"

Dining on beef and potatoes, they hash out several administrations' conduct of war and the media's coverage. Like a Greek chorus, Dr. Barns continues to punctuate the discussion, quoting Churchill. Hunter says little, but Jean likes how he comments. She likes his voice, his smile, his shoulders, his hands, and senses he knows what she's thinking. General Farrand, unaware that his hearing aid battery is failing, drops out of the conversation, thinking everyone is having a wonderful time, and focuses on refilling wine glasses. Ed Broker, who joyously had escaped military service due to flat feet, racks his brain for a way to silence Ursula. Inspiration strikes. He taps his wine glass with a fork. "A toast," he proclaims. "It's been said that an army moves on its stomach. When I was in freeze-dried technologies at Giant, I was responsible for the armed forces MRE's—that's meals-ready-to-eat, Jean—upgrading them till the meals took on a taste and mouth-feel that approximates the wonderful feast we're enjoying here this evening. Let us toast edifying edibles, this evening and always." He raises his glass to Constance, who blows him a kiss.

Clappsaddle turns to Hunter, "Did you mean it when you said Goldwater had the answer?"

"Who knows? He wasn't the only one advocating that we pave the country."

"Belligerent Americans," Ursula hisses.

Emma nearly chokes, "Hunter, did you say pave?"

"That's how they put it. Pave the country and set up basketball courts."

Emma smirks at Clappsaddle. "Might that have been your pro-posal, General? Paving's your métier, isn't it?"

"My métier?"

"Those are your paving trucks parked down at the St. Catherine Sand and Gravel Company, are they not? The ones with the little American flags painted on them." Gotcha.

"I can't say that I follow you, Mrs. Pell. We're talking about Goldwater's proposal."

She stretches her spine to sit even taller and places her hands on the arms of Hunter and Ham, seated on either side of her. "No, General Clappsaddle, I'm asking you about the current paving initia-tive. The highway. I saw you down at the gravel pit yesterday evening. I saw the trucks. I saw the helicopter that picked you up."

Hunter is intrigued, and fascinated by Emma. Clappsaddle, who has no experience dealing with women like Emma, asks for the salt and pepper.

"Yes, of course, it's freshly ground from pure Indian Tellicherry peppercorns. I hope you all like it," says acutely flustered Constance, who has detected that her husband's hearing aid is not functioning.

Ham intervenes. "Now, Emma, you and the General will have to step outside to finish your business if this comes to blows and, mind you, General, you will not win against a woman of Emma's lineage. She traces her ancestry directly to Charlemagne."

"Let the General answer." Emma is determined to extract the truth.

"But, Emma, I'm sure the general would be interested in knowing that your husband, the late Colonel Waldo Pell, served with General Custer. It's true, General. He ran away at age eleven. Joined the Army. Played the French horn in Custer's band. Now, that's impressive."

"And," says Constance, "Mrs. Custer gave Waldo Pell a lock of the general's hair after the massacre." She's at her husband's side, tugging his arm to get him out of his chair for a new battery.

"Impressive, indeed," says Clappsaddle, salting his beef.

Emma won't let go. "I want to know about those trucks, General."

Again, Ham plays diplomat. "Nothing is more relevant than roots, Emma. Isn't that right, Jean?"

Jean shakes her head. "Ham, you know I won't help you derail Emma's train of thought."

"Thank you, dear," Emma says to her, without taking her eyes off Clappsaddle.

Clappsaddle, meanwhile, has thought of a pretext. He explains that he still has not received final plans for the highway but moved trucks into forward position for readiness as soon as he gets the plan and the green light from the governor. "And it's my understanding that the highway will run some distance north of here, maybe thirty miles from New Burford."

Constance leads her husband to the front porch, eases him into a green wicker armchair, and hands him a new battery. Dr. Barnes follows them out, explaining that he's been called to a medical emergency, and lurches down the walk to his aged powder blue Plymouth. In an earsplitting screech, the rubber hits the road, just as Farrand pokes the hearing aid into his ear. Arrgh, he screams.

The Glee Club's serenade brings respite. The guests assemble on the porch, listen appreciatively, or at least politely, to the old military songs, and chat between the selections. Glassy-eyed with sentimentality, Clappsaddle assures Emma that the highway should pose no problem for her town. Hunter and Jean quietly agree to leave right after the serenade.

"It's early," says Hunter as they climb into the Rover. "Can I interest you in joining me and my companion, Freddie, for a walk? He grins, "A handsome spaniel. He's pretty eager to get out of the house right about now."

"Sure. But I can't go for much of a walk in these shoes."

He looks at the shoes, and her legs. "A stroll, then. On easy terrain."

A few hours later, they lie exhausted in each other's arms, under a patchwork quilt.

"That Silver Star means you were a hero?" Now she wants more background.

"Me? No. I was just lucky." He takes her hand into his, closes his eyes, and falls sound asleep. Jean lies awake, listening to the wind, looking at him as he sleeps in his moonlit bedroom, feeling as if she has known him forever, wondering if they would make love again in the morning.

Unable to sleep, replaying the day in her minds eye, Emma gets up, makes valerian tea, plunging an infusion ball into a mug of steaming water, and takes it back to her bedroom.

That morning, Speedy stood at her back door and handed her his writing pad with a self-confidence she had never before seen in him. "Council met in Historical Hall early in the morning. No lights. No sound. Signed papers. Channel L," he wrote.

"How do you know it was the council?" She asked him.

"From shapes, moves," he wrote.

"I have the videotape of that meeting here. Would you watch it with me, show me?"

As the tape was rewinding, Speedy pointed to her laptop.

"You want to use the computer?"

He nodded.

His fingers flew over keys from the moment she entered start. She sat next to him, reading his text, frequently stopping the tape, as he identified each shadowy figure by shape, height, weight, posture, gestures, moves. Worthington, Bertha, Lynch, Standish, all of them, except the short one. He wrote with certitude. But she couldn't discern in the dark blurry shadows any of the features that were so clear to him. To her, the video was still just a dark blur of shadows. That troubled her. How could she base an accusation of high-level town chicanery on a video of shadows that somehow resemble town officials to Speedy, of all people?

Sipping her valerian tea, she envisions a likely scenario. Agatha reported that the highway would go through New Burford. Pease is keeping the route secret because he knows very well that she'll do everything in her considerable power to block it. Pease charms the council and they go into cahoots with him, fully convinced that the highway will benefit the town and, very likely, fully assured that the cement won't get poured in their back yards. As for Clappsaddle? He's in on the whole thing. That was clear form his evasive response to her very first question about the trucks. He hedged everything he said about the highway. Yet the trucks are, in fact, right in the middle of New Burford.

She swirls the tea in the mug, remembering how she once had taken a shotgun and run an unscrupulous developer off his land. He sold the land—to her. Things didn't work that way anymore. It bothers her that Ham tried to mediate when she confronted Clappsaddle. Nobody seems to be able to deal with confrontation these days. She sighs. Have the people of New Burford become complacent, desensitized, tuned out in front of their screens, like the rest of America? No. Not these people. They turn out for town meetings.

Very likely she will have to lead another tough fight. But does she still have the stamina for it? She still has power—property, connections, gumption. But is that enough? Where is the new generation of leaders? For that matter, what's happened to real leaders? Where are the Roosevelts, Trumans, and Ikes, for goodness sake? Humph. These days so-called leaders wrap themselves up in self-promotion, power, and greed, all nicely packaged for the media.

She looks into the mug. Samson simply must enhance that video. And if he can't—? If this isn't nipped in the bud—? Oh dear. Ugh, this is how McDonalds and Starbucks procreate. Only one thing is certain. Speedy is no dolt, and, having sent him home with her extra laptop, she will now be able to communicate with him by e-mail.

A gentle wind sweeps across the Valley of Runs-On-Toes-Into-Wind, whispering through the tall pines. She turns out the light, closes her heavy eyelids, and, pulling the comforter up to her chin, chuckles, "I'm going to blow this scandal wide open, and stick it to 'em. I just haven't yet figured out how." Jenny resettles herself against a pillow.

# 4

## SATURDAY, OCTOBER 12

*New Burford*

Jean lies still, eyes closed, hearing him quietly enter the dark bedroom, unzip, undress. He gets back into bed, lying close without touching her. Where had he been? She feels his breath on her shoulder and rolls over to face him. "Hi. Is it morning?"

Smiling, he puts his arm around her. "Very early. You slept okay?"

"Great. You?" It strikes her how very little she knows about him.

"The best sleep in more years than I care to count." He smiles.

It's the same little smile that melted her last night. "I didn't know what to think when I realized you had gone out."

"Sorry. I always wake up in the middle of the night. I didn't want to disturb you so I went for a walk." He kisses her cheek.

"Insomnia."

"Sort of. Years ago I learned to catnap and never unlearned it." He pauses, not smiling. She waits for him to say more. "Coffee? You get room service."

She grins. "Love some. Black, please."

"Right back." He gets up, into jeans and a sweater, leaves his robe on the bed for her, and goes downstairs, leaving the door ajar. Freddie bursts into the bedroom, leaps on the bed, and plops down next to her.

"Freddie, is this where you sleep—usually?" Freddie rolls his eyes at her, then looks away. She pats the dog. "Do you get kicked out often?" The thought takes hold of her. Maybe he couldn't sleep because he's involved—and missed her. She gets out of bed, shivering, looks skeptically at his robe, puts it on and hurries into the bathroom.

She turns on the shower over the vintage clawfoot tub and tests the water. It is taking forever to get hot. She steps into tepid water, quickly washes and gets out, wraps a towel around herself, and looks in the mirror. You damn fool.

She rushes to the bedroom, locates her panties, puts them on, then her bra. Ugh! This good-looking, middle-aged, charming New Yorker shows up and, wham, into the sack. Part of her still loves every minute of it. He's sensitive, intelligent, obviously works on staying in shape but—Ugh, it was too damn fast! For sure in New Burford. She stands straight, centering herself, folds her hands and, in a flash, stretches her arms over her head, arches her back, takes a deep breath and kicks—mightily—straight up. Ugh! Again she stretches her arms over head, fingers laced, and swings the other leg, kicking even higher. In a huff, she puts on the knit dress, pulling it over her head, as far as her waist and kicks again, powerfully and straight up—

—hitting her nose, hard. "Yow-o-o-o! Ow, ohhhh—" She reaches for a tissue and holds it to her nose. It's bleeding. She grabs more tissues, pulling the hem of the dress to her knees. "Oy. Ice, I need ice." Barefoot, she runs to get it.

Hunter is at the foot of the stairs with two steaming mugs of coffee. "Whoa, what's the rush? It's only six o'clock." Then sees the tissue, red with blood. "What happened?" He puts down the mugs, and goes to her. "Come lie down. I'll call the doctor."

"No! I'll be fine once I get a little ice on it," she insists and they go to the kitchen, where she exclaims through a wad of tissue, "Oh, fantastic!" On the table are two plates, an enormous Mildred's blueberry muffin on each. "But, ugh, this is so horrible!"

"Um, horrible?"

"Yes. You knew I'd be here this morning. Damn, you're just such a—such an incorrigible Damnewyorker!"

"Ouch," he says, closing the freezer door, giving her an ice pack. "You don't mean that."

"Ugh, and I'm clearly still capable of slipping." She presses the ice pack to her nose. "O-o-ow. Thank you. Yes, I meant it. It's true."

He pours two glasses of orange juice, puts them on the table and sits opposite her, looking at her, worried. How did it happen? "Granted, I haven't fully adopted New Burford ways but, as I work on that, let's just keep this between us."

She laughs nervously. "Wish we could. The whole town knows by now that we were together last night." She presses the icepack to her cheekbone. "This is going to be a major shiner. But don't worry. Everyone will know I did it to myself. They all know about my grande battement."

"Battement—? Battering? Beating? My French is lousy."

"In my case, more like chop as in karate chop."

He draws his hand over his face. "Help me out."

She sips her juice. "When I was a kid and got angry or hugely upset about something, I used to literally kick it out, sometimes karate-kicking myself in the face."

"Incredible."

"On rare occasion I still release it that way when I'm angry or upset."

"Angry? Upset? Why? I thought everything was terrific." He's ignoring his coffee, juice and muffin.

"It was. I just —" She removes the ice pack to drink from her mug. "It was just too fast."

"But what's wrong with fast—especially if it's terrific."

"We should talk, but not now. I have to get going. I've got classes."

"Cancel them. You're wounded."

"No."

"So let's have lunch. Let me take care of you and your nose—and we'll talk. What time are you through?"

"Saturdays, I go from nine to one. But— can't today. I'm a mess. I need time, distance."

"Distance?"

"It's pretty clear that I like you, Hunter. It just wasn't good, jumping into bed."

"You're right. It wasn't good, it was fantastic."

"You know what I mean."

"I hear you." He takes her hand. "So the whole town will assume that you got angry at me last night."

"More likely that I got angry at myself." She smiles. "You're pretty neat, you know. But I've got to go now."

He nods.

"Do you have any idea where my shoes are?"

*Barrington, Massachusetts*

In the deeply wooded watershed, under ancient oaks and towering hemlocks, Clappsaddle hunkers over sheets of blueprints anchored by his swagger stick and a few stones, his foreman standing by. The general gets up off his haunches, flips open the laptop on the hood of his Hummer and checks the simulations against the blueprints. "We're good to go tomorrow morning. I'm awaiting authorization. Could be a delay of a day or so." The foreman salutes and trudges off.

Clappsaddle reaches into his sock, pulls out a Lucky, lights it, inhaling deeply, and farts. This covert phase of the job has been a pain in the ass. The route runs through dense woodland, skirting one sparsely populated pocket that is to be surveyed immediately after blasting begins; every precaution had to be taken against being seen. The crew worked from midnight to five in the morning, wearing night vision goggles and camouflage face paint. Now, everything is in readiness to commence blasting and proceed under normal operating conditions.

He drags on the cigarette and coughs. His cell phone is ringing in the Hummer. Shuffling through leaves, he tucks the Lucky behind his ear and reaches into the vehicle for the phone. "Clappsaddle."

"General Clappsaddle, please hold for Senator Donnelley."

"Holding." He takes the cigarette from behind his ear, drags deeply, crushes it out, and field strips the butt. "Good morning, General. Dick Donnelley. Brew Pease informs me you're ready to break ground."

"Tomorrow morning."

"Commendable work under difficult circumstances."

"Thank you, Senator." He senses that the senator is about to lob another complication into the job.

"I'll get right to the point, General. I am advised—and I believe wisely so—to avoid public disclosure of the exact highway route until after the election. We want to keep voters focused on the issues. If construction starts before the election, we run the risk that the blasting, the disruption, and inconvenience might rouse anger, cause people to lose sight of the highway's benefits and possibly generate a form of backlash or protest which might be transferred to other issues. That's a risk we don't want to take."

"So you're postponing the start," Clappsaddle says flatly.

"Just a few weeks."

"So be it." He sighs with undisguised frustration.

"I know delays are always a problem in your business but these contingencies are covered in your contract. And it's imperative that we do this."

"Understood, Senator."

"This change further necessitates a new plan for launching construction. Brewster will give you the details but I wanted to personally alert you to it. And personally thank you. Good work, Clappsaddle."

"Thank you, Senator." Clappsaddle punches off. "That cradle-robbing son of a bitch." He calls the governor's office.

"General Bunker Clappsaddle for Governor Pease."

"I'm sorry, General, the governor is not available. I'll tell him you called."

Bunky puts the phone in his pocket. A red maple leaf drifts from a tree marked for sacrifice, a stripe of garish orange paint on its trunk. A major delay, due to politics. True, they are contractually covered for this kind of thing but every delay brings them closer to hard frost. This will surely enrage Benjamin Tatta, Palumbo's pint-sized chairman. Clappsaddle can hear his tirade, Clappsaddle, if I don't hear that you're pouring cement, you may find yourself supporting an overpass. In this fairly routine exchange, Bunky will then extract from Tatta an admission that such threats are misplaced, but that doesn't make them any easier to tolerate.

The phone rings. It's Pease. The governor gets right to the details of what he's calling his Day One Plan. "What you're going to do, Bunker, is simultaneously detonate every charge along that route. Then bulldoze immediately, starting in New Burford. That's critical. Get that highway route carved out—fast."

"Simultaneously detonate all the charges? You don't mean that, Governor."

"I mean that precisely. If you blast incrementally, there will be protesters out there blocking work before the dust settles from the first explosion, Emma Peters Pell leading the charge. I won't give her that opportunity."

"Governor, I strongly advise against blasting all at once. It would make for one hell of an explosion with high-risk reverberations and it will terrorize the public. They'll think they'd just been nuked."

"I've cleared this with Homeland Security. There's consensus that a drawn-out series of explosions would produce significantly greater public anxiety than one big blast. We don't want to drag it out, we want to get it over and done with, fast. People will be informed immediately after the explosion. And they'll soon forget it. As for reverberations, it's confirmed that no blasting is required near residences, so the risk from reverberations is minimal, well within limits. Did you hear from Donnelley?"

"Yes, I did."

"You understand, then, that you'll get a green light right after the election."

"You know, Governor, that's going to push us into cold weather. A work hiatus will be unavoidable."

"Sit tight, Bunker. Pray for a spike in global warming. Rest up a few weeks for the big, fast start right after Election Day. Then, when the hills freeze over, go marlin fishing. Before you know you'll be back, finishing the job."

Bunky shoves the phone in his pocket, gets into the Hummer, lights up another Lucky, and drives through the woods to the dirt road leading to Route 22. He'll get back to Brass House just before cocktail hour, and can already taste the Jack Daniel's.

# 5

## THURSDAY, OCTOBER 17

*New Burford*

Not even fifty feet from Mildred's old brick arsenal building, behind a row of tall hemlocks, is the reconstructed nineteenth-century stable Jean described. The windows are bright with activity but too high to see what's going on inside. Music faintly wafts into the parking lot. Hunter approaches, sloughing off a tinge of hesitance, then enters the vestibule, a windowed addition to the old structure. Instantly, he recognizes "La Yumba"—and Jean's voice.

"Lead her with your body, not your arms. Slow—slow—quick-quick—slow. Each step rolls off your foot."

Hair pulled into a chignon, she looks spectacular—her pale pink leotard and light gray dirndl skirt worn as elegantly as any twenty-thousand-dollar designer gown. She moves among couples helping them navigate steps, cutting in to demonstrate. At the far end of the vaulting space, behind a wrought iron rail, a fire glows behind the glass door of a wood stove.

"Relax. Knees flexed. Walk, walk, walk, side, step. Gentlemen, you're bending your left leg, sitting on it, for the lunge—yes. Good. Feel the music. Move with assurance. Beautiful. It's all in the feel."

The dance concludes. "You all did beautifully tonight," she says, her eyes drawn from the boom box to the foyer as the "Merry Widow Waltz" begins. "Practice if you can and if you can't just listen to the music and imagine dancing to it. More tango next week—and we'll start the Charleston so bring lots of energy." Couples waltz their way to and out the door where Hunter waits until they've all left. She smiles impishly at him, "You'd like to join the class?"

"I'm definitely interested but may be too advanced for this group," he grins, taking the chestnut necklace from his pocket and presenting it to her in a swag.

"My chestnuts!"

"Turn around. I'll put it on. When I picked it up, they all fell off so I had them restrung. In Barrington. With a clasp. There."

Beaming, she turns back to show him. "This is kinda terrific."

"So that's the last of your Saturday morning shiner?"

"Uh-huh. Almost gone. You should have seen it on Sunday."

"Wish I had."

"Mmm—," she turns up the volume. "So, you're advanced. How's your waltz?" She slips her right hand into his. "Let me lead, for a while," and they move with the music, with each other, turning, circling the room, enchanted. He responds sensitively to her lead, with just enough resistance, as they navigate box turns and hesitations. "Not bad," she smiles, clearly impressed.

"Thank you. And I do a pretty good tango, fox trot, a little salsa, Charleston—but I don't do pirouettes and that stuff." He wants to take the lead, and, as if reading his thoughts, she eases their steps, and gives it to him, her hand resting gently on his arm.

"Dancing lessons when you were a kid?"

"At the downtown Milwaukee Y. My mother said if I was to get anywhere in life I had to get good grades, show good manners and dance like a gentleman."

"They taught you well, and, yes, you're much too advanced for my adult ballroom class."

With his arms and body, he leads her through graceful turns, gliding across the studio floor. "How about private lessons? You'd guide my progress."

"Agreed!" She takes the lead, whirling them with the tender music, then suddenly breaks away in an elaborate improvisation, dazzling him. She returns to his arms, resuming the lead.

"You are absolutely amazing. But do you always prefer to lead?"

"I'm so used to it. But there's one sure way to yield it—." She puts both arms around his neck and effortlessly wraps her legs around his waist as he's waltzing. "How's that?"

"Just fine" he smiles, embracing her, looking into her eyes. The music ends. Silence.

"You know, I could really go for a hot bath in that fantastic claw foot tub of yours."

# 6

## WEDNESDAY, NOVEMBER 6

*New Burford*

Speedy rips off the *Global*'s front page, its barn-door headline announcing, Donnelley by Landslide, its lead photo showing the jubilant senator waving to supporters, Kyle Ludger at his side. He stuffs the clippings into an accordion file, fat with articles printed from the internet and torn from magazines, most recently "Legal Highway Robbery" and "Drive-Ins for Pork Barrel Barons."

With the new laptop he spends hours every night researching the highway, trying to determine its location. He found coverage of the House Public Works Committee and the Intermodal Surface Transportation Efficiency Act. He learned that I-51's federal funding had been approved with passage of the National Lawn Care Act, and he thought he was hitting paydirt when he got into State records. But specific information on the highway's route eludes him. Every day, he e-mails Emma about his progress apologizing that he still hasn't found the facts, but will keep looking. He's also gathering, at Emma's suggestion, a list of environmental groups that would likely support their protest, if it comes to that.

A knock on his door startles him. "Mr. Serika? Mr. Serika?" It's a woman's voice, with a slight accent.

He closes the file drawer. The last one to call him Mr. Serika was the psychologist at the VA hospital who kept asking him, in a similar accent, Mr. Serika, what day is it? Mr. Serika, can you tell me what floor you're on? Who is the President of the United States, Mr. Serika?

"Mr. Serika? I am Misha Hacket. The new girls' custodial matron. Mr. Serika?"

The new girls' custodial matron! He opens the door. She is a large woman, maybe forty years old, with an honest face and hair like straw.

"Mr. Serika?"

He nods. Girl's custodial matron?

"They gave me this to sign and give to you." She hands him the paper. "I will do a very good job, Mr. Serika. I come eight o'clock in morning, yes?"

Eyes wide, he nods again, and she runs up the stairs.

He reads the paper. Employment Agreement. Misha Hacket, Girls' Custodial Matron. Copy to Alvin A. Serika, Director of Building Maintenance and Services. Not fired, not retired, but promoted. He's now Director of Building Maintenance and Services!

Chickadees, cardinals, and juncos feast at the domed feeder hanging from a lower limb of the grandly stark old maple tree, its leaves having fallen away. Emma sets her mug on the butler table, watching them and contemplating the whereabouts of the bats that entertain her in the summer, performing above the lawn, circling and diving for mosquitoes.

She was no more than five years old and terrified of bats when her father explained how the creatures fit into nature's scheme, devouring insects, not people. With that wonderful new perspective, she would run out to the lawn at dusk, lie flat on her back, and watch them swooping and diving, like aerial acrobats in the Lafayette Escadrille and Von Richtofen's Circus.

Sweet memories. They entice her more frequently in these days of precious little good news. Even Donnelley's amazing victory is overshadowed by Agatha's reports of his unconscionable divorce battle with Millie and their daughter just ran off with a Dominican gardener. Then there's all that road-building equipment, still parked at St. Catherine's. Not a single truck has moved north, or anywhere. Speedy checks every day. Very likely, their mission was stalled until after the election, when disclosure of the highway route wouldn't cost votes. And, if that's the case, the public hearing will be called any day now.

Most discouraging is Samson's new theory. As yet unable to enhance the videotape, he now says a mouse or some other animal may have triggered the camera, videotaping nothing more than shadows on a shining night.

Speedy rejects Samson's theory. In her old bones, she knows Speedy's right.

In the cold, gothic chapel decked with battle flags, as cadets kneel, their backs ramrod straight in reverent rectitude for the closing prayers of Evensong, Bunky's cellphone vibrates against his chest. Intuiting that the governor's office is calling with the go-ahead to launch Day One, he leaves the chapel and takes the call by the Old Boy's Oak. It is the governor, giving him the green light and authorization to determine the day and hour of launch. Finally, the waiting is over. Inside the chapel, they are singing the final hymn, "O gladsome light," an old chestnut he knows by heart.

Cadets file out of the chapel in formation. Farrand stops at the old oak tree and the two generals stroll back to Brass House for cocktails. Few words are exchanged.

Farrand hands him a Jack Daniel's on the rocks. "You want to talk about it, Bunky?"

Clappsaddle raises the glass to Farrand, takes a drink, and, sighing heavily, sinks into the wingback chair. "Did you know my father was a Marine? Gunny Sergeant Clarence Clappsaddle. He won the Navy Cross on Tarawa, lugging on his back a profusely bleeding member of the Roosevelt family."

"I had no idea," Farrand says, almost reverently.

"The Roosevelt lived. So Gunny Clappsaddle got the Navy Cross, and thanks from the President himself, together with an appointment for his son to the service academy of his choice." He swirled the ice cubes in the glass and drank from it. "My father didn't much like officers. Neither did I. But when I joined the Marines, like my old man, it didn't take long to figure out that I didn't like being enlisted either. So I exercised my trump card. Went from Parris Island, where they called me 'shithead,' to The United States Military Academy where they called me 'Mister.' A few steps up the social ladder, you might say. Thirty-seven years later I retired with the rank of Lieutenant General, collected a "good-by-and-good-luck" Distinguished Service Medal, and became president of Palumbo Construction Company." He drank from his glass. "Roy, I think I'm ready for a second retirement."

During dinner, Clappsaddle's thoughts drift, the candle's steady flame drawing his gaze. Farrand asks him if he would like to go deer hunting.

Constance chirps, "It's very important to have a hobby like deer hunting."

Bunky swallows a mouthful of meatloaf. "You're quite right, I'm sure."

"For me, it's my collection of china figurines."

"I think I might have some wine after all," Bunky says.

"Certainly!" She passes the carafe to him. "I started with figurines depicting historical events, then the great composers, great ballerinas, state birds, and of course mon general has shown you my gift to him, a set of the fifty-nine generals from West Point's Class of 1915—'the class the stars fell on.'"

"Yes. Very nice."

"Eisenhower and Bradley are especially lovely, don't you think."

"Breathtaking," Clappsaddle says, almost politely, wishing Constance would disappear for a while. In Vietnam, he had blown up anything and everything that got in his way—occasionally drawing criticism for his excesses. Now he has orders to simultaneously set off multiple charges along a ten-mile strip in the Berkshire Hills. He can manage it. But it will be the biggest bang he ever detonated—and unequivocally excessive.

After dinner he selects from Farrand's library King Lakes' *History of the Crimean War*, and reads for several hours. Around midnight he is rereading paragraphs, sentences, phrases, dozing. He turns off the bedside lamp, closes his eyes, and recites, "Now I lay me down to sleep—"

# 7

<hr />

## THURSDAY, NOVEMBER 7

<hr />

*New Burford*

Under a starry, predawn sky, Lieutenant General Bunker Terhune Clappsaddle, U.S. Army, Retired, President of the Palumbo Construction Company, is making his way to town, on foot, in his waxed hunting jacket and tweed cap. A cold wind invigorates him. He speculates how many days they'll be able to work before the deep freeze. For two miles the road winds through woods. He is alone, nary a dwelling or vehicle in sight. For some time he hears what turns out to be Crocker Egg Farm's white delivery van. It passes him, and slows to a stop. The driver pokes his head out the window, asks if he wants a lift. "No, thanks, I'm out for a walk." The van continues toward New Burford.

The woods end, stonewalls enclose gently rolling harvested fields, glistening with frost, then there are farmhouses with barns, orchards, paddocks and more stone walls. Closer to town are handsome Greek revivals, antique capes and saltbox houses. His apprehension grows. He's done a lot of elegant work with explosives since he was a lieutenant at Fort Bragg, when he and his buddies sharpened their skills, blowing up small pine trees, betting on who could fell them with greatest precision between two parked jeeps. But nothing like this.

The stars are paling as he reaches New Burford's center with its copper lanterns, cobblestone streets, brick sidewalks, and tidy shops. He strides purposefully in the direction of a graceful white steeple, towering over simple timber frame buildings, and comes upon an ancient village common, where two early New England clapboard structures, a church and a meeting house face each other from opposite ends. He walks the gravel path joining them, then, tantalized by the aroma of crisping bacon, he is led to a brick building that looks like a reconstructed armory with steamed-up, storefront windows. Mildred's. He looks in.

The restaurant is cheerful, clean, cozy, bustling, appealing in every way. He goes inside, feeling mildly uncomfortable, like an intruder, as he often does when he goes from military to civilian settings. Conversation stops, then resumes stiltedly, eyes darting at him. Assessing the situation, he locates the take-out sign, and asks for black coffee to go. "How about a blueberry muffin? Made 'em myself this morning," says Mildred. Imagining himself having breakfast there at a table behind the steamed up windows, he takes the bag to the Common, sits on a bench near the pillory and, watching people come and go in the morning sun, enjoys a great cup of coffee and a warm blueberry muffin.

He starts back, passing shops, now lighted and displaying American flags. He doesn't want to do it. The explosion will terrify these people. They'll fear the worst. They'll panic. Someone might have a heart attack in the minutes between the blast and the bulletins informing them that the horrific explosion was safe, government approved for everyone's economic benefit.

On the final stretch to WMMA, he wrestles with regrets. He never should have answered a recruitment ad placed by a company headquartered in the Bronx. He couldn't remember ever having heard or read anything positive about the Bronx, not even in the movies. People from the Bronx distinguished themselves by leaving. But this Bronx company had placed its ad in the *Wall Street Journal*, and that, in itself, qualified Palumbo Construction for him. Within seven days, he submitted his resume, met with the chairman, and accepted the offer to become the firm's president. He had been naive. Now, it was his duty to set off explosions ripping open the ancient hills and upsetting peaceful lives.

At Brass House, he changes into his greens, picks up his swagger stick, and sets out for a walk around the campus. He knows he will feel better about things once he is saluted and hears a bugle call. It's the orderliness that's comforting. Orderliness keeps things neat, keeps people out of trouble. Civilians just don't have that sense of orderliness.

Mess Call sounds. Doors fly open from the barracks, plebes run out into formation, followed by the upperclassmen. He considers the countless times he had stood in formation. In formation, he reaffirmed his conviction that the military is a true and honorable vocation. In formation, everyone is where he's supposed to be—and it is always for the purpose of protecting and defending the country. Civilians have nothing like that.

Assembly sounds. He stands still, watching, listening as one by one the first sergeant of each company calls out, "Fall in. Report," for the response, "All present and accounted for." Civilians just wander around as they please.

For forty years, whether or not he agreed, he had followed orders. Sometimes he had tested the edges of defiance, just to keep his sense of autonomy. But disobedience was never an option. Not then, or now.

If charges are detonated at five o'clock in the morning, people might awaken believing they had just dreamed the explosion and they may calm down somewhat by the time government offices open. If it's done on a Friday morning, government offices, starting with Town Hall, could jam the phone lines with busy signals or otherwise deflect complaints, at least through the morning, and perhaps close early for the weekend. By Monday most complaints will have lost urgency.

Bunky returns to his room and makes the phone calls. The charges will be detonated tomorrow morning at five o'clock. With everything set, he grabs his civilian cap and spends the afternoon driving through the Berkshire Hills in his Hummer.

# 8

*New Burford*

It is dark, cold, and still, the gibbous moon resting on black hills. Deer are foraging in orchards and meadows. Raccoons complete their rounds, raiding insecurely fastened garbage bins. Over dark houses, wisps of smoke escape from chimneys.

Suddenly, a deafening explosion shakes the earth and everything on it. Deer dart frantically in all directions. People scream from sound sleep. Children wail. Dogs bark. Cows howl. Car alarms harangue. Phones ring. Constable Turbo Bull gets into his Super Beetle cruiser to investigate. A helicopter thunders into the Valley of Runs-On-Toes-Into-Wind, its oppressive roar rattling windows, pots, pans, china in houses that had just quaked in the explosion. As far south as North Carolina and as far west as Wisconsin, seismographs pick up the blast. In Cheyenne, Colorado, the North American Aerospace Defense Command goes on alert for thirty minutes, while information on the blast wends through channels from Homeland Defense.

New Burford is jolted from sleep—Emma under her comforter, Speedy in the basement of New Burford High, the grandmothers in their bedrooms at Tucker's Chocolate Chip Cookie Cooperative. Hunter, wrapped around Jean in his warm bed, bolts upright, shouting, "Time on target—Jesus Christ, they've got us bracketed." Jean screams. Grabbing her, he dives under the bed, taking her with him, calling, "Freddie, where's Freddie?" He starts to crawl out, on his elbows. A helicopter thunders over the house. He recoils under the bed, pressing his hands to his ears, his arms to his chest.

Jean is terrified. "Hunter?" He doesn't respond, but his lips are moving, as if silently counting, or praying, "Hunter, please." She feels his forehead. Cold, very cold, his face is ashen and clammy. "Oh, please say something." She rubs his arm, his shoulders. No response. She wants to cry, scream, run. The helicopter fades. Downstairs, Freddie is yelping. She takes a deep breath, saying aloud, Pull yourself together, girl. Turn on the news, call Dr. Barnes, call Emma. God, are the phones working? What's out there? Plague? Radiation? What's that stuff for radiation? Potassium idodide? Check the medicine cabinet.

She drags a blanket under the bed and is wrapping it around him when the helicopter returns, nearly grazing the roof. Hunter trembles. She huddles against him.

"My God, it's the big one," Mildred gasps, dropping a "high-test" sign onto each of two large coffee urns. Certain it's the long averted nuclear blast, she starts reciting "Hail Mary," as she had learned it from old movies. Overcome with fear that searing heat is about to blow through the place, she minces toward the window, tears in her eyes, regretting that she had spent her whole life in New Burford. She left town only once, on a bus to New York with Aunt Edith and Uncle George, back in 1956, to hear Frank Sinatra in a reunion concert with the Dorsey Brothers at the Paramount. She was a kid in pigtails. It's still very dark outside. Where is the fireball?

"Sure as heck wasn't an earthquake," Billy states matter-of-factly.

She wipes the tears from her eyes. "Maybe it was a nuclear dirty bomb. Maybe that Arab guy who bought the old Lockwood place is behind this. Could be he's been involved with a terrorist cell, right here, under our noses."

Billy squashes his mouth into one of those I-don't-know-but-I don't-think-so expressions. "You mean the Lebanese guy? He's no terrorist. He keeps sheep, sells cheese and wool. Anyway, that was no nuclear bomb blast. Dirty or otherwise. Shellfire, maybe."

Mildred snaps back, "Don't be ridiculous, I've never heard shell fire, but I sure know it wouldn't sound anything like that. The whole earth shook!"

"You ever read about the Russians at Berlin?"

"No, can't say I have."

`"Well, they had thousands of guns and they shot them all at once at Berlin. That was one big noise."

"You're acting as if you heard nothing more than the toast pop." She shrugs wondering if it's all right for a Congregationalist to recite the Hail Mary. "Ya know, I don't see any fire ball, no flames. Don't hear any sirens. Just that helicopter. I'm thinking we better get things ready. If it's all over it won't matter anyway, and if it ain't over, folks'll probably be coming in any minute. Turn the radio on."

"Um-m, shell fire." Billy saunters into to the kitchen where Hank is taking eggs from the refrigerator and putting them into a basket so they'll look fresher than they really are. Peachpie jumps onto the counter and settles herself by the butter dispenser.

Emma knows what happened. Clappsaddle pushed the plunger.

She waits in the soft glow of a nightlight as the brewer finishes gurgling fresh coffee into the pot. She fills a mug and sits at the kitchen table, scolding herself.

Yes, Clappsadle pushed the plunger, but she blew it, too, by saying nothing. By wasting time trying to gather facts. Why? She's always spoken her mind, even when her opinions were half-baked. People expect it of her. So why didn't she put the highway on the town meeting warrant? Why didn't she present all her evidence at the meeting instead of just asking about the trucks? She could have riled everyone in town into demanding disclosures. They would have fought tooth and nail. Now it's too late.

Outside, Jenny yaps once at the door and Emma quickly admits her inside from the cold twilight. The dog prances, tail wagging. "Oh, Jenny, always so happy to be re-invited in, accepted all over again. Now, I've got to stop stewing. Can't waste energy crying over spilt milk when I need strength to wield the mop. We're going for a ride, Jenny."

Again, the helicopter makes a deafening sweep over the house, but this time it hovers, directly over the field. Hunter opens his eyes, turns his head, and vomits. Jean scrambles out from under the bed. Retching, she grabs her robe.

The helicopter sweeps away, leaving perfect silence. Hunter groans.

"You're going to be okay," she assures him, her voice quavering.

"Oh man, I've got to clean up." He struggles to get up.

"Just take it easy, I'll be right back."

Holding her stomach, she goes down to the living room and looks out the window. Darkness is yielding to twilight. Everything appears normal. She races to the kitchen window and looks out across the back lawn to the field. No sign of danger. The house is very quiet, except for the old clock's steady tick. A tiny green light is glowing on the dishwasher. Electricity! She turns on the radio—Pachelbel!—and scans for the emergency alert system? Freddie is whining to be let out. Damn, where's the news?

"—a failure in the timing mechanism set off...prematurely and simultaneously...the charges that were to have been detonated incrementally along the highway route, after public notice. Tremors rocked the watershed area but no damage has been reported. Repeating the WBAR news flash, construction of Interstate 51, the highway promising a boon to Western Massachusetts' economy, got off to a booming start this morning when charges unexpectedly detonated—"

Outrageous! That's unbelievable, she shudders. People could have died of fright. Hunter—God only knows! Freddy yelps. "Okay, Freddie, but you can't run free this morning." She opens the door, hooks him to the end of a rope anchored to the doorpost, and hurries in to fill the teakettle.

Freddie is yapping. She looks out the window over the sink. The dog is straining at the end of the rope, now barking frantically at bright orange spots moving about the edge of the field. She turns off the faucet. It's three men in orange vests. A fourth comes into the field from the woods. Are they hunters? Investigators, checking things after the explosion? Whoever they are whatever they're doing, they're not trying to hide anything, so there's no reason to mention it to Hunter right away as it might upset him again. She puts the kettle on the burner, then finds a can of household spray cleaner, disinfectant, a roll of paper towels, somewhat shredded by mice, a dustpan, and hurries back upstairs.

He is lying flat on his back, his legs still under the bed, as if he had tried to get up but didn't have enough strength. "You're here!" His voice is shaky, dry, yet happily surprised.

"Of course, I'm here. I was just downstairs. Everything's okay." She kneels next to him. He looks oddly serene, almost a bit spooked, and exhausted. "Freddie's outside, on the rope. Everything's fine. You won't believe what happened. There was a major screw up with the explosives set for blasting out the new highway. They went off prematurely, and all at once. Timing mechanism failed. Idiots. Feeling better?"

"That's incredible." He covers his face with his hand, then slides it away and with a meager, abashed smile and says, "You must think I'm a wimp. A loony wimp."

"No. But I was really worried about you. Still am. And I thought we were under attack and, God, it was awful. But you look much better."

"I am so sorry."

"Nonsense. You got sick," she says, playing down her concern.

"Thanks." He takes a deep breath, and exerts himself to stand. "The highway, huh."

"That's what they said on the news. I really thought it was a bomb. Who says it can't happen here?" She picks up the dustpan and paper towels.

"Give that to me. You're not lifting a finger to clean this," he protests.

"Whoa—. Minutes ago you were violently ill, looking as if you were going through hell."

"No!" He takes the roll of towels from her. "I made the mess, I'm cleaning it up." He's adamant.

Taken aback by this sudden intensity, she concedes, "I'll make coffee. Or tea? Better for your stomach."

"Coffee. Would be great," he says with a thin smile.

"Then you'll tell me what you thought was happening?"

"Come here." He throws his arms around her. "You're an absolutely amazing woman." He swallows, and laughs self-consciously, "I must stink."

"You do. You're also freezing cold—and a little nuts, but otherwise you're pretty amazing yourself." She reaches onto the bed for his robe and puts it on his shoulders.

"Thanks." He puts it on, breathes onto the palms of his hands and winces. "Mephitic."

"I don't know what it means but it sounds about right," she grins, and goes downstairs. "I'll get Freddie back inside."

In short time the bedroom floor is cleaned up, the room aired. They shower, get back under the quilt, and, leaning against a half-dozen pillows propped against the headboard, unwind, sipping steaming coffee. "Those explosions, the helicopter—It was so real," he shivers.

"It was real." She realizes he has told her something. "What did you think it was?"

He closes his eyes, momentarily. "Ugh. Later. I'll tell you later."

"You are so tense. I can actually see the tension in your shoulders. Here, give me your mug." She sets both mugs on the night table. I'm going to show you a terrific relaxation exercise."

"Exercise—?"

"Uh-huh." She throws off the comforter, pushes the pillows aside, lies on her back, her legs slightly parted, opens her robe, places his hand on her abdomen, and stretches out her arms. "Now, feel how I'm breathing from my abdomen—not my chest—my breath is slow and deep. See, my chest is very still."

He grins.

"This is not funny," she says with a big smile. "Now lie back. Close your eyes—and breathe from your belly. Slow and deep—"

They are completely unaware of the surveyors working in his yard.

"Sh-h-h-h. Quiet." Billy shouts, turning up the radio news over the heated debate. Mildred's regulars have arrived early and en masse to argue about possible causes of the explosion—a meteorite, a satellite crashing into the earth, terrorist bomb, dirty bomb, suitcase bomb, long-range missile.

"QUIET," Mildred bellows.

"—that rocked the Berkshires this morning. I'm Barbara Stricter, and this is WBAR, Barrington, where you get traffic and weather every fifteen minutes with a reminder, if you don't like the weather, wait a minute. The time is now 7:10. Repeating the top of the news, it took a big bang to officially launch a big boon to the Western Massachusetts economy. At dawn this morning construction of I-51, the highway to prosperity, got a jump-start in the watershed area east of Barrington when a failure in the timing mechanism set off...prematurely and simultaneously...the charges that were to have been detonated incrementally along the highway route, after advance public notice. Tremors rocked the watershed area but no damage has been reported. Repeating the WBAR news flash, construction of Interstate 51, the highway promising a boon to Western Massachusetts' economy, got off to a booming start this morning when charges unexpectedly detonated. Local traffic will not be affected by the highway construction, which is to be completed in May. However, this morning many area schools will delay opening, among them, Barrington, Egremont, New Boston, New Burford, —"

"Turn that off! What's this 'unexpectedly' talk? They should have told us they were getting ready for that blast."

"Who said that? You're darn right!"

"How do we know as somebody didn't die of fright?"

"Or heart attack!"

"Hold it! That explosion was this side of the ridge. You know what that means? The highway's going straight through New Burford!"

Dead silence. For a second. Then uproar, and a clamor to rush out of Mildred's.

Binoculars hanging from his neck, Clappsaddle tramps across the field, from tripod to tripod, checking prisms, digital transits, and co-axil distance meters. "Well done," he concludes. On his aerial inspection, he saw that everything is moving along in zero tolerances—bulldozing teams shoving the earth from multiple points along the route, and now the crew is surveying the final stretch, pushing vermilion-tipped pins into the ground.

He looks across the quiet expanse to the rail fence, the neat lawn, the white clapboard house, almost pink in the early light. The scene is so peaceful, so inviting, like the kind of place he always wanted to live in with his bride, who spent most of her adult life in military housing, waiting for him. Bunky stares at the vermilion trail cutting across the field, into the lawn, through the garden patch. About twenty feet from the back of the house, the trail curves sharply and returns to the woods—a bizarre detour from the otherwise straight highway. He doesn't know who lives in the house, nor does he want to know. It's none of his business. But he knows the people inside will be furious. His gut sours. "Continue to march," he orders the surveyors, then disappears into the woods.

By seven o'clock, he is back at Brass House having breakfast with Farrand, reading morning newspapers, in the dining room.

He finds it curious that Roy says nothing about the blast. Even if he hadn't been wearing his hearing aid, he surely felt the tremor. Scanning the front section of the *Global*, he breaks the silence, rapping the paper with the back of his hand and snarling, "Take a look at this, Roy."

Farrand slides his glasses to the tip of his nose and examines the photo of the President and Secretary of State entering the White House, a Marine holding the door for them.

"The U.S. military in action as the President's butlers!"

"What's gnawing at your craw, Bunky?"

"I'll tell you, Roy—. From my first day on the parade ground, I was trained to think, 'I stand tall. I am in charge.' They taught us to be deferential, humble, grateful to render service to country. But damn it, this kind of deference—holding briefcases, umbrellas, opening doors for politicians, as if we're valets—is not service to country."

"Thinking of running for office, Bunky?"

"Hell, no," he snaps. "This has always pissed me off. Consider if you will— military people always do as they're told. Generals tell each other what to do, they tell colonels what to do, right down the whole damn excessively long, outmoded chain of command. But, ah-ha, it's civilians who tell the generals what to do. The civilians! And they change places every four years. It's lunacy."

"Let it go, Bunky. You're USA Retired. You do civilian work now. Beyond that you're doing what you can to affect crucial changes in the military. Ease up on yourself."

Clappsaddle doesn't respond. He feels as if he's just wrapped up a search and destroy mission, ordered by unprincipled politicians for self-aggrandizing ends. He excuses himself from the table. All he wants now is to build the damn highway—without getting squeezed between the town's indignation and his own conscience. Then, he'll move on.

At the old Hamilton House, Hunter is making scrambled eggs. Jean turns on Colonial Cable, checking for a school cancellation announcement, which, her students know, would mean that her studio will also be closed. "Emma must be furious," she suddenly realizes. "I'll stop by to see her this morning." She pours orange juice.

"Hold it. Do you hear that?"

She shakes her head.

"That humming sound—like a huge diesel engine, in the distance. It's getting louder."

"Yes," she says under her breath, listening.

He goes to the window—and gapes at the orange trail. "What the hell—?" The noise builds.

Suddenly, three bulldozers roar from the woods, ripping into the field, uprooting grasses, shrubs and saplings, churning up a wide strip of black earth. "My God!" He bolts outside and, in an adrenaline rush, runs across the yard toward the advancing bulldozers.

Running after him, Jean is screaming into the noise, "STOP, Hunter STOP."

Slowly, steadily the bulldozers churn their way across the field.

Hunter stumbles into the field, running toward them, defying them, as if playing chicken. They don't stop. Then, like a sleepwalker, he steps out of their way, staring blankly as the bulldozers shove by him, continuing to rip across the lawn, through the small patch that had been his vegetable garden. Jean grabs his arm and he snaps out of the daze. "I've got to get you out of here," he yells against the roar, the bulldozers continuing steadily toward the house.

"No, we've got to stop them," she shouts, tears on her cheeks. "They're going to flatten your house!"

Twenty feet from the house the three behemoths veer, cutting a hairpin curve in the lawn.

"It's the highway," he murmurs in disbelief. "It can't be!" He watches, shocked, as the bulldozers complete the U through his field and retreat into the woods. The noise fades.

"This is a massive screw-up, Hunter. You've got to go to town hall, like now. You'll probably win a big fat lawsuit. Could be a lucky break—."

"I don't need another fucking lucky break. All I want is peace and quiet. In my house, on my property." He picks up a handful of churned black soil, then releases it. Why?

Dr. Ralph Barnes awakens. The phone is ringing but the service isn't answering. He moans. His central nervous system had shut down during the night when his urinary tract had signaled it for instructions. His pants are wet. Still half-asleep, he glances at the clock—almost eleven. "Dr. Barnes speaking," His voice is composed, highly professional. "Yes, Jean. Does he have a fever, rash, dizziness?" He listens. "Explosion?"

Ralph had slept through the blast in his favorite lounge chair in front of his three television sets. During primetime, he had consumed a fair amount of vodka, a brandy nightcap with the news. Sometime after midnight, when he felt as if he was drowning in his own gut, he stretched a hose into his stomach, pumped out the overflow, and then soothed his throat with another snifter of brandy. He passed out cold the moment he yanked the tube from his throat. "What kind of explosion?"

Jean describes the blast, the invasions of helicopters and the bulldozers plowing almost straight into his house. "He needs a sedative."

"Can you bring him to my office at twelve? Good—. Now stay calm, Jean. Drive carefully."

In the corridor outside the town clerk's office, Hunter studies a framed print of an Indian chief, three feathers in his hair, shaking hands with a white man in a tall beaver hat and knickers. He feels mellow, very mellow from the free sample of Xanax. Wondering what effect the other two prescriptions might have on him, he waits with Jean on a hard wooden bench. The air seems rarefied, oppressive, silencing them. They listen to the rustle of paper, the file search underway in the records room.

"Mr. Barnhill!" Like a school teacher taking attendance, Bertha Harper calls him into her office. He hesitates, then takes Jean's hand, and they go in together. "Nice to see you, Jean," says the Town Clerk as she flips through the topmost sheets in a stack of papers loaded onto the counter. She lays them face down, picks up the next sheet and points to it with the eraser end of a freshly sharpened pencil. "Now, Mr. Barnhill, this says that in 1765 a right of way through the property was granted to Elijah Hawkins and his heirs for the purpose of moving livestock to his non-adjacent properties." She lays it face down on the pile, picks up the next sheet. "This says the right of way belongs to the Massachusetts Department of Transportation. Transferred about a month ago." She goes to the next sheet. "See here, the State located the Hawkins' descendants in Hawaii, and they transferred it. So there it is, Mr. Barnhill."

"But that's impossible," he says slowly, carefully. "At the closing, no one said anything about an old right of way through this property—not even the title people."

"It's been here the whole time. No secret."

"It makes no sense. Why would the highway follow this weird U-shaped right of way? It should be going straight!"

"To protect the splay-footed sapsucker!"

"I don't understand." It all feels surreal.

"An endangered species. This section of the watershed is the only known habitat of the splay-footed sapsucker. Federally protected. Actually that might have been Hawkins' reason for securing the right of way. To avoid those pesky critters. Anything else I can do for you?"

Driving away from town hall, Hunter is numb. "Help me get a grip. My house is on sixty-eight acres—abutting a watershed. Now it's going to be twenty feet away from a major highway so some endangered splayfooted sapsucker can live there undisturbed. I want to be undisturbed, too. I think, as soon as this feel-good stuff wears off, I may be furious." In the back seat, Freddie yaps.

"I'm canceling my afternoon classes. You can't be alone," says Jean.

"No, you're not. Those kids are not going to miss classes on account of me, or the highway. I'll be fine."

"Then do me a favor? Go home, get some clothes, your laptop, whatever, and go to my house. Stay there with me for a while. You don't need to look at that scene."

"Thanks," he manages a smile.

"Good." She kisses his cheek. "If you're really okay, could you to drop me at the studio and come get me later? I've got a class starting in five minutes."

From the studio, he goes on to his house, gathers some things, and flees with Freddie to Jean's, letting himself in with the key under the mat. He drops onto the overstuffed sofa and looks, really looks, for the first time, at the collection of framed photographs on the end table. There are old photos of Jean as a girl, photos of Jean with students—little girls in tutus, teenagers in leotards, middle-aged women in sweat suits, couples of all ages dressed up for ballroom dancing. He picks up the silver-framed, black and white photo of the professional Jean in mid-leap, spotlights caressing the exquisite shapes of her face and body. He wants to be with her. He feels completely comfortable in her house, but has to get away—away from the highway—just long enough to clear his head, to get perspective, and figure out what to do.

He'll find someone to check the house every week or so, drain the pipes, turn down the heat, pack a few things and go. Freddie won't like the city, but at least he will have the yard and the park down the street. But Jean. He looks again at the photos, and reaches for the phone.

Frustrated that she can't access the blasted areas by car, Emma drives over to Colonial Cable where calls are coming in from news producers and reporters covering the explosion story. Some are looking for a base of operation through Monday morning when the governor is holding a press conference at the highway groundbreaking ceremony.

She goes on line to check e-mail, scanning for news from Speedy. There it is.

> *From: aasspeaks@cc.com*
> *To: emmail@cc.com*
> *Subject: Highway*
> *Route goes straight across north end of New Burford through watershed except for a sharp curve that cuts close to the Old Hamilton House. Looks like New Burford access will be right behind the Green. They're already bulldozing. Are you all right? AAS*

Emma rereads his report, marveling at his reconnoitering skill. She clicks reply, invites him for dinner the next evening, asking him to bring his laptop, then invites Hunter and Jean.

Delicious aromas are wafting from the kitchen when he brings Jean home from the studio. He grins, "I figured you didn't feel like eating out, not even at Sparkie's—so Sparkie's delivered."

"Sparkie's delivered? Sparkie's does take-out about like Four Seasons."

He shrugs. "Hey, Sparkie is a Marine; Marines take care of each other. Now, I'm going to follow his very specific instructions. So if you will give me about ten minutes."

"Fantastic, I'll go shower," she beams, convinced that he's recovered from the day's ordeals, not just hiding in the haze of medication. When he picked her up at the studio, they danced for a while, even a tango, which he couldn't have done like that on meds.

He sets the table with the supplied tablecloth and napkins, a centerpiece of miniature roses, and candles. He spills from a plastic bag sliced endive, yellow pepper and avocado chunks into a bowl and tosses them with the supplied dressing. From the oven he takes two covered aluminum pans and a baguette. Everything is ready.

"Flowers, linens, candlelight, this is lovely," she exclaims as he opens a bottle of wine.

He says nothing about his decision until dessert, individual pots of crème brûlée, which he barely touches. He puts down his spoon.

"Not more bad news—."

"I called Ben this afternoon," he pauses. "A friend of his has been subleasing my apartment in New York."

"You kept your apartment—?"

"It just happened to work out that way. I was about to sell when Ben told me about this guy, a TV producer. He lives in L.A., works a lot in New York. He offered me a good deal."

"Ugh. I know where this is going."

"I never had any intention of going back but—"

"Not consciously." She gets up from the table and paces. "Damn." She laces her fingers, stretches her arms over her head, slightly swinging a straight leg.

Immediately he's up from the table and holds her. "Damn it, don't even think of those karate kicks, battements. Please understand, I do not want to leave but I can't think straight here. I've got to get away for some perspective, to figure out how to unload that property—and finish that damn book, which I certainly will not be able to do while watching my yard get paved."

She sighs. "I do understand. It's just very crummy."

"Come with me."

"I can't. The irony is I just turned down an offer to do a festival, rehearsing in the city in December, because I can't just up and leave my students. Or you." She pauses, looking down. "When are you leaving?"

"Monday morning. The tenant's in L.A. He won't be using the apartment till February, maybe March, but I should be back before then."

She can't look at him.

"It'll be fine, really."

# 9

## TUESDAY, NOVEMBER 11

*New York City*

As Governor Brewster Pease officiates at the I-51 groundbreaking ceremony, the Rover is cruising through Westchester County toward the city. The closer Hunter gets to New York, the more certain he is that he's made the right decision.

He smiles, remembering how Jean had told him she'd be in the city in December. She had bounded into the house after her Saturday classes, pealed off her sweater, and headed for the shower, saying I've got great news, come wash my back and I'll tell you. In all the cascading water, lather and steam, not much else was said except that she had called back about the festival job, it was still open, and she's doing it.

On Saturday they were invited to Emma's for dinner and, after hearing his plan, Emma and Speedy offered to check the house while he was gone. "Don't worry about a thing," Emma said, "—just do what you have to do and come back soon." The next morning they together toured the house, Emma with a clipboard, Speedy with his note pad, both taking notes. Speedy asked about all the unfinished projects, scrawling, "Do you want those pipes wrapped? Windows glazed? Consider it done." Unbelievable.

About fifty miles from the city, on the Sawmill Parkway, he slides a Gershwin CD into the player. New York in the thirties. Black tie dinners and dancing. Romantic movies. A New York without fear, tension, without subway doors closing in your face, without cabs racing by you in pouring rain, without always rushing—without always needing to convince yourself that everything's okay.

He imagines the old Hamilton house next to a highway—like living on the Cross Bronx Expressway without a fast commute—and recalls the ghostly video he saw at Emma's. Speedy had presented a plausible scenario, writing like mad on his laptop, identifying the members of the town council, including charming Bertha Harper. But his theory is convincing only if you want to believe him. And even if, by some miracle, everyone in town believed him, it wouldn't matter. The right of way transfer was unethical but legal. He had been screwed. The town, too.

He cuts off the CD and angrily accelerates into the passing lane at 85 miles an hour. Emma's right, the town will never be the same again. More people, more cars, malls, developers will buy up land. Including his. The house might be salvaged as professional office space. No. He slows down.

The Rover crosses the toll bridge from Riverdale into Manhattan, speeds down the Henry Hudson to the Westside Highway, and exits at 96th Street. Dodging pedestrians, skateboarders, bikers, and potholes, he speculates the odds of finding a parking space near the apartment building so he won't have to make several trips to carry all his stuff from the garage, two blocks away.

As he turns the corner from Central Park West, a car pulls out of a space right in front of his brownstone. At eleven a.m. on a Tuesday, this is miraculous! He laughs. Either this is a good omen or the car was just stolen, or both.

He swings the Range Rover into the space. It all feels so familiar. But not like coming home. This was never home. New York had taken care of him, praised his frivolous, vapid copy with the Golden Ladder

Award, given him lavish remuneration, increased every time he re-signed, provided an abundance of beautiful, easy women. Unreal. Unreal—until that day, on his way to a business lunch at the Sky Club when he saw, right in Grand Central Terminal, that old homeless woman urinating on the floor, squatting like a mamasan, next to her five shopping bags filled with neatly folded newspapers. He imagined her sitting in the Colony Club having tea. Who was she? Why wasn't anyone helping? Why wasn't he helping? He wasn't helping because he was too busy walking through Grand Central carrying a $1200 box made out of a dead steer. And people who carried dead steer boxes didn't help people who sit in their own urine. Nor did they see them.

That's what he had left. He turns off the ignition. At least Melanie doesn't know he's in town. Freddie stretches in the back seat, looks out at the street, and gives Hunter a disapproving look.

"It's only temporary, Freddie."

Freddie farts and slowly, very slowly gets out.

In the foyer, nothing has changed, except the name added to his mailbox— DeCarlo. He unlocks the foyer door, and, in the hallway, unlocks four locks on the apartment door.

The apartment is exactly as he had left it. He goes across the living room, through his study, unlocks the back door and the metal secu-rity door to the enclosed yard. Freddie follows. The adjacent brown-stones and their fenced in yards look no different. Freddie marks the yard and hurries inside.

Settling on the couch, Hunter first checks in with Ben, then, like Pavlov's dog, calls Babs Mahoney at *Jock Illustrated*. Babs always used to give him instant updates on whatever was going on in town. She made it her business to know everyone else's business, who's in, who's out, who's moving up, getting canned. It's not that he cares about any of that anymore, but reentry to Manhattan triggered the old habit.

A desultory voice answers, announcing that Babs Mahoney doesn't work at *J.I.* anymore. Impossible. He calls the main number and is im-mediately connected to her.

"Hunter, you mangy son-of-a-bitch. Oh, thank God you're here. But, of course, you're here! You were his star! Oh, you must be devastated."

"Stop." Hunter cuts her off, as he learned to do with her long ago. "Know what?"

"About Ruggie."

"What about Ruggie?"

"My God, you don't know. He died last night, early this morning, actually. Oh, it's so awful. He was so wonderful. Hunter? —Are you there?"

He can't grasp what she had said. Ruggles Wheelwright Wilmot was one of the founders of Dasher, Wilmot and Epstein, and at fifty-four, is not supposed to be dead. "What happened?"

"Chronic media overload syndrome."

"What the hell is that?"

"Well, I'm told it's like manic-depression but much worse because it can complicate or trigger other conditions, especially when goes undiagnosed—which is what happened to Ruggie. Very scary. They didn't know he had it, and Ruggie just kept doing it all. That's who he was. I mean Ruggles Wilmot was The Business. The ultimate expertise-ceo. Ugh, I don't have to tell you. He gave a shit about everything but, they're saying when he got to cyberspace, he started burning out his own circuitry."

"When's the funeral?"

"Is that all you can say? Tomorrow at eleven. Go with me, Hun? Ruggie had just promised me 24 pages from Cavemate Underwear. Maybe you could help me hit Epstein for them. I'd hate like hell to lose 24 pages."

"Where's the service?"

"St. Thomas. Fifth Avenue. I can hardly wait to see you, Hunter. I've got so much to tell you. Things got really rough here after those greedy sons of bitches plundered and sold us down the river in that fantasyland deal. They pocketed obscene megabucks, leaving us

peons, what was left of us anyway, to mop up the financial hemor-
rhage, ugh, don't get me going, but you know all that, it's ancient
history. What's important is that, at some point, the big boys noticed
that the stodgy old print rags were actually performing damn well.
Even in down cycles. So, would you believe?—they went into a huddle
and emerged with a commitment to launch a fabulous new magazine.
And here's the best. Guess—you get one shot at this—Guess who's
publisher.

"Uh, Babs Mahoney."

"Yessssss! Aren't you proud of me?"

"I always knew you'd get to the top." He wants to tell her he
doesn't care anymore about new magazines, shaky 24-page deals, or
Cavemate Underwear—but if he did, she wouldn't hear him anyway.
Babs had honed occupational skills of listening selectively and do-
ing all the talking most of the time. He will ask the right questions.
"What kind of magazine?"

"It's about dogs and puppies. About these wonderful creatures
and their owners and the relationships between them. The relationship piece is key. Right on a hot trend, a new category that's got legs,
very long legs. And we're right on it, with this new rag."

"What's the name?"

"*Sit!*"

"*Sit*," he repeats. It fits with the other L-W publication names—
*Pulse, Folks, Jock Illustrated, Rich, Sit*.

"Yes, *Sit*! Isn't it perfect? They've made a solid financial commitment, all things considered. And now we're ready to go into full bore."

"Congratulations." Hunter always marveled at Bab's ability to pick
words and phrases from miscellaneous lexicons and toss them into
her speech like little chunks of blue cheese in a salad.

"We've taken over an entire floor and built an enormous kennel.
Staff can walk their dogs to work and leave them in *Sit* Day Care &
Kennel, free of charge. And we're got videocams and two-way voice
communication from the kennel to each office so staff can practice

voice commands and have quality time with their pets throughout the day. How's that for editorial involvement?"

"It's terrific. I'm really glad for you." He can't take any more. "Babs, I gotta run. I'll meet you in front of St. Thomas. Make it 10:30 so we'll get good seats."

"Grrreat. Love you, Hunter. And don't forget. I've got to see Epstein."

"Love you, too, Babs. See you at 10:30." He leans back into his old couch and looks out into the yard. The ivy climbing on the six-foot fence is exactly like the ivy climbing on trees near the old Hamilton house. How does it survive here in this effete soil, minimal sunlight, and foul air? Certainly better than some of the people.

# 10

*New York City*

The granite sky threatens rain. It feels colder than it is as Hunter waits on the church steps, watching mourners emerge from taxis and limousines. He remembers the weddings here, two of them Ruggie's, and a few Christmas Eves, when he was transported by incense, a world-class boy's choir and the rector's English accent. Ruggie was a member of the church and will certainly get an impressive funeral. For that matter, Ruggie had been a member of just about every organization for which he qualified and every private club that accepted him. No wonder his circuitry got jammed.

A vender hawking hot pretzels and roasted chestnuts pushes his steaming cart through the crowd. From around the corner, a woman in a full-length mink coat and unnaturally red hair approaches with an angular man in a Chesterfield. She struts up the steps, arms outstretched and air-kisses him, exclaiming, "Harvey, it's Hunter! You're back! You look terrific!"

"Nice to see you, Marcie. Harvey," Hunter says, smiling. Marcie had been a junior copywriter with him at DWE and, after changing agencies, was catapulted to the position of global creative director. Harvey, her intermittent lover, is, or at least was, general counsel for ABG Video Enterprises. She quickly moves on, Harvey trailing her when an old friend and squash partner, tall and darkly handsome, greets Hunter.

"Hey, Jack. This is tough."

"A real bummer. How about a game sometime soon? Like tomorrow, at six?"

"I'll reserve the court," says Hunter, somewhat distracted by the beautiful, elegant blonde waving to him from the sidewalk. She is upstaged by Babs, who has just arrived with a large dog, about eighty-pounds of mixed breed.

With effusive greetings, Babs leads the dog up the steps to Hunter and plants an audible kiss on his chin. "Hunter, this is Brandywine. Shake hands, Brandy." The dog obeys and Hunter takes the paw. "Isn't she gorgeous? Half Saluki and half short hair German retriever, much to the dismay of her birth owners."

Hunter straightens. "You can't take a dog in there, Babs."

She lowers her voice, "You bet your sweet ass I can. The entire ad community is here, all the trades, *W*, *Quest*, you name it. We're great photo fodder in this sea of suits. Smile, Hun. They're shooting us as we speak." She takes his arm, reins in Brandywine, and grins widely.

"Babs, it's Ruggie's funeral. You can forget about image building for an hour."

"Are you kidding? This is a promotion opportunity par excellence. Listen, Hun, you look great, we all miss you terribly. Now don't start getting all hung up on the wrong stuff. This is an Episcopal Church. Anything goes—in a formal sort of way. Hell, I've still got framed on my office wall that *Newsweek* article on the female Jesus up at the Cathedral, St. John the Divine. Nailed to the cross, loincloth, big breasts, the whole nine yards. And that was years ago. Believe me, these people will have no trouble with Brandy. Now let's pay our respects to Ruggie. Heel, Brandy."

If the dog's a problem, the ushers will handle it, Hunter tells himself, going inside. They sign the memorial book and start down the long center aisle, Babs taking Hunter by the arm and Brandy by a short lead. Hunter recognizes a fair number of media people peering at them through sunglasses and wishes he were wearing shades, too, at least for this promenade.

Halfway down the aisle, Babs puts on her best smile for the reporters who are bobbing about, identifying faces, and signaling their photographers. She presses forward to the third row, where she shunts people sitting on the aisle toward the other end of the pew, and moves in. "Sit," she commands, in stage whisper, and Brandywine climbs onto the red cushioned pew. Babs beams.

Seated on the aisle, next to the large, panting dog, Hunter is annoyed—not by the dog, who seems pretty neat but by Babs, who is ripping ad pages from the funeral program, and by all the media people, seasoned chameleons ever shifting and modifying to accommodate clients and now assuming reverential, respectful postures.

The choir files into the chancel. The rector appears from the sacristy with two acolytes, one carrying a censer, the other a crucifix. Some stand, everyone else imitates.

"Stand," Babs commands. The dog obediently jumps to the floor, and on hind legs, rests front paws on the back of the next pew. The organ sounds. The rector and acolytes solemnly walk the center aisle to meet Ruggie's remains at the main entrance, then turn and lead a procession of priests, deacons, layreaders, honorary pallbearers rolling the casket, a host of flag bearers, and six men in tuxedos, each carrying what appears to be an oversized pepper grinder.

The congregation turns to face the procession. Babs slips her program into the rack and leans across Brandywine to whisper, "Reception's at your club, right after a private family interment—perfect time to nab Epstein for the Cavemate spreads."

He doesn't answer, his eyes on the procession. The dog's eyes are on the swinging thurible, spewing thick, fragrant smoke. Eventually, the procession reaches the front of the church. The choir sings "Battle Hymn of the Republic." The rector seats the congregation. In row three, Brandy scrambles onto the pew.

Dan Dasher is at the lectern.

"My friends. We gather to mourn the loss of Ruggles Wilmot and to celebrate him—his person, his genius, his humanity. A lion among admen, Ruggie had extraordinary energy, enthusiasm and indefatigably demonstrated the ability to get it done, whatever it was. He brought in business, built business, sustained business because he unerringly knew what mattered, and addressed all matters that mattered. He attracted the best talent. He understood genius. And he knew what worked—in television, print, direct mail, outdoor, transit, skywriting, newspaper inserts, hang tags, menu clip-ons, shelf-talkers and then on the internet—leaderboards, pushdowns, sidekicks and sliders. He was among the first to take the pulse of the e-economy and master digital branding. He had an instinct for effective advertorials, championed heart-rending pro bono work, and gave of himself to make the world safer for global commerce.

"When he observed that war gets in the way of marketing, he founded his Samples of Peace Foundation, now in its second year orchestrating airdrops of product samples into the world's crisis zones, inspiring combatants everywhere to lay down their arms and enjoy consuming.

"Ruggie took great pride in DWE's countless awards, among them Clios, Andies, Effies, Golden Marbles, and the highest honor: the Advertising Academy's Golden Ladder Award. In his final days, he created a montage of DWE's award-winning ads and commercials. This montage we are about to see is introduced by a series of audio clips from his answering machine archive. It concludes with Ruggie, himself, in an extraordinarily moving farewell." An enormous screen is slowly descending, covering the reredos of sculpted saints and angels. Applause ripples through the nave. Dan holds up his hand, the applause subsides.

Hunter picks up the program, a slick magazine, *IN MEMORY, The Funeral Program Magazine*, Ruggie on the cover with a banner, Special Issue, Ruggles Wheelwright Wilmot—On to his Great Reward. He quietly flips through it—lots of ads, pages and pages of ads, a few stories about Ruggie, his school days, career highlights, the order of service, and more ads. The flags in the procession, he learns, represent the twenty-six genealogical societies of which Ruggie was a member—Colonial Wars, Colonial Governors, Sons of the Revolution, Flagon and Trencher, and so on. The six men in tuxedos are maitre d's of his favorite restaurants. The lights dim. Brandywine plunks herself on the floor, resting her muzzle on a kneeling pad.

The montage begins with clips of phone messages from Ruggie's mother, from Dasher and Epstein, from mother again, from ex-wives, from grateful clients, and then, against a soft soundtrack of Pachelbel's Canon, longer messages, presumably from Dick Cavett, Barbara Walters, Bono and others, all praising his initiatives to promote world peace. On the huge screen above the high altar, print ads and commercials extol the qualities of hand cream, foot powder, careers in the Federal Bureau of Investigation, motor oil, chewing gum, British gin, Polish vodka, fat-free cheesecake.

The screen suddenly is dark for several moments. Then Ruggie appears, tan and serene in a white turtleneck sweater, seated by the fireplace in the living room of his Fifth Avenue co-op. "Thank you for taking time from your very busy schedules to attend my funeral. I greatly appreciate your presence on such sort notice. Timing, you all know, is always critical. At this moment timing is a matter of life and death. Which is why I am taking this opportunity to focus your attention on the life-saving organ donor program and I'm doing this in a way that, I trust, will inspire your support and participation." He pauses for a sip of water. The church is perfectly silent.

"When I died, my vital organs were immediately harvested by a team from the University of Pittsboro Medical Center and flown back to Pittsboro for transplantation surgery—simultaneous with my funeral. ABG Special Productions is broadcasting, live, the surgery and my funeral. Proceeds from the sale of broadcast and video rights are going directly to my Samples of Peace Foundation. Certainly, this is the most important presentation of my afterlife. From the bottom of my heart, I thank you for watching, and for considering the gifts you can give. My warmest wishes to you all. For DWE, for the industry, for the global marketplace, the best is yet to come." Ruggie's image fades.

Applause erupts. Brandywine yelps.

"Quiet, Brandy," Babs commands.

The dark screen fills with a yellow-white light that dissolves to an image of Melanie Atwood, sunny blonde hair, high cheekbones, Armani suit. Hunter momentarily turns his eyes, fidgeting with his necktie knot.

"Good morning. I'm Melanie Atwood, live from the University of Pittsboro Medical Center. We are at the transplant surgery theater, where a seven-organ transplant is in progress. All seven organs were donated by global advertising doyen, Ruggles Wheelwright Wilmot. His wish is that you, his family and friends gathered in New York at St. Thomas Church for his funeral, and audiences throughout the world might share and be inspired by this momentous television event. The recipient of Ruggie Wilmot's organs is Willis Duncan of Nome, Alaska, who was flown here yesterday when the National Organ Transplant Center identified him as next in line for the big seven—one heart, one liver, one pancreas, two kidneys, and two lungs." A nurse appears and helps Melanie into a surgical gown and mask. The camera follows them through swinging doors into the surgery theater.

There they are. The seven organs, and some twenty gowned and masked anesthesiologists, surgeons, and nurses adroitly wielding scalpels, tubes and clamps.

Suddenly, the head surgeon triumphantly raises his arms, thumbs up. All seven are in. Melanie whisks off her surgical mask for the camera's extreme close-up, and joyously reports, "It is accomplished! All seven safely inside Willis. Thank you, Ruggie, for your great gift. This is Melanie Atwood at the University of Pittsboro Medical Center in Pittsboro, Pennsylvania." The choir is singing the "Hallelujah Chorus" as the camera returns to the surgical team, high-fiving each other in time with Handel.

The huge screen ascends and the rite proceeds and concludes according to the *Book of Common Prayer.* Synchronously, they lift their pepper grinders over the casket and give them three smart turns, sprinkling fresh pepper over the casket. The celebrant sneezes. Sniveling he leads the recession, the pallbearers with casket, Ruggie's third ex-wife, his mother, the Dashers, and Epstein and, starting with the first row, the congregation joins the solemn recession. Taking Brandy's leash and stepping into the aisle, Hunter prods Babs who is checking with reporters, making sure they have enough photos of her with Brandywine. She quickly takes Hunter's arm for the recession.

They emerged from the dark Gothic church into bright sunshine, New York at its autumn best. "What a gorgeous, perfect day," says Babs. "Let's get a drink. We've got time to kill while they're doing the interment. The St. Regis, the King Cole Bar—like old times. The doorman will take care of Brandy, no problem."

Babs orders a vodka and tonic, Hunter a scotch and water. Furtively she lights and drags on a cigarette, and says, narrowing one eye against the smoke, "I'm so glad it all worked out like this."

"It was disgusting."

"What was disgusting?"

"The whole bizarre funeral-transplant-telecast. Bad taste. And put that out, please."

"Oh, so now you're the self-exiled arbiter of good taste. What's the matter, Hun? All's not sweetness and light with Melanie?" She fishes a small silver box from her bag and crushes the cigarette in it.

"Melanie has nothing to do with it. It could have been Walter Cronkite up there and my opinion would have been the same. It was inappropriate."

"My, you're testy!" She blows smoke toward the floor. "So what didn't you like?"

He glances at the next table where two Japanese men and a voluptuous blonde are doing martinis. "It trivialized a major ritual."

"How could you say that? You probably just resent like hell that you weren't around to take credit for the concept."

"That's not only way off base but cruel. Maybe I borrowed but I never took credit for ideas that weren't mine."

"Whatever. The surgery show was fabulous and you know it. Broadcast around the world. Maybe even got more viewers than Di's funeral. A real coup for ABG. For the whole industry. This big agency principal donating not just money but his major organs, seven of 'em. And all the benefits go to Samples of Peace. It was Ruggie's ultimate signature. Big, bold, beautiful—."

"Give me a break."

"Really. Think about it. Advertising people never get to sign their work. You guys do brilliant stuff, but nobody out there knows who did it. My name is always on the masthead. Everybody who works on a magazine doing something at least somewhat significant gets on the masthead. So Ruggie got to sign off—big time. And it was glorious."

Hunter is playing with their mixing straws. "It's what he wanted."

"May I also point out that today I got you farther down the aisle, closer to an altar than any other woman." She smirks.

He drops the straws and laughs, "Another score for Babs Mahoney."

"That reminds me, Hun, I need a favor."

"Epstein and your twenty-four pages?"

"No. This is even more important to me. And in the church I realized—you're actually the only person I can talk to about this—."

"Hard to believe. Tell me."

"I need you to come to the rescue."

He grins, expecting a joke. "Okay, how can I rescue the publisher of the hot new *Sit*?"

"You know my story—"

"I do," he winces slightly, hoping she won't get into it again.

She does. "—I was one of the very first women to sell magazine advertising at Luz Inc. I was a kid, 21. Just out of Briarcliff. And I got into it with both feet."

"You were a star, Babs. Still are."

"I wanted to do it all. And I did, pretty much. I was on the cutting edge of the feminist movement. Weekends I burned my bra. Weekdays I took men to lunch and dinner. I used my gut, my company credit card, negotiated, and entertained well. Got strategic. Now I'm proud to say I'm a publisher—as well as a mother."

"A mother? You're a mother?!" He can't imagine it.

"Thanks for being shocked," she snaps indignantly.

"I just never thought of you having time for a family."

"Fair enough."

"So when did you adopt?"

"Adopt? Hell no. I gave birth to her—"

"A girl?"

"A daughter. Yes. And very pretty. I gave birth to her sixteen years ago, right in the Luz-Werner Building. On the thirty-first floor. All by myself."

He thought she might be serious till he heard this. "By yourself?"

"Well—I had L-W Book's Midwife to Motherhood series."

"Right. What's her name?"

"Paraphernalia."

"Paraphernalia! Cool!" He laughs.

"Ugh, you're impossible. It's a terrific name!"

"Calm down, Babs. What's this got to do with your rescue?"

"Actually her rescue."

"Paraphernalia's?"

"Bingo. For some weird reason I feel I've got to talk to a man about this and you're it."

"What about her father?"

"She never needed a father. Except for the jump-start."

"Is that right?" He's annoyed again, sensing she's setting him up for another one of her unfunny jokes—with a male-bashing punch line.

"Yeah. That's right." She takes out another cigarette and taps the filtered end on the table.

"So there's some guy out there who doesn't know he's got a daughter?"

"That's not important." She drags on the unlit cigarette and puffs out.

"So, what is important, Babs?" He wants to get up, leave the bar and New York but suddenly thinks of the times he ended up in the sack with her. Years ago. After media parties, after they both had consumed too much alcohol. They were not good together. She had made love like a field hockey quarterback, her favorite position of her favorite sport in prep school. But for some reason, they salvaged the relationship. Nursing hangovers in harsh morning light, they agreed to keep their friendship out of bed, which they did. That was close to seventeen years ago. He is staring at her. Not likely, but possibly he is this girl's father. If she exists, which he doubts.

She flashes the lopsided grin that tells him she's about to change her tack. "What's important is getting her out of the Luz-Werner Building."

"Getting her out of the building? I don't get it." Now he's convinced the Paraphernalia story is nothing more than a weird mind-game.

"It's where she lives, Hunter. She was born and raised there. Remember? She's never been outside the building."

"Pretty limited childhood." But why did she say he was the only one she could talk to about this?

"Limited? Not at all. She reads every issue of every magazine, every Werner book, every L-W Books series, has listened to every L-W recording, viewed every video. She's smart as a whip, set up her own web site, never disturbs anyone. It's worked out fabulously but—"

"But what?"

"The problem is she doesn't have an employee identification card."

He roars.

"You have a sick sense of humor. This is no laughing matter. There's no record of her having had an appointment. She has no pass to turn in at the security desk. They'll nab her. Security is tight these days—."

"Oh, come on Babs," he humors, now certain this is a bizarre joke. "People come and go in and out of the building every day, all day, all night. Security may be tight, but this isn't insurmountable. On the other hand, why should she leave now? It's been good for sixteen years, why not go for seventeen?"

"Why? Because she's spending every waking minute on-line. She's got to get a life!

"So put her name on a masthead and let her start building a career."

"No. She's got to get out."

"So here's what you do. Have a friend, a female friend, go to the reception center in the lobby and give her name as Paraphernalia Mahoney. Reception calls upstairs to confirm, fills out the visitor's pass and hands it to her."

"But they'll take the pass at the elevators when she leaves."

"Your friend isn't going to get in any elevator."

"She isn't?"

"No. She's going to wait for you to come down to the lobby where you will get the pass from her and take it up to Paraphernalia. Paraphernalia's on her way."

"Oh, Hunter. Love of my life. Why couldn't I have thought of that?"

"You're under a lot of pressure. I wouldn't worry about it."

They order another round of drinks. Babs tells him about *Sit*'s rate structure, special issues, its web site, fashion line extensions. He tunes out. Misses Jean. Looking at his watch, he announces, "You know, I've got to be on my way," and signals the waiter.

"You're not going to the reception? You promised to help me corner Epstein."

"You don't need me to close that deal."

"That's true." Her tone is brittle.

The check arrives and she grabs it. "This one's on *Sit*."

"Thanks." He feels guilty. "Come on. I'll walk you to the club—and Brandywine."

"No, go ahead. I'm just going to collect my thoughts, and take a cab."

"Sure," he smiles, getting up from the table. "Good luck, Madame Publisher."

"Not so long next time, okay?"

He kisses her check. "Okay."

As he leaves, she motions to the waiter for another drink.

# 11

*New York*

Day breaks into the bedroom, through the window's iron security bars, smog-glazed panes, and wooden blinds. Stirring from a dream, disoriented, Hunter gropes the sheets for Jean. Is she fantasy? The invasion an illusion? No.

They had talked on the phone last night before he turned in. He had told her about the funeral, about Babs and the creepy Paraphernalia story. He told her how strange it feels to be back in his old apartment and how much he misses her. She told him her friend Martha Kindle had guessed that she will be staying with him in New York and cautioned that if other mothers figure it out they'll likely say she's a negative role model for their girls. She dismissed it as petty talk but sounded a bit uneasy about it. Neither mentioned the highway.

He gets up, splashes water on his face, puts on jeans and a sweater, leashes Freddie, grabs his jacket, and they charge outside, up the sidewalk to Central Park. Jogging along the Bridle Path, Freddie stops frequently, exploring new smells. Runners and walkers, in packs, pass them, a few say good morning. Later, after coffee and checking the news he'll do his run.

Returning, he instantly recognizes a heady fragrance in the foyer. Freddie, unleashed, sniffs the hall like a tracking bloodhound and, as the apartment door clicks open, barges inside and stops short. Tossed on the carpet is a beige fox coat, then, in a trail, a leather boot with a three-inch heel, then its mate, leading to the couch, to Melanie, in a black cardigan and cropped leather skirt, reclining, slowly swinging her long, golden-tan leg. She pouts, "Welcome back."

"Nice tan," he smiles.

"I missed you," she coos, fending off an energetically curious, panting Freddie. "But please put your friend in the yard."

"You don't remember Freddie?"

"Of course. But I've developed an allergy to fur."

He dispatches an obstinate Freddie to the yard, then eyes the coat. "Allergic to fur?"

"Fur on living creatures." She's playing with the top button on her cardigan, pops it open, moves her fingers to the next. And the next. Her cleavage deepens.

"This isn't—a good time—" He knows he doesn't sound convincing. He's fully aroused, and she knows it.

"Whatever it is, it can wait." She gets off the couch, shedding the sweater, slides the skirt to the floor and stands naked before him.

He looks at her, touches her bright blonde hair, and pulls off his sweater.

She unzips his jeans. "Everything's really good right now, except it's been too long without you."

As always, it was good sex. Nothing less, and nothing more. He feels hollow.

"Ughhh, I've got to run. Come see me tonight," she says, wiggling into the skirt, buttoning herself into the cardigan.

"Can't."

"Can't?" She yanks on one of the boots.

"Got a—commitment."

"A date? So reschedule or come afterwards. I'm on L.A. time. After ten is good. I go back to L.A. tomorrow—for two weeks, maybe longer. So tonight is it for a while."

"I can't. Really. It's a little more than a date. Someone's coming, staying with me for about a month."

"Arriving tonight?"

"Soon. It's just—" He pauses, and goes to the window, searching for the words.

"I don't believe it. You're letting her pressure you." She tugs on the other boot. There is silence. "So, I'm going to make it easier for you." She rummages at the bottom of her purse, takes out a set of keys and jingles them. "I'll leave these with you so won't have to make another set for her, and you won't have to worry about my dropping in while you're entertaining. That's because I adore you. And I look forward to getting them back. From you—or Frank."

"Frank?"

"DeCarlo. Your tenant. What a connection he turned out to be. He's the best. It's largely because of him that I'm about to sign a fabulous contract with ABG."

"Congratulations. Now you need a new goal," he says with a faint smile, wondering why it annoys him that she's been screwing around with someone else in his old apartment.

She drops the keys into his hand, folds his fingers on them. "We both know it just doesn't get any better than this." Her voice is silken. "But it's fun to keep testing."

He holds the fox coat for her and kisses her cheek.

"Have a good time."

"You too. And good luck out there."

He walks her to the foyer. As she steps outside, the engine starts in a navy blue town car double-parked across the street. She gets into the back seat and the car speeds off. The fragrance in the hall has faded somewhat.

He lets Freddie in, then shaves, showers, and scrambles eggs—the whole time thinking about Jean, about Melanie, about the bizarre funeral—but mostly about Jean. Too drained to go running and in no mood to work on the Kennedy Graveside Memorial Companion, he hooks Freddie to the leash and they head out again, this time walking for hours.

&#10021;

*New Burford*

Having arrived at Emma's to go for a walk with her, Jean waits in the living room as Emma concludes her phone with Samson. On the coffee table is a newly potted scented geranium. She rubs the tip of a leaf between her fingertips, releasing a lemony fragrance. Inexplicably anxious all morning, she feels somewhat comforted in the unstuffy graciousness, the quirky elegance of Emma's home. Free verse lettered in tempera paint on windowpanes and the old vacuum cleaner bag on the mantel relax the otherwise formal look of ancient Chinese vases, brass sconces and the large oil painting of wire haired terriers.

"Disappointing news. Samson says he can't do a thing with that videotape." Emma marches into the living room, Nikes in hand, and plunks down in her corner chair to put them on. "Says if you've got nothing but mud to start with, it doesn't matter what you do to it, all you're ever going to get is digitally enhanced mud."

"Maybe that's why I'm feeling down today."

"Nonsense. Pick yourself up. We're resourceful." Emma gets to her feet and stretches her arms over her head. "Let's be on our way. You tell me walking is just as good exercise as jogging and easier on these old knees, so let's give it a try." She whistles through her teeth. "Come, Jenny."

The air is cold and damp, their breath visible, as they walk briskly through the pine grove, Jenny running ahead.

"What about the bank?" Jean asks. "Would Willard tell you if any of the selectmen had made suspicious deposits?"

"No. Tried that already. My guess is the contents of those envelopes weren't deposited in a local bank, and, for all we know, the envelopes contained transaction slips, not money. They're no fools, doncha know."

"Ugh, it's so sleazy."

"Now m'dear, sleazy things inevitably unravel. It's the nature of sleaze. When the scoundrels realize that we know what they've done, things will sort out. Trust me. Now, what's going on with you? The bulletin says you changed the dates of your holiday recess."

"Starting earlier this year. "

"What's up?"

"I've been meaning to tell you. I'm going to do that festival with Nelson. We're doing Agnon for a college workshop, and repeating it this summer at Jacob's Pillow."

"That steamy pas de deux? I thought you were over him."

"Completely, but we've always worked well together, which you know. And at my advanced age—."

" Hogwash!"

"He and Truda are happily married."

"I'm glad he settled down. I wish the same for you, but going off with an old beau is hardly a step in that direction."

"I went after this because Hunter's in New York."

"Now that's what I wanted to hear," Emma grins, then stops in her tracks. "As long as you both come back."

"We will. At least I will."

"Then he will too. He's head over heels for you."

"I don't know."

"Trust me."

Their steps cushioned in fragrant pine needles, they walk in silence, deep in thought. Emma is remembering when Jean retreated to her family's cottage just before her fortieth birthday. At the end of her career and with no family, she was lonely and depressed. So Emma suggested she start a dance studio and showed her the stable in New Burford center. The new work renewed her, and professional jobs still came her way. The only downside for her was the dismal paucity of attractive eligible men in the area. And then Hunter Barnhill showed up.

"Somewhere I read," Emma muses, looking up into the branches, "the pine is to conifers what the apple is among fruit trees, and the oak among broad-leaves. Words to that effect." She pauses. "Waldo and I planted all these pines, don't you know, just after the war."

"They're magnificent."

"Some day Waldo and I will both end up here."

"He's buried here?"

"Here? Good heavens, no. That's Waldo on the living room mantel."

"In the Ming vase?"

"No—the vacuum bag. I never told you?"

"Uh-no, I don't think so."

"Oh, for goodness sake. Well, Waldo had emphysema, don't you know. Poor soul was sick for years, shuffling and staggering about till he finally died—out in the herb garden. I found him in his Pendelton robe, lying on his back in the sweet woodruff, a little smile on his face, a rosette— Flagons and Trenchers—pinned to his lapel. He was clutching a small bouquet of marigolds and lamb's ears. I think he had just picked them for me."

"Ohhh, Emma."

"And jostled from his robe pocket was the ubiquitous pack of Luckies."

"He smoked? Even with emphysema?"

"Like a chimney," she said, bristling. "Anyway," her voice softened. "Waldo wanted to be cremated and have his ashes spread on the Revolutionary War parapets over there, beyond that rise." She points. "A week after the service, Mr. Munson of the Munson Funeral Home came to deliver the ashes. Unfortunately, I was in the shower when he cranked the doorbell.

"You weren't expecting him?"

"No. He just came by. So, soaking wet, I went running to the door in my bathrobe. He handed me the package, offered condolences. I accepted and offered tea. He declined, turned on his heel, and left. I shut the door, turned on my heel, and slipped right there on the wet floorboards, spilling Waldo all over the front hall and into the dining room."

"No!" Jean covers a grin with her gloved hand, trying not to laugh. "Were you okay?"

"Land sakes, I was just fine. But, heh," Emma chuckles, "I had a mess on my hands. Without thinking twice, I inserted a new bag into the vacuum cleaner and collected him up. When I removed the bag, I didn't know what to do, then, a few days later it dawned on me and I put the bag on the mantel."

"And that's where he's stayed," Jean says, thinking how bizarre.

"Yep. Except for fifteen minutes in 1965 when Theophilus, our cat, pawed him off onto the floor. Theophilus was constantly bolting from imagined terrors and taking refuge on high places like the mantel. Anyway, before long Waldo and I will be together again. You'll be here for Thanksgiving dinner?"

"Wouldn't miss it. I leave the week after. Emma, I'm just worried about gossip. Martha knows what I'm doing and she's worried that if other mothers figure it out they'll gossip and, in this town, that could close the studio."

"No one has to know what you're up to or with whom. They know you go out of town for performances. Rest assured, that's all they'll know. Count on it." She takes Jean's arm.

"Thank you."

"Don't give it a thought. I thank you and my knees thank you for the walk. When can we do this again?"

*New York*
Hunter stands at the red service line. The white chamber is cold, and every square inch of its thirty-two by seventeen by sixteen-foot

dimension feels constrictive. He hits an easy lob. The small hard ball comes off the front wall, glances off the sidewall, in an almost vertical trajectory and bounces on the floor, close to the back wall. Jack instantly judges where to take it and hits it directly to the front wall, a few feet above the red line. They rally. Hunter gets the point.

It's not what Jack had expected. "Hey, been playing up there in the woods?"

He tries to recall when he had last played. And why he had kept his membership. The negligible non-resident dues—like the apartment lease, was an offer he couldn't refuse. He switches to a hard serve. His favorite shots come back to him. He keeps the advantage and wins the first game.

By the second game, Jack is used to his serve and takes the advantage. Hunter momentarily loses concentration, remembering the New Year's Eve party when he and Melanie slipped away from the dinner table with their champagne glasses and, in this darkened squash court three floors above the party, made love before returning for dessert. Jack wins the second game by two points.

Tired, playing on borrowed energy, Hunter's concentration breaks again, this time on the image of the necrology card on the club's bulletin board in the lower lobby, the white card with a heavy black border, *Ruggles Wheelwright Wilmot* elegantly lettered by the club calligrapher. Ruggie had brought him into the Gotham Club, proposed him for membership, lined up seconders, pushed his nomination through the admissions committee, and got him on committees so he'd get to know people, make contacts for DWE. Jack gets another point.

Hunter refocuses, crouches into position, anticipating the next shot and, hits a low backhand. Jack isn't ready. Hunter gets a point. A rally begins. His thoughts drift again, to the club's main entrance, to the doorman's welcome—Mr. Barnhill, good to see you, sir, we've missed you—and feeling dropped into a past life as he grasped the uniformed arm to shake hands. He wipes his face with his shirt and checks his grip, his mind replaying images of the main lounge, its familiar massive oil paintings and wingback chairs but no familiar faces, the billiards room, men playing in shirtsleeves, ties loosened, an attractive woman in a teal blue suit sitting at the bar, his gym clothing, clean folded and ready for him as if he had played yesterday.

Jack easily wins the next two games and the match.

"You did me in," Hunter says, panting, patting Jack on the back.

"Could've been your match but your responses were really erratic. Heineken?"

"Perfect."

Emerging from the shower, Hunter grabs towels from the shelves, wraps one around his waist, drapes another around his neck, and spreads a third on a chair before dropping into it. The fitness facility had been completely renovated with fruitwood lockers, new shower room and sauna, plush carpeting in the dressing area, comfortable chairs clustered around low tables, and an array of computerized rowing machines, elliptical trainers, and lifecycles.

"What do you think of all this fruitwood?" Wrapped in towels, Jack sits down heavily and pours water from a carafe.

"A bit cushy for a locker room."

"Finally removed those old colonic irrigation hoses but gone also are the supplies of white paper slippers and Egyptian cotton hand towels with the club crest. It's a new era." He quaffs the water, examines the empty glass, then looks Hunter in the eye, "So what's goin' on?"

"God, I don't know where to start. In effect, I was evicted from my place. Property rights violated, but, as it turns out, I never had any rights. So I'm here because I can't rationally deal with it, figure out how to bail out of the mess, as long as I'm in the middle of it. But even here, I can't concentrate. Which makes everything even worse. It's hard to describe."

"You could come in a little tighter on the details."

Hunter heaves a sigh. "I've got 68 acres up there that abuts a state watershed. A highway's going through the watershed, paralleling and very close to my property line. Actually that wouldn't have bothered me, but they had to divert the path to protect the only known habitat of the splayfooted sapsucker—"

"The what?"

"Some endangered species. The diversion cuts through my property, like a giant U-turn, clearing my house by about twenty feet. It follows an old right of way I didn't know existed. The variance wasn't included when I bought the property and nobody picked up on it, not even the title insurance people, nobody. So, the state bought it, and, because they anticipated heavy local resistance to the highway, they kept the transaction and the route sub rosa right up to the start of construction. Now the highway's in my back yard. I'm fucked."

"It's got to be illegal."

"No, unfortunately, it's quite legal. And it gets worse. Last Friday morning, about five o'clock, there was a massive explosion along the back end of my property."

"That Berkshire's explosion!"

"Brutal. Right after the explosions, a helicopter buzzes my house. Several times within minutes. Then bulldozers, three abreast, like tanks, crawl out of the woods, and head straight for my house, ripping a four-lane strip through my backfield and lawn, nearly razing the house. It was insane. I was crazed."

"You have a lawyer?"

Hunter shakes his head.

"Why the hell not? What are you going to do? Unload the property. Take the loss."

"I don't know what I'm going to do. But I'm going back. There's this woman—"

"So what else is new?"

"No. This is different."

Jack scrutinizes him. "You know, I don't think I ever heard you say that."

"She's really beautiful."

"That's standard."

"She is not standard. She walks in the room and everyone notices, but it's not just her looks, it's the way she moves, sometimes the way she doesn't move—it's the way she is." He pauses. "We're really good together."

"Ah-ha, you're actually in love."

"When I freaked during the invasion, I was a mess. She hung in there—."

A waiter arrives with the beer and two glasses, pours some as Jack signs the chit, and leaves.

Hunter takes a long swig from the bottle. "That morning my head was right back in Vietnam. Does that happen to you?"

Jack wipes his face with a towel. "I wasn't there the way you were. I just flew a lot of hairspray and Tampax from Manila to Saigon for the nurses. Navy fliers didn't go through what you went through." He pauses. "But I remember wanting to be a Marine so I could carry a revolver."

"Piece, we called it."

"Right. So I bought a .357. Blew out the light switch one night in the bachelor officer quarters." Hunter laughs. "And I had a sailboat that I kept at the Saigon Yacht Club."

"Not bad."

Jack's face falls. "It wasn't fun."

Hunter gets up and paces. "You know, I never let myself think about it. Then, when all that fire power let loose in the hills behind my house, I was back there." He pauses. "Survived a Sea Stallion crash. Then, seventy-two hours later, I was a second lieutenant running a reconnaissance platoon, and the next thing I knew, we were in a big one against a battalion-size force. Eighteen of us. We were told we had won. I was never sure but we were credited for some 200 killed. Lost only one." He goes back to the chair and drinks the beer. "Sometimes it comes back at me, like fragments from an old movie. You know what I'm talking about? "

Jack nods.

"This woman I was telling you about—Jean. She'll be here—staying with me through the holidays, I think."

"Terrific!"

"Definitely. Hey, let's get something to eat."

It's nearly midnight when he gets back to the apartment and checks his e-mail. Three messages.

Ben writes, *Where is it?*

From Marcie Greene—*Great seeing you if only briefly and under such sad circumstances. Harvey and I would be so pleased if you and guest could join our table at the Samples of Peace benefit on Tuesday at the Metropolitan Museum of Art. In his last days, Ruggie was so busy with the organ transplant project that he never got around to designating someone to take his place at his table on Tuesday. I'm sure Ruggie would have wanted you. It's an interesting table including José Fernández, Director of Special Peace Initiatives at the UN, Howard Lambert who, with Harvey, set up the transplant-funeral simulcast, and Dasher. Please, please say yes. Black tie/haute gowns. Cocktails at six. Table 2. xox/mmg*

From Speedy, cc: Emma—*Your house is OK. They've paved about five miles, including the curve by your house, installed support posts in your yard for sound-baffle wall. Continue to march. AAS*

*PS, Emma's helping me get a driver's license.*

The image of bulldozers ripping up his land kaleidoscopes with images of the house, helicopters, the crash, Ruggie's casket, bulldozers, Melanie, organs lined up for transplant surgery, Babs, the house, Jean, the squash court. Goddamn it, Ruggie isn't supposed to be dead. Dying is for later. Except lottery dying, sacrificial dying, in Vietnam.

He clicks out of cyberspace, opens a new file, and writes,

> *Back in New York, my narcotic. Back in the past but I don't belong here. Back in my old apartment but I don't live here. Moved on. Found a home. Invasion. Couldn't stop it. Couldn't control it. Injustice. Focus.*

He clicks back to reread Speedy's message and replies, thanking him for the update, then adds— *Did you serve in the military?*

The answer comes back while he's still on line—

Korea, 1952. I was 14. Lied about my age to enlist. I was a big kid. A bullet entered my helmet, ricocheted. Couldn't speak after that. Got a purple heart. They put me in a VA hospital and treated me like a stuffed animal, which wasn't bad. Then, when I was in the middle of getting transferred to another VA hospital, I got off the bus when it stopped in Barrington. The bus took off without me. I walked to New Burford. What about you?

He rereads the message, and hits reply.

*Vietnam, just before it ended. I won the lottery and went straight to hell from high school. More later.*

He signs off, shines his shoes, and writes for hours.

# 12

*Burbank, California*

Executive producer Howard Lambert flicks off the screen. "I've seen enough, Frank. Too risky. Advertisers wouldn't go near it. Affiliates would refuse it. It's a legal minefield and we've never done anything like it before. Aside from that it's golden."

"Never done anything like it? Howie, this is totally recombinant." Frank is talking faster and louder. "A mutant of *Wheel of Fortune, Sixty Minutes, Survivor, Millionaire,* and *Your Favorite Home Videos,* plus *ER.* A life and death, docu-reality-game show in a magazine format. Sexy. Fun. Meaningful. It's got a reeeally big prize—life. And speaks to a major issue."

"How does *Favorite Home Videos* fit in?"

"It's right up front. Here it is again, quickly. *Transplant Time* opens with show host Melanie Atwood, in front of the audience, presenting, narrating tear-jerking home videos, photos, stories supplied by contestants who need organs and about the organ donors. The contestants, and-or family and friends, and the donors' family and friends are in the audience. A hunky but gentle male nurse type comes on the set. He and Melanie go to the big wheel and give it a spin to see who gets the organ, who gets to live. Big tension. The winner, or representative, comes up and hugs the family of the donor. A lot of weeping. Next segment is at the operating room. Melanie talks to the doctor, to the family, and if possible, to the patient. The show ends with a follow-up interview with the recovering patient ideally during a visit by the donor family. Hugs. Tears. That's it."

"I like the broad. A mix of Claudia Schieffer and Diane Sawyer fifteen years ago."

"Melanie Atwood. She's an anchor on your New York station. Her agent's pushing for her to do network news, but she's too much eye candy for that. This show is perfect for her."

"No, it's not. Unlike the show, the broad's got potential." Howard picks up his phone. "Who is it, Amy? Yeah, I'll take it, but then I don't want any interruptions for twenty minutes." He punches to another line. "Lambert. That's right, I want Bentley off it. He's a total putz—."

Listening in, DeCarlo gets off his chair, ambles across the private conference room to take in California's sunshine, and returns as the conversation winds down.

"So where were we?" Howard is holding his head, as if it were splitting.

"*Transplant Time*. The concept came out of Ruggie's funeral. You were there."

"Yeah, I was there for that posthumous grandstand. What a piece of work. I should have figured they'd develop something from it. But a pilot for a transplant game show?—jeeze. Totally not safe."

"You think you can slow your prime time audience erosion playing safe?"

"I know exactly how far we can push the social envelope with any show, I've got a strong survival instinct, and I avoid like the plague unsupported risk such as this. That's why we're still milking this medium."

Frank is shaking his head. "You're milking it all right. Sucking on a dinosaur tit while every other medium, hell even radio, keeps getting fatter, grazing on bigger and bigger audiences. Listen, Howard. What you need is a calculated, well-supported risk. *Transplant Time*. Consider the audience involvement."

"Gambling for body parts? Think of the legal complications. It wouldn't stand a chance of getting through Standards. And if it got through, the religious whackos would go crazy."

"Since when have you worried about a handful of Hasidim and Christian extremists? Anyway, if they protest, news'll cover it. Actually, that's a good promotion. I'll remember to set it up. As for Standards, no problem. Hear me, Howard, *Transplant Time* was created specifically to address a top priority issue on the national policy agenda."

"Right." The tone of sarcasm and tedium did not conceal his curiosity.

"You need to know the background." DeCarlo lowers his voice. "The government monopoly running the transplant market is a disaster. It doesn't satisfy demand. Back in the seventies, they centralized organ distribution. Then the National Organ Transplantation Act set up a registry for donors and recipients. It also prohibited doctors from selling organs. A doctor can't even make his own deal to get an organ for a patient. So they have no incentive."

Howard yawns loudly. "So they should switch to cosmetic surgery."

"What I'm saying is even if an organ's available in his own hospital where it's needed, the doctor can't touch it. He has to turn it over to the organ bank."

"This is boring, Frank."

"Hear me out. It's not just the doctors. There's no incentive for anyone to cooperate. The procurement coordinators have a helluva time selling grieving families on the idea of donating their loved one's organs to a stranger. They can't offer any compensation, can't even offer to cover funeral expenses. Meanwhile, the religious whackos won't donate, its' against their laws. And prices are astronomical because of hospital mark-ups."

"Get to the punch line." He forces another yawn.

"Here's the key piece. Demand keeps growing, but if the government's out, the black market goes in, and costs will skyrocket. Congressional leaders and the Administration agree that the government has to get organ supply up to just the right level. The first step is to change public opinion, create a climate for public participation in the organ donor program. It's a priority on the national agenda, and policy makers expect *Transplant Time* will do the job. Howie, this is a big deal."

Howard's eyebrows arch, corrugating his forehead, as he contemplatively messages his jowls. "*Transplant Time.*"

"We did some testing and audiences love it—18 to 35, 18 to 49, 18 to 54, males, females. What I'm saying is it grabs the younger people, the hardest to reach. Everything indicates it will be a monster hit. "

"Testing doesn't mean shit. People think they're supposed to like something like this. So they tell us they love it, and we move ahead on a loser."

"Remember the audience at Ruggie's funeral? Did they love it, or what? They sucked it up. The place was quiet as a tomb."

"I can't argue with that."

"It scores big on the toughest test. Ourselves. If we love it, America will love it."

"But there are unknowns. Like can you be sure of a steady stream of product, er, organs for scheduled production?"

"The program will generate it. That's the point. It'll set a new trend for organ donation. We believe people will be lining up to donate organs just for the fifteen minutes of fame."

"Jesus."

"Then it's a go."

"I didn't quite say that." He pauses. "It's still no, Frank." He grins. "A qualified no. This has potential. Now buy me a bagel and a Coke."

"You're beautiful, Howie. Melanie Atwood's joining us for lunch. You'll love her."

# 13

*New York*

In the stainless steel kitchen of his terraced penthouse apartment overlooking the Hudson River, Ben is slowly stirring a pot of fennel risotto simmering on an eight-burner professional range. "So you drove to Prince Street, into a freight elevator that delivered you to the party," he says, somewhat distracted, repeating what Hunter just said, and ladling more broth into the pot. He had invited Hunter and Jean for lunch to meet her but that was the pretext for his intention to read Hunter the riot act about missed deadlines.

Hunter knows a reprimand is in the offing—but later, when it won't interfere with the enjoyment of lunch, as Ben's true love is creating and sharing culinary masterpieces that satisfy his shrewd palate. "We parked among Lamborghinis, Porsches, even an old Bentley at the end of this cavernous living room-studio."

"When I rsvp'd," says Jean, "Julian asked what Hunter drives and requested the honor of the Range Rover's presence at his soiree. He's so pretentious."

"What's his name?" Ben asks, slicing portobello mushrooms.

"Julian Yeager," she says. "Pretentious isn't quite it, because he's really turned pretension into an art form, and proudly admits it. He's another fine artist turned entrepreneurial showman. Now he laughs all the way to the bank when critics say his work is shallow."

"So what's his shtik?" Ben asks, tossing arugula, goat cheese and walnuts.

"Smart marketing," says Hunter. "He creates product on the sales floor, so to speak. When we arrived, the studio walls were lined with enormous blank canvases. Then, once the party got into full swing, three groups—quartets—of guys in white slacks and turtlenecks entered from the parking area, singing what sounded like a combination of Gregorian chant and doo-wop, and carrying paint cans, rollers, and paint roller trays. They went directly to the canvases and proceeded to spread terrific electric colors on them. Then a bunch of naked dancers, men and women, entered, loped up to the canvases, two or three to each canvas, rubbed their bodies against the wet paint, danced to another canvas, rubbed and pressed against it, introducing a new color, leaving impressions of body parts, then moved to the next canvas, and so on. Then, Julian appeared with a can of black paint and a huge brush, added a few grandiose strokes to each canvas, actually sort of unifying the color smears into something interesting. Finally, the dancers, totally covered and slick with wet paint, embraced the singers in their pristine white outfits and they all struck poses with Julian for a half dozen photographers."

"Were you one of the dancers, Jean?" Ben asks, turning mushrooms on the grill.

"Actually, I was asked, but declined."

"You didn't tell me! That explains why for a moment it looked like two of the dancers were about to drag you into the paint. I don't know how I would have dealt with that."

"That's why I didn't do it." She grins, cuffing his shoulder.

Ben spoons risotto onto three plates. "Clearly it was a fairly interesting diversion."

From the way he said diversion, Hunter senses Ben is about to get on his case. "Ah, but most interesting is the point of sale. After the applause, an auction started. Bids opened at $25,000. All twelve canvases sold—. Add it up. And presumably the photos will be sold."

"Nice work," says Ben. He pours San Pellegrino into stemmed glasses.

"But it was a benefit," Jean qualifies facetiously, "this time for unemployed countertenors."

"You mean a racket," Ben roars. "So who bought the canvases? Let me guess. Intellectual wanabes, aspiring art connoisseurs, assorted glitterati."

"Exactly, the upscale philistine market."

"You guys are so jaded. Some very distinguished academics were there and legitimate high art types, too" says Jean.

"Like yourself," says Hunter. "And that was smart marketing, too. You, the NYU professor, the curator from MOMA, others like that, scattered around the sales floor, supplied validation while the philistines, whatever they are—the kind that drive some people to places like New Burford—wrote checks."

"You're turning into a backwoods curmudgeon, Barnhill," says Ben.

"It's the Berkshires, not the backwoods," Jean corrects, "and some find a better life up there. Come visit some time," she says warmly, "if only for some fresh air."

Jean and Ben get along as if they were old friends, discovering they once had lived on the same block, and identifying mutual acquaintances. Eventually, the conversation turns to business and the time comes for Ben's inevitable tirade. "Barnhill, I'm going to lock you up in a hotel room in Buffalo if you don't get cracking on this," He's punching a schedule with deadline extensions marked in red.

Like a mischievous small boy, Hunter grins at Jean, "You want to go to Buffalo for a few days?"

"You're gonna drive me out of my gourd," Ben bellows. "Supposedly you've been working on this. Where the hell is it? What the hell have you been doing?"

Jean and Ben are looking at him with the same somber expression.

"I thought you came to the city expressly to get this done," she says.

"So you're coming down on me, too."

"It's business," she says. "You're under contract. Maybe I should leave you alone, go home, come down just for rehearsals."

"Why? You had nothing to do with this. You just got here."

Ben leans back, crosses his arms, and watches their volley.

"I don't want to be a distraction," she insists.

"You're not. For that matter, I've actually done some work since you arrived. The truth is, it's not finished because I'm writing something else."

Ben turns red. "What the hell are you saying?"

"It's an article. Could be a book. Certainly it's more compelling than this Kennedy thing."

Ben is glowering at him. "Right now, I couldn't care less if this new project of yours were to land you a Pulitzer—it's not what you've contracted to deliver."

"This isn't good, Hunter," Jean declares, sympathetically but firmly. "You keep escaping. From New York, from New Burford, from this work, from—. You have trouble, um, staying with things."

"That's harsh. I—" He starts to defend himself, then cuts himself off. "I admit, I've neglected my obligation here, misplaced priorities—"

"That's an understatement." Ben is thoroughly exasperated.

"But I promise you, both of you, I'll be back on track, tomorrow. I'll put this other thing aside. I've gotten a good start and it can wait now." Silence. "Trust me."

Ben gets up for his pipe, thoughtfully puts its stem in his mouth. "Marcie tells me you're going to that thing at the Met Tuesday."

"Yeah. It'll probably be an uptown version of the scene on Prince Street. But we're going for Ruggie."

# 14

*New York*

Klieg lights sweep across the granite facade of The Metropolitan Museum of Art, stretching into the clear, cold night sky. Limousines and taxis in long lines inch toward the carpeted strip on the stairs to the main entrance.

In an idling taxi about thirty limousine lengths from the carpet, Hunter remarks, "This is tedious. The big names are staggering their arrivals for the photographers, security's maxed. It could be an hour before we get inside."

"So let's go to the side entrance," says Jean.

"Brilliant! Driver, pull out of line, pass all this and turn right."

At the south entrance, security guards stop them to check identification with the guest list and direct them into the route through corridors lined with more guards, up flights of stairs lined with still more guards, and across exhibit halls of ancient Greek and Roman treasures. Finally, they emerge into a sea of sweeping ball gowns, heavy-duty jewels, tuxedos, society matrons behaving like starlets in their major dresses with names as big or bigger than their own— Wang, Herrera, De La Renta, Valentino, Cavalli, Chloé, Klein.

Hunter takes two glasses of champagne from a waiter's tray and gives one to Jean, who is getting checked out in her vintage, midnight blue, deeply-V'd Balenciaga gown, a string of cranberries around her neck, her hair pulled up in a twist. "You are, without a doubt, the most beautiful woman here," he whispers to her. Remote acquaintances and people they can't recall or place effervescently greet them as the crowd funnels them through the receiving line and into the dining room, lavishly decorated with thousands of tiny lights, ivy, boxwood and lady apples. Marcie, stoic Harvey at her side, beckons them to their table where they've gathered José and Isabel Fernández, and Dan and Ellen Dasher. Isabel, an amateur Flamenco dancer, and Jean instantly connect. Marcie and Dan tell Hunter he's the only one who could appropriately take Ruggie's place here tonight.

"Quite an exaggeration, but thank you. So where's Epstein?"

Marcie takes him aside, "You don't know? A few days after Ruggie's funeral, he demanded an exit deal. I think Dasher squeezed him out but don't tell him I said that. Effectively, it was totally unexpected and some say highly reminiscent of your stunt."

As Jean is talking with Isabel, she peripherally sees Hunter drawn to a streak of skin-tight gold lamé, a backless dress, topped with a mass of blonde curls, tan arms claiming a hug from him. Instantly, she knows Hunter and this woman have been lovers. She hears an artificial laugh as the blonde, Hunter, and a sullen-looking guy approach.

Hunter clears his throat, "Jean. I want to introduce Melanie Atwood. Howard Lambert."

"My pleasure," says Melanie, nearly bursting from the plunging gold neckline. "I was just telling Hunter about my new contract with ABG." She turns to him, and in perfectly modulated tones says, "My role as host is bigger by far than any evening news or morning show anchor job. And the show has a true and crucial mission which I will tell you about, later." She looks at Jean. "And what do you do, Jean?"

"Perform and teach dance," Jean says, scrutinizing Melanie, then Hunter.

"I'd love to see you dance," says Howard.

"Jean was with the New York City Ballet," says Hunter with a smile for her, placing his hand on her back. "Now she does festivals, master classes, runs a dance studio in the Berkshires. She's phenomenal."

"Too old or not quite good enough to stay in the big time?" Melanie condescends.

You bitch, Jean refrains from saying as she counters, smiling, "Neither. I achieved artistic independence. You work for ABG?"

"About to star in a new prime-time show."

Howard adds, "They say her show is going to change the face of prime-time."

"A facelift for prime time," Jean says sweetly. Howard laughs.

Ignoring it, Melanie checks out the crowd and, with spontaneous delight, blows a kiss and waves. "Howard, Michael's here. We've must say hello before everyone sits down." She whispers in Hunter's ear, kisses his chin, and moves on, dispatching Howard to get her more champagne.

"Charming," says Jean.

"She knows what she wants," he answers objectively, wiping off the lipstick.

"And you're on her list. It looked as if she was going to scoop you up into that gaping bodice of hers and swallow you."

"Forget her. I have."

"Find your places, please," Marcie announces. She has arranged the seating, placing Hunter next to her with Melanie on his other side, and, on the other side of the table, Jean is between Howard and Dan.

Melanie breezes back to the table. Hunter holds the chair for her and takes his seat as she intones, "Amazing how things work out. So is that your houseguest? Jan? She's cute."

"It's Jean. And, no, I wouldn't say cute. Stunning, exquisite. Not cute. So how's L.A.?"

Marcie answers for Melanie. "She's arrived, Hunter. Her show's going to be the next network phenomenon—-reality-drama-maga-zine-game show!"

"It's got a green light for the summer season," Melanie explains, "and then goes to the fall line-up. It won't miss because its purpose is to promote a good, important cause and build awareness of a major national health issue."

As she's telling him about the pilot, he glances at Jean who is bantering with Dasher and Howard. Jean glances back and they exchange little smiles. Melanie notices, but ignores it, continuing her briefing. The next time Hunter looks across the table Melanie abruptly turns to Harvey, on her left.

Marcie, sensitive to table dynamics, immediately asks Hunter, "Did you hear about Arnie Martin?" Arnie had been copywriter at Dasher Wilmot Epstein and at just about every other major agency, never managing to stay anywhere for more than six months. "He finally dropped out of the business, completely, and founded something called the Slow Society. Its mission is to slow down everything and everybody. They do it with kinetic community art. He got a grant from the National Endowment for the Arts and now he's doing fabulously."

"On grants?"

"That, plus workshops, contributions, and member dues, rather, companion dues. They call themselves—companions. Anyway, members go around the city entering apartment and office buildings and ride the elevators, pushing all the floor buttons—that's the kinetic community art piece—and they collect data for projecting 'slow factor' based on the number of elevators and floors, et cetera that can cause delays."

Bored, Hunter drains his wineglass. "I remember Arnie used to get a big kick out of pushing all he elevator buttons and then asking, Doesn't everyone push all the buttons at least once in a while when all alone in an elevator?" Relieving his boredom, Melanie leans toward him, pressing her breasts against him, and coos in his ear, "Tell me, Hunter, haven't you missed all this even just a teeny bit?"

On the other side of the table, Howard and Dan are very attentive to Jean. Dasher regales her with stories about Hunter's career and his Golden Ladder Award. Howard tells her she's a natural for the screen and offers to get her a bit part in a movie currently on location in the city. Jean thinks Howard is a sleaze, Dasher a suit rack, but gives them her undivided attention while Melanie is blatantly coming on to Hunter.

"She's some piece of work," Howard says to Jean as if reading her mind, pointing at Melanie with his fork. "This show will change a lot for her but not that relationship, which is solid, for years." He leans over to her and says, his breath hot on her neck, "The nice part is that they always give each other plenty of room to enjoy transient hedonists like us." He laughs. "We're in the same club, sweetheart."

Jean feels walloped. In a frozen split second, she steels herself to respond calmly. "Her diction is remarkable."

"Diction? Yes, that, too. She does have excellent diction." He pauses, almost thoughtfully. "I understand she was a natural—good tone, believable, authoritative from the get-go. But she always worked at improving her craft. Then, she had that special surgery on her vocal tract, along with a few tucks—"

"Vocal tract surgery? Sounds extreme."

"Well, the doctor who does the operation—and he's made a fortune on anchors—he states right up front, results can vary. For Melanie, it was a total success. Her vowels roll out of her mouth with uncommon resonance and simultaneously, her eyebrows arch. It's intensely sincere. Then, when she got that fabulous full balcony—."

"From a surgical theater?"

"Ah, you ask because you've got the real thing and a truly great set at that, especially for a ballet dancer. Now, don't get me wrong, I've got nothing against synthetic knockers but look around. Did you ever notice how so many breasts look alike these days? I much prefer 100% natural. In a heartbeat I'd get in line to see you dance, showing off your yummy boobies."

"Sorry, Howard." Jean laughs thinking he's so boorish it's almost funny. Waiters are removing plates, sweeping the crumbs from the table in preparation for dessert. Marcie stands for an announcement to Table Two. "Please, may I have your attention? For desert let's be congenial and rearrange ourselves. Gentlemen, you do the moving. Exchange chairs. Take your glass. And have fun!"

Harvey kisses Jean's shoulder, and dashes to Melanie's side as Hunter hustles to take the chair next to Jean. "Missed you," he whispers.

Either because of the wine consumed or the more compatible rearrangement of personalities, the mood at Table Two immediately becomes more subdued, intimate. After dessert and a brief address by the executive director of Samples of Peace, the biggest names of new and old New York society vanish into the night while the revelers follow distant music and the red carpet path into the Temple of Dendur. Hunter and Jean indulge in the moment, their style immediately attracting glances. And when Jean begins a sensuous improvisation, revelers, Howard among them, gather to watch. Melanie sidles over to Howard, and leads him off into the night.

Snow flurries rush the windshield as the taxi barrels across Central Park. Jean rests her head on his shoulder. "You astound me. The Advertising Academy's Golden Ladder Award."

"I should have known Dasher would recite my resume to you."

"Just the highlights."

"As it turns out, that Golden Ladder is now sitting on the bottom of a cold toilet tank in New Burford, Massachusetts."

"No. Why would you do that?"

"It's a Plexiglas brick. I put it there to conserve water."

"Sometimes— I don't understand you at all," she says with a heavy sigh.

The cab pulls up to the brownstone. Hunter gets out, gives her his hand, and arm in arm they navigate the slippery white dusting of snow and go inside. Ella Fitzgerald is singing, replaying in the CD queue. Hunter takes their coats to the closet and lets Freddie out into the yard. Jean slips off her shoes, goes to the window, and watches as Freddie shakes snowflakes off his back, then dashes to the door where Hunter is waiting for him. She continues looking out the window at the falling snow, slowly removing her hairpins.

"What's the matter, Jean?"

She combs her fingers through her hair. "Hunter, let me get this straight. You earned medals in Vietnam, and sent them back—. You won a Golden Ladder and put the award in your toilet tank—."

"No, Jean, I see what you're aiming at, but that's not the way it went. You don't have the whole picture. Just a fraction."

She crosses her arms. "Not because I haven't asked."

"True. It's just so complicated, maybe inexplicable." He pauses. "Where do I start? The Golden Ladder thing? It was entirely political."

"Mmm."

"Really. Before and after me, everyone else elected was either dead or retired. I was 35."

"You were outstanding."

"Hardly," he says, loosening his bow tie. "The campaign that got me elected had already won a bunch of awards. None of them made any sense either. Because the campaign quite simply was not great work. Anything but." He unfastens the wing collar and sits on the couch, elbows propped on his knees, clasping his hands.

"Oh, stop this modesty thing."

"It's not modesty. I know mediocrity when I see it. There was surely a pretext for singling out that campaign. One rumor was that the committee thought it was time to contemporize the award." He pauses. "And some said my election was part of some energy policy public relations ploy. Who knows? Sit with me."

"Energy policy?" She sits on the hassock, opposite him.

"Yeah. The campaign was for Big Jim's Oil Company. It was everywhere in just about every medium."

She looks at him, blankly.

"See? Not exactly high on your list of most memorable ads."

"Back then I wasn't paying attention to anything but dance. But you must have been a top performer to get assigned to that job."

"No. Actually, before that, my work was remarkably undistinguished. Hell, I was hired at DWE only because of a chance meeting with Ruggie's father—a blue-blood Wall Street lawyer, World War II veteran, big military supporter. He got me the job in his son's agency simply because I was a vet. I'm not saying I was incompetent. I did okay. Dressed trendy, lunched, partied well. And that seemed to be enough."

"Amazing way to make a living. And Big Jim?"

"Oh man, what did he tell you about Big Jim?"

"So there really was a Big Jim?"

"Larger than life," he chuckles. "He was the impetus behind my stellar success."

"Sooo—?" She gives him a smile.

He grins. "So, it all started at Big Jim's ranch house, out in Tulsa. Around the pool. Big Jim liked to hold meetings at his house because, he said, everyone was more comfortable and worked better there."

"I can imagine."

"Anyway, I had flown out for a creative strategy meeting with Big Jim and his director of public affairs. Wilmot was there. Epstein too. And a senior account guy. Hal Sirano was his name. I remember compulsive Hal refused to take of his suit jacket. And it was hot. Tulsa hot. You really want to hear about this?"

"Absolutely."

"So a *Forbes* reporter was sitting in on the meeting, writing a profile of Big Jim, who was truly enormous. And there was this bikini-clad redhead Big Jim introduced as his administrative assistant. Shirley. That was her name. She was waddling around the pool in high-heeled sandals, contemplating a swim. Sirano was writing like crazy on his yellow lined pad, getting down all the agreed upon next steps. The meeting was essentially over. Nobody was talking. So the reporter grabs the window and asks Big Jim. What's it like, owning the biggest oil company in the world? At that moment, Shirley is waddling by him. He reaches out, smacks her behind, and bellows in his sugary drawl, 'It's a gas!' It was an epiphany."

"Huh?"

"Yup. I didn't need any of the backgrounders or research. One week later I went back to Big Jim's ranch house with Epstein and Wilmot to present the new campaign with the golden slogan."

"Which was—?"

"A big picture of Big Jim and his pledge— 'It's a gas.'"

She hesitates, baffled. "That's it?"

"See what I mean? But Big Jim loved it. He approved it along with a media budget nearly twice the proposed amount. Next thing I know Big Jim invites me on a private moose hunt. And after that I was the only one Big Jim would talk to from the agency. So they promoted me to Executive Vice President, gave me huge salary increases every few months, figuring I was the only reason the agency kept the account, which previously switched agencies every time Big Jim didn't like some thing, or some one."

"And when did you start winning awards?"

"Almost immediately. The campaign took off and, God knows why it had staying power. Articles in the trade press analyzed it. *Pulse* magazine quoted some Harvard sociology professor who designated the slogan an artifact of popular culture. Then one day about a thousand well-wishing associates packed into the Waldorf's Grand Ballroom to hear the ladder speech read to me by the President of the Academy of Advertising."

"You must have loved it."

"Not really. Then, like now, it didn't make any sense to me. But what could I do? DWE became the hot shop. Clients signed on faster than we could handle them. It was unreal. Sometimes I'd say, guys, I don't belong in this business and invariably they'd give another bonus or raise. The ads were nothing special. When were back home I'll show you. You'll see what I mean."

Back home! The thought would have delighted her, but not now that she knows about Melanie.

"At least I put that chunk of Plexiglas to good use." His expression becomes somber. He gets to his feet and paces. Ella is singing softly. "As for those medals—." He stops at the window, makes a fist with his right hand, and punches his palm. "First, you should know that just about every guy who served in Vietnam was heroic in ways few can imagine. Yet awards were given only when it was possible to get the paper work done. When there were enough eyewitnesses to an action and they had enough time to prepare the documentation, then an award was made. Figure from that how many guys, in the chaos of war, didn't get the credit they deserve." He pauses. "Anyway, I didn't refuse the medals. I sent them back because I was pissed—about another issue. There's a difference."

"I see," she says, unconvinced.

"One of these days, I'd like to read you some of what I'm working on now."

"I would like that. I really would like that," she says wistfully, getting off the hassock, and picks up her shoes.

"What else is bothering you? Talk to me, Jean."

"Nothing. It's late."

"It's not nothing. What is it?"

She hesitates. "I don't know how to talk about it. So what can I say? I'd ask but—I just can't." She starts for the bedroom.

He takes her arm. "Ask what? Put it out there."

"Are you in a committed relationship with Melanie, like open marriage?"

"You really did get an earful." He shakes his head. "No. Emphatically, no! Whatever there was between us, it's over. And, believe me, it never came close to what we have."

She looks him in the eye. Distrust dissolves. A shoe in each hand, she slips her arms around his neck. He holds her. Ella is singing Cole Porter, *I am in Love.*

"And what about you? At that Prince Street soiree, I heard you and your dancing partners could be pretty casual about intimacies—breaking up in the morning, re-coupling by evening."

"I left all that, quite some time ago. But—" They're swaying with the music.

"But what?"

"The moose. What happened to the moose?"

"Immortalized him."

She steps back, aghast. "Noooo."

"Yup. Shot him with a thirty-five millimeter. Telescopic lens."

She grins, throwing her arms around him.

"Do me a favor, drop the shoes."

# 15

## THURSDAY, JANUARY 23

*New Burford*

Its headlights turned off, the vintage gray Mercedes disappears into gloomy mist, slowly veers off the road, and comes to a stop behind thickets. They get out—Emma in her hooded, black, boiled wool cape, Speedy in his hooded Army field jacket, the dog in red bandanna—and trek to the edge of a clearing, a smoothly graded slope jabbed with rows of vermilion-tipped stakes marking the access road.

Speedy tugs on a stake. After three days of intermittent rain and dismal drizzle, temperatures hovering just above freezing, the cold mud readily yields the stake. Triumphantly waving the stake over his hooded head, he returns to the car for burlap bags, gives one to Emma and starts up the slope with the other. They bend over the ground like farm laborers gathering winter rutabagas and methodically bag their harvest. Jenny dashes between them, then, growling, she grabs a stake in her jaws and yanks it from the ground.

Icy raindrops begin to fall just as Speedy bags the final stake. He takes Emma's arm and hustles her to the car, then goes back for the three burlap bags full of vermilion-tipped stakes, stashes them in the trunk, takes out a long handled lopper and heavy-duty pruner and goes over to the bramble. With a keen eye, he selects, cuts and drags branches from the thicket to the clearing, inserts them into the mud, and moves rocks of various sizes to the base of his new thicket. The access roadbed between I-51 and New Burford is perfectly camouflaged.

Suddenly, the leaden skies open, releasing a downpour. He runs back to the car, slowly drives it on to the macadam road, and then turns on the lights.

"The gods are with us," Emma chortles. "This rain'll wash away footprints, any trace of our having been here. Well done, Speedy. Now, let's get the bags over to my place."

Her long driveway traverses an orchard of neatly pruned dwarf apple trees, precisely spaced on a rolling, expansive lawn. She gazes at the dormant trees, pondering the likelihood of the general's discovering their little environmental protection project. The Mercedes stops by a whitewashed door on a stone retaining wall at the back of the house. Speedy takes the bags from the trunk and Emma holds the door for him as he deposits them in the root cellar. "I'll get started destroying the evidence while you go check on the old Hamilton house. We'll have tea and spice cake when you get back. How's that?"

He smiles.

As he drives off, she loads stakes into a basket and carries them from the root cellar, through the kitchen, down the hall, to the fireplace in the living room, dropping one on the way. Jenny retrieves the dropped stake, prances into the living room, and gnaws on it. Emma snatches it from her. "Thank you, Jenny. That one just might have gotten us caught."

She crumples several sheets of newspaper, sets them on the grate, tops them with a few stakes and a bit of dry kindling, and strikes a match. The paper blazes, but the pine stakes smoke and sputter. "Too wet," she coughs, waving smoke away from her face.

Suddenly, flames burst through the smoke. "If nothing else, he'll get the message that we won't tolerate an access road into New Burford."

Not about to take any chances with Emma's car or his new driver's license, Speedy drives slowly. The rain has stopped, but the visibility is still poor. Turning into Hunter's driveway everything appears to be in order. The kitchen light is on, which means there has been no power outage, which means the basement sump pump is negotiating any elevated ground water from the thaw. Approaching the house, he sees the unmistakable shape of a Hummer in the driveway. He comes to a stop behind it, writes down the license number, grabs his flashlight, and gets out.

A whoosh of enormous, flapping wings startles him—a turkey buzzard, taking flight across the new concrete highway, into the woods. Speedy tries the lock on the kitchen door. Secure. Then goes to the back of the house where the posts recently installed to support a noise baffle wall stand in the gray mist like sentries along the smooth concrete strip. He freezes. From the one short post, a glowing ember arcs to the ground. He stares into the mist. The post is moving toward him.

"Barnhill? Are you Barnhill?" The voice is tough, hoarse.

Speedy doesn't move, recognizing the walk, the cigarette mannerisms, the stick under his arm. He was at the gravel pit, picked up by the helicopter the day the equipment arrived, and in Mildred's the day before the blast. It's Clappsaddle.

"No. You're not Barnhill." He walks up to Speedy. "Do you know where he is? I've stopped by a few times to see him but he's never here."

Speedy holds his fist to his ear as if using a telephone and points to it.

"I tried calling," says Clappsaddle. "He's got an answering machine, but I'd prefer to speak to him. You lost your voice?"

Speedy nods and takes out his notepad and writes, "I'm Barnhill's friend."

"I'm Bunker Clappsaddle. I'm involved with this highway job here." He looks at the old house, its white form clearly discernable in the mist. "This is a regrettable situation for Barnhill. I, uh, I just want him to know I had nothing to do with putting this road here. I followed orders."

Speedy writes, "I'll tell him you said that."

"Would you? Thank you. I appreciate that."

They walked back to the house and their vehicles.

"What's your name?" asks Clappsaddle.

"Serika," he writes.

"Thank you, Serika."

Clappsaddle gets into the Hummer with the American flag on the door and starts the engine. He backs it around, driving onto the grass, leaving tire prints in the soggy earth, and heads down the driveway. Speedy tries to smooth the tire impressions, pressing the furrowed sod with his boot. Shaking his head, he gets into the Mercedes with a story to share with tea and homemade spice cake.

# 16

## THURSDAY, FEBRUARY 13

*New York*

The antiquated steam radiator hisses under its sleek custom cabinet enclosure and shuts off with a loud clunk. Sleet prickles the windows. Hunter pops vitamin C and zinc tablets into his mouth, and gulps them down with orange juice. He feels miserable. Stuck in New York when he wants to be in New Burford. He can't blame the Kennedy Graveside Memorial Companion, which is finally in production, despite his ever-diminishing enthusiasm for the job. In a way, the Kennedy thing gave him an excuse to postpone the inevitable, choosing from options that are no less grim or limited than they were the day he fled.

Friends, real estate agents, lawyers tell him to unload the property, sell to a developer. But he can't do it. It would be better to donate it to the Nature Conservancy, ideal stewards of the splay-footed sapsuckers' habitat. But he can't do that either. The problem is that beautiful, plain, old, ordinary farmhouse by the super highway, where it doesn't belong. It may remain there for a while, perhaps for years, before it is torn down. He simply can't abide the idea of releasing it into perdition. The agent says there are better houses coming on the market in the New Burford area, but that's not the point. The point is that he trusted his lawyer at the closing, and blindly signed everything, including the continuation of the right of way. It was like clicking *agree* to a standard software licensing contract without reading the fine print only to learn later that the fine print gives Bill Gates rights to your left kidney. A chilling thought, no doubt inspired by Melanie's big new show. He sneezes, grabs a tissue, as Freddie, stretched out on the rug, sighs heavily.

"My sentiments, precisely, Freddie. I've got to leave this town. Got to go home, face reality, cut my losses." He grabs his Blackberry to contact the real estate agent. New mail has piled up. He scrolls down, sees aasspeaks@cc.com, and opens it.

> *Saw some old photos today in the school library. Did you know that when they built the reservoir, they put houses on wheels and hauled them to new sites on the other side of town?*
>
> *You could move your house. You got plenty of land and some beautiful sites far from the highway. Like that hill over-looking the pond. AAS*

"Move the house?" He rereads the lines and exclaims, "Move the house! If it were on other side of the property, the highway would be almost a mile away. Freddie, we're out of here."

# 17

*New Burford*

Three hours from the surrendered New York apartment and four-tenths of a mile from the old Hamilton House, the Rover crosses the ridge into the Valley of Runs-On-Toes-Into-Wind and comes to a stop on the side of the road. Hunter leashes Freddie and, spurred by a blustering wind, they follow a recently hacked path through the woods to the top of a knoll. The wind plays with him, tousling his hair, gluing his jeans to his legs. He sits on the ground to take in the view. The knoll slopes to a clear, spring-fed pond. At the far side of the pond is a flat rock, his retreat on many sleepless nights. From there, the meadow stretches to the ridge, green with hemlocks. Beyond the ridge, beyond the range of sensual detection, lies the highway.

As soon as Speedy gave him the key to the puzzle, the pieces started sliding into place like Rubik's cube. Atlas Building Movers, located on-line, told him the overbuilt farmhouse with strong floor joists and frame could be moved safely and fairly easily, given the short distance with no overhead utility wires along the route. After signing the Atlas contract, he called DeCarlo, who bought the apartment, furnished, for an even million. He can almost intuit how the last pieces of the puzzle will come together.

They return to the Rover, take off, go four-tenths of a mile down the road, and turn into the driveway. The vehicle slows to a crawl. Freddie is panting, yapping, drooling on the window.

"Oh—my—God—" Hunter holds his breath. The farmhouse is severed from its environment by a massive, twenty-foot wall jutting from the woods.

"Un-fucking-believable," he repeats under his breath. He parks by the house and goes to investigate. Freddie runs to the wall, sniffs, and lifts his leg. "Well done, Freddie." He turns to look at the old house, unmoored, severed from its environment.

Inside, a penumbra reasserts the overwhelmingly dismal presence of the wall. Seasoned coziness is put asunder, but defiantly, long sprigs of forsythia, prematurely blooming indoors, burst from a Ball canning jar on the kitchen table. Against the jar is a note, elegantly penned, the first and last words of each sentence decorated with filigrees and flourishes. He picks it up and smiles.

*Welcome home, Hunter. I would be delighted if you and Jean would come to my place for dinner tomorrow, Sunday evening, at six. Affectionately, Emma.*

A postscript is boldly printed. *This morning I pushed up the thermostat, turned on the water and the gas, and lit the pilot light on the water heater. You're all set. AAS*

Vestiges of doubt leave him as he unpacks the car and puts things back where they belong. In his office, too, the wall casts its shadow. He closes the shutters and goes upstairs with his bag. On the landing he sets it down. Something isn't right. The air feels oppressively close. Straight ahead through the open bathroom door, the window presents a panorama of the U-shaped wall and the strip of concrete engraved across his property, incongruously set against the bucolic hills tinged reddish with stirring sap. Grossly intrusive and ugly, but still peaceful.

In his bedroom, the highway dominates the view from three windows. The lawn, vegetable garden, and rail fence are gone. He opens a window for fresh air and stares out, then unhooks the tie-backs, releasing the curtains to cover the window, gets sheets and pillowcases from the linen closet and makes the bed. Freddie jumps on the smoothed blanket, and rolls onto his back, expecting a belly rub. Atop the dresser the cell phone sputters. "Hey, classes over?"

"I just closed," says Jean. "Where are you?"

"At the house. I got on the road earlier than expected."

"You okay?"

"It's grim. But, yeah, I'm fine. Can't wait to see you."

"I'm in the car, on my way," she says. "Emma told me Speedy was going to stop by to get your heat and hot water going."

"Yes, they left flowers and a note. Emma invited us to dinner tomorrow."

"She has her Tupperware party in the afternoon. Ladies only. I always go. But dinner will be just us and Millie Donnelley."

"As in Millicent Donnelley, the senator's ex-wife?"

"She's the daughter of Emma's cousin, Agatha Peters Warwick, and she's visiting for a week or so. Actually, she's a neat person but these days very angry and hurting. Donnelley's been a real bastard."

"I've got an axe to grind with him, too. This highway is here in large part due to him."

"Are you sure you don't want to come to my house?"

"No, not now, anyway. I sort of need to be here. But if it's too depressing for you—"

"All I need is to know that your hot water is back on so I can take a bath when I get there."

"It should be fine," he says, going into the bathroom, wincing at the highway, and turns on the faucet. "The only problem with taking a bath here is the view but I will do my very best to keep you distracted." He drops in some bath crystals. "Where are you now?"

"A minute down the road."

"Your bath will be ready for you." He winces again at the highway, then laughs. "Hey, I'm thinking we might get a couple of skateboards."

"Or roller blades."

He hears the car and runs downstairs.

# 18

## SUNDAY, MARCH 16

*New Burford*
      *Notice!*
   *Who loves this land for what is there*
   *Not only mine, not only theirs,*
   *Rest assured they are WELCOME here,*
   *Whether cursed for color or damned for deed,*
   *Whatever their race or creed,*
   *In night or day, in foul, or fair!*
   *But those who careless or with will*
   *Presume to do one square-foot ill,*
   *Let them BEWARE the lean were-bear;*
   *The man-half-bear with a belly to fill*
   *Which is not dead though it lie still*
   *For a thousand years at the heart of the hill*
   *In the ageless fault where it makes its lair!*
      *1939,* Montgomery Hare

Scribed in white paint across the panes of the bay window, the poem draws Hunter's attention. Shown into the living room by a late-teenage girl in black slacks and white blouse, he is waiting as the last to leave the Tupperware party prolong their conversations on the terrace.

"The poet was an old friend of hers. A neighbor, more or less," says Jean entering the living room and collecting a quick kiss from Hunter. Emma enters close behind her, hands outstretched, welcoming him, and bids him take a seat. As they gather around the coffee table, Hunter thanks her for having kept an eye on his house, with Speedy.

"That's what friends are for," she says, perching herself on the Chippendale corner chair, drawing it closer to the coffee table where there is a tray with four stemmed crystal glasses, a decanter and a plate of canapés. "Thank you, Cornelia," Emma says to the decorous teenager. "Before you leave, please go upstairs, knock on Mrs. Donnelley's door and ask her to come join us; the Tupperware crowd has left." She is pouring sherry into the glasses. "I apologize for the hangers-on, Hunter. They didn't start yakking, really, till the party ended and then it flowed like sap about every trivial topic you can imagine. Please, have some sherry." Jenny plops down on the rug. "So, Jean, who do you think was the wet blanket this afternoon?"

"Bertha, for certain. She intimidated everyone, sitting there like a storm cloud ready to burst. No one dared say anything."

Hunter asks, "Bertha Harper, town clerk? Best supporting actress of the midnight video?"

"The same," says Emma, "She certainly wasn't herself this afternoon."

"Maybe I'm a little too paranoid about all this," says Jean, "but if looks could kill, Bertha would have annihilated me this afternoon."

"Interesting," says Hunter. "When I arrived our paths crossed on the terrace. I said hello, friendly enough, and she walked by without a word, nose in the air."

"A guilty conscience!" Emma grins, rubbing her hands together.

"Guilty conscience? No such thing anymore." The comment is from a tall, thin woman, with stylishly short, graying blonde hair, and keen, deep-set eyes framed in dark circles. At her side is a black standard poodle. Jenny lifts her head to observe them. Hunter stands.

Emma introduces. "Millie Donnelley. Hunter Barnhill. Millie is my cousin, once removed."

"Hunter Barnhill," Millie repeats with sure recognition. "You've got a highway on your property."

"You might say I got paved," he says, standing to shake her hand.

"Likewise." Her voice is petulant. "No doubt you've heard I'm gay."

Emma interrupts, "That's unnecessary, Millie.

"To the contrary, it's quite necessary that I make it clear, right up front: I am profoundly heterosexual. Now I'll drop it." She sits in the armchair opposite Jean.

"So am I," Hunter uncomfortably chuckles then quickly adds, "Guess we never heard your side of the story."

"That's for sure! May I introduce Rousseau?" She proudly pats the impressive dog sitting obediently beside her and, with eyes much like hers, apparently following the conversation.

"Rousseau," he says, "Are you named for Jean Jacques or Henri?"

"Jean Jacques, *certainement*. So, your Town Clerk is feeling guilty about what?"

"About our highway travesty," says Emma. "Evidently, she is suffering pangs of conscience about what she did to the town, especially to Hunter. A good sign that justice will prevail."

"Justice? I don't follow." Hunter sets his sherry on the coffee table.

Emma has a twinkle in her eye. "You get justice when people become heartily sorry for what they've done and want to make amends."

"Don't hold your breath. Imagine Dick Donnelley heartily sorry. I think not."

"And Bertha was clearly trying to make me feel like a guilty party," Jean protests.

"She was looking to dump her guilt onto you—to lighten her load," says Emma. "But she can't get rid of it that way. In a way she's looking for punishment but she won't get it. Punishment fits the crime but apparently—apparently," she repeats, emphasizing, "no crime has been committed. Technically, no one did anything wrong. There's no evidence to speak of, no money trail, no fingerprints, no footprints. So, no crime, no punishment. No defendants, no trial. But justice. That's something else, don't you know."

"Ah, poetic justice." Hunter half-smiles. "The lean were-bear, the man-half-bear with a belly to fill may come out of its lair. Ill has been done to vastly more than one square-foot."

Emma is obviously pleased that he's read the poem. "But the lean beast may not have to stir if, as Speedy believes, we keep letting the scoundrels know we're on to them—without directly accusing them. I believe he's right. Bertha's not the only council member who is uncomfortable. Justice is wending its way already."

"Thanks to Speedy, I'm going to salvage most of my property. That doesn't change the fact that an injustice has been done by those who determine what's fair. They determined that it's fair to swindle in order to protect the splayfooted sapsuckers' habitat. They give a sapsucker a better than even chance and to me a check for $387, fair compensation from the Commonwealth of Massachusetts for my confiscated strip of land along the variance that is now part of the highway system."

"Oh-my-oh-my," Emma gravely shakes her head. "That check is an insult."

"When did people lose a grip on knowing what the government is doing?"

"When they stopped knowing what's really going on," Emma exclaims. "But people haven't abdicated; we're the government! It's our business to secure rights, protect the innocent, the law-abiders, the peace-dwellers. The people are sovereign; government leaders can keep us in the dark only when security is jeopardized."

Millie snaps, "And like any king, people can use their sovereignty for the good—or for abuse. People who abuse shouldn't be allowed to govern. But they do. On every level. Because nobody knows what's going on.

Emma huffs. "That's why I get so upset when people act as the ladies did this afternoon. Not one of them would take my bait and talk about the highway or anything of significance. And finally, after Bertha left, they just talked about covered dish recipes and Michael Douglas's marriage and cold frames."

"That's why the incorrigible types get and keep the power, working the system to their advantage, abusing anybody who's in their way, with impunity."

"Yes, until the rest of us get the gumption to exercise our rights," Emma counters.

Millie erupts. "I say bring the self-righteous, manipulative bastards to trial!"

"Millie, Millie! Even if you could try them and find them guilty, what good is it—unless they feel remorse and decide they'll never do such a thing again."

"Emma, you just don't get it. People like Dick Donnelley do not feel remorse."

"Now, just a minute, Millie. He's not some pathetic, disabled soul who injures people because he has no conscience. He went through a moral degradation to make these actions part of his life. He and Pease and Bertha and all the others have to go through emotional gymnastics in order to feel okay about what they've done."

"Point of order," Hunter interjects. "I happen to prefer Donnelley's politics, for the most part. Pease's too. And I have a hunch I'm not the only here who thinks like that."

"Good for you, Hunter," says Emma, pounding the arms of her chair with an optimistic finality. "Having said that, I will also urge you all to mark my words. Somehow, those two will also get their just desserts. They're not immune." Invigorated, she gets to her feet. "Now, I'm going to put our supper together."

"Let me help," says Jean, going with Emma.

"Thank you, m'dear. We don't have much to do. The casserole is in the oven. I have some nice mustard pickles—" She turns to Millicent and Hunter, "We'll call you in a few minutes."

Millie relaxes her grip on the cocktail napkin she had crushed in her fist during the controversy. In the moment of awkward silence, she takes a deep breath, then asks, "It's none of my business, but did you vote for Dick?"

"I did. I was clueless about all this on election Day." He pauses. "And you?"

"Would you believe it? I couldn't bring myself to split the ticket. Yes."

"And if you had it to do over?"

"He would not get my vote. Nor would I be a compliant pushover with the lawyers who assured me that if I would just kept quiet, the whole thing would quickly blow over. The allegations will fade fast, they said. It's for your own benefit, they said. Ha!" She tells him her story, and he listens until Jean calls them to the dining room.

Seated at the center of a table that would comfortably seat eighteen, Emma and Jean opposite Hunter and Millicent, they talk about the way things used to be in Boston and New York.

"That looks divine," says Jean as Emma tosses dandelion and other young leaves with ramps and snippets of lovage, chives, sweet cicely.

"All from my cold frame, except the ramps, which are very early this year."

"I caution you, Hunter, some say Emma's salads are a bit peculiar," says Millie. Her distinctive flair with greens comes from Rebecca, her eighth, my ninth great grandmother."

Jean explains to Hunter, "The story is, or I should say historical rumor had it, that Rebecca skirted an accusation of witchcraft on account of her creative culinary use of herbs."

Millie joins in telling the tale, "She had a penchant for chopped raw vegetables tossed with a variety of herbs, flowers and seeds which evidently produced an exotically stimulating effect."

"What year are you talking about?" Hunter asks.

"1630's, there about," says Millie.

"It was 1638, to be precise, according to Rebecca's diary," says Emma. "Captain Duty Peters, her husband, and Rebecca had just left

Hartford under a gathering cloud of suspicion. Some believed that eating flowers was akin to eating your young. Hartford wasn't much into witch hunting, per se, but, when the rumors reached Duty's ears, he decided they must move on, just in case the hysteria spread."

"However," says Millie, "According to Duty's diaries, he was more than ready to get out from under Hartford's Hookers and the Hosmers and start his own town."

"I believe he wrote that much later," Emma clarifies, "but Rebecca was quite agreeable to leaving Hartford, and it was she who chose the route, northwest, landing them here in the Valley of Runs-On-Toes-Into-Wind—named after Chief Agitated Bear's wife, doncha know."

"And, as the story goes," says Jean, "Runs-On-Toes-Into-Wind ran away from Bear right after he sold the valley to Captain Duty Peters."

Millie sighs, "Alas, we don't know what happened to Runs-On-Toes-Into-Wind."

"Unfortunately, no," says Emma. "But the rest is history. The Peters were very enterprising. Painfully frugal. Others followed them here, and before long they incorporated the township of New Burford, named for the town of our English ancestors."

"So," says Hunter, "New Burford might not have existed at all, had it not been for Rebecca's salads."

"Quite right," says Emma, again looking quite pleased.

"Delicious," says Jean.

"Bitter," says Millie.

"Robust," says Hunter with a big smile.

# 19

*New Burford*

In camouflage battle dress and campaign hat, swagger stick tucked smartly under his arm, leather map case and laptop bag beside him, Lieutenant General Bunker T. Clappsaddle, U.S. Army, Retired, and President of Palumbo Construction, waits on the sideline of the New Boy Drill Field for the Black Hawk.

For two and a half months, his crew worked round the clock to make up for the delays. Now, right on schedule, he is making an aerial inspection of the completed job. If it looks good, the grand opening of Interstate 51 can be scheduled for Memorial Day weekend as originally planned. He looks to the horizon, then at his watch.

Invited along for the ride, Brigadier General Roy Bolton Farrand, in his starched camouflage battle dress and campaign hat, hustles across the drill field and exchanges a salute with Bunky. From behind the treetops a National Guard chopper thunders into view, whacks its way around the New Boy Drill field, and hovers a moment before touching down. The door slides open, and, precisely on time, Lieutenant Colonel Marvin Norwocki, Massachusetts Army National Guard, leaps to the ground. Saluting, he crouches and waddles out from under the blades. Out of decapitation range, he straightens, marches up to Clappsaddle and Farrand, and comes to attention.

"Good morning, General, General. We're all set, Sirs, if you'll follow me, please."

The two generals follow Norwocki back under the whirling blades and hoist themselves into the chopper.

"You're in good hands, Generals," says Norwocki, introducing the pilots. "As civilians, they fly for American." They all nod respectfully, buckle up and Norwocki gives the Cavalry hand signal for charge. The chopper lifts off over soft green mounds of budding treetops. The morning sun is brilliant, the sky cloudless. In seconds, the chopper clears the ridge along the western side of New Burford. And there it is—a ribbon of cement looking like a limp noodle dropped by the Jolly Green Giant.

Bunky presses field glasses to his eyes, scanning the highway. "Uh-huh. Very good. Uh-huh." General Farrand, having turned off his hearing aid when the helicopter took off, is dozing.

Suddenly, Bunky lunges, the chopper lurches. "Where is it? Where the fuck is it?" Frantically, he refires the questions, almost choking. He thumps the pilot's helmet with the swagger stick. "Turn around and drop to fifty feet. Now!"

Norwocki grabs hold of Clapsaddle's jacket with both hands and shoves him back into his seat. "General, as the senior state officer aboard this state military aircraft I must ask that you restrain yourself, Sir."

"Norwocki, tell that fucking idiot flying this thing to turn around and go down for a closer look. Now! That's an order!"

Norwocki yells the order to the pilot. The chopper banks, and descends.

"Now, tell him to set down on the highway, there, between that road and the village green."

Norwocki leans forward and cups his hands around the pilot's ear. The chopper touches down onto the new surface of I-51.

The map and laptop cases swinging from his shoulder, Bunky stomps to the highway's shoulder. He scans the strip of cement, checks and rechecks the plans, on the computer, and on the blueprints. "Holy fuck."

"Sir?" Norwocki is standing at attention, exactly two steps to the left and one step to the rear of the general.

"Norwocki, there's no fucking turnoff here. There's no fucking way to get off this fucking highway into New Burford. It's on the fucking plan, but it's not here where it's fucking supposed to be. The access road never got fucking built. This is fucking impossible. I checked every fucking detail myself. Every fucking stake." Clenching his teeth, rapping his boot with the swagger stick, he paces a few feet, and stops. "Norwocki, my foxhole is full of shit." His voice is hoarse.

"Yes, Sir."

Punching his cell phone, Clappsaddle walks out of earshot. The conversation is brief. He pockets the cell and strides directly to the chopper. "To the State House."

"Yes, Sir!" Lieutenant Colonel Marvin P. Norwocki, Massachusetts Army National Guard, salutes perfectly.

*Boston*

"Are you telling me, Bunker, that there is no access ramp for New Burford?" Pease's determined jaw masticates the possible ramifications. His elbows are planted on his tidy desk, his fingers rigidly steepled.

"Affirmative."

"Otherwise the highway is completely constructed? Ready for traffic on May 23, the target date?"

"Affirmative. Here are the options. One, open the highway as scheduled and, after the holiday weekend, commence round-the-clock construction of the New Burford access. The drawback: traffic will slow construction and construction will slow traffic. The alternative is to postpone opening till we finish the access road. We'll work round the clock and get it done in record time but not for the Memorial Day weekend."

Pease raises an eyebrow, the corners of his mouth turn up. "New Burford, eh?" A Machiavellian grin spreads across his face. "Brilliant. Positively brilliant!" He gets off his chair, and throws his arms around Bunky. "General, I most highly commend your bold engineering blunder."

"Hmmmph." Clappsaddle is uncertain as to how to respond to the backhanded compliment, let alone the bear hug.

"I-51 will open on schedule, without that access ramp. To hell with New Burford! The town's nice on the eyes, but some of the people are so peculiar, so ornery, you might say they constitute a counter-tourism cell. Frankly, Bunker, I'm so pleased with this outcome that I'm asking the legislature to award you the Commonwealth Cross for Conspicuous Service."

"Thank you. What colors are the ribbons, Governor?"

"Green with pink and yellow stripes. The medal has a little Chickadee, our state bird, with the state flower, a little Mayflower, in its beak. You'll like it, General."

# 20

*Barrington, Massachusetts*

Governor Brewster Pease is personally directing the pubic relations campaign for the grand opening of Interstate 51. The governor wants news cameras aimed at a long line of out-of-state vehicles stretching from a ceremonial ribbon across the new highway. He wants coverage of his speech and Donnelley's congratulations. He wants coverage of his presentation of the Commonwealth Cross for Conspicuous Service to the first driver on the new highway and of the first car bursting through the ribbon, leading a stream of cars, full of tourists, smiling and waving, eager to spend big bucks in western Massachusetts. The governor does not want locals flocking to the event, causing traffic congestion and delays that would aggravate the out-of-staters, so advance publicity is targeted exclusively at the tri-state New York metro media. Intrastate media are to receive releases a half hour before the ceremony.

An hour before the ceremony, everything is in readiness. The reviewing stand constructed at the highway interchange is decorated with red, white and blue bunting. Cadets from Western Massachusetts Military Academy march into position behind the ceremonial ribbon. At the Mill Race Inn, dignitaries arrive via Black Hawk shuttle from Boston. Norwocki, in his dress blues, white gloves, and scabbard, trots out, under the chopper's blades, to officially greet them— members of Congress, state and county representatives and transportation officials, the state director of tourism, the adjutant general of the Commonwealth of Massachusetts, bankers and real estate developers. Senator Donnelly and his bride arrive with Governor and Mrs. Pease. They all gather at a cocktail reception and then, fifteen minutes before the ceremony, are driven in motorcade to the interchange, and seated in the reviewing stand. Clappsaddle takes his seat next to Betsy Pease, who hands him a molded black box. The Conspicuous Service medal. Looking forward to the ceremony when he will receive his, he opens it, to take a peek.

At precisely seven o'clock, the Massachusetts Army National Guard Band sounds attention, Pease goes to the podium and, leaning toward the microphone, gets a piercing electronic squawk. He pulls back a few inches, attempts to say Good evening, only to get another deafening squeal. The governor is livid. Clappsaddle calmly strides to the railing and barks, "Norwocki!"

Norwocki dashes up the stairs, his white-gloved hand steadying his scabbard. With a smart salute, he presents himself to the governor who hisses a terse order through a tight smile pasted over clenched teeth. Norwocki snaps a salute and skids down the stairs, shouting, "Sergeant Major, Sergeant Major!"

A team of Massachusetts National Guardsmen determines that the speakers behind the microphone are feeding back into the system. They move the speakers. Pease returns to the podium. It is now dusk and the governor sees that lighting is inadequate. Again Norwocki is called to the platform. He salutes and flies down the stairs, shouting, "Airborne!"

Behind the reviewing stand, engines rev up. Deuce-and-a-half trucks, Humvees, government vans, and official limousines drive into a semicircle formation, backing into position to beam their headlights on the podium. Satisfied, Pease smiles broadly, accepting the dignitaries' applause.

A horn sounds. Then another, and another, the signal spreading like contagion down the line of cars backed up for twenty miles. Out-of-staters waiting to get on the new highway are not tolerating the delay. Suddenly a great surge of honking sweeps up to the reviewing stand and drowns out the proceedings. Pease shoves his notes into his pocket, signals Clappsaddle, and, closely followed by Norwocki and news teams, he and the general blaze their way to the lead car, its hood kissing the ribbon.

It's a 1990 Ford LTD Country Squire station wagon, heavily rusted, the muffler wired to the fender, the left rear window sealed with gaffer's tape. The tires are new. Inside are the Delaneys—Paul, Madge, Beverly, and Scott, bound for their cabin in Sandisfield, Massachusetts. The night before, in their ten-room, rent-controlled apartment on Manhattan's east side, Paul and Madge saw on the news aerial views of a new highway that would cut twenty minutes off their commute to the country.

An impatient man, Paul Delaney checks his ferocious temper which he is wont to hurl at anybody or anything that gets in his way of his getting anywhere. It is now forty-five minutes since the white-gloved lieutenant colonel had asked him to stand by to receive an award from the governor of Massachusetts. Paul is glowering at the preposterous-looking cadets, in capes, shakos, and white gloves, lined up behind the ribbon, barricading the highway.

As the cacophony of horn honking continues, Pease takes the award from Clappsaddle and together they approach the vehicle. News teams surround them. Paul Delaney is gripping the wheel, his eyes pinned straight ahead. Bunky raps on the window with his swagger stick.

"Ick, Daddy, it's a bone," shrieks Beverly Delaney in the back seat.

Paul Delaney lowers the window.

"Good evening. I'm Governor Brewster Pease."

"Uh-huh."

"And this is Lieutenant General Clappsaddle."

"Uh-huh."

"And you, sir, are—?"

"I am more than an hour behind schedule," Delaney responds icily.

"Well, I have something for you that should handsomely make up for your delay. You will be the first to drive onto Interstate 51, and the People of the Commonwealth of Massachusetts wish to recognize you and show our appreciation.

"Governor, the best way for you all to show your appreciation is by removing that blockade so my family and I can get on with our weekend."

"That will be done. But first, if you would just step out of the car, please, you and your family. This will only take a moment—."

Grudgingly, Paul gets out. Madge opens her purse, quickly combs her hair, applies lipstick, cologne, and corrals the kids, barreling out from the back of the wagon along with a 156-pound Great Pyrennes. Instantly, the dog bounds, growling, for Clappsaddle's swagger stick.

"Paul, get the dog! Quiet, please, Fella," says Madge.

"Madge, he doesn't understand 'Quiet, please,'" says Paul. "Sit. Sit, Fella."

Fella sits and the family gathers around Paul.

The governor unrolls the parchment, quickly summarizes the citation from the Great and General Court of the Commonwealth of Massachusetts, and loops over Paul's head a satin ribbon bearing a gleaming Commonwealth Cross for Conspicuous Service. The medal rests on Paul's t-shirt just below a Yankees logo. The formality concluded, they shake hands, and pose for cameras. As Norwocki takes the Delaneys' full names and address, in order to mail them the inscribed citation, an even louder wave of honking surges. Paul deftly removes and drapes around Fella's fluffy neck the Cross for Conspicuous Service and the family piles back into the Country Squire station wagon, Fella first. Accompanied by a groundswell of honking horns, Paul accelerates onto the open road, and, making up for lost time, gets the old wagon up to 85 miles per hour.

*New Burford*

"Hey, congratulations," says Jean as they linger after dinner at the candlelit table. "How many times did that helicopter fly over us this afternoon? And you didn't get sick, or even look sick, even after that raw steak."

"It was black and blue--perfectly grilled," he says, unconvincingly. "I'm cured," he almost smiles. "Or desensitized? I didn't even get queasy today. But I've got a sinking feeling that the helicopter traffic is about the highway. That it's about to open, any time now."

"Impossible. There's been no announcement. You and Speedy check every day."

He shrugs. "Freddie, how about a walk." The dog yaps and runs to the door.

Jean snuffs out the candles. "Before we go, I'm closing windows. It feels like the temperature just dropped twenty degrees in a half hour."

"I'll close them upstairs, get sweaters, hit the john, then, Freddie, we're yours." He dashes upstairs into the bathroom and turns on the light. Relieving himself, his eyes are drawn out the window to two tiny specks of light—enlarging, fast. My God, a car—speeding straight at us. Christ, where's the turn?

At its top speed the wagon is rattling toward the curve when suddenly, straight ahead, there appears against the darkness an illuminated billboard of a man urinating. Paul gapes at it just as the old Ford wagon heads into the apex. Reflexively, he sharply turns the wheel, overcompensating, steering the car into a spin, propelling it into the immense wall. Fella lunges forward, his neck breaking on impact with the rear view mirror. Behind the Country Squire wagon, a Toyota Highlander barrels into the curve, brakes too late, and crashes into the Delaney vehicle, compressing it like an accordion. The steering wheel pierces Paul's chest like an apple corer. Madge's severed head is wedged in the glove compartment. Beverly and Scott are flattened between the seats. A loose hubcap continues rolling, wobbles, settles on the new pavement.

In deafening crashes, sheet metal compacts against the huge wall. Glass shatters. Sparks fly. Then silence. Darkness. Just like that. Like Vietnam. Standing at the toilet, holding his penis, he stares into the darkness. Again, headlights zoom toward the house, tires squeal. He snaps to full alert, zipping up, as metal crunches against metal. Another crash. From the foot of the stairs, Jean is calling him, terror in her voice. "Let's go, we've got to help," he says, racing down the stairs into the kitchen and picks up his cell phone. She's right behind him, cringing upon hearing yet another crash, then another. "Call Turbo," he says, "I'm calling the state police." She dials. He grabs a flashlight from a drawer. "Tell Turbo I've got a flooring plank that'll probably reach from the bathroom window to the top of the wall, and a ladder—"

Another crash. And another. Like dominoes.

"And tell Turbo—"

She gives him the phone.

"Turbo, a massive-multiple car collision is in progress. Get ambulances, Doctor Barnes. Right. It's just below my bathroom window. I've got a plank that'll span the distance and an extension ladder. Okay, we'll call Barnes and tell him you're picking him up."

After the phone call from the old Hamilton house, Constable Turbo Bull calls State Trooper Monohan, then turns to his commercial style milkshake maker, giving it two more seconds to bing ice cream, raw milk, malt powder, and chocolate syrup to the consistency of wet cement.

With the frosty stainless steel beaker securely nestled between his legs, the Volkswagen Super Beetle squad car, lights flashing, siren wailing, speeds through town on its steel-belted radial tires. At the end of a long, deeply rutted private road, the squad car stops in front of a white, aluminum-sided Leisurama mobile home with brick-red vinyl skirting. At the window, a frenzied Jack Russell terrier yaps a warning.

Turbo gulps the milkshake, preparing himself to fetch Barnes, which involves throwing ice water in his face, and coffee down his throat. The usual routine. "Ahhhh." He licks his lips, wipes his mouth with the back of his hand, and releases a hearty belch. Comforted, he sets the beaker between the bucket seats, drags on the emergency brake, lifts himself out of the squad car, and goes inside.

"Quiet!" Barnes snaps at the dog. The doctor is sitting on the edge of his lounger chair, facing three abutted television sets, all showing the same extreme close-up of blood-red tissue manipulated by gloved hands while a hushed voice-over explains the action.

"Doc, there's been a bad accident out on the new highway. Let's get on it!" Turbo soothes the high-strung dog, scratching its ears, while assessing Ralph's level of inebriation.

"Shhh. I know. I'm coming." Ralph gets to his feet and, without taking he eyes off the show, slowly tucks his shirt into his trousers. The video cuts to Melanie Atwood, wrapped in green surgical garb, her eyes gleeful as she whisks off the mask and joyously congratulates the surgeons. Then, with a flourish, she strips off the drab smock, revealing a glossy, skin-tight yellow jumpsuit, the show's logo emblazoned on her bosom. In time with the pulsating theme music, she struts through a cheering audience, to a chrome stage set with a glowing neon wheel, a red serpentine needle, spinning around it, lighting a digital number at the end of each spoke. At the edge of the curved set she blows kisses to the audience.

"Now that's good television," says Barnes, buttoning his shirtsleeves.

"Let's speed it up, Ralph." Turbo is perturbed.

"Calm down, Constable, you'll live longer." He checks the contents of his medical bag and gathers supplies, while keeping an eye on the show.

The needle slows to a stop. Number forty-five! The camera swerves from the number on the wheel, into the audience, to the same number on a t-shirt worn by a gaunt man in a wheel chair, grinning feebly. His wife and three children, all wearing "45" t-shirts, jump up and down, hug him and each other, as the audience cheers, sighs, and sobs. Melanie intones, "You can participate in this great joy, experience fame and glory just by saying: Yes, I want to be an organ donor. Be a donor. Call 1-800 ORG SHOW or log onto www.org.org. If you're waiting to receive an organ, tell us your story so the wheel can spin for you. Again, that's 1-800 ORG SHOW or www.org.org."

"She is some knockout," Ralph exclaims, turning off the televisions. "Great show! A triple tonight—heart, liver and kidney— flown from San Diego to The Pittsboro Medical Center." He puts on his corduroy jacket. "Around here, the closest I came to doing a transplant was when old Henry Harper's testicles got cut off by the rip saw over at the lumber yard. They put 'em in a bucket of ice and drove 'em with Henry to the hospital." He picks up the glass of amber liquid, chugs it and announces, "I'm all set, Constable."

"I've got a thermos of coffee for you in the squad car."

"That won't be necessary. Just crank up the siren. Now where's Incision. Incision!" The dog leaps onto the lounger chair. "Incision, guard the house."

In front of the old Hamilton house, Jean paces, anxiously clutching herself, watching for Turbo and Barnes, wondering why they're taking so long. She trembles, imagining the suffering on the other side of the wall. Needing to do something to help, she goes inside to find Hunter. Hearing noises upstairs, she runs to the bathroom, and directly into the end of an extension ladder stretched across the room, its other end disappearing through the open window.

"I'm out here, Jean."

She goes around the ladder to the window and gasps. He's outside, sitting astride a plank spanning the distance from the windowsill to the top of the baffle wall, easily twenty feet above the ground, and struggling to leverage the ladder through the window. She instantly grabs the end of the ladder to guide it.

"Thanks," he says with a quick smile, and, rung by rung, pulls the ladder through the window until it reaches the top of the wall. Then, making his way down the plank, he lowers the end of the ladder to the ground, leaning it against the wall. He tests it, then gets on. Halfway down, he takes a flashlight from his pocket, turns his shoulders, and slowly pans the beam across the wreckage. It is quiet, so very quiet. A column of smoke is drifting into the wind. Overwhelmed, he shuts his eyes a moment. Then slowly he climbs back up the ladder, across the plank to the window where Jean is waiting.

"It's worse than you can imagine," he says, swinging inside. "I don't know how many cars are down there. Crushed. It's one huge wreck. And so ominously quiet." He presses the heels of his hands to his temples.

"My God," Jean murmurs, "where are the ambulances?"

"I saw some emergency lights flashing, way down the highway. Probably cars that avoided the crash but can't turn around to get out. If that's the case, they may be blocking the rescue vehicles. It's a total disaster." He shakes his head and puts his arm around her. "You okay?"

She nods, feeling wretched.

"Look, as soon as the police find another way of getting to the scene, let's get out of here and go to your house—"

"Barnhill?" Turbo's husky voice booms from the ground below the window. "I've got Doc Barnes here."

Hunter yells, "Come on up. You can get over the wall from here."

Turbo and Barnes stomp through the front door, and up the stairs to the bathroom, passing Jean on her way down. They halt a few feet from the open window, where Hunter is clamping the plank to the sill.

Hunter's eyes widen when he sees them. Their girth is a factor he hadn't considered. The doctor's weight is mostly in his belly, a cumbersome load but not too heavy for the plank. Turbo's entire body is massive, his arms, legs, and neck as well as his gut. "You know, Turbo," says Hunter, "I can get the doctor down there, but I don't know if this plank can hold you."

Turbo needs no convincing. "Just get the doctor down there. I've got to meet assistance when it arrives, which should be any minute now." He backs out of the bathroom.

"Let me carry that, Doctor," Hunter offers, reaching for the black leather medical bag.

"No, thanks, I can manage it."

"Okay but let me show you how to move down the plank. Hug it, like this. I'll be in front of you the whole time, talking you through. When you come to the ladder, I'll grab your ankles, and put your feet on the rung. You all right with this?"

"Uh-um, fine."

Hunter gives him a reassuring smile and goes through the window.

Barnes quickly opens the medical bag, pulls out a flask, and takes a swig. Fortified, he puts it back, buckles the bag, and, grasping its handle, watches Hunter's demonstration. There is no way he can manage the heavy medical bag. He drops it onto the plank, shoves it into Hunter's hands, and climbs through the window.

Perspiring heavily, he inches his way along the thin aerial bridge, only once daring to look down. Finally, he feels Hunter gripping his ankles, connecting the soles of his shoes to the rung of the ladder. Safe. He goes down a few rungs, then rests, leaning against the ladder, and looks over his shoulder. Hunter is beaming a flashlight across the wreckage. The enormity of the disaster stuns him. He grabs a deep breath from his belly and takes the next rung, continuing to the ground.

In his routine check of CB radio police bands, Samson Feddicker picks up Turbo's communication with Monohan and immediately contacts Emma for her approval to launch Colonial Cable's all-channel news bulletin.

"Do it!" Emma says instantly. "And Samson, take the remote truck out and get live video going. Go to the head of I-51, in Barrington at I-50, and follow it as far as you can."

*Barrington*

After Turbo's call, Trooper Monohan calls Headquarters, Massachusetts Army National Guard, requesting helicopter rescue assistance at the accident scene. The duty officer puts Monohan on hold while he locates New Burford on the map and checks the computer to identify the senior military officer in the area. "It's Lieutenant Colonel Marvin P. Norwocki. He's in the vicinity, assigned to the governor's detail at the I-51 opening. I'll put you through to the governor's traveling staff."

Norwocki is at the Millrace Inn where the governor and Clappsaddle have just learned about the accident from the bartender who has been watching the bulletins on Colonial Cable. Monohan states the situation to Norwocki, who then requests the adjutant general's chopper for relief service. Governor Pease considers the request. He is now relieved that media turnout for the ceremony was less than he had expected, especially since he's just learned from the bartender that all the reporters who had been hanging around for a press briefing following the ceremony are now descending upon the accident scene. He immediately decides that greater attention would be drawn to the accident if the helicopter were redirected to a rescue mission; it will continue transporting the dignitaries back to Boston and New York from Barrington.

Norwocki gets back on the line with Monohan. "No go." The request for helicopter assistance goes back to headquarters.

*New Burford*
Colonial Cable's alarming bulletin rouses the curious folks of the Valley of Runs-On-Toes-Into-Wind to check out the situation. Some go to the highway juncture. Most head for the old Hamilton house, where they soon discover that the best view of the action is on television and they gather around Hunter's screen for Colonial Cable's coverage.

The New Burford Defense Battalion musters and, in new camouflage battledress uniforms, purchased on-line, they march in formation, under the command of Hamilton Gerard Goodwill, VII, to the old Hamilton house. Leaving his troops at parade rest in front of the house, Hamilton goes inside, marches upstairs to the bathroom, and offers the Battalion's assistance to Turbo. Turbo accepts, saying, "Stand by for a signal from Doc Barnes."

Police cars, fire trucks, EMS vehicles, ambulances and towing trucks line the driveway at the old Hamilton house. Rescue workers trek into the house for further instructions, having been directed to the old Hamilton house as the point of access to the accident scene. Reporters arrive and interview individuals as they view Colonial Cable's live coverage and arrive at the front door.

Jean retreats to the kitchen to make coffee. The aroma instantly draws a crowd of cops, firefighters, flatbed truck operators, and rescue workers. She squeezes her way out of the kitchen, only to find even more people in the dining and living rooms, milling around, watching television, munching on chips, doughnuts, guzzling beer and soda. Gloria, the town wag, feigns surprise at seeing Jean there. Jean mirrors her catty grin and flees to Hunter's office.

On the other side of the wall, Hunter climbs up a few rungs to track Dr. Barnes by the beam from his flashlight. Looking out over the debacle, he sees that Barnes has reached the vehicle rammed against the wall.

Barnes looks inside the crushed Country Squire wagon. A white male is impaled on the steering wheel. Next to him is a female body without a head and between them a large dog with a ribbon around its lifeless neck. The air is heavy with fumes— burning engine oil, leaking gasoline, antifreeze, window solvent, and a scent he had long forgotten, Eau de Chanel No. 5. Liszt's "Reminiscences of Mozart's *Don Giovanni*" is faintly playing on a Walkman headset, saved from destruction by a sturdy Igloo Playmate ice chest. The back seat is compressed against the front seat, young arms and legs sticking out from between them—three legs, two with matching socks and shoes and two arms not matching. Eyeing the chest, Barnes reaches for his medical bag, and takes a long swig of scotch from the flask. Of course! *Transplant Time* needs organs. And he, in the midst of terrible carnage, equipped with a medical bag and ice chest, he can help.

He pulls the ice chest through the broken rear window and opens it. Six cans of Diet Pepsi, a head of Boston lettuce, a package of ground round, a gallon of skim milk, a pound of butter, a half-gallon of not-from-concentrate orange juice, and some individually wrapped slices of American cheese, all resting on a bed of ice. He tosses the food back into the wagon, saving the ice.

The middle-aged male is an easy operation. The heart and lungs are badly damaged but the pancreas, kidneys, and liver are in excellent condition. He puts them in the Igloo Playmate ice chest and closes the lid. Then he goes to the headless woman. She yields one heart, one kidney, a pancreas, a liver and a left lung. Barnes slides them into the ice chest. He tries, without success, to pry the back seat from the front seat, regretting that he did not pack a crow bar. Making a mental note to strap one to his bag whenever called to an auto accident, he glances again at the dog, picks up the ice chest, and moves on to the next car.

He works quickly, gathering as many organs as possible before the imminent arrival of EMS and rescue teams. He finds a sufficient number of coolers for his harvest but how will he transport them? Hunter will help. Others too. New Burford people won't question him, but very likely others are around who might be justifiably suspicious of the coolers moving up the ladder, through the house, and into the squad car.

Sirens wail. Helicopters thunder overhead. Barnes peels off the latex gloves, takes a Handiwipe from his case and wipes the blood off his wrists and arms. Hunter is nowhere to be seen. He carries two coolers to the base of the ladder and goes back for two more. They are heavy. His arms ache but he is overcome with a sense of power. He will become a purveyor of fine organs to the transplant industry. He will call *Transplant Time*'s 800 number, possibly get connected to that great looking Melanie Atwood. That's her name. Yes, he'll call her and make a deal. But can he trust her? Is she for real? Jesus, maybe *Transplant Time* is a hoax. No. Those operations aren't staged. He'll deal in strict confidentiality. It's their business to do that, just like his. But they'll have to move fast. That's the beauty of it, he realizes. The whole thing can be negotiated, delivered and paid for in just a few hours.

Standing at the base of the ladder, among the coolers, Barnes sees Hunter where the plank meets the ladder, and waves to him just as he hears Jean calling him, distress in her voice. Hunter drops out of sight. "Hunter!" Barnes yells. "Hey, Barnhill. C'mon down and give me a hand."

Hunter shouts to him from the window. "Ham's ready to assist, Doctor. He's got the whole battalion here." Swinging off the plank, into the bathroom, he calls ahead, "Turbo, tell Ham that Barnes just signaled. He needs help. I can't help him now."

Search lights beam from two hovering helicopters as fire trucks, police cars, tow trucks and rescue vehicles swarm onto the field defined by the U-curve in the highway. From the apex of the great wall, the wreckage extends a quarter mile down one arm of the curve. The other side of the U is pristine, untraveled concrete. A helicopter lifts off from the field. Another approaches.

In the old Hamilton house, Ham Goodwill complies with Turbo, who had responded to Hunter, who had reported that Doctor Barnes needed their assistance, and organizes the New Burford Defense Battalion into a relay line. Without questioning and instantly, the battalion obeys the order and begins moving four Igloo Playmate ice chests, three Coleman ice chests, and one Cool Baby Cooler along the line from the foot of the ladder, across the plank, through the window, into the house, down the stairs and out the front door to the Volkswagen squad car.

Getting out of the way of the relay team, Jean waits anxiously on the landing as Hunter pushes through the crowded bathroom. "Freddie's missing. I can't find him anywhere. With all this noise he can't hear us calling. He may be very disoriented."

"We'll find him." In the hall, about to head down the stairs, he senses something moving in his dark bedroom. "Give me a second, Jean. I'll meet you outside."

"And as soon as we find Freddie, please, tell these people to get out of here unless they're helping."

"Count on it," he says quietly, as he starts toward the door, slightly ajar. He discerns two women in there, one of them poking around the closet. He barges in and flips the light switch. "Bertha Harper, Town Clerk! You want to tell me what you ladies are doing in here?" He stands in the doorway.

The woman at the closet squeals, dropping a hanger along with a red cashmere robe. Bertha answers for them. "We're looking for the stairs. This must be the way, Dottie."

"You know, Mrs. Harper, I had no trouble identifying you in the dark after seeing you in the video of that midnight town meeting."

"Wh-what are you talking about?" Bertha Harper is flummoxed.

He presses his hand to the doorjamb, blocking their exit. "First my property rights are invaded and now it's my privacy." He pauses. "I just saw bodies in those crushed cars out there, on the highway, what used to be my field. Who's responsible?" He studies Bertha's impassive expression. "You know the way out." He stands aside and the two women leave, passing him, eyes downcast.

As he follows them downstairs, the Defense Battalion's relay line is breaking up, the last ice chest moving along into the squad car. Turbo emerges from the bathroom and calls out, "Barnhill, I shut the window on the board and turned off the light so you won't get any more bugs flying in."

"Thanks," Hunter calls out as he sees Jean at the front door, saying goodnight to Bertha and Dottie as they sheepishly scurry off. "And, Turbo," Hunter adds, "before you go, would you ask everyone to leave. My house is off limits now."

"You got it, Barnhill."

Turbo paces a few yards from the old Hamilton house, withdraws his .357 from its holster and fires a round into the night sky. "Okay," he hollers, "I want everybody off these premises by the time I count to three. One."

People pour out of the house.

"Two."

They scramble into their cars and the exodus begins.

"That should do it for you, Barnhill," says Turbo. "Any stragglers, you've got my permission to kick their butts out the door." He eases himself into the squad car, next to Barnes, turns on the siren, and peels out, passing the line of cars in the driveway. There, where the Volkswagen was parked, is Freddie, sniffing around.

"Freddie!" exclaims Jean, rushing over to the dog. Groveling, as if caught red-handed the dog wiggles up to her for a reassuring pat. Hunter grabs his collar and walks him inside. The dog balks to gobble a morsel of food dropped on the doormat.

The house is a mess, strewn with soda and beer cans, donut and pizza boxes, coffee mugs, napkins, wrappers, chips. They start cleaning up, loading trash onto the pizza boxes. Taking the first load into the kitchen, Hunter discovers two reporters working on laptops.

"Out! This is not a pressroom!"

"We'll be finished in just a few minutes. We're with the *Crier.*"

Infuriated, he speaks softly, distinctly, clearly threatening them, "I wouldn't care if you were with the *Washington Post*, get out of my house. The story's on the other side of the wall— unless you're writing about abuses of privacy and property rights." He takes a deep breath, "Leave!" A helicopter takes off over the house. They pick up their things and go without saying a word.

He's reaching for a bottle of aspirin as Jean comes in with a pizza box piled high with garbage and dumps it into a bulging, plastic trash bag. She washes her hands and accepts the aspirin bottle from him. "We've got to get out of here," she says resolutely. "Let's just take out the garbage; everything else can be cleaned up tomorrow."

Turbo and Barnes unload the ice chests and coolers from the squad car, and stack them in the mobile home's living room. Tail twitching, Incision eagerly sniffs the containers, slowly circling them, and yaps.

"What's in there, Doc, if you don't mind my asking?"

"Not at all. Medical waste. Debris, bandages, stuff that shouldn't be left around. It's best that I dispose of it."

That makes perfect sense to Turbo. He bids the doctor good night and departs.

Barnes pours himself a glass of bourbon to steady his shaky hands. He fumbles among magazines, newspapers and junk mail on the end table, locating the VCR remote control. Clutching it in his sweaty hand, he rewinds the evening's programs back to *Transplant Time.* There it is, 1-800-ORG-SHOW.

He gulps from the glass, picks up the phone and punches the number. After several rings, he hears switching, then several more rings. A recorded voice comes on the line.

"Thank you for calling *Transplant Time.* If you are donating an organ, press 'one.'"

Barnes presses "one."

"Thank you. If you are donating a heart, press 'one.' If you are donating a pancreas, press 'two.' If you are donating one kidney, press 'three.' If you are donating two kidneys, press 'four.' If you are donating a liver, press 'five.' If you are donating a lung, press 'six.' If you are donating two lungs, press 'seven.' If you are donating a heart/lung combination, press 'eight.' If you are donating any other body part or combination thereof, press 'nine.' If you require an organ, please call our Recipient Screener, Monday to Friday, 9:30 a.m. to 4:30 p.m., Eastern Time, at 1-900-NEEDONE. The call is $9.95 for the first minute and $7.50 per minute thereafter. If you wish to speak with an organ associate, please remain on the line."

Barnes remains on the line.

"Thank you for calling *Transplant Time*. This is Joyce. How may I help you?"

"My name is Ralph Barnes. Doctor Ralph Barnes. I'm calling from New Burford, Massachusetts. I may have access to organs for your show."

"I see, Ralph."

Barnes smarts at hearing this voice named Joyce calling him by his first name.

"Possibly a considerable supply of organs. Fresh ones. The hosts having expired within the hour. You do refer to them as hosts."

"Yes, Ralph, we call them hosts." Her voice is energetic.

"If you're interested, you've got to move quickly before they spoil."

"Ralph, I'm going to have to call you back and verify you. I mean you could be just anybody, now, couldn't you?"

"I am Ralph Barnes, MD. I live in New Burford, Massachusetts. I am sitting in my living room with four Igloo Playmate ice chests, three Coleman ice chests and something called a Cool Baby Cooler. They are filled with fresh organs. Now get someone on the line who can use them." He takes a swig of bourbon.

"One moment please."

"Hi, Doctor Barnes. This is Larry Ruben from *Transplant Time.* How ya doin'?"

"Ruben, I'm doing fine. Now listen. I've got enough organs here to choke a horse, so to speak. Harvested within the hour. Hearts, lungs, livers, pancreas, kidneys."

"This is legitimate!"

Barnes takes another swig. Incision is licking the side of a Coleman ice chest. "Incision, get away from there."

"Incision?"

"My dog. His name's Incision."

"Doctor Barnes, I know our producer would personally like to take those organs off your hands but he's in Las Vegas this week at a convention. So I'm sending an escort team to, uh, New Burford, asap. Now, Doc, what are they worth to you? I mean, we're dealing, right?"

Barnes says the first number that enters his head. "$100,000."

"You got it. The Organ Escort team will bring you a certified check for $100,000 unless you want us to deposit it somewhere."

He wonders if he should ask for cash. "No. Just make the check out to Ralph Barnes, M.D. However, Ruben, this is in strictest confidence or we don't deal."

"That's how it works, Doc. Now I'm going to put our logistics team leader on the line, and you tell him where you're located in New Burford. He needs to know where they can land a helicopter."

The deal concluded, Ralph has a few nightcaps and dozes off. In what seems like mere moments, helicopter thunder, reverberating through the mobile home, wakes him. Incision yaps wildly. Mildly disoriented, Ralph focuses on the ice chests, remembers *Transplant Time,* and lurches to the door, squirting breath freshener on his tongue.

A man in a bright yellow flight suit emerges from a cloud of dust churned up by the whirring blades. "Hi, there! Doctor Barnes?"

Incision growls, showing his teeth. Barnes eyes the red *Transplant Time* logo on the flight suit's sleeve. "Easy, Incision."

"I'm Bobby Smith, the Organ Escort Team Leader from *Transplant Time*, America's favorite prime time show!"

"Yes, I'm Doctor Barnes. Come right in."

The young man in the flight suit steps up into mobile home and points at the ice chests. "So, the organs are in these coolers?"

"That's right. There's an inventory list in the Cool Baby Cooler."

"Excellent. But I'll have to take a look," he says, squatting to open them.

"Certainly. But let me first get Incision into the bedroom. He's been sorta high strung ever since I brought these things in. It's the scent that gets him excited."

"I'll say. A dog could really have a pig-out on this."

Ralph drags a headstrong Incision into the next room and closes the door. The barking persists. As Smith opens the Igloo Playmate ice chest, Barnes pours himself another bourbon.

"Will you join me for a drink?"

"Thank you, Doctor, but, when I'm flying, I don't touch spirits."

"Suit yourself."

"Say, Doc, these are fresh! I've seen a few organs in my day, and I know when they've been sitting around too long. These look really good. Boy, I'd love to know how you got 'em."

Barnes has been preparing for that question since making the first cut. The best answer is no answer. Tell no one. Not even this golly-shucks Bobby Smith kid. "Mr. Smith, you know confidentiality can't be broken." The bourbon was bringing him back into an alcoholic comfort zone. "You have a check for me?"

"Of course. Your check." Smith unzips the pocket on the upper arm of his yellow flight suit and withdraws an envelope. "Here you go, Doctor. A certified check from TTP Inc.— that's *Transplant Time* Productions."

Barnes holds the envelope up to the light, opens one end with a scalpel and shakes the check from the envelope. It falls to the floor. In a swift exertion, amazing himself, he bends over and snatches

the check before perky Mr. Smith can see the amount. There it is—
$100,000. Son of a gun!

"We're all set, then. I'll just make sure these lids are tightly closed,
and then I'll be right back with my crew to load 'em into the chopper."

# 21

## SATURDAY, MAY 24

*New Burford*

The Medevac airlift is still thundering overhead as Mildred's regulars, sleep-deprived and irritable, gather for breakfast. Turbo is in his usual place at the counter, digging into a double order of blueberry pancakes, fried eggs, bacon, sausage and ham. Next to him, Speedy is sipping coffee, waiting for his egg and muffin, watching the reflected activity at the tables.

"Thought I'd see you and the Widow Pell down at the old Hamilton house," says Turbo.

Speedy shakes his head.

"Just about the whole town showed up there. Except you and Emma."

Speedy nods without taking his eyes off the mirror.

Willard Cornwall, in his dark blue suit, comes in, locates the "specials" blackboard propped on a counter stool and carries it to its easel. Everyone hushes as he erases the death total at the top of the easel, above the apple walnut pancake special. He chalks a new number—115. Worthington, at a table with Bertha Harper, signals Willard, who joins them, wipes his chalky fingers on a paper napkin, and studies the menu, unchanged for twenty years.

Gradually conversation resumes. Speedy listens in, and around—

"Seems to me we ought to cancel the Memorial Day parade."

"Can't do that. But it might be fitting to march in silence."

"Why should we change our Memorial Day activities on account of those accidents? They have nothing to do with us."

"This town is going to be crawling with outsiders, just wait—"

"Down at the Barrington morgue they found eviscerated bodies—"

That gets Speedy's attention. And everyone else's.

"What's that? Wha'd he say?"

The place falls silent.

"Organs. Cut out of some of the bodies," a volunteer fireman reports. "That's what the EMS guys were saying. But the next thing we know the medical examiner is saying it wasn't so, just a wild rumor. Wild or not, the rumor got quashed mighty fast. Some reckon it was witchcraft."

"There's no witchcraft around here," declares Bertha. "But it ain't right what's going on down there at the old Hamilton house." Every head in Mildred's turns to her. "Jean Glick isn't just dating that New Yorker. She's living with him. That's why she hasn't been here mornings since Barnhill got back from wintering in New York."

"Eat your heart out, Bertha. Never too old for a touch of envy, eh?" Mildred quips, eliciting a ripple of snickers.

"This is no laughing matter, Mildred. I'm concerned for our young girls, especially our impressionable teenagers. This kind of thing starts innocently enough with our little girls in ballet lessons, but before you know it, she's teaching them that decadent, indecent dancing. And you know what that leads to."

"Nonsense. You want to see decadent dancing? Do a little channel surfing sometime, Bertha. That is not what Jean Glick teaches."

"Excuse me," snaps Bertha. "But Jean Glick is a role model for our young people. Unfortunately, underneath her charm, that woman is a Damnewyorker, like him. Together they're trouble, exposing kids to Damnewyorker immorality."

"That's enough, Bertha. You've gone too far." Martha Kindle speaks out.

"Not I!" Bertha's in a huff. "Did you see the poster for Jacob's Pillow? That's Jean Glick and some guy with his hand on her thigh, holding her leg straight up. Indecent."

Enraged, Speedy swivels to get up. Turbo clamps his enormous hand on his shoulder and quietly, sternly admonishes him, "Find out where this is going before you get riled up."

Two men in khaki suits and aviator sunglasses walk in. Everyone silences. Mildred greets them, "Looking for the accident scene?"

"Yes, ma'am." They get directions to Barrington, two containers of coffee, two blueberry muffins, and leave.

"I won't stand for this," says Martha. "Jean and I have been friends since we were kids. My girls think she's the best and they learn more than dance from her, like self confidence. Bertha, I suggest you go on over to the studio next Saturday morning and see for yourself. And go to the kids' ballroom class, too, where they're waltzing around like little ladies and gentlemen."

"It takes two to tango," says Worthington. "Personally, I believe Barnhill's urban immorality is the core problem. He should make an honorable woman out of her or keep his hands off. If he can't do either, then he belongs back to New York, away from our youth."

The door swings open and in walks a gray-haired woman wearing a turquoise prairie dress, Teva sandals, inches of bangle bracelets on both arms, silver rings on most of her fingers, and chunky turquoise earrings. With her is a tall, gaunt, younger man with a shaved head, wearing faded black jeans, sandals, a brown leather vest over a tattooed chest, his ears are pierced with rows of small gold hoops, his nose with a turquoise stud. In silence, everyone gawks at the couple as they go to the take-out counter, order coffee and ask directions to the crash site.

"Ya can't get there from here," says Mildred. "Gotta go back to Barrington. How about a nice blueberry muffin?" They leave with two large coffees, two blueberry muffins, and directions to Barrington.

Ham Goodwill resumes. "Barnhill seems all right to me. His character was put to the test last night, and as far as I'm concerned he passed. However, Farrand tells me he's not marching with us in the parade. He should. He's a veteran. I can't imagine why he would decline to march, and that troubles me."

Members of the Defense Battalion grumble in concurrence.

"Hold on. I've got to put in my two cents," says Turbo, easing off the stool and facing Mildred's patrons. I worked with Barnhill last night. Before I even got to the accident scene, and I was the first, Barnhill had set up a rig and managed to get Doc Barnes over the wall to treat victims long before any ambulances showed up. And he stood by, ready to assist Doc Barnes, till the Defense Battalion relieved him. Now, if his heart's not in marching on Monday, I can't say I blame him. He's got to be pretty upset about that highway going through his land and all the fatalities in what used to be his back yard."

"That's beside the point, Constable," says Bertha. "We're discussing morality, Barnhill's shenanigans with Miss Jean Glick, and their negative influence on our young people. Although I've never observed her dance classes, I have made observations at the old Hamilton house, and I know that her clothing is hanging in Barnhill's closet."

Speedy wipes his mouth with a napkin and throws it on the counter. This time Turbo doesn't stop him as he slides off his stool and goes to the blackboard. He picks up the eraser and holds it, looking for Mildred's approval. Everyone is watching, not knowing what to expect. "Sure, Speedy, go ahead," says Mildred.

He erases the specials board, leaving only the death total, takes the chalk and circles the total. Then he draws a square at the bottom of the board, a shaded band across the top, a U looping from the shaded band to the square, and a dotted chalk line around the U. He labels the dotted line *Wall*, and marks the square old H house. Inside the curve he prints—*Unethical. Who approved? Who gained? Who paid?* He carries the blackboard through the restaurant holding it for everyone to see, places it on the empty chair at Worthington's table, and starts back to the counter. "That'll be enough, Speedy," Worthington says, crossing his arms over his chest as Speedy returns to the counter, leaves a few dollars by his plate and, with a pat on the back from Turbo, heads out the back door.

"I don't know what's come over him." Worthington breaks the silence. "We got him an assistant at the school, Emma's got him driving. Now the half-wit's too big for his own britches." Mildred's patrons are staring at him. Bertha is smoothing her hair.

Up in the control chopper, hovering over the accident scene, Norwocki is still on duty, fighting fatigue, commanding the Massachusetts National Guard Troops, directing the evacuation below, observing on an array of monitors the action captured by surveillance cameras on the belly of the chopper. A few prickly turf disputes have required his intervention, but, for the most part, his troops cooperate well with the Massachusetts Highway Patrol, Homeland Security, FBI agents, firemen, EMS teams and the State Police, as the joint teams evacuate victims and clear debris. He logs activity in detail, mindful that he might be heading the rescue operation following a terrorist attack.

Eleven hours after the event, as the sun was lifting over the hills, he had ordered breakfast with three large coffees, shaved, changed out of his dress blues into battle dress, and got back to work. Now, twelve hours after the event, the crisis zone is normalizing but the monitors show the action entering a new phase.

POV's, personally owned vehicles, and unmarked vehicles with official plates are driving into the U-shaped field. A small crowd is gathering at the edge of the wreckage. He zooms in on it. There, in the eye of the swarm, is Clappsaddle, vigorously waving his swagger stick. The general is giving a briefing. Norwocki orders the pilot to set him down. It's time to fight on foot.

*Boston*

"Dammit, John, what the hell is the *New York Trib* trying to do to the Commonwealth of Massachusetts?" Pease flings the front section at his media adviser, who had been called from his bed to the Governor's residence. "If their aim was to undermine my economic stimulus initiative, they've achieved it. And worse. Christ, this could decimate Berkshire's tourism for the entire summer." He picks up a refolded section of *The Boston Global* and snaps his finger on an inside story. "Go figure. The *Global* didn't even put it on the front page. Just two, three-inch columns and a photo. What's going on here?"

Cassler, sitting on the other side of Pease's desk, glances at the front page, then calmly folds the paper, places it on the edge of the desk, and listens without interrupting as Pease continues to rant.

"Look at these photos. Articles throughout the whole damn front section. A whole lot of tangential, circumstantial crap. Precious few relevant facts, heavy innuendo that this was a terrorist attack. No one clued me in as to why they're blowing this into something it's not." He glowers, his jaw masticating.

Waiting to see if he continues, John mutters into his cupped hand, "Great story," then asks directly, "Do you suspect terrorism?"

"Of course not. But now the entire nation will suspect it," Pease says, clipping each consonant.

Cassler knows the clipped diction is a sure sign that the governor is on the verge of one of his rare displays of hot temper. "But all the ink says accident. The National Transportation Safety Board and state transportation officials are investigating."

"As are the FBI and Homeland Security. That's hardly reassuring," Pease is speaking painfully slowly, enunciating very crisply. "This would have been significantly less damaging if they had used the press material, the facts we spoon-fed them. We gave them all the research data. That highway passed every safety test. And just about every optional test. Did they balance the gruesome aspects of this fiasco with our research? Did they? No. Did they mention our tight security?"

"We didn't announce our security measures," Cassler states flatly.

"Then do so, now." Pease nearly spit the words into his face. "Make it clear that there wasn't the remotest chance of terrorist activity on that highway."

"I say fuck it."

"Fuck it?" Pease's jaw drops.

"Yeah. The public has an attention span of about twenty-four hours, if that. Yes, it's longer for those directly involved, but, proportionately, that number is always very small. Brew, most of the people you want to see driving back up here will have forgotten this accident in a few days. If you remind them by announcing in the media what you're doing to determine the cause of the disaster, you'll keep their fear alive. They won't come. Leave it alone, and you'll probably be able to reopen by the Fourth of July weekend. So drop it."

"Impossible. Do you have any idea how many investigations are getting underway?

"No, and it doesn't matter, because you're going to fully cover your ass. No, you're going to steal the collective thunder of those investigations by authorizing your own battery of investigations, which will get the preponderance of media attention. You are going to follow your own rule for handling bad press. Ignore it. And refocus attention where you want it."

Pease is stroking his chin. "Yes. I need a list of everyone who has shown up at that curve. I will personally keep on top of the investigation. We'll push to get safety tests done as quickly as possible. And I want simulations done in all weather and traffic conditions, at all times of day, at speeds from 40 to 100 miles per hour."

"Exactly."

"As soon as we get conclusive reports that the highway meets safety standards, we reopen."

"But—no fanfare. No announcements until after it's been open and safely traveled for a week, or longer, without any accidents or delays. I assure you, Brew, vacationers, country home-builders, city escapees will get right back on I-51 and they won't give a thought to the highway's safety as long as it gets them where they want to go— faster."

"So, we're back in business on the Fourth of July weekend."

*Springfield, Massachusetts*

At a grey metal desk in 26th Infantry Brigade Headquarters, Norwocki scoops the last bits of foam from the bottom of a Starbuck's latte grande, tosses the cup into the trash, removes the lid off another, and gulps half of it. Sleep deprived for now forty-eight hours, he had stopped at two Starbucks on the road to Springfield. At the second, in Longmeadow, he drank one cup in the shop so he wouldn't fall asleep at the wheel and got three to carry out—one to get him to headquarters and the rest to see him through the completion of the job.

He separates sheets and scraps of paper into two piles, each in chronological order. The caffeine kicks in again. His task is to prepare for the Office of the Governor a comprehensive listing of all the investigative teams, state and independent agencies, auditors, watchdogs and inspectors that had checked in at the accident scene. As standard procedure, he had made notations for every entity that entered the disaster area, with the time of arrival and departure. He can do it. He bows his head. Holy Mother, this is for the governor. It's got to be as perfect as humanly possible. Please help this very tired mortal. Thank you. Amen.

He boots the computer.

First to arrive on the scene were Bruno Fitzsimmons, State Director of Highways, and teams from the Massachusetts Department of Transportation and the Massachusetts Turnpike Authority. Five minutes later the director of the Massachusetts Office of Homeland Security and FBI inspectors arrived. By ten o'clock inspectors had arrived from the National Transportation Safety Board, The National

Highway Traffic Safety Administration, the National Safety Council, the Highway Loss Data Institute, and the Insurance Institute for Highway Safety.

Then came representatives from the Motor Vehicle Manufacturers Association, the Department of Transportation, the Center for Auto Safety, the Highway Users' Federation, the American Association of State Highway and Transportation Officials, the National Motorist Association, and the Federal Highway Administration Traffic Systems Division. A representative for the Senate Chairman of the Public Works and Transportation Committee showed up with two CIA agents.

By noon, representatives had arrived from the EPA's Office of Mobile Sources and from California's Program for Advanced Technology for the Highway, Path One. Then Clappsaddle's buddy, a retired lieutenant general, who now heads the National System of Interstate and Defense Highways showed up with his friend, the representative from the National Automotive Center at the U.S. Army's Tank-Automotive Command.

There were representatives from the Center for Auto Safety, the Urban Policy Research Institute, and the Italian Argo Project, which they said had been inspired by the Program for European Traffic with Highest Efficiency and Unprecedented Safety, known as Prometheus. Two men presented identification with the Security & Exchange Commission. Representatives from the Owner/Operator Independent Trucking Association, the American Trucking Association, and the Army Corps of Engineers arrived at the same time. During the next half hour representatives arrived from the American Association of State Highway and Transportation Officials, the Texas Transportation Institute, the ENO Foundation for Transportation, and The Intelligent Vehicle Highway Systems Program.

By mid-afternoon, investigators had shown up from the National Council on Public Works Improvement, the Program for Advanced Technology for the Highway, the North Carolina Highway Safety

Research Center, the Transportation Research Board and from the National Academy of Sciences. One of the senators on the Transportation Subcommittee of the Senate Committee on the Environment sent staffers. A fleet of limousines arrived with a team from Detroit representing the big three auto manufacturers. Two women had said they were looking to investigate compliance with the Transportation Equity Act for the 21$^{st}$ Century, Public Law 105-178.

Representatives arrived on behalf of Physicians for Automotive Safety, The American Association of Automotive Medicine, The National Association of Minority Contractors, the New York Thruway Authority, the Highway Trust Fund, the Interstate Highway System, the American Road and Transportation Builders Association, The Bureau of Motor Carrier Safety, The American Automobile Association, Owner-Operators Independent Drivers Association of America. The Chairman of the Senate Subcommittee On Water Resources, Highways and Infrastructure arrived with staffers. The spokesman for a team with the National Rifle Association informed that they were there to rule out the possibility that the accidents had been caused by hunters or snipers.

More than 300 had inspected the crash site, all taking notes, and all, presumably, preparing reports. Norwocki wonders if any of them would share their reports, integrate their independent findings. Unlikely, since no one was in charge.

# 22

## MONDAY, MAY 26

*New Burford*

After the morning's parade, speeches, prayers, and rifle volleys, the old, respectfully groomed Burying Ground is quiet and colorful, its headstones and monuments decorated with crepe paper poppies, bouquets of lilacs and peonies, wreaths of red, white and blue carnations, and American flags waving from thin sticks planted in the grass. In the treetops, crows cryptically call to each other.

Hunter walks the rows in the oldest section, reading names, connecting to symbols and artwork carved hundreds of years ago—winged souls, hearts, thistles, goblets, wilting tulips, hourglasses and gourds shaped like breasts. Many of the words they had chosen are illegible with time. Those still legible are of love and faith; some beautiful, some obscure and mysterious.

Absorbed in thought, Hunter walks through an arched opening in the perfectly trimmed boxwood hedge and enters a section of more substantial headstones, dating from tha early twentieth century. A gray haired woman in a navy blue and white polka dotted dress, is seated on a granite bench, a straw hat on her lap, an orange crepe paper poppy pinned to its navy ribbon. As he turns, respecting her privacy, she calls him by name.

"I'm AnnaBelle Jordan."

"Oh, yes," he says, remembering well her tactful sense of timing at the Farrands' dinner party, the first evening with Jean.

Straight away, she asks, "You weren't here for the ceremony this morning?"

"Uh, no. I had a conflict."

"Conflict. Yes. I had a conflict, too. That's why I'm here now." She pauses. "It's just awful what happened to you and your property at ground zero, as we say these days. And a shame, a terrible shame what's happened in this town."

"But unavoidable, I guess."

"The Widow Pell had a hunch that highway was destined for these parts. She tried to pin down General Clappsaddle, you recall. I never thought I'd see the day when the wool got pulled over Emma Pell's eyes. But she's gettin' on." She shakes her head. "It's not good. The Widow Pell gets hoodwinked and the rest of the town doesn't know what hit it, until it's too late. These accidents never should have happened."

"Who hoodwinked the Widow Pell?"

"Politicians, top to bottom."

"The town council?"

"Ay-yuh. And the ones who told them what to do."

"Who's that?"

She puts on the straw hat, shading her eyes from the slanting, afternoon sun and looks him in the eye.

"You have my word," he says. "I won't betray your confidence."

"Sit down here." She pats the bench and when he's settled beside her says softly, "I've heard the generals talking. Farrand, Clappsaddle, others come by Brass House. They talk about a lot of things they'd never discuss outside their circle. You can be sure they don't know I'm listening." She looks at him for reassurance.

"They'll never know. Promise."

"The generals don't like what's going on. Not one bit. They'd give their eyeteeth to upset the politicians' applecart just long enough to straighten things out but they can't do that 'cause they got where they are by climbing into that applecart. Makes 'em mighty frustrated these days. Especially the one they call the Renegade. Sad thing is, the generals get all fired up about fixing things when they talk together, and that's as far as it ever goes."

"Guess they aren't much different from the rest of us."

"You got a point." She pauses, cupping her hand over her mouth as if a breeze might broadcast her disclosure. "General Clappsaddle got orders from the governor, who is in cahoots with Senator Donnelley. The town council did the governor's bidding. He charmed them, possibly bought them. That part's vague." She hesitates. "I never told you any of this."

"You've told me nothing."

She folds her hands. "You know, there was a time when people around here used to talk and talk and get all riled up about everything under the sun. That's how we worked things out. Not now. These days, if something's really important, we worry for a bit. Maybe get angry for a while. Maybe. Then we forget it. This is not a big town. We all should know what's going on. But we don't."

"You sure seem to know what's going on."

"'Cause I'm a nosey old lady, but I don't dare talk to anyone about what I know."

"You're talking now to me."

"Yes, here in the Burying Ground, I'm speaking my mind to somebody who's seeing the same view."

The raucous crows take flight into the woods. "What would it take to get people involved, riled up again? "

"If not this highway, I don't know what could do it." She gestures toward a headstone. "There's my George."

"A Tuskegee Airman!"

"And proud he was of it. He used to say that when you visit here on Decoration Day you're paying respects to everyone who ever served his country, no matter where they were laid to rest. I couldn't bring myself to follow the parade here today. But I had to come visit today."

"I agree with George. And I think I pretty much know how you feel."

She sits taller, straightening her shoulders. "You know, right after nine-eleven people were singing *America the Beautiful* on TV, for a little while anyway. Do you know the second verse?"

He shakes is head.

"*O beautiful for heroes proved in liberating strife, who more than self their country loved, and mercy more than life! America! God mend thine ev'ry flaw, confirm thy soul in self-control, thy liberty in law.* We all ought to sing that before our town meeting. Whistling's fine, but I think it's time we add some words to our music."

"At the next meeting, why don't you suggest we all sing, or at least recite it? I'll second your motion," he says, a glaze in his eyes.

"How about the other way around. You propose it. I'll second it. No one would vote against it."

Smiling, he extends his hand in agreement.

"You should run for town moderator," she says, placing her hand on his shoulder.

He laughs. "A Damnewyorker as moderator?"

"You're eligible. Think about it. You'd have my vote. And you'd be surprised how many others would support you, not least among them, I happen to know, the Widow Pell."

They sit in silence for a while.

# 23

*New York City*

J ack Weinstein feels heavy and old, like a fossil, which is what Lola, the ad coordinator calls him. He can't remember when he last went for a two-hour, two-martini lunch at Palm Two. But after the long, harrowing weekend, he needed a strong dose of that old-fashioned, mid-day remedy to ease his hyper-sense of vulnerability and mortality. All morning, everyone in the department was talking about the disaster, suspecting terrorism, making him feel even more spooked about the possibility that, if things had gone as planned, he would now be stretched out in Riverside Memorial Chapel. Amy too. It was her idea to set their departure time, aiming to be the first to drive on the new highway, and she was furious when a client crisis kept her in the office until seven o'clock, ribbon-cutting time on I-51.

Crossing Lexington Avenue, he feels even more vulnerable than he did before lunch. The irony is that Amy had convinced him to buy with her the place in Stockbridge so they'd have a refuge. She had planned where they would meet to go there in the event of a terrorist attack, mapped alternate routes out of the city, bought two collapsible bicycles, even an inflatable raft. For him, the house was a first step toward realizing his dream of living and working in a gentler town, as gentle as a martini haze. And as soon as he figures out how to make enough money there to meet overheads and pay off the five advanced degrees earned by his four kids from three defunct marriages, he will stay there, in the Berkshires, in their sanctuary. Which is why he had called his old client buddy, asking him to lunch at Palm Two for reassurance: Terrorists don't hit on bucolic, non-sectarian sanctuaries. Do they?

He shouldn't have had the steak, or the second martini. His mind is spinning backwards. Damn martinis. His boss introduced them almost thirty years ago, took him to lunch at the Algonquin on his first day, ordered martinis, and lectured him about the Roundtable writers who gathered there in the twenties and thirties and about the separation of editorial and advertising powers at the *Trib*. Jack was a quick study. He had ordered his third martini with the aplomb of his boss, "Straight up with no garbage." Just about as quickly, he had acquired his boss's conflicted sentiments about editorial staffers, those production line laborers who create and cobble product, but, except for the stars, make lousy wages, inversely proportional to the influence and respect they wield and command. The ad staff gets none of their stature but with responsibility for the bottom line, the sine qua non, their inferiority is salved by substantially higher remuneration and, for a lot of years, fat expense accounts. When did things start changing? Looking back, he nearly bumps into an overflowing trash receptacle in front of his building. Vowing to go up to the Berkshires some weekend and stay, phoning in his resignation, he goes inside, back to his office.

"Jack, oh mah-gawd, Fossil!" Lola rushes at him, her enormous bust bouncing ahead of her spindly frame as she waves a fistful of yellow message slips over her head of thick bright red curls. In her other hand is a tightly clutched pack or cigarettes. "You're wanted in the front office, like an hour ago. Get your ass in there. Last call was ten minutes ago." She gives him the slips, knocks a single cigarette up from a new pack, and takes it into her mouth. "I'm going for a smoke."

Circulation is still slipping, but this quarter's ad sales are trending up in some categories, and at least holding in the rest. Jack figures he's about to get the old "it's time to go the extra ten yards" speech. Or maybe an edit announcement is in the works—hirings, firings, another new section, which means he has to make yet another round of phone calls, personal calls, and lunches with clients to inform them before the news hits the trade papers. God, he is sick of it all.

Approaching the office, he cranes his neck to be sure his bleary eyes aren't playing tricks on him. Edgar Posthorn, the obits editor, and Leslie Berger, editor of the Leisure section are meeting together with the associate publisher. That combo is peculiar enough, but why the hell is he getting called into this meeting?

"Come on in, Jack. Close the door behind you, and have a seat." The senior vice president and associate publisher for advertising is semi-reclined in his ergonomic chair, buttressing himself with the soles of his shoes at the edge of the desk. "Edgar, take it from beginning, give Jack the gist of it."

Edgar Posthorn pushes his half-glasses up into his thinning hair and grimaces slightly. He doesn't like Jack Weinstein. He never had to. He is clearly uncomfortable, hemming and hawing.

"Take it easy, Edgar." The shoes drop to the floor, the chair springs upright, "Jack, this tragedy Friday night, up your way, took the lives of nearly two hundred New Yorkers. It could kill us too, certainly pile more straw on the camel's back."

"What are you saying?" Leslie snipes.

"Point blank, we created a monster with the 9/11 obits. Set a precedent. It was the right thing to do. But do you want to take a wild, rectal-reach guess at the edit lineage, the paper and ink consumed on mass tragedy obits—with virtually no direct ad support? Now we have another disaster on our hands, and it too will wreak havoc on the bottom line. However, we've come up with a tourniquet to stop such hemorrhaging." He unscrews the cap from a bottle of Vintage water, and takes a swig. "We're envisioning a new special section for Edgar, here. Mourning Times."

"That's mourning with a 'u'?" Jack asks.

"That's right, Jack," says Leslie, scrunching her face. "No confusion on that in print."

The briefing continues. "The concept, with mock-up, has actually been on the ice for years, ever since we repackaged the then so-called society pages into Trends. Edgar, show Jack the layout and design options. One of them's pretty nifty. It's a rubbing from an old tombstone. An angel head or demon head. Whatever. It's great for this weekend's Massachusetts disaster but ultimately we'll need to go with something more generic.

Posthorn slides his glasses onto his nose and flips through sheets of designs. "I'm having trouble with this."

"Me too," says Leslie who is on the edge of her chair, legs crossed, the upper one kicking with impatience. "If you want my opinion, this whole concept sucks. Totally inappropriate."

"Hold on. Don't get ahead of yourselves. It needs tweaking. But with tasteful graphics, this is the kind of thing that we could submit for design awards. There will be separate guidelines for this ad category, which we'll call condolence advertising and we'll refuse ads that are inappropriate. What do you say, Jack?"

"You want my opinion?" Jack pauses, thinking through what he's supposed to say. "Promoted in the right way, you know, *appropriately*, you'll get ads from the companies the deceased worked for, their professional associations, that kind of thing. The business press does this all the time."

"You're right on it, Jack."

Edgar gets to his feet. "If you all don't need me any more, I've got a lot of work to do."

"Likewise," says Leslie. "And this is now way off my turf."

The associate publisher dismisses them. "Go. But, Edgar, leave those designs here with me." As they dash out, he leans back into his chair, hands clasped behind his head. "Jack, that accident was near your place up there."

It suddenly occurs to Jack, "Are you expecting me to sell ads into the obits from last weekend's disaster?

"No. I've got something else to discuss with you." He pops forward, and tightly holds his hands against his chest. "Jack, it's tough, very tough for me to do this, but I'm about to make you happier than a pig in shit."

"I'm listening." Jack is leery, half expecting to hear that he is about to be replaced by a well-connected GenX-er.

"We are doing a special Leisure section devoted entirely to Berkshires tourism. The new highway, as you know, was to have been a major economic stimulus and boost tourism, but instead of stimulus, they get set-back. The tragedy will hit tourism hard up there."

"Until the highway reopens."

"There's no telling when that'll happen. So we're going to give them a business boost with this big Leisure section on June 27, a week before the Fourth of July weekend. "This is your baby, Jack. Go on up and sell the pants off it. Real estate, resorts, inns, spas, restaurants, galleries, music festivals, you name it. Hell, I don't have to tell you what to do."

"You got it," Jack grins.

"Make whatever deals are necessary. I'm counting on you to pump up some ad lineage with this. So give me your projection by the end of the day, and now get out of here."

Jack goes back to his office, stuffs his briefcase with media kits, and calls Amy. For two and a half lovely weeks, he will be living and working in the Berkshires.

# 24

*New Burford*

The night it happens all over again, Jean is soaking in the clawfoot tub after a day of rehearsing. "What's wrong? You've got that look on your face," she says when Hunter, clenching a bag of baby carrots in his teeth, pokes his head into the steam filled bathroom. He eyes the window, then abruptly withdraws, shutting the door. She turns off the faucet with her toe, listens, then calls out, "Hunter, what's going on?" She knows he's right there. "Hunter?"

He opens the door and comes in holding a glass of wine, which he places with the carrots on a footstool beside the tub. "I thought I heard something out there. Like traffic." He goes to the window, removes the shutters propped on the sill, ready for installation, sets them on the floor, and peers through the escaping steam into total darkness. Nothing.

"No way can there be traffic," she says, and takes a sip of wine. "There's been no announcement. Come join me." He kisses her on the forehead, undresses, and gets into the tub. Sensing his preoccupation, she hands him the glass and, pushing her feet against his legs, sits up. "Did it bother you? Seeing me dance with Nelson?"

"Bother me? You were fantastic. Exquisite. Dazzling. Even beyond what I expected, or could have imagined." He did not expect to see her in a hot *pas de deux* with the younger, adonis-ly muscled guy she once lived with. He could watch just so much, averting his eyes, reminding himself that it's her business.

"I'm not looking for more compliments. Just want to know if it bothered you."

Drinking from the glass, his mind's eye replayed the duet. "Well—I guess at times I felt something other than, shall we say, pure appreciation for the art of dance."

"Like?"

"Like—You knew this was going to happen."

"That's why I wanted you to come to the rehearsal. So tell me."

"Tell you what? You want to hear that I got aroused?"

She grins.

"It was actually pretty strange, sitting in a dark theater, an audience of one, watching you and some dude climbing and sliding all over each other." He half smiles.

"I just want to be sure you understand that whatever it may look like, it's a totally professional thing. Nothing more."

"Understood. And it was a pleasure to meet this guy while the two of you were still panting, skin glowing with perspiration as if you had just achieved multiple simultaneous orgasms."

"Whoa—! You were jealous!"

"Not at all! Well—. Who am I kidding? But it wasn't exactly ordinary, garden-variety jealousy. It was like watching your wife making love to another man while somehow knowing you don't have grounds to get upset about it. "

"Like watching your wife?"

"That's not a stretch."

"That's how you think of me?"

"I've as much as said that a thousand times."

"As much as said it?"

"I love you, Jean."

"I love you, too, but—"

"But—?"

She looks down at the water, then back up at him. "Hunter, will you marry me?"

"You're proposing?" He shakes his head. "Unacceptable," he smiles. "It's only proper that I propose marriage to you."

She beams. "So?"

"So will you marry me, Jean?"

Water splashes out of the tub as she throws her arms around his neck. "Yes!"

He kisses her. "You can live with all my eccentricities, my hypersensitivities to weird noises and all that?"

"I already do," she says with joyous confidence.

"Let's get out of this tub and celebrate." He reaches for two bath towels and drapes one around her, pauses, and asks, "Show me how Nelson lifts you? So I can experience one of those delicious slides."

She laughs, delighted. The next moment, he is lifting her high, her buttocks in his hands, and slowly lowers her, easing her body down across his face, sliding her against his chest, her breasts against his forehead.

Suddenly, screeching brakes shatter the moment. Crash. Her feet touch the floor. Crash. In horror, they gape out the window into the darkness. Screech—crash. Crash. Hunter pulls Jean from the window and hits the light switch. Screeech, screech—smash. In the dark, the persistent monstrous cacophony overwhelming their sensitivities, they hold each other for a moment, trembling, knowing.

"Throw on some clothes," he says picking up his. "Let's go straight to your house. I'll call Turbo from the car."

Doc Barnes picks up the call on his new police band radio, the only purchase he made after depositing the $100,000 in a Boston bank. With a crowbar strapped to his medical bag, he heads over to the old Hamilton house, expecting that Barnhill would again rig up the plank to the wall. Halfway up the driveway, he is taken aback. The house is dark. He parks, gets out and rings the bell. No answer. He tries the other doors, then goes to the barn. "Barnhill?" He snoops about, and sees a sixteen-inch chain saw. It's razor sharp and full of fuel. Perfect.

Chain saw in one hand and medical bag with crowbar in the other, he strikes out for the wall, and finds a spot well covered by dense growth of weeds and bushes. He pulls the choke and yanks the starter cord, once, twice, several times. It coughs, refusing to turn over. One more time he works the choke and tugs on the cord. The machine roars, raring to cut, and he guides it along an invisible line from the base of the wall, up a few feet, over, back down. Plop, a hatch opens. He doesn't need Barnhill for access but how will he transport the harvest without the militia?

Racking his brain, he checks the time. About a mile down the road is Colonial Nursery where they keep, out front, their fleet of little red Radio Flyer wagons. He trots back to his car and speeds to the nursery, praying they haven't locked up the wagons. Pulling into Colonial's parking lot, he sees them lined up, no chains, no locks. He pops open his trunk, grabs two, and races back to the hole in the wall.

Forty-five minutes later, Ralph Barnes, MD, returns to his mobile home, this time leaving the harvest in the car. Secured in the screen door is a folded sheet of paper with his name scrawled on it. He goes inside and unfolds it, as Incision frantically greets him. "Thursday, 9:15 pm. Stopped by for you. Another accident on I-51. Same place. Hoping you're already there. Turbo."

Sweating profusely, he fills a glass with bourbon, gulps half of it and drops into his lounge chair. It feels like a mental hologram. The kick off of a holiday weekend. Out-of-state cars packed with Igloo Playmates, Colemans and Cool Baby coolers. He reaches for the phone, presses 1-800-ORG-SHOW and when the recording begins, presses 1 through 9.

"Welcome to *Transplant Time*. It must be you, Doctor Ralph!"

He recognizes Joyce's voice.

# 25

*Boston*

Governor Brewster Pease is awakened at four in the morning by a phone call from Bruno Fitzsimmons, the State Director of Highways. Another massive accident—another chain reaction collision—on I-51. The same place. His heart pounding, Brewster stretches out between the sheets, dropping his head on the pillow, and stares into the darkness as the pounding subsides. Betsy stirs, and rolls over with a grunt. He gets up and heads into the shower.

At five o'clock a.m., the governor is downstairs in his office at his desk. Confounded. The highway was to have been one of his greatest achievements. How could this happen? How could it backfire? Twice! He can't downplay this kind of carnage. But he must finesse it. Somehow use the crisis to demonstrate leadership. How? In the morning light he stews to no avail.

"Good morning, Governor." Cassler comes in, sits on the other side of the desk, directly facing the glowering Brewster Pease. "Déjà vu, eh?" Cassler quips, then leans forward and, slapping the desk avows, "This time we take action."

Pease straightens. "You're damn right. This is a massive fuck up. What's the spin? Terrorism. It might have been an attack."

"You want people worrying about terrorists in western Massachusetts? No indications of fowl play surfaced from the last wreckage, and they won't find any this time, either. It's the fucking Curve, Brew. The Curve's the core problem but not the problem you've got to address." He withdraws a single sheet of paper from a leather portfolio.

"What are you proposing?"

"This is a draft of your statement. It reads, I speak to you in the shadow of another terrible tragedy. Under my authorization, the National Guard is working with state and local police, firemen and rescue teams at the disaster site. To the victims and their families, to everyone who is suffering loss, I offer my deepest sympathy, prayers, blah, blah. While we are fortunate to live in Massachusetts under an umbrella of security that grants us peace of mind in our daily lives, this accident is another jarring reminder of our vulnerability.

"A mission has been placed squarely on my shoulders. This morning I renew my commitment to you. As your steward of the public trust, as leader of the Commonwealth, I will continue to provide the strategic direction, tools, and aggressive support needed to secure highway safety on our highways.

"Last month, I launched a major investigation, assembling eighteen action teams of top experts who conducted exhaustive research and comprehensive highway risk analyses. The teams submitted risk abatement recommendations, which were implemented with zero tolerance. Much work was done. Much work remains.

"I am now launching the Second Stage Investigation. I am assembling twenty-four action teams of experts to evaluate and analyze all challenges to accident prevention and safety protection and to solve problems associated with the widest range of highway hazards. The findings of the Second Stage Investigation will be presented at a major conference. Their solutions will be aggressively implemented in this state and demonstrated as a model to the rest of the nation.

"My goal is to maximize highway safety and security. I will proceed toward that goal with steady focus and determination. I am confident we will make every adjustment required to achieve that goal, serving the mission of assuring safety and peace of mind for our families, for our fellow citizens, for all who travel our highways. Thank you very much."

Pease runs his fingers along the wood grain of his desk. "You know, John, my great-great-great grandmother served tea on this table to General Howe. Murray Hill. Manhattan. Allowing General Washington to escape through Harlem Heights and save the Republic."

Cassler tugs at his earlobe, then leans his elbow on the desk. "Brewster, this is the only way to handle this fiasco."

"Tell me, John." The governor is displeased that Cassler didn't comment on the genealogical significance of his desk. "About this conference."

"A symposium on highway safety. Scheduled as soon as possible. But we don't limit the focus to these accidents. The scope has to be larger. Comprehensive. National. Highway safety as a national issue. The time is right for this. People feel impotent. They need an outlet, a tangible way to perceive that something concrete is being done to make things safer. Effectively, we shift the focus away from I-51 and Massachusetts to a national frame. The entire country collectively will share our load."

"Making this a national disaster, not Massachusetts-specific," Pease says looking out the window at the perfectly tended garden, a smaller version of The Orangerie at Versailles.

"Exactly." Cassler pauses. "It's your best shot, Governor."

"National media attention."

"Yes. We'll ratchet the program with some big names. Get a celebrity shrink to talk about road rage, its societal causes, that kind of thing. A glitzy babe will embrace the cause for cameras. You'll come across as the leader in time of national crisis."

Pease, still gazing out the window, interrupts. "John, is there a hereditary component in witchcraft?"

"Say again?"

Pease turns from the window and fixes his penetrating eyes on Cassler. "Witchcraft. Sorcery. Is it an inherited ability? Genetically linked?"

"Are you back on that rumor of eviscerated bodies?" Cassler gets to his feet, and waving his hands, emphatically declares, "That was a crazy rumor and we quashed it. People in crisis, in an emergency, sometimes get psychotic, and think they're seeing things that aren't there. None of that evisceration stuff happened. None of it."

Pease thoughtfully examines his fingernails.

"Brew, drop it, let's get back to the conference."

"John, calm down. Your conference proposal is excellent. It's the way to go." He slowly glides his hand over the highly polished desktop, then adds, "And I think the conference might be a good opportunity for me to personally extend an olive branch to a certain individual who just might be at the bottom of this mess."

*New York City*

Melanie Atwood kicks off her shoes and pours a glass of mineral water. She is exhausted, having just returned from an intensive vocal training session in London with a diaphragm specialist, the commander in charge of Trooping the Color for the Queen's Birthday Celebration, who is renowned for coaching rising stars of the Royal Opera. She drags her bag into the bedroom and drops onto her bed.

When she scheduled the training session, she had no idea that production for *Transplant Time* would continue, non-stop, after the bumper harvest of organs over Memorial Day weekend. In record time, they produced more than half the season's shows plus a two-hour special, putting them way ahead of schedule. Then, just as she was about to cancel the London trip, production went into hiatus. Organ donations dropped off, ceased, so she made it to a hugely important party on Martha's Vineyard, kept the London appointment, and contacted her agent to book a few promotional appearances.

Now, at last, despite exhaustion, she can bask in sweet success. Her show is a winner, a meteoric success. *Transplant Time* is number one in overnight ratings, a go for the fall season. Audiences love her. In the operating room, her commentaries and interviews with doctors are authoritative, professional. With patients she has a sensitive bedside manner. With families of recipients, she is supportive and compassionate. In the roulette sequence, she is enthusiastic and hopeful. In the biographical segments, she is warm and sincere. Melanie Atwood is star, a brand, and the brand is hot. The media are boosting and cashing in on her appeal. Her face has appeared on covers of dozens of magazines and her name in all the major gossip columns. She was even photographed with the vice President of the United States when she was named spokesperson for National Transplant Week. Not exactly her kind of guy but it was her first taste of political power. And she loved it.

A realist, she also has to reckon with *Transplant Time*'s one potential downside. After the initial surge in organ donations, the producers assumed that the trend would continue. It was expected that people would go for elective surgery, donating a lung, a piece of liver, just to get on the show. It's not happening. Which may mean curtains, the hook, cancellation. But she is not the problem. By every other standard, her show is a mega-success, and she'll flourish, regardless of organ donation trends, as long as she plays it right.

She rolls on her back and check phone messages:

First, Jason, her agent, had left word confirming the *Vanity Flair* cover story. She is to get back to him as soon as possible and schedule the photo session. "They see you in a string bikini made of surgical masks—two masks on the breasts and one on the crotch." The second message, also from Jason, confirms an interview and cover story for *Rogue* magazine.

She punches past several messages and hits DeCarlo's. "Melanie, love, another batch of organs came in. We're back here in scenic Pittsboro, taping surgery segments. Get yourself here, asap, but don't bust your ass. We'll tape you whenever you get here and drop you in later, which is what we're doing with the winners and the audience segments. A little fucked up, but it works. Anyway, same hotel. I'm in 803. See ya later."

The next message is from a John Cassler in the office of the Governor of Massachusetts, Brewster Pease. He says she will be receiving a letter from the governor requesting that she be a keynote speaker and the governor's personal guest at a national conference, July 24 and 25, in Barrington, Massachusetts. The subject: Safe Highways Save Lives. "We'll have in attendance members of official Washington as well as our state legislators and business leaders," says Cassler. "Our speech writers are available to you, and we've contacted your agent regarding the honorarium. Governor Pease feels that your participation would ensure the success of this important conference, and he will be most grateful if you accept. I'm calling in advance of his letter because of time constraints. We'll need your answer no later than Monday—"

She replays the message. Barrington. She once got lost in Barrington, driving back from Hunter's place. Brewster Pease, Governor of Massachusetts. He was in *Folks* for something not long ago, she recalls. She can't remember what he looks like but the possibilities are luscious—a personal guest of the governor in Hunter's back yard.

She picks up the phone to call Jason and leaves a message. "Jason, it's three o'clock-ish. I just got in and will be on my way to Pittsboro within the hour. Meanwhile, I got an interesting call, which I'm forwarding to you. It's from a John Cassler in the Massachusetts' Governor's office. He's calling about a conference in Barrington, end of July. He's already contacted you. Jason, I want to do this one. Get back to him and confirm. Tell them to write whatever they want me to say and get it to you in advance. The usual. I'll talk to you about the other stuff when I get to Pittsboro, and, uh, don't haggle with Cassler over the honorarium. Ciao, babe."

She punches into the network's car service and orders a pick-up in forty-five minutes.

# 26

*New Burford*

Emma's herb garden is at its peak, mounds of artemesia, santolina, lavender, lemon balm, and thyme, in geometrically arranged beds, yielding a heady fragrance within the high walls of wattle and rugosa roses. A tall frosty glass of iced raspberry tea tinkling in each hand, she elbows the iron latch on the gate, and Jenny pushes it open. "Let's call it quits, Jean," she says, setting the glasses on a small cedar table. "You've done a yeoman's job, clipping to beat the heat. I've got the harvest washed and drying on paper towels. This afternoon I'll do tinctures." She pinches off two sprigs of mint and adds one to each glass. Jenny settles down in the sweet woodruff.

Removing her gloves, Jean joins her at the table, leaning back in the weathered chair, stretching her legs in the mid-morning sunshine. "I can't imagine the Lawn Maintenance Organization taking care of your grounds."

"Nor can I. Certainly, no LMO worker will ever deadhead a single withered bloom here. Why, I 've never trusted anyone else but you to so much as pull a weed in this garden, let alone harvest. Not even Mr. Prichett. And as regards grounds maintenance, I've given it much thought. When Mr. Prichett told me he was about to take a supervisory job with the regional LMO, I realized I couldn't possibly train, retrain and supervise the no-doubt ever-changing crews that would be assigned to maintaining these grounds. Goodness sake, I'd sooner mow every blade of grass myself than let bureaucrats take charge here."

"But you can't opt out. It takes power equipment to mow all this lawn."

"Not to worry." Emma sips her iced tea and with a satisfied smile explains, "Mr. Prichett is not taking that LMO job. What's more, he got a so-called transitional waiver to use power equipment here through your wedding day. Everything will look perfectly beautiful. After that, what he can't manage manually will revert, in part, to meadow and Mother Nature's mowers will take care of the rest."

"Sheep?"

"Yep. We had sheep here when Waldo was alive. Goats, too. But you've got to watch goats. They've got lots of character and voracious appetites. Never satisfied with mere grazing, they keep going, defoliating, ground clearing if you don't stop them." The phone is ringing in her pocket. "Emma Peters Pell speaking. Hello, Doctor, I trust this is a social call. Certainly, you may have a catalog. That would be fine. Yes. See you in a bit, then."

Perplexed, Emma tucks the phone back into her pocket. "Hmm, maybe he's got ants. Doctor Barnes wants to buy Tupperware. Quite odd."

"That's not so odd. You only invite women to your parties so he's never had an opportunity to order any."

"You have a point."

"Was he ever married?"

"Oh yes. To a pretty New Burford girl, Norma Noddin. He and Norma were very bright kids. Phi Beta Kappa-, *magna cum laude*-bright. She became a pediatrician, and he, doncha know, became a fine surgeon. At Bay State Hospital he was renowned for open heart surgery."

"What happened?"

"Much. It was a storybook wedding. They had a baby girl. Poor little thing, no more than eighteen months old, she choked to death on an open safety pin."

"Ugh, that's horrible."

"Certainly was. So horrible the marriage died with the child. Norma left Ralph and Boston, joined the Peace Corps, went to Botswana and never returned. Ralph came back to New Burford, bought old Doctor Farley's practice, and moved into the house he grew up in, which he inherited when his parents died of botulism, from a swollen can of Bon Vivant lobster bisque soup. Four generations of Barnes had lived there. Then, wouldn't ya know, the house burned to the ground."

"This is just awful. Is that when he got the mobile home?"

"Yes. He could live in that darling house in town where he has his office but prefers that cramped, isolated mobile home."

"I wonder if he ever misses doing major surgery in a big city hospital."

"Who knows? But he once told me he was glad to be rid of the legal and insurance pressures at Bay State. I know he's still very adept with his scalpel, doing quite a bit of out-patient surgery, and I'd imagine he could walk into a surgical theater today and do a fine open heart operation. That is when he's steady." She pauses, watching the bees on the lavender. "Hmmph. I got another odd phone call this morning. From Brew Pease."

"Really!"

"He called about a conference in Barrington, the end of the month. Safe Highways Save Lives, something like that. Experts coming from all over the country. He wants me to be honorary chairperson."

"Rapprochement."

"I don't know. And, frankly, I don't get it. Why is he so ingratiating?"

"He wants you to bury the hatchet. Needs your support."

"For what? He got his highway."

"So what did you say?"

She purses her lips, restraining a big grin. "I said yes!" "Now, what do you think about those lamb's ears? They're getting a bit invasive, wouldn't you say?"

ॐ

Locked up for four days, the old Hamilton house is hot and stuffy. Hunter drops rolls of blueprints on the kitchen table, opens windows, and takes a beer from the refrigerator. The phone rings and continues beyond the count for intercept by the answering machine. There's been a power out. He picks it up.

"Hunter, I've been trying to reach you for days." It's Ben.

"We're staying at Jean's. It's been a little crazy here."

"Yeah, your old buddy at DFC told me Jean was at Jacob's Pillow. Good for her."

"DFC?"

"Your old agency. Dasher Ferguson Cohen. Epstein cut out just before Ruggie died."

"You know where he went?

"To another planet. Enrolled at General Seminary. So Dasher took on Ferguson and Cohen."

"Ferguson. If nothing else, he's resilient."

"Hey, he speaks well of you. Saw him at benefit dinner. Said he's trying to contact you. They're gearing up to sell the agency and want you back on retainer, for appearances. Said I'd give you the message. But the real reason I'm calling is because since I saw the *Trib's* Leisure section on the Berkshires, I've been thinking you should do a creative non-fiction article on those accidents. The paranoids here believe terrorists are behind it all. You could find out what the locals think, how they feel. Cobble it; an editor will clean it up. It would be a good way to get your name out there before the promotion of your Kennedy book. What do you say?"

"Uh, this is tough." He rubs the back of his neck. "Can't do it, Ben."

"Come off it. Just write up a few interviews. For you, it's a piece of cake."

He sighs. "Here's a thought. Come up here and we'll talk about it. It might even do you good to get out of the city for a few days."

He laughs. "Do I have to drive on that cursed highway to get there."

"You can't even take a wrong turn onto it, because it's closed."

"So tell me when and how to get there. I'll be there."

The powder blue Plymouth arrives at Emma's house just as Jean is getting into her car to leave. Doctor Barnes asks her how Hunter's doing, reminding her that his prescriptions can be renewed as needed. At the front door, he collects his thoughts before turning the hand-bell. Emma shows him into the living room, offers him a glass of iced tea, which he declines, and hands him the catalogue, opened to the container section.

"Would you like to see samples, Ralph? I have them in the pantry."

"Yes, thank you." He follows her down the center hall and through the kitchen, where the counters are covered with batches of herbs, and the table with dozens of tiny bottles and funnels, a liter of Popov vodka in their midst. "I see you're preparing your tinctures," he says. "New research confirms that barberry is good for the bowels."

"Here they are, Doctor." One side of the pantry is stocked with Tupperware samples—bowls, mugs, tumblers, serving and salad sets, kitchen utensils, Tuppertoys and a wide variety of containers. Emma senses his uneasiness. "Look it over, Ralph, and take your time. Here's an order form. I'll be on the terrace. Holler, if you have any questions."

He thanks her, and, when she's out of sight, reaches for his flask to soothe his flaring frustration. The energetic Joyce voice had called to inform him that *Transplant Time* nearly went into a crisis when a TTP surgeon mistook a pancreas for a liver. The doctor and the producer had blamed the packaging, so in the future the show will only accept organs individually packaged according to TTP's specifications.

Inserting his fist into containers, stretching his fingers to approximate organ sizes, he obsesses on the implication that he could mistake a pancreas for a liver. He selects containers, writes item numbers and quantities and tallies the order. It's steep, but the cost is re-billable. For that matter, he'll start charging TTP on a unit basis.

He emerges from the pantry and goes to the terrace, where Emma is working on her laptop.

"I'm all set, Emma. Here's my order."

She examines it. "Looks right. But it certainly is a lot of Tupperware."

"My Tupperware needs are great. I was initially interested in these air-tight containers for re-organizing my office, but they'll also be handy in my kitchen, slowing the onset of mold and mildew, preventing invasions of microorganisms, ants, bees, mice, and whatnot. How long before I get them?"

"About a week or so. Just a few days if you air ship."

"Air shipment, then. I want to get started." He smiles. "Well then, I'll be on my way, Emma. No, no, don't get up. Thank you so much." They shake hands, and he starts off down the fieldstone path to the driveway.

"Very odd," Emma says under her breath. Suddenly, she springs from the chair and chases after him. "Ralph, Oh Ralph—. Yoo-hoo. Yoo-hoo!"

He turns, and apprehensively retraces his steps.

"Ralph, I have a request. Governor Pease is convening a highway safety conference on the 29th and 30th, at the Millrace Inn, and I've agreed to be honorary chair of the event. Would you be willing to serve on my event committee? All that's required is that you show up for the opening and closing sessions. I'd be most grateful. What do you say?"

# 27

---

## WEDNESDAY, JULY 23

---

*Barrington, Massachusetts*

On Main and Church Streets, overhead banners proclaim, *Barrington—Proud Host of Safe Highways Save Lives.* Security teams are combing the Millrace Inn and environs. Mobile television production units and up-link trucks are rolling into position behind the inn. Conferees are checking in at the inn, a day early, and fanning out to explore the countryside. Melanie Atwood groupies are converging at the inn's main entrance, awaiting the arrival of their star, squealing whenever a blonde head emerges from an arriving limousine. Their noise reaches the pressroom where Lieutenant Colonel Marvin Norwocki is securing coaxial lines with gaffer's tape. He goes to investigate.

Pushing the door into the crowd, the screaming swells, "It's Elvin! Elvin's here!"

Norwocki orders them to step aside but they continue pressing toward him, chanting, Elvin, Elvin! "Silence" he shouts, "I am Lieutenant Colonel Marvin P. Norwocki, Massachusetts Army National Guard, in charge of logistics for Safe Highways Save Lives." They boo and groan.

Norwocki quickly ascertains that the crowd has mistaken him for Melanie Atwood's hairdresser, who always arrives in advance of his client to check the tap water's pH rating and always wears camouflage, the name of his unisex cosmetic line.

Although flummoxed at having been mistaken for a hairdresser, he comes up with a tactic for managing the crowd. "Listen up," he shouts. "I'm informed that an advance man will select Atwood's entrance and, as the officer in charge of logistics for this conference, I can tell you that the only entrance he will not choose is the main entrance, which, by state and local fire laws, is disallowed to crowd-attracting celebrities. I therefore suggest you split up, cover the other entrances."

They boo, mouthing a few obscenities, but obediently split up.

Norwocki follows a splinter group to the back terrace, then veers off, across the lawn, to a yellow and white striped tent, his headquarters. It is his duty to anticipate and supply conference needs, great and small—video systems, bleachers, and Portosans, platforms, signage, shuttle buses. When registration exceeded the inn's conference capacity, he booked Barrington High's auditorium and the American Legion Hall, rented LED video panels, 32" monitors and plasma displays, and supervised closed circuit television hook-ups.

He picks up a clipboard, makes a notation, then reviews the multicolored schematic laid out on five easels: status charts of provisions for two-day's of lectures, panel discussions, luncheons, refreshment breaks, and workshops concluding with auto exhibitions on the Curve. The closing cocktail party and dinner, sponsored by the Department of Tourism, is not his responsibility. Tourism has handled lodging arrangements, bumping reservations with make-good offers to book the Millrace Inn for VIPs, The Valley Resort and Spa for the media, and for the conferees scores of hotels, inns, and bed and breakfasts within a thirty-mile radius of Barrington. When Tourism came up short on lodging, he contacted General Farrand, president of Western Massachusetts Military Academy in New Burford, who came up with a Rusticator's package at $36 a night, including fitness breakfast, optional sunrise hike, and an authentic reveille with bugle call. In all, more than eight hundred are registered for the conference, plus media.

Standing back to survey the situation detailed on his easels, he takes a highlighter and circles the final two events. A snag. After the driving exhibition at the Curve, conferees will make a mass exodus, returning to their lodgings to change for dinner. They'll need extra buses for at least an hour, an unforeseen expense that will bring costs over budget. If he can slow the flow between these events, the additional buses won't be necessary and he'll accomplish mission under budget. He highlights "cocktail hour," draws a line between the inn and the Curve, and ponders. It can be done by setting up two cocktail tents—one at the Curve, the other at the Millrace Inn. Most conferees will gladly wait if offered a free cocktail, and the cost of drinks and tents can be charged to the Department of Tourism.

He goes to his laptop, checks the 3-D USGS topo maps, then switches into the land modeling CAD program which displays the U-shaped wall, highway and field with elevations. He adds the tent behind the bleachers. That leaves no room, whatsoever, for parking. The field stops at the woods, a solid, arbitrary line. Where the hell will he put the VIP-limos, the buses, and a hundred cars? Possibly more. He puts on his helmet. A-ha! Chainsaws and a bulldozer will do it. But how will he get a bulldozer through the horrendous traffic? There's only one way. He thrusts his hand into his ACU jacket and, with a flourish, pulls out his phone. "Thornton?"

"Hooooah!" The voice bellows on the other end.

"Listen up, Thornton. Get on the net, round up some of your boys. Tomorrow morning you're going to hitch a front-end loader to a Chinook and do some combat engineering."

"Sir, yes, sir."

"You're mission is to airlift that thing into New Burford. Come in over the new highway, looking for the U-curve. There will be bleachers there, and a tent, yellow and white striped. Set it down right there. You're going to open up that field, push it into the woods. Take trees as necessary to achieve the objective, which is to level the ground for a parking lot that'll hold sixteen buses and a hundred fifty cars. The space is to be cleared by tomorrow, 1200 hours. Is that understood?"

"Sir, yes, sir!"

" 'Make your way by unexpected routes,'" he quotes Sun Tzu.

"What's that, Sir?"

"Carry on, Sergeant Major. Out!" Norwocki puffs up his chest, sucking in his gut, and tips his helmet.

The Jack Russell terrier lunges against the window screen, yapping at the Federal Express deliveryman who is pounding on the door of the mobile home. He waits, hearing from within a television audience wildly applauding. He climbs onto a dilapidated lawn chair to peer inside. Through the screen he sees three television sets showing a blindfolded chef decorating a cake.

He gets off the chair and calls out, "Doctor Barnes. Doctor Ralph Barnes." The terrier presses against the screen, growling, showing its teeth. The deliveryman gives the finger to the dog, and again pounds on the door, setting off wild barking. No response. This is the third time he has driven up the long, rutted driveway at the designated time, only to find the same vicious dog, the same old powder blue Plymouth with MD plates, and no one to sign for the delivery.

Two failed attempts are not uncommon, even understandable when a busy doctor is the recipient. But a third time is inexcusable, especially for an extraordinarily large order like this. The dog has quieted, evidently as worn out as he is by this exercise. He unloads the truck, stacking the boxes in front of the door, and drives away in a cloud of dust.

An hour later Ralph regains consciousness. Opening the door for Incision, he shrinks back, shielding his face with his arm. A wall of light brown boxes looms like an ominous psychotic vision. He squints at them, and picks up the box nearest him. The Tupperware!

He hadn't considered the total volume. Where would he store them? Contemplating the problem, he makes a pot of strong coffee. Of course! Tupperware is impervious to natural elements, so he can stash them under his Leisurama home, neatly arranged by size, with labels affixed for efficient packing. Suddenly, it all feels very complicated. He dumps the coffee, pours vodka into a tall glass and consults his other self, the one who feels good about things. Maybe he should retire soon and move away—where it's warmer and life is simpler. He feels lonely.

॰॰

Constable Turbo Bull drags a barrier across eastbound Route 22 and sets up a sign— ROAD CLOSED—with flashing amber lights. Traffic had been building all morning— conferees determined to get an advance look at the fatal Curve—giving him no other recourse but to close the road. He eases into the Volkswagen Super Beetle squad car, contacts Colonial Cable, and initiates a crawler bulletin: Due to high-risk traffic conditions, residents are instructed to redirect back to Barrington anyone asking for directions to the accident scene.

A navy blue Lincoln town car pulls alongside the squad car. The driver, in white short-sleeved shirt, pencil-thin neck tie and wrap sunglasses asks for directions to the Barnhill residence.

"You can't get there from here," says Turbo. "You've got to go back to Barrington."

The darkened back window lowers, revealing Melanie's bright blonde mane and beguiling face. "Hello, officer. Do you know the old Hamilton house? That's what they used to call it."

"Hmmm, the old Hamilton house, you say."

"Actually it's the Barnhill house. I'm looking for Hunter Barnhill. The house is near here. But I don't remember where to turn and I'd call but the cell connection keeps fading."

He knows that face. "You're that woman from *Transplant Time.*"

"Melanie Atwood. I'm stopping here on my way to the highway conference. Governor Pease invited me to speak."

"It would be a pleasure to get you oriented, Miss Atwood. I'll personally escort you to the old Barnhill house." He raps at the driver's window. "Follow me."

At precisely the speed limit, the Volkswagen squad car leads the Lincoln to the driveway, where Turbo thrusts his large arm out the window, pointing. The Lincoln turns, the squad car peels onward into town. His heavy foot to the gas pedal, Turbo is itching to tell someone about his exchange with Melanie Atwood. But he can't. Rumors would fly if the word got out that she and Barnhill are friends, and that she visits the house. Speedy. He can tell Speedy.

Melanie waits in the driveway. It was dark when she was here in 2001, and she barely remembers the house, which is actually fairly large but plain and old or, as he used to say, charming and unpretentious. But why would he install this gawdawful humongous wall, and so close to his house? Maybe it keeps deer out of his precious garden. In the Hamptons, the deer fences are barely visible and very tasteful. This is a monstrosity, and so un-Hunter. If only he had settled in the Hamptons. Or Connecticut. She begins to feel wistful, impatient, depressed, angry. It's been ten minutes. She takes a business card from her purse, writes a note on the back, reads it, rips it up, writes another, reads it, reconsiders, and rips it up, too. The Lincoln takes off, turning right at the end of the driveway while, from the left, the Rover arrives.

Hunter and Jean haven't stayed at the old Hamilton house since the crash on July 3, but because their anxiety about the highway has been easing as the house-moving date approaches and as Jean's house won't comfortably accommodate Ben's visit, they're returning, at least for the long weekend. Having just met with the architect to sign off on the plans, they unroll the renderings on the kitchen table and look them over again, envisioning every perfect detail. The foundation is to be poured next week. Then, after the house is moved construction will begin on new bathrooms, a new kitchen, and a solarium.

Against a background of silence, the steady ticking of the old pendulum clock lulls Jean into delicious drowsiness. Succumbing, she goes upstairs to nap. Freddie tags along, jumps on the bed, and nestles against her.

An hour later the peace is disturbed. On the other side of the wall, a fleet of buzzing power mowers begin sheering the field, a generator revs up, planks dragged from a truck plunk into stacks, air hammers pop. Awakened, Jean pulls back the curtain. "Oh, no," she gasps. A crew is setting up bleachers and a large yellow and white striped tent on the other side of highway, facing the Curve, the wall and the house. Freddie at her heels, she goes to tell Hunter who is still at the table, sound asleep, head cushioned on arms folded over the *Berkshire Crier*. She kisses his forehead. He stirs then straightens, on edge. "What the hell are they doing out there?"

"They're setting up bleachers and a huge party tent inside the curve. Come upstairs." Freddie scampers along with them. "The bleachers will face this way," she says, drawing the curtain from the window. "All those people are going to be looking straight at us. And Ben's going to be here!"

"Drop the curtain, Jean. I just read the program. There's only one event out there and that's Friday, late afternoon. We're not going to be here then, and, as we carefully planned, we're not going to be here the whole time that conference is going on—except to sleep and grab a cup of coffee in the morning. Please, don't worry about this."

She lets the curtain fall back over the window and sits on the edge of the bed. "But when Ben leaves, let's go back to my place."

"Absolutely." He sits next to her. "Look, this whole thing will be behind us very soon."

"I know. And this sweet old house is going to be wonderful." She brightens as he lies back, and pulls her on top of him. "But I'm having a tough time with this noise, with the whole scene out there, not knowing when the highway will reopen." She tucks her hands under his shoulders and closes her eyes, enjoying his touch. "How long before Ben arrives?"

"An hour. Probably longer. Plenty of time to take our minds off the bleachers and the hammering outside." He rolls her aside to get up and let Freddie out of the room.

Long ears aerodynamically slicked back, stubby tail like a propeller, Freddie bounds down the driveway to the red Jaguar sedan and chases it back to the house.

"So this is it!" Ben stretches, and throws his arms around Jean. "How are you, you sumptuous creature? Hunter, you don't deserve this woman. And, my God, this air! I may have to start smoking again just so I won't o.d. on oxygen." Freddie yaps and wiggles up to him. "Refrain from drooling on me, Freddie, and I'll give you goodies," he says, opening a gold bag of Doggie Biscotti and then opens the door to a back seat, loaded with Zabar's shopping bags.

"What's all this?" Hunter asks.

"Smoked salmon, oysters, sturgeon, paté, a couple of cheeses, Roquefort, boucheron, a wheel of brie—" He pays no attention as Jean, grinning, keeps repeating, I do not believe this. "—niçoise, cerignola, calamata olives, beautiful Spanish olive oil, extra virgin, balsamic vinegar," he rubs his hands, "a dozen bagels, rye bread, a sourdough baguette and last, but not least—," he goes to open the trunk. "Voila! A case of select red and white wines and a basket of perfectly ripe peaches, grapes, and a few mangoes.

"Did you think we'd starve you?" Jean asks.

"No, no. It's just that four days is a long time for me to survive a deprivation of my essential soul foods, and I figured you'd enjoy some treats imported from the big city. So I brought a supply for all of us."

"Looks great," Hunter laughs, clasping Ben's shoulder. "Now let's get all this and you inside and settled. Then we'll have a champagne aperitif here before dinner at Sparkie's, nine o'clock reservation."

"Sparkie's? What kind of a place is that?"

"The Berkshires' best. Sparkie was a cook in the Marines. On Marine Corps birthday, he always makes a huge Marine Corps emblem with pimentos and green olives set in cottage cheese."

Ben groans. "That's supposed to impress me?"

As they unload the car the phone rings several times, each time cutting off. Again, it rings. "It's an unidentified caller, and it's getting annoying," says Hunter, joining Jean in the kitchen where she's arranging Ben's smoked oysters on a plate. Ben comes downstairs, and Hunter pops the champagne cork. They toast his arrival in the Berkshires, friendship, and then announce their wedding plans. Jean takes Ben's arm, "Will you please honor us with your presence?"

Ben glowers. "You got to be kidding. I'm here not even ten minutes, after schlepping all the way from New York, and the two of you want a commitment from me to come all the way back in just a couple of weeks?" He pauses, eyebrows raised, calling his own bluff, and smiles warmly. "Mazeltov!" He kisses Jean and hugs Hunter. "I thought I saw a rock on your finger," he says to her. "Let me see that." She holds up her hand. "You did okay, kid." He raises his glass, "To the bride and groom. Every happiness," he toasts. "So who's marrying you?"

"Thanks to you," says Jean, "The Reverend Doctor Mrs. Tiffany Wallingford Epstein and Rabbi Feldman, the Epsteins' therapist."

"Thanks to me?"

Hunter explains. "You pointed us to Epstein, Ben, when you told me he was at the seminary. I called him to ask who might marry us and he suggested his new wife."

"He remarried?"

"Uh-huh. Two months ago. Tiffany Wallingford. A former model—we're talking Victoria Secret, *Jock Illustrated* bathing suit model. Turned public relations executive, then went to seminary, got ordained, got a Ph.D. in Biblical Studies, and now teaches Eschatology, I think he said, whatever, at General Theological Seminary. Epstein said when he met her, it was a coup de foudre. The image of an *JI* swimsuit body in a clerical collar drove him wild. He moved into seminary housing, quit DWE, started taking courses so he could communicate with her and a few months later they were married."

"No shit," Ben joshes, lasciviously twitching his eyebrows. "I look forward to meeting Reverend Tiffany."

"Easy, Ben," says Jean. "Tiffany's a towering intellect and very nice."

Hunter grins. "She is impressive. We had a pre-nuptial counseling session with her. What's more, Epstein looks happy." He looks at the clock "Now, let's get you settled and ready for dinner."

Arriving at Sparkie's parking lot, Ben is somewhat comforted to see a preponderance of luxury cars with District of Columbia and New York plates, many of them press and official. Inside the restaurant, the aroma of roasting garlic and beef and the well-dressed crowd in the bar, waiting for tables, reassure him that his palate may be satisfied.

Hunter makes his way over to Sparkie, who is standing at an antique schoolmaster's desk, checking reservations, and quietly asks, "What's going on tonight?"

"Hey, jarhead," Sparkie greets him, voice lowered. "It's a zoo tonight. Big conference over in Barrington. The hospitality guide listed us as the best restaurant in the Berkshires. People are coming out of the woodwork. And the egos—unbelievable! Glad you're here on time. Your table's ready, and tonight it would not have been easy to hold it." Sparkie shows them into the dining room, glowing with candlelight, a fire crackling in the stone fireplace, elegantly framed oil paintings on forest green walls, dark wood chair rails, oriental rugs on wide board floors, slat-back chairs, somewhere a roving classical guitarist and, despite the crowd, the corner table, the best in the house, reserved for them. The burly restaurateur seats them and, upon scanning the tables and noting that all the waiters are fully occupied, he presents a big jovial grin and announces, "Hi, I'm Sparkie, I'll be your waiter tonight." Sparkie takes their drink orders, describes the specials, answers Ben's questions, makes suggestions, and, as he turns to moves on, tosses up a riveting question, "So, Hunter, do you think all these experts will figure out what caused the accidents in your yard?"

"In your yard?" Ben is dumbfounded.

Jean eyes Hunter who stiffens slightly and answers, "It all happened about twenty feet away from the house."

"From your house?"

"Uh-huh."

"So that wall behind your house, that huge ugly wall, which I politely did not ask about earlier, is concealing the highway, the Curve?"

Hunter doesn't answer, his attention drawn to another table. He leans back trying to eavesdrop. Jean answers Ben. "Yes."

"God. I know people who know people who were killed out there."

"It is truly tragic, horrible, grotesque," she says. "Tomorrow morning, take a look from upstairs."

"And I read that the highway goes in only one direction. Fairly irregular."

Hunter sits forward. "About as irregular as it gets around here. The good news is that we're having the house moved a half a mile. A beautiful ridge will separate us from that God forsaken highway and—" He cuts himself off, listening, and turns as if looking for a waiter. "Jean, look directly over my left shoulder. Is it Clappsaddle?"

"It is! I'll bet he's involved in the conference."

"I just read in the *Crier* that he's a speaker. Tell me about the dude with him. The sleezy-looking one with the Hollywood haircut. Do you recognize him?"

"Hollywood haircut, huh," says Ben.

She glances again at Clappsaddle's table. "No, he's right out of a bad movie. The general's poking the sleezeball's chest with a weird stick. Looks like he's giving him a piece of his mind."

Hunter leans back again to listen as Sparkie arrives with a bottle of cabernet sauvignon and a waiter appears with escargot for Ben and gazpacho for Hunter and Jean. Ben sighs with delight, inhaling the garlic. "I don't know what the hell you two are talking about, but this looks divine."

"I may be over the top on this," says Hunter, "but I've studied that video with Speedy, and I could almost swear the sawed-off guy with the general was at that midnight meeting. He's the one with the briefcase, who left the pile of payoff envelopes on the table."

"Now this is getting interesting," says Ben.

Jean looks again. "I can't tell, but Speedy would know." She turns to Ben, who is mopping up every drop of melted garlic butter with French bread. "Sorry, Ben. We should explain but it may be too complicated."

"Try me."

"Later," says Hunter. "Better that we tell you what's planned for your visit."

"Planned? I've come to enjoy a long, lazy, sybaritic weekend feasting my eyes on Jean, indulging my palate, sleeping, reading, and engaging in conversation. I'm a simple man."

"You'll do all that, but tomorrow morning we're giving you a tour of the area. In the afternoon a long walk or we'll set up a hammock for you in the Peters Pell pine grove, and you can read and snooze while Jean and I take a hike. Tomorrow night we have tickets to see Arsenic and Old Lace at the Williamstown Summer Theatre. Friday we drive to Sheffield, pick up a lunch at the Sheffield Gourmet and picnic at Bartholomew's Cobble. It's back to New Burford for dinner and then off to Tanglewood to hear Yo-Yo Ma."

"Terrific!"

"On Saturday—"

"Hold it, camp counselor." Ben is feeling managed, and doesn't like it.

"Nope, I'm almost finished. Saturday and Sunday you can do whatever you want, whenever you want, because the conference will be over, and we won't feel the need to stay away from the hubbub— and the house."

"Ah-ha. An ulterior motive. All right. I'll cooperate. It's two days of structured leisure, but—," he pauses. "I just realized you're talking about the National Highway Safety Conference. Melanie's here for that! She's a keynote speaker! We should all get together for a drink."

Jean's eyes widen.

"Good for her," says Hunter. " But I'll pass on getting together."

"Me too," Jean quips, with deadpan expression.

"Aw, you guys are no fun," Ben ribs. "At any rate, at least I now understand why you didn't want to do that story on the accidents."

As their entrees arrive, Dover sole for Jean, prime rib with Yorkshire pudding for Hunter and Ben, Jean bows her head and whispers, "Hunter—! Don't turn around, but it looks like General Clappsaddle is heading to our table."

"Barnhill? Hunter Barnhill."

"General," Hunter says, pushing back his chair to stand.

"No, no, stay seated."

Hunter stands and they shake hands.

Clappsaddle nods to Jean, greeting her by name as she eyes his stick. "I don't mean to disturb your dinner—"

"Not at all, General," says Hunter. "May I introduce our guest from New York, Ben Newman. Ben, General Bunker Clappsaddle." Their greetings are perfunctory. Clappsaddle then turns his back to Ben and Jean and lowers his voice, "Barnhill, I'm wondering if you received a message from me through Serika."

"Yes, I did, General. Thank you. I appreciate it."

"After the second accident, I did some research and ascertained that the splay-footed sapsuckers migrated north some time ago. Based on those findings I recommended that the Curve be straightened. Unfortunately, my argument was not sufficiently persuasive." He clears his throat. "However, I subsequently learned that you're moving the house."

"Yes, Sir."

"I wish you the best in your new location. Seems like a fine place to live. A nice town."

"Thank you, General. Yes, it is a fine town. Just somewhat misguided lately. I've been encouraged to run for town moderator. My hats going into the ring."

"Then allow me to shake the hand of the next town moderator of New Burford. Semper fi, Barnhill."

"Semper fi, General."

Clappsadle returns to his table and Hunter sits down, replacing the starched napkin on his lap, pondering the exchange.

"You show him such deference," says Jean.

"I just told him I'm running for town moderator."

She beams. "When did you decide?"

"Just now."

"The beef is excellent," Ben exclaims.

"I heard that," says Sparkie, reappearing to check on the table. "How's everything else?"

"Terrific," says Hunter, glancing at the uncleared table where Clappsaddle and his party had dined. "Sparkie, was that table reserved under the name Clappsaddle?"

"Clappsaddle? No. But, without looking at the book, I can tell you the name was Tatta."

"The short, fat guy with the slick haircut?"

"Yeah, that was Tatta. And did you catch Clappsaddle's swagger stick?"

"Sinister," says Jean.

"Bones," says Hunter.

"Homo sapiens bones," Sparky specifies.

"Ugh!" Jean shivers. Savoring every morsel, Ben is not listening. "Clappsaddle's been here several times," Sparkie adds, "with old General Farrand from the military academy and a big guy, tall, early fifties, a colonel they call the Renegade. A few others are always with them, but they're different faces every time."

# 28

## THURSDAY, JULY 24

*Barrington*

**E**lvin picks up a fine, thin brush, applies a soft line to the upper lid, a lighter, finer line to the lower lid, momentarily studies his work, then shuts the eye shadow palette.

"That's it?" Melanie flares. "I hate it. I want more eyes, that smoky liner."

"You want to be the highway angel or Catherine Deneuve in *Belle de Jour*? It isn't television today, sweetheart," he says, using a light touch on her brows. He whips out the mascara wand. "Now be still."

Obediently, she freezes as he sweeps her upper and lower lashes, then blurts, "Maybe no TV cameras, but the place is going to be loaded with photographers. The governor's going to be here, probably Senator Donnelley, and God knows who else—so dammit, I want great eyes."

"Trust me, this is the look you want." He shakes excess powder from a fat sable brush and applies a bronzed blush along the cheekbone to her ear. "There. Very nice. You're gonna be in a lot of natural light." She poses, chin up, chin down, left three-quarter profile and right, examining the effect in the mirror, as Elvin pours a dime of oil into his hand and rubs his palms together. "But if you don't stop frowning and wrinkling up your face, you're gonna have to schedule emergency botox work."

"Fuck you! Just finish and get the hell out!"

"This snit of yours is totally unnecessary. How long ago did I tell you that your numero uno has walked off your game board? Now can you hear me? And he won't be circling around again. Stop frowning. It'll ruin your face!" He runs his hands through her hair, lifting and smoothing it. "There. Beautiful! Now if you're ready to listen—"

She still can't grasp it. Yesterday. He wasn't at the house, but could not have been gone for long because the dog was there, alone, barking when they drove up. She left a message on his cell phone but it was probably turned off, as usual. She called the house, several times, only to reach the answering machine and hung up.

"Melanie, darling, focus. Do you or do you not want to know what your chart says?"

"Dammit, yes."

"Good girl. The outlook is actually quite promising, but first there's work to be done. You've got to use this month's obstacles to analyze past problems. If you can do that, things are poised to turn around for you."

"Obstacles? Give me a break. Everything's been just fine for me, thank you. The problem is your charts. These days they suck."

"You don't have to accept my readings," he snaps back, waving a styling brush. "But, face it, your personal life is a mess. What have you got to lose? Analyze what's been going on in your life recently. It'll not only lessen the sting of rejection, but give you a clearer perspective, freeing you to explore new options which may lead to surprising developments, intriguing encounters."

"Bullshit. It's all bullshit. You and your absurd charts."

"Hush up, princess, so I can do your lips."

She faces him, chin up, pouting.

"Maybe a tiny bit of shimmer—, yes, nice. Anyway, I'm betting you weren't happy last night, all alone, cooling your heels in this obscure little hotel room. Admit it."

"I admit it. I felt caged. But only for a split second. I immediately redirected my energy and rehearsed my speech." She won't give him the satisfaction of knowing that she had felt utterly miserable, but then, almost in accordance with the chart, talked herself into preparing for a performance that would dazzle every power-person in the room, starting with the governor. She had meticulously marked up the speech with her codes for emotions, inflection, pauses, pacing, body movements, facial expressions, and for eye contact with audience, dais, and, most important, the governor.

"You could have accepted the dinner invitation from the Secretary of the Commonwealth, which very likely would have been an intriguing encounter, or at least might have led to an interesting development. Did you actually believe Hunter was going to call you last night?"

"Go. Get out! Now! I've got to go over my speech."

"Fine, I'm out of here. But get the glassiness out of your eyes. Don't ruin my artwork with selfish tears." He scoops jars, bottles, brushes, pencils, and palettes into his Louis Vuitton satchel. "You can't have it both ways. Shoo me away and I won't be around to fix the smudges and smears." With a wise smile and a beneficent wave of the hand, he ducks out, quietly closing the door.

"Ugh!" She throws a box of tissue at the door. "Damn you, Hunter!" She huffs, takes a deep breath and goes to the full-length mirror to checks her image. The lean, raspberry red suit, just snug enough on the bust, is perfect. Her make-up, too, is perfect, though she wouldn't acknowledge it to Elvin. Nor would she admit to him that he's right about her personal life. It's time for a hard look at reality, a new perspective on options. A knock on the door startles her.

"Lieutenant Colonel Norwocki, Massachusetts Army National Guard, reporting to escort you, ma'am."

She looks at her watch. He is precisely on time. She had objected strenuously to this escort nonsense when informed of it on arrival, but was told the conference committee would overrule her objection due to the crowds of fans she had attracted. She picks up her speech and opens the door. "Good morning, Lieutenant." Behind Norwocki are two men wearing what appear to be uniforms from the American Revolution, large epaulets, swords, medals covering their chests.

"Let's go," she snaps, starting down the hall. One atavistic warrior marches ahead of her, the other follows her, Norwocki is at her side. She hands him a folder. "I'm giving you my speech, which is to be on the podium for me, in perfect order. Is that clear, Lieutenant?"

"It's Lieutenant Colonel Norwocki," he corrects her, willing to overlook the mistake once but not twice. "Yes, ma'am. The speech will be on the podium." As they walk, he briefs her on her part in the opening proceedings. She doesn't respond but huffs in disdain, never looking at him. A real piece of ass, he's thinking, but tougher than nails.

After delivering Emma and three, bakers'-dozen boxes of Mildred's blueberry muffins to the VIP breakfast room, Speedy finds his way through the Millrace Inn lobby to the main conference room, which is set up with three hundred chairs in rows facing a dais and large overhead screens stationed at every tenth row. Forty-five minutes before the conference begins, no one else is around, except for a technician testing the microphones. Speedy has never experienced anything like this. With time on his hands, he selects a seat for himself—fourth row, aisle, right side—, reserves it with his jacket, and sets out to explore the great lawn and gardens Emma had mentioned.

He exits to a flagstone terrace where handsome people at small iron tables are having breakfast. Beyond is the great expanse of perfectly flat, emerald green lawn, glistening with dew in the morning sun. He imagines walking barefoot all the way across the lawn to the garden and the white trellises, covered with pink, red and yellow roses. He squints. Just ahead, three men, one with a briefcase, are gathered around an Adirondack chair beside the precision-cut croquet lawn. One of them is wildly gesturing, shaking a stick. The physique, posture, and especially that stick are unmistakable. It's Clappsaddle.

Speedy steps back to the terrace and sits at a table where he can inconspicuously watch them. A waitress approaches cheerily asking, Continental for one? Speedy shakes his head, pointing to his watch. She trundles off with the coffee pot just as the short guy sets his brief-case on the Adirondack chair, withdraws a large manila envelope, and hands it to the third man. They shake hands. In a flash, Speedy identifies them. It's the video's guest star, the stout guy. It's the same briefcase. And he's shaking hands with—Percy Standish, Secretary of the Commonwealth. Standing aloof from them, Clappsaddle raps his leg with the swagger stick, then tucks it under his arm. The three start toward the terrace and, passing Speedy, go inside. Speedy gets up and follows them.

Melanie's expression instantly softens as she and Norwocki enter the room where members of the dais are assembling for continental breakfast before the opening session. Norwocki escorts Melanie directly to Percy Standish who is talking with Emma Peters Pell. Percy introduces himself, lavishing her with praise and gratitude, and introduces her to Emma. The formalities concluded, Norwocki asks for a word with the secretary. They turn aside and speak briefly. Standish promptly excuses himself. Norwocki sees him to the door, leaving Melanie standing with Emma.

Marginally aware of the tall, dignified old lady, Melanie's eyes dart around the room. Observing her, Emma warmly asks, "Won't you have a blueberry muffin? They're very good."

"Uh, no, thank you. Blue tongues are for bears, not public speakers," Melanie says, loftily, eyeing the door.

Emma insinuates a smile. "Are you expecting someone?"

"Aren't we all? Expecting the governor? He should be here by now. He's late."

Emma chuckles, "My dear, it would be out of character for the governor to arrive on time. But mark my words, Brew will arrive at precisely minute before it would be too late."

"Sounds like you know him well," Melanie says, recalling that Emma Peters Pell is chairman of the event, and therefore well connected, at least in Massachusetts.

"Since he was in diapers. And his father before him. And my late husband was a good friend of his grandfather."

"Are you from Boston?"

"No, I'm from these parts," says Emma, "a stone's throw east of here. New Burford."

"New Burford!" Melanie exclaims. "Do you know Hunter Barnhill?"

"For goodness sake, yes, very well. And you know, Jean, too?"

"Uh, yes. We met in New York last winter."

"Their wedding is going to be at my house, in the garden, weather permitting. I am so thrilled."

Melanie blanches, then fixes a broad smile on her face as she concentrates, though obsessively preoccupied, on the details Emma is relating. "Only three weeks left to get everything ready. But those two have things well organized, as you might expect. They're perfect for each other, doncha think? —and look who's here, not a moment too late. Governor Brewster Pease." Emma puts on a smile for him, much like Melanie's, as the governor directs himself through hand-shaking VIP's to greet Emma.

Color returns to Melanie's cheeks as the governor glances at her, and then focuses on Emma. "My dear Emma Peters Pell, how delighted I am that you're here," says Pease, extending both hands to her. "Your chairing this event means more to me than you can imagine."

"Ah, but I can, indeed! Nonetheless, kind of you to say, Brew."

"In all sincerity, Emma, your presence here underscores the integrity and resolve of this conference in pursuing the goal of maximized public safety on our nation's highways."

"Please, Brewster Pease, save your highfalutin words for the more impressionable. Allow me to introduce Miss Melanie Atwood, who has observed your tardiness."

"This is indeed an honor, Governor," she says smoothly, shaking his hand, looking coquettishly into his eyes. She likes what she sees. Tall, about six, two. A bit of a good-life paunch, but otherwise in good enough shape. Strong chin. Distinguished graying at the temples. A little stiff, but she can loosen him up and senses he's ready for that.

"Call me Brewster, please. And the pleasure and privilege are mine. Thank you so much for your participation, and, if you don't mind my saying so, you are even more beautiful in person than on television, Miss Atwood."

"Brewster, please, it's Melanie. And I want to thank you for inviting me here because it's opportunities like this that give real meaning to my work."

Pease is charmed. "I'd like to talk more with you. At lunch we should be—," he glances aside at Percy who is signaling him, "—seated together at the head table."

Without taking her eyes off his, she purrs, "We'll talk then."

His mouth curls in a slight smile. "Actually, dinner would be better, if you're free. Senator Donnelley and his wife are arriving this evening. It would be just the four of us. An early evening. Dick's the first speaker tomorrow morning. What do you say?"

"I'd be delighted, Brewster."

As the governor is whisked off by Percy, Norwocki calls everyone's attention and reads off the order in which the VIP's are to file onto the dais. Melanie turns to Emma as they get into the line-up. "Well, Mrs. Peters Pell, you and I are front row, center."

"Yes, where we'll have to behave ourselves," Emma says, a twinkle in her eye.

With a fair amount of confusion the VIP's find their places in the line. Norwocki bellows, "You, Miss Atwood, step out of the line. You don't belong there." As she obediently steps aside, Norwocki continues instructing her, relishing it. "You'll be escorted down the center aisle, to the podium where you'll find your speech in perfect order and, on an additional cover page, you will find one sentence, announcing the National Anthem. Read it. After the National Anthem, deliver your speech. When you finish, take the chair next to Mrs. Peters Pell. Is that clear, Miss Atwood?"

"Yes," she responds, as the military escort appears beside her.

"Excellent." The broad just needs to be told what to do, Norwocki concludes.

In the lobby, Speedy's nose is in *The Berkshire Crier*, while his eyes are on Standish, Clappsaddle and the short guy who are killing time, scanning complimentary copies of *USA Today* and *The Global*. Standish suddenly starts down the hall. A few minutes later, he returns, signaling Clappsaddle and the short guy and together they head down the hall. At a distance, Speedy follows. They cluster outside the VIP breakfast room. Standish goes inside. The governor emerges with Standish and has a brief exchange with Clappsaddle. Standish opens the manila envelope, shows the governor the top page, and slides it back inside. The door to the breakfast room opens. Percy, Clappsaddle and the short guy hustle down the hall as the VIPs leave the breakfast room, processing to the dais. Speedy goes after the trio through the exit, across the lawn, to the parking lot, where they disappear in a sea of cars. He watches a few moments, unable to discern them, then hurries back to the conference room. Members of the New Burford Defense Battalion, Melanie Atwood in their midst, are standing in the doorway. A bugle sounds.

"Ladies and Gentlemen," a voice booms through the speakers. "It is a great privilege to present to you the keynote speaker for Safe Highways Save Lives, one of the most respected and trusted names in television, Melanie Atwood. Continental soldiers flanking her and the Defense Battalion's Color Guard bringing up her rear, Melanie steps down the aisle, regally waving to conferees on the left and to the right as they applaud and come to their feet. At the podium, she adjusts the microphone, waits for the applause to subside, then begins. "Deformed at birth with a harelip—" She pauses, glances at Emma who is nodding to her, rolling her hands, signaling her to proceed. Melanie starts again. "Deformed since birth with a harelip, thereby gifted, and blessed with perfect pitch, Willard Cornwall of New Burford will now whistle our National Anthem."

Everyone stands. As Willard steps forward, Speedy hurries down the aisle to the seat reserved by his jacket.

A runway swagger in her hips, Melanie struts behind Sparkie to the corner table where Governor Pease, Senator Donnelley and his wife, Kyle, are talking in earnest over drinks. Melanie feels every set of eyes in the restaurant following her and loves it, as much as she loved arriving in the governor's limousine, and the warm greeting from Sparkie, who remembered when she was here with Hunter. Brewster looks up and, with an irrepressible smile, watches her approach the table, stands, as does the senator, and introduces her to Dick and Kyle, who compliment her for the success of *Transplant Time*.

"Thank you so much but, please, don't let me interrupt your conversation," she says, noticing what the others are drinking, and ordering a kir royale.

"Hardly an interruption," says Brewster. "I was just putting these two to sleep presenting a case for increased government purchasing on the internet."

"That's fascinating," she breathily exclaims.

"Brew has an internet fixation," Kyle says flatly.

"I wouldn't call it a fixation. However, I accept the inevitability of digital democracy, and the multitude of benefits and disadvantages, many as yet unknown. I've got an ever-increasing concern about cyber-terrorism threats, which are still vastly underestimated."

The senator comments, "There are also those who reasonably maintain that such threats are highly exaggerated, given the fact that military systems, nuclear weapons, CIA and FBI computer systems, et cetera, are inaccessible to hackers."

"Frankly, it's unwise to rule out the possibility that so-called unassailable systems might be targeted," says Pease, "I'm keenly aware of the damage that can be inflicted because I've done a bit of hacking myself.

"You? Hacking?" Kyle and Dick are amused. Melanie is agog.

Brewster pauses as a waiter delivers Melanie's drink. "I wanted to understand it better. And, in the course of my trial exploration, I downloaded codes and got into State—for starters."

"You didn't!" "Department of State?!" "When?" They are incredulous.

"Back in the nineties. Do you recall the Love Letter virus? A Philippine hacker inflicted damage totaling around $15 billion. It even hit our own Labor Department."

"Like wiping out a city the size of Springfield," says Dick.

"I had the same thought. Which is why I looked into it. The public didn't hear much about the specific damage done but, for example, it took almost 3,000 hours for the Department of Labor to get back on its feet. Later, it fell out that the hacker was arrested but released because Philippine law isn't designed to prosecute these crimes, and we did nothing to prosecute or recover damages. Upon learning that, I felt compelled to grasp this hacking thing, this stealth threat, about which I knew nothing, and managed to get some hands-on experience."

"How'd you do it?" The senator is riveted. "Inasmuch as you are no fifteen-year-old, which, I understand, is the average age of the most facile hackers."

Brewster laughs. "I had a mentor, but it wasn't a fifteen-year-old. Emma Peters Pell walked me through it."

"Emma?" "Emma Peters Pell?" Dick and Melanie are stunned. Kyle roars.

"That's right. Over the phone. And since then, she's brought me up to speed on exportable data-encryption, e-wire-tapping, and cyber-defense issues."

"I'm almost not surprised," Dick chuckles. "Years ago she talked about creating an interactive community with her cable system."

"And she did that, to a degree." Brewster confirms.

"I remember," Dick continues, "she wanted to see the point at which people would accept or reject interactivity. I didn't know what the hell she was talking about at the time. Later I learned her system was blocking media signals, filtering out violence and objectionable programming, and then running the cleaned up version, somewhat delayed."

"That's terrible—and illegal," Melanie protests.

"She's ferociously protective of the town and for some time she was its gatekeeper. Her system reached nearly 100% of the households in the valley because television signals couldn't get over the hills." Brewster pauses. "Satellite technologies eroded her exclusive, so now she's talking about creating safe, snug, efficient wireless societies—real and virtual communities. She's very knowledgeable and, as I said, very much up to speed on cyber-defense issues."

Sparkie arrives, suggests specials, takes their orders, and leaves.

"The big question, Brew, is what did you do once you got into State?" Dick asks.

"I browsed. Surely you don't think I would rearrange information?"

"Certainly not," Dick smiles.

"But I can tell you that when I got into those files, I instantly knew that hackers, with over-the counter stuff, acting on their own initiative or on behalf of governments or private interest, could change government bids, outcomes of elections, interrupt 911 systems, turn off the power grid in Chicago in the middle of winter, insert false data into battlefield information systems, and much worse. Unchecked, this threat could change the world by 2010."

"Every computer is a strategic weapon," Kyle coolly observes.

"Potentially. And, as voters increasingly cast ballots over the net, consider the possibilities." Brewster eyes Dick who seems preoccupied.

"Instant feedback," says Melanie, gazing at him. "But the media will still manage and interpret the feedback, making sense of it for the people."

Brewster gazes back with a slight smile. "So, I suggest we toast the media. Do we have a wine list?" Kyle hands it to him. He scans it, glancing at Dick, makes a selection, and pointedly asks, "What's on your mind, Dick?"

"Something's occurred to me—on this hatcheries bid," he says, lowering his voice.

Kyle picks up the cue and turns to Melanie, "I've been wondering, since you went to *Transplant Time,* has your orientation shifted away from news?"

"My orientation will always be in broadcast journalism. I'm versatile, of course, but my versatility is grounded there," she answers, aware that Kyle is deliberately trying to distract her from hearing what Brewster and Dick are saying. But, skilled in carrying on dialogue while listening to an earpiece, she can discern that they are discussing a fallback plan—an environmental initiative that will convert slabs of concrete into fishery spawning reefs. Donnelley is to get the bid into appropriations.

The hushed conversation is interrupted by the arrival of appetizers, Brew comments so Kyle and Melanie can hear, "It's reasonably safe to assume, Dick, that the exhibition road test will go without a hitch. All last week there were trials, day and night, and they've done simulations in snow, sleet, fog. Nary a skid, I'm pleased to report."

"Terrific," Dick says blandly. "Sorry I can't rearrange tomorrow afternoon's schedule to be here for the road show."

Over dinner, as they talk about the Federal Reserve chairman's next moves, immigration reform, and new research on home-schooling, Melanie concludes that Brewster is not only brilliant, but very likely presidential material—and a good lay.

Dick and Kyle decline coffee. "I've got to go over my speech," says Dick. "There won't be time in the morning. The interviews on the highway are at the crack of dawn."

"You're sticking around for the panel immediately following your speech?"

"Yes," Dick says, "but by two I'll be back in D.C. On the outside chance something ugly happens, yet again, when the rubber hits the road, I'll bail you out from there."

The derogatory edge irritates Brewster. "Nothing ugly will happen."

"But isn't it nice to know someone's there to cover your ass if and when you need it?" Kyle grins at Dick and they noisily smooch.

"We've got to run," Dick announces, and they exchange pleasantries. As they leave, heads turn to watch them, and then swing around to check out the governor, who is now alone with Melanie Atwood.

"They're still in heat," Brewster says to her.

"You're jealous," she smirks.

"How would you know?"

The guitarist is playing in the next room. "I'd like some decaf espresso," she says.

He orders two. "These interviews in the morning might be something of a switch for you," he says. "Instead of dishing out questions you'll be fielding them."

"Actually, with the success of *Transplant Time*, I've been interviewed quite a lot. But I've never been in a group interview with a governor, a senator and a general."

"Your peers can be tough."

"They'll be good to us."

"I have your word on it?" He's smiling.

"Mmm, I'm betting you've already submitted the questions."

He takes a folded paper from his jacket pocket and gives it to her. "Here they are." As she glances at it, he leans his elbow on the arm of the chair, and looks at her. She tucks the paper into her purse. "So,

Melanie Atwood, where do you go with *Transplant Time*'s meteoric success? Another season?

"Very likely. The ratings are unprecedented."

"What about donor numbers? Are they up?"

"They come in spurts, unlike the ratings, which steadily climb."

"Because of you. You are phenomenal."

"Thank you, Brewster," she whispers.

"Do you enjoy doing the show?"

She nods, "Very much. What's most gratifying to me is that the program has an important mission." She shakes her head. "However, my mission with *Transplant Time* is dwarfed by the work you do. I was so impressed this evening by your knowledge, your wisdom. Brewster you are amazing."

"That's humbling," he says, a facetious curl on his smile.

"Please. You're not humbled. You know you're amazing."

"As you know you are. Amazing. Intelligent, savvy, highly professional, keenly in tune with your audiences, whether they number in the millions—or just one. You have charm, finesse, and luscious beauty—"

"Brewster—,"

"Don't tell me you're humbled to hear that."

"Frankly, I don't know what would humble either of us. Certainly not compliments."

"We know each other, Melanie."

The guitarist rounds the corner, strumming a pulsing Catalan song. She is imagining the world she could inhabit with him. "Brewster, I shouldn't say this, but I'm suddenly terribly conscious of the fact that you're married."

"I am too."

"But, Brewster, I've never felt like this before. Really."

He takes her hand. "It's mutual then."

"Mutual and impossible. We must get back to the inn. To our respective rooms."

"If that's what you want."

They ride in silence, looking straight ahead through the windshield at the macadam road winding through woods, the limousine headlights illuminating an endless verdant canopy. Brewster touches her chin and turns her face towards his. "One kiss?—for an ardent fan."

She almost guffaws, wondering if, according to politically correct etiquette, he will continue to ask permission every step of the way. But she won't find that out tonight. She feels the smooth cloth of his hand-tailored jacket, as he takes her into his arms and kisses her. She likes it—a lot. The Governor of Massachusetts!

Fingering his jacket lapels, she looks at him with longing and coos, "I know I could make you sooo happy, if you were available."

"Then I shall have to arrange for that. "

The limousine pulls up to the Millrace Inn. In the lobby, they formally say good night and Melanie starts across the lobby to the elevators. Feeling his eyes on her, she turns, flashing a smile at him and knowing: Governor Brewster Pease, you are hooked.

# 29

*New Burford*

As day breaks, the Black Hawk is soaring over the Berkshire's Hills, carrying Senator Richard Donnelley, Governor Brewster Pease, television star Melanie Atwood, and Palumbo Construction's General Bunker Clappsaddle to the Curve, where they are to be interviewed at the apex, on live television in a half hour. Their escort, Lieutenant Colonel P. Marvin Norwocki, Massachusetts Army National Guard, is pressing his cellphone headpiece to his ears, straining to hear New Burford's Constable Turbo Bull, who is requesting assistance with a Curve-related situation at a local diner.

Bull is detailing the situation: "A TV crew arrived here at Mildred's Diner about fifteen minutes ago. Not for breakfast but lookin' for volunteers to say 'Happy day, America.' Four guys. They got some resistance. Folks gave 'em the silent treatment. The TV people thought there was some misunderstanding and again asked nicely enough if a few folks would step outside and wave at the camera. Still, no takers. I advised 'em to leave well enough alone. Then one of 'em announced from the take-out counter that every good American wants to wish everybody a happy day on television. Everybody's is silent. Then one of the TV guys says, 'Hey you people, what's your problem?'" Good question, Norwocki is thinking, as the chopper heads into the Valley of Runs-on-Toes-Into-Wind.

Bull continues, "Well that gets their dander up. A few get kind of verbally hostile, maybe even antagonizing the crew, saying no one watches morning shows except truants and inmates. I told the camera guy it's nothing against the show, it's just that people in this town got a different drummer. They're real private."

"Constable, what kind of assistance do you need from me?" Norwocki asks, craning his neck as they swoop over the Curve. He doesn't like what he sees below. Sandwiched between the apex of the Curve and the wall are dozens of television production trucks with satellite dishes, and three towering scaffolds laden with video equipment. He feels a chill. The media is all set for a spectacle; ready for live coverage of more fatal accidents.

Turbo answers, "Colonel, I'm calling on behalf of these TV people, asking your assistance in locating some people who will say, Happy day, America."

"No problem, Constable. Tell them to hustle over to the Curve. Melanie Atwood will say Happy day. She's arriving there now." He hang ups, assigns the mission to her, and, to his astonishment, she salutes him, and says, "Certainly, Colonel," with such lovely warmth in her voice and eyes that for a split second he doesn't realize that her graciousness is entirely for its effect with the governor and the senator. No matter. Now he's got his hands full.

As soon as the chopper touches down, he is confronted by a crazed sound crew, screaming obscenities about some dog barking in the house on the other side of the wall. He ascertains that they have been trying, unsuccessfully, to make contact with the occupants. With only minutes till airtime, the go-fer who was to drive to the house has just phoned, totally lost. General Clappsaddle is waving his stick, ranting that they set up the interviews far enough from the Curve and the house to get out of earshot.

The barking dog leaps into view momentarily at the second story window. As Elvin is attempting to style Melanie's chopper-blown coif, she freezes, distressed, staring up at the old house. Repeatedly she exclaims, "Is that a Spaniel? A Spaniel! It's a Spaniel!!" Pease gently assures her the dog will be all right, commending her compassion for animals.

They're all nuts, Norwocki concludes, trotting off to the wall, determined to get through or over it, somehow. By sheer luck he sees behind a thicket sunlight shining through a large hole. A hole in the wall, roughly sawed! Moments later, the dog is silent. Norwocki scrunches to return through the hole, the morning sunshine behind him, and emerges triumphantly shouting, "All clear. The people in the house are leaving for the day—taking the dog." Aside, he comments to Melanie, "You really know your dogs, Atwood. It was a spaniel."

"Oh my Gawd," she gasps. "Elvin, that's Hunter's house!"

"Life goes on, sweetheart. You look great!"

The interviews go well. At the conclusion, Melanie and the governor, together, greet the country, saying, Happy day, America. The camera stays with them as they climb aboard the chopper with the senator, the general, the hairdresser and the colonel. The chopper lifts over the hills and heads back to Barrington for the opening of Safe Highways Save Lives—Day Two.

*Barrington*

So far, every event, every speech, workshop, panel discussion of Day Two has proceeded without a single glitch. Which makes Norwocki very nervous. In front of the Millrace Inn, he paces, bullhorn in sweating hand, awaiting the conclusion of the research summation speech. If something goes wrong during the driving exhibition on the Curve, it'll be nationally televised. Conversely, if all goes well—. Hearing a muted burst of applause from within, he stops in his tracks. This is it.

The doors of the Millrace Inn burst open, conferees pour out. The guardsmen move into position, escorting the conference committee,

Emma and Dr. Ralph Barnes among them, to the lead bus and then funneling the crowd into a single line to successively load the sixteen buses. When the conferees are all aboard, Norwocki escorts the governor, general, and Melanie to a limousine flanked by state police motorcycles. A Humvee pulls up alongside Norwocki. He climbs into the front passenger seat and, as the Humvee sprints forward, heading for the lead bus, Norwocki's arm stretches out the window to mount a flashing red light on the vehicle's roof.

From around the Church Street corner, a fleet of state police motorcycles thunders from the Millrace Inn's parking lot into formation around the caravan. Four motorcycles speed ahead to progressively stop traffic for the caravan as it advances. Norwocki signals the lead bus. It rolls forward and the rest move along behind it. The limousine trails at a dignified distance.

*New Burford*

Chatting merrily, enjoying the scenic ride through the green hills, the conferees suddenly silence as the sixteen buses consecutively reach the I-51 interchange. For two days they have seen and heard conclusive evidence and exhaustive research reports confirming that the highway exceeds all safety standards, but now that they are passengers, riding on the infamous concrete strip, unspeakable doubt seeps through those negligible margins of error, and looms as they approach the Curve. They gaze through tinted windows at the vehicles getting set to test-drive the Curve, and at throngs of spectators and reporters, and at Melanie Atwood fans. Slowly the buses traverse the new concrete. At the point where the highway veers into the U-Curve, they stop, and then proceed straight ahead, driving off the highway into an enormous parking lot hacked into the woods.

The door of the lead bus opens, Thornton leaps aboard and announces to the conferees, "Welcome to Safe Highways Save Lives Driving Exhibition. You are now within the Curve. When you disembark you will see a cordoned path that will take you to the bleachers. Along the way, there is a yellow and white Hospitality Tent, which you can see from here on your right. You are welcome to stop there for refreshment, cocktails and snacks. At the conclusion of the program, this Hospitality Tent and another like it at the Millrace Inn will remain open until six o'clock, compliments of the Massachusetts Department of Tourism. At the bleachers, cadets from Western Massachusetts Military Academy will direct you to your assigned seat and assist you in any way. Questions? Please, watch your step. Thank you." He dashes off to the next bus to repeat his speech.

Ralph's face lights up. "Can I get you a little sherry, Emma?" He offers his hand to her as she steps off the bus.

"No, thank you. I've got my water here," she says, patting her capacious straw bag. As Barnes heads for the tent, a cadet ushers Emma to a cordoned section of the bleachers, and shows her to her assigned seat—an index card bearing her name is taped to it. She looks around for Ralph's seat, and, spotting it four rows away, rips the card from the seat next to hers, climbs up the bleachers and switches them so Ralph can sit next to her. Back at her seat, she takes a cushion from her straw bag, settles herself on it and leans back, surveying the arena, the empty highway, the television rigs, the ugly wall, and the sadly exposed second story of the old Hamilton house.

Conferees are scrambling up the bleachers, balancing drinks and paper plates loaded with finger food, excitedly anticipating the driving exhibition. The limousine pulls up in front of the bleachers, delivering Clappsaddle, Atwood and Pease, who receive applause as they are seated among speakers and other dignitaries in the two rows of folding chairs next to the podium, facing the bleachers. Emma wonders what's keeping Dr. Barnes and then sees him, a large plastic glass in each hand, ushered by a cadet. She flags him with her white hankie and he settles next to her, just in time.

"Ladies and Gentlemen," invokes the Chairman of the Massachusetts Transportation Board, "Welcome to the Safe Highways Save Lives Driving Exhibition. Under the leadership of Massachusetts'

Governor Brewster Pease, this conference has focused on the mission of reducing fatalities, injuries, and economic losses resulting from motor vehicle crashes in Massachusetts and every state in the Union. In pursuit of the safest possible transportation systems, we have examined an exhaustive body of the highest caliber research. We have peered through the lenses of engineering, weather, and behavioral factors. We have reviewed and proposed education and enforcement programs that address issues of aggressive driving, distracted driving, impaired driving—."

"Why doesn't he just get on with it," Emma whispers to Ralph.

"You know how it goes. Now they tell us what they've told us for two days." He sets one of the glasses under his chair and drinks from the other.

Emma is studying the upper story windows of the old Hamilton house. "Is it true, Doctor, you crawled out of one of those windows and climbed down a ladder to the accident scene?" Hollow-eyed, he looks directly at the Curve, the wall, the bathroom window. His mouth drops open. Like an agonized saint in a Renaissance painting, his eyes penitently roll upward, his shoulders helplessly slouching. "Ralph? Are you all right? Oh dear, it must be shocking to see what you did. Careful, you're spilling your drink. Let me take it and put it down for you."

"No, thank you." he mutters, dropping the plastic glass. Then slowly, deliberately he pours the second drink through the bleacher planks onto the ground below. He looks up at the house. "How could I do that? How? How could I?"

"You know, Ralph, that in times of crisis sometimes we are able to draw on an inner strength we never knew we had and find ourselves capable of doing things we thought impossible, even unimaginable in our wildest dreams. You were very brave, extending your helping hand in dreadful, terrible circumstances."

He does not respond. His eyes roll over to the dignitaries. He pats his brow with a tissue and mutters, "*Transplant Time.* Melanie Atwood. Geeze."

"She's no prize. Ralph, you might be more comfortable if you take off your jacket."

The transportation chairman is droning on, summarizing construction algorithms and data from the tests in simulated weather conditions. "In addition to the scientific research, we also commissioned Charlotte Schambra, the cement reader from Woodland Hills, California. She found a few hairline fissures in the syntax, nothing even remotely hazardous. She, too, concludes that the highway's structural elements are sound. And, according to her reading, the fatal crashes resulted from a quirk of fate—what some Massachusetts residents centuries ago might have called 'a visitation by God.'"

Everyone applauds.

"We expect the exhibition we are about to see will reconfirm the findings of the massive body of distinguished research presented at this conference. The vehicles participating in this exhibition are sponsored by the National Association of Automobile Manufacturers in cooperation with the New York, New Jersey, Connecticut, and Massachusetts Car Dealers Associations. These associations have screened and qualified today's drivers to provide a representative sample of the drivers on America's highways. We give special recognition to the Leather and Chain Motorcycle Club from Ossining, New York, who volunteered to ride the Curve today. Let's give all the drivers and their sponsors a round of applause."

"Get on with it," someone shouts over the applause.

"Why do you suppose all these car dealers are taking the risk?" Ralph wonders aloud, still dazed.

"Promotional stunt," Emma states flatly. "A safe, well calculated promotional stunt. They all got the engineering reports. If they had seen any risk at all, they wouldn't be here. Once BMW and Volvo signed up, all the other dealers jumped in. Now I'm hearing some of them want to make this an annual event." She eyes Ralph, shaking his head. "Maybe you'd like to rest in the bus or we could ask a cadet to find you a ride home."

He insists he's fine and focuses on the transportation chairman who is still reading, "Vehicles will be driven solo, in packs, in drag duets, and other formations—reaching speeds of 85 miles per hour at the apex. Possibly faster. The exact speed at which the vehicle takes the apex will register on the digital scoreboard.

The conferees are impatient, talking among themselves, as he continues. "This afternoon's exhibition is a celebration of American highway engineering, a celebration of the progress we have already made in improving the safety of our highways, and an inspiration to all of us here today as we go forward from this conference, to work tirelessly on performance-based safety programs. So, with no further ado—."

They applaud vigorously. The first car, a 1956 Ford Thunderbird races past the bleachers and takes the Curve at 82 miles an hour, according to the LED digits. The crowd cheers.

Then, a new model Subaru Outback speeds down the highway, racing through the Curve at 82 miles per hour. Loud applause. A Toyota powered by hydrogen fuel cells leads an ensemble of alternatively fueled, environmentally friendly vehicles. Enthusiastic applause. Four BMW's, in diamond formation, take the apex at 92 miles per hour. The crowd roars.

In all, one hundred eighty-six vehicles speed safely through the Curve, to the audience's delight. Then, the Ossining Leather and Chain Motorcycle Club's four hundred goggled biker guys, each tightly hugged by a biker gal, thunder toward the Curve, scarves flying, and careen around the apex in a V formation. The crowd goes wild, whistling, hollering, clapping, stamping their feet. The display reads 05—105 miles per hour!

Finally, a high mobility multi-purpose wheeled vehicle, a Humvee, with a 7.62 mm coaxial machine gun mounted on the cab, approaches the Curve. At the wheel is a Guardsman, a speedy-four, and behind the cab, at the gun, is Lieutenant Colonel Marvin Norwocki, Massachusetts Army National Guard. As the Humvee whizzes past the bleachers, Norwocki fires a celebratory salute of blanks over the crowd. Some cheer. Most gasp. Two spectators collapse.

Cadets scamper among distraught conferees, crying out, *Get a doctor, call EMS.* Ralph whips around and, straight away, clambers up the bleachers to assist.

The Chairman of the Massachusetts Transportation Authority, returns to the podium. "Ladies and gentlemen, what a success we have witnessed! I want to thank you all for your commitment to making highways safe, because," he pauses, "safe highways save lives. Interstate 51 is a masterpiece of highway engineering and, it is my great pleasure to announce that it will officially reopen as soon as this area has been cleared. Now the time has come to celebrate. See you at the Hospitality Tents and at the Safe Highways Save Lives gala dinner. Thank you, all!"

Having successfully administered mouth-to-mouth resuscitation as the Chairman of the Massachusetts Transportation Authority announced I-51's reopening, Barnes now is comforting his conscious, bewildered patient. He recalls having told Emma he wasn't keen on attending the dinner dance. Now he certainly wouldn't go. He will be at home, sober as a judge, on call to help.

Overcome by fresh air, Ben drops onto the sofa and watches Hunter build a fire in the wood stove inserted in the fireplace. "Why is it so damn cold? It's July," he protests.

"You'll be plenty warm in a minute," Hunter puts on a Miles Davis CD, freshens Ben's drink, and goes to the kitchen, where Jean is sprinkling alfalfa sprouts into a salad. Whiffing the rosemary marinade, he picks up a deep platter filled with a butterflied leg of lamb studded with slivers of garlic and takes it outside to the hot grill.

After two servings of lamb and a fair amount merlot, Ben confesses that as much as he would love to hear Yo-Yo, he couldn't possibly

stay awake for the concert. He looks so completely relaxed that neither Hunter nor Jean makes any effort to dissuade him.

For the urban denizen, solitude in the quiet house is an unexpected pleasure. Far from the incessant whir of air conditioners partially
masking the perpetual street cacophony of sirens, horns, alarms and
garbage trucks, he makes himself comfortable on the sofa, reaches
into his tote bag of newly released books, and selects one. Freddie
curls up at the foot of the sofa. The warmth from the stove comforts,
the cheery flames and steady tick of the old pendulum clock mesmer-
ize. Rosy evening light streams through the windows. He sets the book
and the mug on the end table, removes his shoes, and stretches out,
sinking into the sofa, into the tranquility, into deep, dreamless sleep.

He awakens in pitch darkness, chilled and confused. He is not in
his apartment. Freddie licks his hand, orienting him. But what time is
it? Ugh. To determine the time, he will have to move his person and
find a light source. He feels utterly incapable of the former, which is
an unconditional requisite for accomplishing the latter.

Shivering, he sits up, fumbles in the dark for the lamp on the end
table, gropes for the switch, and, "Aagh," cringes from the brightness.
The pendulum clock reads 9:15. He has slept for more than an hour.
Wondering where he might find the thermostat, he sees the stove's
darkened glass door. The fire is out. This is not the way I would write
this scene, he grumbles. The fire is supposed to merrily dance all
night. Reality sucks, he mumbles, dragging himself to the stove.

He gets on his knees and opens the stove door. Smoke escapes.
Shrinking back in disgust, he sees red-hot coals in the ashes, and beside the stove is a brass, kindling pail. He crumples up a few pieces of
newspaper, stuffs them into the stove, tops them with a few logs, closes the door, and watches. The chamber fills with thick, rolling smoke
that suddenly, miraculously clears as flames leap from the coals, blaz-
ing through the paper, burning into the wood. "What a boy scout," he
chuckles, pleased with himself. Absorbing the warmth, he feels deli-
ciously drowsy, ready for ten more hours of sleep. He shuffles across
the living room, up the stairs to bed.

At the top of the stairs, he hears a powerful, almost frightful gust of wind. Wondering why he hadn't heard it downstairs, he goes into the bathroom and opens the shutters. The wind abruptly subsides to absolute stillness. He shrugs, turns on the light and, as he relieves himself, the wind again gusts in a fearsome burst. In that instant, headlights pierce the darkness, zooming toward the house, closely followed by more headlights, all speeding directly toward the house. He shuts his eyes, tight, and freezes.

As their Infiniti approaches the Curve, Alice Rench says to her husband, "Donald, look! Up there! —"

At the Millrace Inn the party is in high gear, champagne flowing, music filling the hall, lavishly decorated with roadside wild flowers, tall grasses, and highway signs —SPEED LIMIT, YIELD, SLOW VEHICLE LANE, WRONG WAY—all lit by beaming headlights. Buffet tables groan with roasts, platters of cold half lobsters, huge bowls of jumbo shrimp, salads, fresh fruit, cheese boards, and an array of desserts. Over the drink bars are bright yellow banners, "Driving tonight? —No imbibing tonight."

The sense of triumph and relief is palpable. Interstate 51 is blameless for the tragic accidents. The automotive industry is blameless. The cement is blameless. The drivers are blameless. Palumbo Construction is blameless—at least as far as I-51 is concerned. Governor Brewster Pease is not only blameless but, according to the evening news, "has demonstrated strong national leadership ability in his handling of the tragedies."

Media people, many of whom had accepted a weekend junket offered by the Massachusetts Department of Tourism, outnumber conferees, association executives, safety researchers, and government agency people. Although the news teams didn't get a live crash story, the event did give them lots of live automotive action and ample opportunity to interview each other.

For Emma, the evening is tiring, but she does not want to leave without speaking to Brewster, who has not yet appeared. She mingles, pleased that Speedy, her escort, is in no rush to leave. Taking it all in, he's enjoying multiple trips to the buffet table, and when he does not have a plate in his hand, he's busily writing on his notepad. Emma introduces herself to an Ossining biker and they chat about Rolling Thunder until the band music, sixties rock, becomes so loud they can no longer hear each other, and the biker asks her to dance. Emma accepts. On the packed dance floor, Lieutenant Colonel Norwocki, in evening mess dress, winks at her as he frenetically frugs with the somewhat sedate Mrs. Norwocki. Emma laughs, thoroughly enjoying the chance to shake herself out a bit after two days of confinement in conference rooms.

Suddenly the music stops, thunderous applause erupts upon the arrival of Governor Brewster Pease, Melanie Atwood, in a one shouldered, skin-tight, red dress, Lieutenant General Bunker Clappsaddle in mess dress, and, just behind Pease, the deferential Percy Standish. Clappsaddle appears aloof, dissociating himself from the limelight. Melanie and Brewster bask in the ovation and wade into the crowd, shaking hands, receiving congratulations.

"Emma!" Brewster exclaims, clasping her hand and kissing her cheek. He calls out to the crowd. "Your attention, please. My heartfelt gratitude goes to each and every one of you who participated in this important conference. I also want you all to know how particularly grateful I am to the Honorary Chair of Safe Highway Save Lives, Emma Peters Pell. She is an extraordinary woman, and an exemplary community leader. Let's give her a big hand."

She smiles, acknowledging the applause with patrician poise. "Congratulations, Brew. To you and to your staff," she says patting his hand, then extends her hand to Clappsaddle, and to Percy. Melanie smirks, waiting for Emma to compliment her, and she does, taking her hand. "Melanie, dear, I so enjoyed our chats. Like school chums, eh? My best wishes to you."

"Thank you so much, Emma. I am honored to know you," she says, trying to imagine her on the phone, guiding Brewster as he hacks into the State Department.

"Thank you," Emma says with a mischievous glint in her smile. "Now, if I can find my dear escort and pry him away, I shall be on my way."

"But the band is now playing a foxtrot, your music, Emma," says Brewster, "and the night is young,"

"Not for me." She glimpses Speedy timidly hanging back from the group and beckons him. "I would like to introduce you all to my good friend, Alvin Serika. Governor Brewster Pease." Speedy nods and they shake hands. Emma explains, "Alvin doesn't speak, but hears and perceives ever so keenly. For that matter, in many ways, he's like another set of eyes and ears for me. This is General Bunker Clappsaddle."

"We've met," Bunky says, shaking Speedy's hand. "Good to see you, Serika."

"And Melanie Atwood." Emma quickly qualifies to Melanie, "Alvin is a good friend of Hunter Barnhill."

"Well!" Melanie gushes. "I am delighted to meet you, Alvin."

Speedy's eyes swell like saucers beholding Melanie Atwood in all her bright red voluptuousness. His mouth rounds and then clearly, distinctly shapes the words, "My pleasure." He wonders if she owns a bicycle.

Concealing astonishment at his unprecedented attempt at speaking, Emma next introduces Speedy to Standish. Narrowing his eyes, Speedy cocks his head in aversion, awkwardly sensed by the others. Brewster brightens the moment saying, "We can't let this foxtrot pass us by. May I have the honor, Mrs. Peters Pell?"

"Your charm is irresistible, Brewster Pease," she says taking his arm. Melanie turns to Speedy. "Would you dance with me, Alvin?" He blushes, bites his lower lip, and off he goes, led by Melanie to the dance floor. Photographers circle the two couples.

"I don't know how to thank you enough, Emma," Brewster says, then slowly twirls her. At easy arms length, he tells her, "Your participation in the conference means the world to me and you went well beyond the call of duty in helping to make this conference a success."

"We do not always see eye to eye these days, Brew, which is why I felt it was especially important for me to accept your olive branch and chair this event. Participation in public forums is a duty. Furthermore, I always appreciate opportunities to make new acquaintances, discover what's on people's minds, share thoughts." She glances over at Speedy, dancing remarkably well, back straight, chin up, though stiffly holding Melanie at a distance as she animatedly chats at him.

On the sidelines, Clappsaddle checks his watch. He wants to leave, too, but the sight of Speedy dancing with Melanie inspires him. He strides over to Speedy and taps his shoulder. Speedy stops in his tracks, bows to Melanie, and rushes from the dance floor, grinning from ear to ear.

Bunky tries to keep his eyes on Melanie's face, haloed in bright blonde hair, while marveling at the round breasts almost bursting from a slither of red-hot dress.

"General, you are a marvelous dancer," she gushes.

"Competence in ballroom dancing was required at West Point, Miss Atwood. In some ways it was a remarkably liberal education."

"Liberal? You're serious?"

"I'm always serious. And I can boast I was better at ballroom dancing than the vast majority of my classmates."

"Maybe it's a talent that earmarks generals, General."

"Very insightful, Miss Atwood. As a matter of fact, bayonet fighting requires footwork and grace of movement quite similar to sophisticated dance steps."

Watching from the sidelines, Percy decides it is now his turn to dance with Melanie. He cuts in, dismissing Clappsaddle, and takes her into his arms. "This is a great pleasure, Melanie, however fleeting it no doubt will be, as I expect Brew will cut in momentarily." He turns with her to check on the governor. "Actually he appears to be quite engrossed, dancing with Emma."

"Maybe they're talking about your video."

"My video?"

"Mmm, the one with you and Clappsaddle's boss at that New Burford town meeting in the middle of the night. Shaaame on you," she smirks.

"WHAT!?!"

His response baffles her. "Uhh—yuh, like you don't know what I'm talking about? Helloooo. Mr. Secretary, it was that meeting when you cut the deal with the selectmen. They've got it on videotape. You and a guy named Tatta. Emma said it was devious and highly un-ethical, though technically within the letter of the law. I'd be embar-rassed to repeat what else she said. Not ladylike."

"Emma has this on video?" He is visibly shaken.

"Don't worry. I don't think she's going after you guys except to keep you in line. But she definitely intends to weed the corrupt cul-prits out town government." She looks over his shoulder with a seduc-tive smile. "Time's up. Here's Brewster. And, uh, Percy, for whatever it's worth, if I were you, I wouldn't mention the video to him unless he brings it up."

"My turn, Percy." He smiles at Melanie as she wraps her arms around his neck. He holds her close, barely moving with the music. Photographers come in tight.

"You don't mind if they photograph us dancing like this?" she asks.

"Mind? They can run it on the front page of the *Global*, I'd love to supply the headline."

Suddenly, Norwocki appears. "Sir. Mr. Governor." Failing to get the governor's attention, he taps him on the shoulder. Brewster turns away. He will deal later with the colonel's audaciously inappropriate effort to cut-in.

Norwocki persists. "Mr. Governor. Sir, a word—. It's urgent, Sir." He clicks his heels and salutes. "Urgent!"

Still holding Melanie, Brewster stops dancing to incline his ear. Norwocki cups his hands around his mouth and whispers.

The governor braces. "Get Percy. And Clappsaddle," he orders, softly.

"Clappsaddle's left, Sir. The helicopter is here."

"Keep trying Clappsaddle. Where's Percy. He was just here. Tell him to get Cassler."

Norwocki salutes, executes a smart about face and departs.

"Another accident!" Melanie gasps.

"I've got to go, Melanie," he says gravely, starting off the dance floor.

"Brewster, wait!" She goes after him, and says under her breath, "Take me with you. I'll manage the media. You can trust me."

Without stopping, he shrewdly eyes her, assessing the offer and says, "Keep walking, keep smiling, act like you're having a great time, and tell me what you have in mind. Fast."

"Cut off access to all media. Governor's orders, Norwocki will handle it. Give me permission to file an exclusive report for ABG. We'll frame it together. We only need two technicians and they're here." They stride through the doors to the great lawn, where a helicopter is waiting, blades turning. "One phone call, actually two, and I'll have it arranged. Let me do it, Brewster, please. Give me your phone."

He reaches into his pocket, eyes fixed on the helicopter, and hands it to her. She flashes a smile at him, punches a number and, mincing across the lawn on stiletto heels, yells against the noise into the phone.

Norwocki gives them a hand to board the chopper. Percy is right behind them. Two men race from the inn's terrace to the broadcast remote truck, grab equipment, sprint to the helicopter, and climb on board.

The helicopter lifts off. Brewster huddles with Norwocki and Standish, Melanie makes more calls, then announces, "Brewster, it's set. I'm doing an exclusive report. Now talk to me. Who's got pen and paper—?"

Brewster takes off his jacket and puts it on her shoulders. The temperature has dropped, easily ten degrees since sunset, but she doesn't seem to notice. "This is horrific! Devastating." He presses his palms to his forehead.

"Yes, it is terrible, Brewster. But it doesn't have to be terrible for you. We just need the right frame on this."

The governor steeples his hands, and thoughtfully brings the tips of his fingers to his chin. "These are the key points," he says, with calm authority. Norwocki hands Melanie a yellow lined pad and pen, and she starts scratching notes.

Horror lies before them, mangled vehicles, broken glass, metal debris, small fires, the smell of motor oil and gasoline, victims moaning.

Melanie winces, holding her mouth. The sound technician hands her a wireless mike, asking, Do you need a minute? No, she answers without hesitating, attaching the microphone to her dress. "But give me that, too," she says, grabbing the hand mike from him. She sheds Brewster's jacket, swigs water from a quart bottle, takes several deep breaths, swivels her head, rolls her shoulders and, dropping her jaw, forces a yawn. "Okay, let's do it," she says, taking complete charge. "I'm going to walk along the tops of the cars, and don't tell me it's dangerous. That black Acura looks good. I'll go from there to the Jeep. Boost me up there."

They get her onto the Acura's roof, check sound, clear a path for the camera operator. Ready.

Melanie is on. Sirens wail in the distance. Flares sparkle behind her. A windshield shatters at her feet. Danger emboldens her.

"With an ABG exclusive report, this is Melanie Atwood on Interstate 51, New Burford, Massachusetts, where a chain-reaction collision has occurred minutes after the highway's reopening to traffic. At least twenty-five vehicles are involved in this collision, which is the third on this new highway. Massachusetts' Governor Brewster Pease immediately ordered the highway closed and rushed here by helicopter from a conference in Barrington Massachusetts to personally oversee the rescue efforts.

"In my interview with the governor en route here, he asked, first, that I convey his deep concern and sympathy. His prayers are with all the accident victims, their families, beloved others, and friends." She pauses, considerately. "Governor Pease said that this disaster is particularly shocking because comprehensive investigations and rigorous testing have confirmed conclusively that the highway not only meets, but far surpasses the highest national safety standards. These findings were presented in all-day sessions yesterday and today at the Safe Highways Save Lives conference, convened by Governor Pease, and attended by hundreds of highway safety experts, transportation and elected officials from across the country, as well as private citizens concerned with highway safety, myself included as keynote speaker."

She pauses, dolefully shaking her head as a siren wails then, stretching her tight red dress, strides from the Acura to the crushed hood of a Toyota Corolla and nimbly sidesteps to a mutilated Ford Explorer. "As you can hear from the sirens, emergency medical vehicles continue to arrive where just a few hours ago, safety experts observed successful demonstrations of the highway's safety. Easily two hundred vehicles sponsored by U.S. automotive dealerships, with drivers representative of the diverse populations on America's highways, smoothly took this very Curve at speeds up to 105 miles per hour."

She steps down onto a Mini Cooper, kicking out of her way a rigid arm reaching from the shattered rear window. "Governor Brewster Pease is calling for a continuation of investigations into the causes of the accidents. However, he said, and I quote," she reads, glancing down at her notes, "Dire, unknown and remote factors somehow, once again, evaded the most exhaustive and sophisticated research and investigative methods. Immeasurable suffering has been caused. This is a time to override scientific evidence and instead use judgment. Which I am now doing. With deepest respect for the victims of these dreadful accidents, in sympathy of all who are suffering loss, I hereby order this highway closed—permanently."

With cool professionalism, she strides from the Mini to a Jeep Grand Cherokee. "I understand that the governor, who is at this time involved with the rescue teams, intends to explore the possibility of recycling the highway, dismantling the concrete slabs for deposit in the Massachusetts Bay where they will serve as fish spawning reefs. Tomorrow morning, Governor Brewster Pease is holding a press conference when he may elaborate on this environmental initiative.

"In order to maximize access for rescue operations, Governor Pease is disallowing media access to the accident scene. Stay turned for further coverage of this developing story and for the governor's press conference tomorrow morning. Reporting from New Burford, Massachusetts, this is Melanie Atwood, ABG News." She tosses the hand mike to the camera operator and takes off the wireless mike.

"Melanie!" Brewster scrambles across the smoldering wreckage, leaps atop the Jeep Grand Cherokee, embraces her, smothering her with kisses. "My God, I adore you!"

"Oh Brewster. I've done it! Real substance, hard information, in an action setting." He kisses her hair, her face, her neck, her shoulders, as she enthuses. "I just know it's an Emmy! A Peabody! DuPont-Columbia! Clarion. Matrix." He silences her with a long, impassioned kiss. "Yessssss—," she pants, her iconic breasts heaving, "this is almost unbearably exciting."

"Yes, yes it is," he moans, caressing the ravishing curves in the tight red wrap.

"Make love to me, Brewster. Oh Brewster —"

"Yes! Yes!"

He jumps from the crushed Jeep. She leaps into his arms. Nothing exists except their lust and illusions about each other. Urgently, yet carefully, they step through the wreckage, carnage, searchlights, and sirens, to the waiting helicopter that sweeps them up, out of the chaos, across the dark and silent hills to the inn. There, undisturbed by the distant fury, power politics and power media make power love till the dawn's early light.

# AUTHOR BIOGRAPHY

R. E. Laurence cobbled words, mostly non-fiction, at Time Inc., Broadcasting Magazine and Young & Rubicam in New York City, crafted fiction, *Spare Parts*, in western Massachusetts, and currently writes mostly creative nonfiction in central Mexico.

www.ingramcontent.com/pod-product-compliance
Lightning Source LLC
Chambersburg PA
CBHW070853180626
46817CB00003B/758